'By the devil! You're a pretty sig…

She flinched, pra… at her. A man moved … face. He was smiling … of green sparkling like … pened.

'Please excu… rges to attend to.'

She tried to … ay. The man caught her …

'What's the hu…

'Please leave m… he kept her voice low. 'I am chaperone to Mrs Didcott's young ladies. She will be distressed if she sees you detaining me.'

The man laughed at her distress and bowed with a flourish of insolence. 'Ward Trenchard at your service, m'mselle.'

Nicole snapped her fan open and fluttered it briskly. 'Ward Trenchard!' she gasped aloud in a delayed reaction. The flush stole over her cheeks again.

Everyone knew how evil he was. He was reputed to be as wicked as his late father, an American slave-trader. The scandal about his wife being caught with a black lover matched his own nefarious deeds.

'You are scared of me?' Ward's question challenged her.

She shook her head but before she could answer, Emma jostled her aside.

'Nicole, come away at once! She is my chaperone, Mr Trenchard, and I have need of her.'

'Indeed?' Ward's eyebrow arched. 'I doubt she has need of you,' he said sardonically. He bowed to Nicole, deliberately ignoring Emma and her companions. 'We shall meet again, m'mselle, without the cabal.' It sounded like a threat as he turned and strode away.

Also by Raynard Devine

THE FLESHTRADERS, Volume One
MASTER OF BLACK RIVER

RAYNARD DEVINE

The Flesh Traders

Volume Two

Black River Affair

Futura

A Futura Book

First published in Great Britan in 1985
by Futura Publications, A Division of
Macdonald & Co (Publishers) Ltd
London & Sydney

ISBN 0 7088 2541 9

Photoset in North Wales by
Derek Doyle & Associates, Mold, Clwyd.
Printed in Great Britain by
Hunt Barnard Printing Ltd, Aylesbury, Bucks.

Futura Publications
A Division of
Macdonald & Co (Publishers) Ltd
Maxwell House
74 Worship Street
London EC2A 2EN

A BPCC plc Company

For

Lindsay & Josim,
Laval, Clovis & Jocelyn

Port Louis

CONTENTS

Prologue
BLACK RIVER
April 1816

The seasoned slave accepted his condition, in the same way that Ward, as the months passed, accepted his. Slaves obeyed him and consequently he came to expect their obedience. In the curious way that slavery had of affecting everyone involved with it, Ward was being seasoned too, as a Master.

From: '*Master of Black River*'

Prologue

As the frenzy calmed, Ward let his seed pump into the wench lying beneath him. He sighed, not with the pleasure or satisfaction of a contented man, but with a weariness that was born of frustration. He lay lodged deep within the female, waiting until she stopped writhing and he was drained completely.

The girl groped in the gloom of the cabin for his head. She tried to pull his face around so his lips would meet hers.

'By the devil!' he cursed with disgust. 'None of that!' He jerked away roughly, leaving the girl panting.

'Damned wench,' he muttered as he swung his legs over the edge of the bed. 'You better get me a whelp for New Year or I'll ...' He left the threat unspoken as he reached down and pulled up his breeches from where they hung around his ankles.

'Get back to the quarters.'

'Thank yo', massa,' said the slave politely. She had been taught by Ellen, the plantation housekeeper who schooled all the female slaves on how to behave when the master bedded them.

The warmth in her voice soothed Ward's anger. He leaned over and slapped her thigh. 'That's enough, doudou. You're a'right.'

The wench grinned broadly. She would repeat the compliment in the quarters, where it would give her status. At the Black River plantation it was an honour to lie with the master. If she got full, there would be extra rations, less work toiling in the hot sun of the cane fields and, if she bore him a child that lived, a bolt of cloth to make dresses to wear on Sundays.

'Get out, wench,' he said again, annoyed by her glance of affection. He could not remember her name. He had called her from the fields as he returned from the mill. It was enough that she had the broad hips of a childbearer, her face was pleasing and she was young.

She knew the routine because of Ellen's careful instruction. She had bathed herself in the swift-flowing Black River that gave the plantation its name, and had been annointed with sweet smelling oil by some of the older slave women.

She had approached the pavilion where he had his own quarters without fear, ignoring the proximity of the great mansion at the other side of the courtyard. Ward had watched her walking in the gathering dusk with her head held proudly. Gina, his wife, had watched too from the mansion's long veranda.

Gina was still watching when he strolled out of the room onto the balcony of the wooden cabin which had once been the guest pavilion. He stifled his yawn and tried to look like a man who was pleased with what he had done.

The girl slipped past him, smoothing down the coarse calico material of her slave frock. She tossed her head boldly, not afraid to be seen by Gina. The female slaves sensed that they were in no danger from his wife. Ward was Gina's master, as well as theirs.

As the girl sauntered towards the path that led to the compound by the river, Ward stared back at Gina. She was glaring at him, opening her mouth to speak.

'You can't make me feel guilty!' he shouted to stop her reproach before it began. He strode the few steps across the courtyard to the mansion, affecting a swagger. He did not want Gina to see how disappointed and empty he really felt.

'I'm a slave breeder, ain't I? That filly's goan give me a fine whelp come New Year. Mixed breed sells for a high price in Port Louis.'

'Hah!' Gina turned away as he stepped onto the veranda.

Ward wondered how much rum she had drunk. In the three years since their son, Garnet, was born, Gina had changed. She was no longer the enchanting girl he once loved. She had gained weight until it obscured the trim beauty and grace of her youth. Her radiant complexion was lost, replaced by the artificial bloom of beeswax and powder. Her manner, once charming, now revealed her true self as hypocritical and harsh. She was a haggard, blowzy, evil woman.

He sighed, for a moment succumbing to a pang of remorse. Yet she was the one to blame. By lying with a slave she had destroyed not only his love, but his life as well. He could never be a husband to her again, however long they remained married.

'You can do what you like for all I care!' Gina hissed as he strode past her.

The challenge in her voice halted him. He turned to gaze at her. Instead he saw Ellen, his loyal and loving regular bed wench, hovering in the shadows behind Gina. She was always close to protect him. Her presence now blunted the curse he was about to utter at his wife.

'I shall!' he snapped. 'I don't need your blessing.' Suddenly a feeling of despair overwhelmed him. 'I'd be obliged if you don't spy on me,' he added wearily.

'Spy!' Gina's laugh was a harsh cackle. 'I don't spy on you. I know everything you do without having to spy. You think you're smart but you're not. I know the desire that's gnawing at your heart. But I am the mistress of Black River, Ward Trenchard, however much you wish I wasn't.'

'Desire?' His eyes flickered with concern before he could disguise his shock at her remark. With a shrew's uncanny instinct to wound, she had found his weakest point.

'You're drunk! Where's the houseboy. Where's Dell? I want a drink too. You've had enough already.'

'Dell's upstairs in my chamber with his britches off, waiting for me.'

Ward flushed, stung by her retort.

'Hah!' she shrieked, her eyes glinting. 'If you seek solace in a slave's arms, why can't I?'

'Gina, for God's sake!' He raised his hand and moved towards her. 'Mother's in the sewing room. She'll hear you.'

'Let her hear. Do you think she doesn't know what you are?'

He lowered his hand. 'Whatever I am,' he said forlornly, 'you're the one who made me this way.'

'Am I?' Gina cackled again, delighted by his troubled mood. 'I'm glad! I thought you were proud of yourself and your black wenches.'

'They're better than you!'

'You don't believe that, Ward. They aren't white, however much you'd like them to be.'

'What do you mean?' He tightened his hands into fists, holding them rigid at his side, daring her to provoke him.

'You poor bugger!' Gina thrust her body at him. 'You long to lie with me again, don't you? You can't feel you're a man when you ride those black sluts. They only lie with you because you'll flog them if they don't.'

'Why!' He prepared to strike her. She held up her chin, gazing at him disdainfully.

'Go on,' she said, taunting him. 'You can't hurt me any more, Ward. You long for the love of a white woman. Look at yourself. You're hollow without me.'

He felt the energy draining out of him. He lowered his hand and gripped the veranda railing. She was right. It was why even Ellen's devotion was unable to quell the disillusion that plagued him.

He had never been at peace since the night he discovered Gina and the slave in bed together.* The memory still rankled, despite his attempts to avenge himself with his ruthless bedding of his slave wenches. If only there was another way to rid himself of Gina's hold on him.

The solution came to him without warning. 'You're not the only white Creole woman in this colony, Gina,' he said softly. 'There's plenty could be mistress here.'

She laughed in his face, the foul odour of rum gusting

* See: 'Master of Black River'.

under his nostrils. 'You're mistaken, Ward. For all your wealth, there is not one white lady, British, French or Creole, who would change places with me.'

'That's not true!'

'Yes, it is. White women aren't slaves. You can't lash them to love you. They know you're a failure, Ward Trenchard. A despicable, heartless slave-holder, no better than the hapless slaves you force into your bed every night.'

'Ballocks!' He brushed his hand through his dishevelled locks. 'Besides, why should I want a white woman? If they're like you, I'm better without.'

Gina's mocking laughter infuriated him.

'I'll show you,' he said, breaking away and storming inside the house.

He dashed into the drawing-room and grabbed some of the invitation cards that were lying on top of the mantel piece. He hurried back to the veranda and flung them at Gina. They fluttered to the floor around her skirts as she grinned mockingly.

Ellen was frowning, trying to make him keep calm and not let his wife goad him. He ignored her.

'See these!' he shouted. 'The season starts soon. Everyone wants me to dine with them, attend their blasted veranda affairs, go to their balls –'

'You're the wealthiest man in Mauritius, Ward. You hold liens on the sugar crops, mortgages on plantations and slaves and have coffers of money to lend. That's why a hostess invites you, not because she wants you to bed her.'

'I'll show you,' he said again, stooping down and plucking up one of the invitations. 'See this.' He thrust it at her.

'Mrs Didcott's veranda affair at her Academy for Young Ladies. We'll go there. You'll see how the women want me. I'll be under the skirts of the most beautiful white lady in Port Louis before the season ends. I don't care if she's virgin, married or a bitch like you. I'll have her with ease.'

He gazed out over the courtyard to where the cane was growing. He was excited by his scheme. At last he saw a way to get even with Gina and end her constant mockery of him.

Darkness had descended. Dell, the houseboy, was hanging lanterns in the trees.

Gina was right. He had everything a planter could want: a prosperous plantation, a herd of two hundred prime slaves and a nursery full of niggerlings being reared for sale, abundant wealth, a grand mansion ... everything except the loyalty and love of a white woman.

He would show Gina she was wrong. He did not need her.

When he looked back, Gina was moving towards the stairs that led up the side of the house to her chamber. He had not entered her room for nearly three years.

A slave stood at the foot of the staircase, watching her devotedly. His broad shoulders were covered in a shirt of the sheerest silk, lace ruffles at his collar. He bowed as Gina approached, then extended his arm to escort her up the steps.

It was Clovis, the negro Ward had castrated when he caught him in bed with her.

Gina, Ward vowed as he watched them walk up the stairs together, was not going to neuter him too.

Book One
A VERANDA AFFAIR
1816–1817

The greatest charm of Port Louis is not in the set festivities of the season but in the pleasant little parties on the veranda after supper; at these veranda affairs the visitor finds himself flattered and enchanted by the gracious and urbane courtesy which prevails ...

Auguste Billard, 1817

ONE

Nicole was determined that she would attend the veranda affair; Mrs Didcott was adamant that she would not.

'It's out of the question,' Mrs Didcott said. 'What will people *think*?'

Nicole was dismayed by her remark. She stared at Mrs Didcott as she sat on the edge of the couch nonchalantly pouring herself a cup of tea. She was English and the insult to Nicole was uttered without shame.

Mrs Didcott's lips twitched with a hard smile. 'I'm glad you understand, my girl. With the cream of society on my veranda, how can I possibly allow you to be seen? You shall stay in your chamber and attend to your lessons.' She finished pouring the tea and with deliberation placed the silver teapot on the table. She raised the cup and its saucer towards her.

Nicole wanted to dash over and thrust the cup in her face but she remained standing awkwardly at the edge of the circle of chairs. She glanced around the cluttered drawing-room and wondered what to do. Although she knew she should bob a curtsy and withdraw from Mrs Didcott's presence, a spark of defiance made her linger.

'Is it because you think I'm too young?' she demanded. Then she added, before Mrs Didcott could take the cup from her lips, 'In this country, girls make their first appearance in public at fifteen. Minette de la Morinay was only thirteen when she married Major Lindsay and I'm sixteen already –'

'Nicole!' Mrs Didcott's voice stung her to silence with the force of a slave whip snapped across her buttocks. The china figurines in the glass-fronted cabinet where the bible was kept seemed to tremble at the harsh sound.

Nicole refused to be intimidated. She was glad she had upset Mrs Didcott although she expected she would soon feel the lady's tawse on her knuckles.

Mrs Didcott's cup clattered into its saucer as she puffed herself up to deliver her rebuke. 'I have seen,' she said in a tone of outrage, 'certain females in this country seated astride horses like gentlemen. It is not done, *Miss Genave*, in *English* society, even if girls do marry at thirteen in the Creole community. In this house, we conduct ourselves with propriety, in behaviour and morals.'

'Yes, m'm.' Nicole bowed her head. Again the English lady had by insinuation made her feel unworthy.

Nicole failed to understand what connection there was in riding and her desire to attend the veranda party. It was simply part of Mrs Didcott's general disapproval of her. Before she had come to live in the house as companion to Mr and Mrs Didcott's daughter, Emma, she had no misgivings about her conduct, or about being a Creole.

'Go to your room, *Miss Genave*.'

The command was uttered sarcastically and Nicole tried to ignore it because each time Mrs Didcott referred, even obliquely, to her shame, she felt crushed. She raised her eyes and gazed with appropriate deference as Mrs Didcott regarded her disdainfully. She began to speak, then changed her mind.

'Yes, m'm,' she whispered, curtsied briefly and hurried from the room, relieved to have escaped without a stroke across her knuckles from the tawse.

Mrs Didcott wore the tawse dangling on a ribbon at her waist where a Creole matron would wear scissors. She used it to emphasize the words of the Lord when she was instructing her class of ten young ladies, and Nicole, in her schoolroom. She applied it vigorously, especially on Nicole, when any of her pupils asked questions she considered impertinent.

'A young lady,' she would say with a switch of the short leather thong across a girl's hand, 'does not bother her head with unnecessary matters.'

Nicole dawdled now she was out of the fiercesome woman's presence. It was Mrs Didcott's habit to take tea and relax in the drawing-room until it was time for her husband to return from the court-house where he was acting Receiver of Registration Dues. Nicole calculated he would not arrive for another thirty minutes; she had time to plan her next move.

It was not her wish to be disrespectful to her benefactress. She was prepared to look on Mrs Didcott's refusal to let her attend the party as being born out of her ignorance of local customs. The season would be starting properly in one month's time, in June, and people would think it very odd if she did not appear in public beside Emma. She was, after all, born in Mauritius whereas Emma came from England.

'I *shall* attend,' she vowed to herself as she walked slowly up the stairs. Emma's father would give his permission if she asked him. He was so well meaning he would never consider that her presence would be a disgrace. Unfortunately what Mr Didcott agreed could be overruled by his wife.

She was a *Tartar*! Nicole shivered at her boldness in abusing the lady who had helped her. Yet it was hard to feel gratitude in the face of Mrs Didcott's hectoring manner. Even her appearance was frightening. She towered above the girls in her academy and was built like a boatswain. Her hair, cut unfashionably short, was steel grey and accentuated the sternness of her face. Hair sprouted from a mole on her upper lip, just under her nose, like a moustache.

She was a formidable woman. It would take all Nicole's wiles to convince her she should be allowed to attend the veranda affair. She paused at the top of the stairs and listened.

From the chamber she shared with Emma came the sound of Emma ham-fistedly practising the guitar. She sighed at the clash of cords. Emma was like her mother, too brash to be successful at anything sensitive.

'You're strumming,' she said, pushing open the door.

'Play it gently. It's supposed to produce music, not earache.'

Emma looked up with a grim smile. 'Mamma says I must learn, so I *will* learn.' She struck another chord.

Nicole winced. 'You're fighting it.' She held out her hand for the instrument. 'Like this.'

She played a few notes and began to hum the words of a popular French air. The music soothed her while Emma's admiration helped revive her squashed confidence.

'You play so well! I wish I could. Are all Creoles musical?'

Nicole smiled. 'We enjoy singing, dancing, the sound of a military band. Doesn't everyone?'

'Not everyone can play as divinely as you.' Emma looked so woebegone, Nicole laughed.

'Everyone is good at something,' she said, laying the guitar aside.

'No, give it to me.' Emma held out her hand. 'Mamma wants me to play at the party. I've simply got to practise.'

'You?' Nicole was flabbergasted.

'Isn't it awful? I'm sure I'll drive all the guests away.'

'No, you won't. They'll love it.' Nicole walked to her bed and sat on it while Emma resumed her heavy-handed strumming.

Music was important to the success of any social occasion in Port Louis. Every evening, after the decline of the sun, families gathered in their gardens to enjoy the cool air, chatting gently among themselves while one of the young females of the family played guitar, accompanying the instrument with her voice.

Emma's voice, thought Nicole glumly, was as raucous as her mother's, and as incapable of holding a tune as her fingers were of plucking one. As she listened to the dreadful sound, Nicole wanted to tell the girl to stop it but she was loath to upset her. Emma, despite her physical resemblance to her mother, was rather simple-minded and hated to be criticized. She was like her father in many ways.

Mr Didcott was a vague, obliging man who spent much of his time away from his wife. Every evening when he returned from his court duties, he listened to his wife's complaints about her day, ate his supper and then, with a cry of 'My goodness, I'll be late, must be off,' he would excuse himself and return to the town.

Nicole had Emma to thank for being invited to live in the Didcott home. Mr Didcott had wanted Emma, his only child, to have a companion when they arrived in Mauritius three years previously. Nicole had been chosen because she was recently orphaned.

At that time there were few white ladies, either English, French or Creole, in Port Louis. Later, when settlers arrived from Great Britain and officials brought out their families, there were sufficient pupils for Mrs Didcott to start her Academy for Young Ladies. It was her own idea and one which received the whole-hearted support of Robert Farquhar, the colony's governor.

The veranda affair that Mrs Didcott was planning would herald the unofficial start of the social season. Being a snob, she chose her guests for their status. They were all British, with the exceptions of two. One was the United States commercial agent, William Buchanan.

None of the French, however important they judged themselves to be, were invited. Creoles too, as the white people born in Mauritius were called, were excluded, except for one, Ward Trenchard.

Mrs Didcott felt obliged to invite him because of his influence. Since he was known never to accept invitations, she had no fear that she would actually have to entertain him and his brazen wife on her veranda.

The official commencement of the season was in June, when the first race meet was held in the Champ de Mars. It marked the start of winter, with the cyclone season safely over and the temperature in the town dropping to the seventies.

Ball succeeded ball rapidly and dinner parties were given by the British nearly every night. Mrs Didcott depended on the success of her veranda party to give her and her nominated young ladies entrée to every event of the season's social calendar.

Nicole sighed at the thought of the excitement. The season was the sole topic of conversation among the young ladies of the Academy. Curiously, in previous years, Nicole accepted being excluded from the festivities and took a worldly attitude at the foolishness of girls who were 'coming out'.

Now she was resentful because it was to be Emma's turn, not hers. She sighed loudly.

'Oh dear! Is my playing as bad as that?'

Emma's cry of concern broke into her thoughts. 'No,' she replied quickly, sitting up and blinking.

'You gave such a sigh, I thought you must be bored with it.'

'Forgive me.' She rose from the bed and walked over and touched Emma's shoulder. 'I was thinking.'

'What about?' Emma put the guitar on her own bed with a sigh of relief. 'Do tell me. Have you seen a young man?'

'Of course not.'

'What a shame. I do wish our house was closer to the Champ de Mars. Every evening the most divine young men promenade around its perimeter. If we were just a bit closer we could see them from the veranda.'

Nicole frowned at Emma's frivolity, although she envied her carefree attitude. Everything was a game for her yet perhaps this very season she would meet a dashing army officer or government writer and be married. She would have to sail 'home' to England and there raise a family.

'How dejected you look this evening, Nicole. Quite a sourpuss.'

'Shh! If your mother hears you –'

'Fiddle!' said Emma. 'I've had quite enough of Mamma for one day. She's determined to turn me into a model young lady so I can be a credit to her. I don't *feel* like an exemplary young lady at all.'

'Yes, you do!' Nicole was shocked by her outburst.

'Do I? Perhaps I will when the season starts. Isn't it wonderful? At last I'll be able to go to all those balls and dance with a different man every time. I'll be able to sit on the veranda while the moon shines and a beau whispers sweet nothings in my ear.' She giggled.

'I'll have my first kiss, first *real* one I mean ...' She paused, then added, 'I'll be sure to tell you all about it.'

'You knew!' she gasped.

'Knew what?' Emma opened her eyes wide, pretending innocence.

'You knew I'd be excluded from the party! Your mother told you I wouldn't be allowed to come out!'

'Oh, that!' Emma shrugged her shoulders in an unladylike manner. A strand of hair drifted across her eyes and she brushed it back, taking her time to say, 'Is coming out really important?'

'You seem to think it is.'

'Well, perhaps it is for the British. The French are different. They have their own parties and so forth, quite a different season.'

'I'm Creole, not French.'

'Oh yes ... Are you banned from the French parties too?'

Nicole dismissed the remark before she let it hurt her. She watched Emma carefully as she reached for the guitar again. If she played at the veranda party, Nicole thought, she would drive away any beau who might otherwise be prepared to ignore her plain features.

It was curious how English girls lacked a talent for music. All they thought of was men and horses and any activity that combined the two, such as horse-racing or stag hunting or picnicking at the foot of Pouce Mountain.

'Oh bother!' Emma said, slapping the guitar strings angrily. 'Mamma insists we have music. I've simply got to do it.'

The sound jarred Nicole's nerves. Suddenly an idea so bold it caused her to catch her breath sprang into her mind. She stared at the flamboyant tree, gripping the window-ledge with her hands. She was aghast at her wickedness.

'You all right, miz?'

Nicole shut her mouth and looked around. Fidou, their maid, was standing beside her. 'Yes, of course,' she said trembling. 'I was thinking.'

Fidou sniffed suspiciously. She was two years older than

Nicole and Emma but seemed a century wiser. Nothing escaped her attention. Nicole faltered under her stern gaze.

'You an' Miz Emma quarrellin'?' she demanded.

'What a funny idea,' laughed Emma. 'We've never done that, have we, Nicole?'

'No.' Nicole shook her head vigorously. She had an uncomfortable feeling that Fidou could read her thoughts.

'I shall go to bed early tonight,' she said, moving away from the window and Fidou's scrutiny. 'Perhaps I do have a slight headache. Do you mind very much leaving the guitar alone for this evening, Emma?'

Nicole had the greatest difficulty keeping calm and acting normally during the ten days until the party. Emma, of course, noticed nothing. She prattled about the men she was longing to meet, how she would captivate them and win the handsomest for herself. All day she practised the guitar, being excused her other lessons by her mother, who was anxious that she should perform at her best.

It was Fidou whom Nicole feared. It was silly to be afraid of a slave but she dreaded what might happen if Fidou saw through her plan and reported her to Mrs Didcott. She made every effort to be especially nice to her just in case.

She brooded all week on her idea although outwardly she appeared as cheerful as usual. Her good humour almost led to her undoing when Mrs Didcott commented on it.

'What a relief you've accepted your position at last, Nicole,' she said. 'You'll get on well now you know you are Emma's companion and can never be her equal.'

'Yes, m'm,' Nicole replied, assuming a sulky expression to make Mrs Didcott think she really was unhappy about missing the party.

The evening finally arrived. Over thirty guests were expected, including the governor, the garrison commander, the chief justice and the accountant general. Mrs Didcott was in a state of high excitement as she prepared herself, shouting orders to the house slaves and causing everyone to feel flustered.

In her chamber Nicole watched Fidou helping Emma to dress. She was nervous as she summoned up the courage to carry out her plan. 'Emma, dear,' she said, trying to sound sad. 'I shall be thinking of you on the veranda enjoying yourself.'

'You'll hear the music and chatter from up here,' said Emma moving to her side to embrace her. 'You can imagine you're on the veranda too.'

'Ah yes ...' She tried to look tearful. 'Would you do me a favour, Emma?' she asked softly.

'Anything!'

'Wear my handkerchief. It's the one I was saving for my first season. It's very pretty.'

'Where is it?'

'In the chest, I think. Help me look.'

She opened the chest and waited until Emma's hands were on the edge of it and she was about to reach inside to search through the contents.

'What colour is it?'

'Oh, there it is.' Nicole peered into the chest over Emma's shouler and pretended to stumble. She caught at the lid to steady herself, at the same time making sure it slipped from her grasp. It slammed down with a sickening thud on Emma's fingers.

Emma shrieked with agony and pulled away.

'Miz Nicole,' said Fidou with a puzzled frown. 'What *have* you done?'

'My fingers!' wailed Emma, holding up her bruised hands.

'I'm so sorry,' said Nicole. 'I slipped.'

Emma burst into tears as her mother bustled into the room.

'Do stop that noise!' shouted Mrs Didcott. 'My head!' She gaped at Emma. 'For heaven's sake, child, you'll ruin your dress.'

'Emma's hurt her fingers.' Nicole held her breath and waited. 'It was an accident.'

'I can't play tonight!' gasped Emma between her tears.

'Of course you can! We *must* have music.'

'I can't,' she said unhappily. 'Look.' Her hands were blue where the lid had struck them. Nicole felt a twinge of guilt.

'What will I do?' Mrs Didcott croaked with despair at the prospect of her party being ruined. She glanced helplessly from Fidou to Nicole and back to Emma still shaking with tears.

Nicole waited a few moments while Emma sobbed and Mrs Didcott fussed about the room, then she spoke up timidly. 'If you like, I could play. I don't mind.'

Mrs Didcott looked at her with relief. 'Why, of course! Thank the Lord for that.' Her expression changed to dismay at the thought of Nicole's background. 'But you must sit in a corner out of sight. You're not to speak to anyone!'

Nicole lowered her head to avoid Fidou's glance. 'Yes, m'm,' she answered, amazed that her wickedness had succeeded.

TWO

Jonathan tightened his stock and was about to turn away from the looking-glass when he halted. He faced his reflection in the full-length mirror and scowled at himself. He looked perfectly acceptable now but in less than an hour the stock would be wilted, his shirt soaked in perspiration and a rash of tiny pimples would prickle his arms and neck in the heat.

It was nearly six years since he stepped ashore on the beach at Black River with Mr Farquhar, yet he was still not accustomed to the high temperature, the humidity, the mosquitoes, the brashness of the Creoles, the cunning of the slaves. His catalogue of complaints about Mauritius would appal Governor Farquhar if he knew.

Jonathan shrugged, brushed back the lock of hair that habitually flopped over his brow, and stared carefully at his reflection in the fading light entering the room from its single window.

When he first took up residence in Government House, he had an apartment that overlooked the courtyard. French windows gave a view down the avenue of magnificent palm trees lining the Place d'Armes to the harbour. Now he lived in a chamber the size of the governor's dressing-room, located at the back of the house, over the slave quarters.

There had been many changes since those exciting days when the British took possession of Port Louis from the French and he marched through the town behind Mr Farquhar as his unofficial aide-de-camp. He was young then, only twenty-two, and full of hope. The optimism had died in the eyes of the person watching him glumly from the mirror.

His face was dominated by his nose, which seemed to weigh it down. It gave him a hangdog appearance that lifted only when he smiled, which was rarely. He was a modest man without ambition. In a gathering or at a meeting, he liked to merge into the background without being noticed.

He smoothed down his coat to remove its wrinkles. He was dressed soberly in clerical grey with freshly laundered breeches and shoes that he had polished himself, instead of trusting a slave to do it. Alas, after a few minutes in the streets of Port Louis, the gloss would be smothered in dirt, his coat would be creased and his effort to appear smartly dressed would be in vain.

He turned from the mirror with a sigh. All day he had been copying Governor Farquhar's dispatches into ledgers. It was clerk's work. Gone were the days when Mr Farquhar would confide in him. Now he read the governor's views from someone else's script.

He blamed the coterie of self-seeking military men with whom Mr Farquhar surrounded himself at government expense for pushing him aside. It was a shame after he had served Mr Farquhar without salary or thought of personal aggrandizement for ten years.

His door swung open and he glanced in annoyance at the slave who strode into the room. He had never succeeded in getting the house slaves to knock on his door before they entered.

'Guv'nor want yo',' the boy said, nodding his head along the passage that led to the front of the house.

' "Sir," ' said Jonathan with exasperation.

The boy gawked at him.

'Say, "sir"!' Jonathan scowled. 'You must address me as "Sir".'

'Yessah!' The boy backed away with a smirk, not bothering to conceal his contempt.

It was galling for Jonathan to know that not even the blacks respected him. Somehow they sensed he was no longer important in the hierarchy. Why was it so, he wondered. He had served Mr Farquhar well; he spoke only when he was spoken to, not like those hearty people like Dr Telfair and Captain Lesage who were the governor's confidants now.

He hurried along the corridor, smoothing back his hair, feeling a trickle of sweat seeping down his spine. Government House was a large and lofty building, forming three sides of a quadrangle with balconies along each of its three stories. The ground floor, built of coral, was constructed under the direction of La Bourdonnais, a Frenchman who was governor eighty years previously. The superstructure was completed by the British after the capture of the island.

Governor Farquhar's quarters were at the front of the house, where a wing on either side extended out towards the harbour. Jonathan had to walk the full length of the corridor past the governor's office before reaching his private suite. He knocked on the door and waited.

'Come in, come in!' called a voice. 'No need to knock. Door's always open.'

He pushed open the door gingerly and peered behind it. Mr Farquhar stood at the window, with its splendid view of the harbour. The chandelier and the candelabra were lit and the room was bright with light. He held a sheaf of dispatches in his hand and was scanning through them. Jonathan slipped inside and stood by the door. He was surprised to see that Mr Farquhar was alone.

'Hah, Mr Rendye!' The governor grinned at him after he had finished perusing the papers. 'Glad you haven't gone out to supper. I've just received these.' He waved the dispatches at him.

'Yes, sir?' Jonathan was puzzled and glanced beyond the governor's shoulder to the harbour, wondering what ship had newly arrived.

About four British vessels a week entered the port together with occasional ships of French or American registry. Only a few of the British vessels came from England and the arrival of a ship with mail was an event for the townsfolk. Jonathan was surprised he had heard nothing about it.

'HMS *Tyne*, Captain Curran,' said Mr Farquhar, guessing what was on Jonathan's mind. 'Yes, Royal Navy! Top secret.'

Jonathan nodded, understanding the lack of excitement over the ship's arrival. It was so unexpected that even Mr Farquhar's group of toadies was ignorant of its presence. Dr Telfair, with his love of intrigue, would surely have been at Government House if he knew.

'The *Tyne*'s at my disposal, Mr Rendye. To catch the flesh-traders.'

Jonathan watched as Mr Farquhar strode up and down in front of the windows, reviewing the contents of the dispatches in his mind. It was the governor's habit to develop his ideas aloud to help him reach a decision. He did not expect comments from his listeners.

Jonathan enjoyed those moments when he was privy to policy being formed. Alas, such confidences were infrequent in recent years. He suspected he was only being honoured by Mr Farquhar's soliloquy that evening because there was no one else to hear it.

'With a ship,' Mr Farquhar said, striking the papers clasped in his right hand against his left, 'I can be seen to be taking action against the slave-trade. That will satisfy

Ward Trenchard's criticism of my not doing enough to stop it. Oh, I know,' he added as though Jonathan were about to contradict him, 'I know Ward is *breeding* slaves to sell. There's no law against that.' He looked at him expectantly.

'A shortage of slaves on the island would create a demand for Ward Trenchard's Black River breed,' Jonathan said on cue.

'Exactly.' Mr Farquhar stared out of the windows which were open so the breeze could cool the room. The muted sounds of vessels creaking in the harbour drifted up to them.

'This colony cannot survive without regular importation of slaves from Madagascar yet I am obliged by my own law to ban the slave-trade. We need the crops that the slaves produce for the tax those crops bring the treasury. Am I to cut my own throat ... to bring about the destruction of this colony ... to force the settlers to abandon their plantations?' He turned back into the room and glared at Jonathan as though he had dared to suggest it.

'By the devil, no! I have to keep the French settlers agreeable. Thank God, it's only one ship. That can't stop the slave-trade. Ships will still slip into our bays at night and unload their cargoes. Yet I *will* be seen to be making an effort.'

Jonathan was unperturbed by Mr Farquhar's hypocritical reasoning. It had become second nature to him. The governor was a man of charm whose warm brown eyes twinkled with ease. By personality he had won over the French and Creoles who were the island's inhabitants. He retained their support by twisting every directive he received from the British government so he could accommodate the settlers' wishes. He argued that the terms under which the island was capitulated to the British by the French were inviolable.

This attitude to the arrival of a ship that was supposed to stop the slave-trade was typical. Jonathan suspected that the governor's well-known dislike of Ward Trenchard was one reason why he was prepared to tolerate the importation of slaves. He was more interested in harming Ward's sales than in placating the French who also happened to be slave-holders.

The governor's conflict with Ward Trenchard was deep rooted. In the days of Ward's father, Jonathan collected on the governor's behalf a commission on the sale of every Black River slave. Ward had refused to pay the bribe when he inherited the plantation and was open in his criticism of the governor.

Jonathan thought Mr Farquhar seemed troubled. He was holding a single dispatch in his hand. The others had fallen to his desk.

Jonathan longed to sit down. He had been on his feet since six and worked without a break until it was time to dress for supper. This unexpected summons from Mr Farquhar indicated that he was going to be kept up late.

He glanced at him surreptiously as he sat deep in thought. Robert Townsend Farquhar, at forty, retained the enthusiasm with which he had governed the colony since his arrival. He was making up for the lost years when his career had run aground after a bright start.

When he was twenty-three, he had been made governor of the Moluccas. His impetuosity led him to clash with his superiors and he resigned in high dudgeon. For eight years he waited for a new posting and it was only due to his father's connection as physician to the Prince of Wales that he was given Mauritius.

He seized the opportunity eagerly. He had learned from his mistakes and was tactful when disagreeing with official policy. He acted first, doing what he thought was best. He governed the colony with the well-being of the British and the settlers as his objective.

Reconciling the frustrated aspirations of the French with the idealism of the British was not easy. By charm and subterfuge he succeeded.

Jonathan, meanwhile, had become disillusioned by Mr Farquhar's increasingly cavalier attitude towards the demands of the British Government. He believed it was his duty to obey official instructions, not ignore them. He resented being drawn into Mr Farquhar's schemes.

Glancing again at Mr Farquhar, he saw he had slumped backward in the chair at his desk. The sight of such a great man lost in despair stirred him. He felt a love for the man that made him blind to his duplicity.

Mr Farquhar was handsome, with thick black hair that he wore brushed back from his aristocratic forehead. His side whiskers were cut short, one inch below his ear. He had a dynamic and sympathetic nature that won the loyalty of all he encountered. He was interested in people, innovative, courteous and accessible.

Jonathan was ashamed of his lack of faith in him. It had grown gradually, increasing when he was being crowded out of the governor's circle by men who were trying to manipulate him. Now that he and Mr Farquhar were alone he felt the rapport they had shared exerting its bond again.

Suddenly the governor dashed his hand against his brow and uttered a loud moan.

'Is something wrong, sir?' Jonathan stepped over and poured a glass of water from the carafe on the desk. He offered it but Mr Farquhar waved him away irritably.

He stood with the glass in his hand, uncertain what to do.

'Damn! Damn! Damn!' Mr Farquhar banged his fists on the desk and rose to his feet. His chair toppled over, falling to the floor with a loud crash.

Jonathan backed away, still holding the water. He gulped it down rapidly and placed the glass on a table close to the door. He had never seen Mr Farquhar in such a furious mood.

'Close the port?' Mr Farquhar shouted. 'It's impossible!'

Jonathan's heart sank. For years it had been the governor's dream that Mauritius would become a clearing-house, with its port open to ships of all nations. This conflicted with British law that prohibited all but British ships using British ports.

Mr Farquhar had so far avoided compliance with the law by procrastination and by utilizing the civil service ploy of requesting clarification whenever his attention was drawn to something he had deliberately neglected to action.

'I've lost!' he said, coming to rest at his desk. 'All this,' he gestured out of the window at the forest of masts in the harbour, 'for nothing.'

Jonathan waited with bated breath for his anger to calm.

'We're trying to build up trade here. To make the colony prosper so it can stand by itself, even contribute to the British exchequer ...' Mr Farquhar's voice died; he had expounded his arguments in dozens of dispatches to the secretary of state.

'Can't they see the restrictions they are placing on us by forcing me to close the port?' he cried in frustration.

'Perhaps,' whispered Jonathan, 'they view Mauritius as fulfilling its place in an overall policy of which we know nothing?'

'Policy? Bah!' Mr Farquhar glared at him as though he were stupid. 'You credit the British government with a policy! There's none. Some confounded clerk in London disagrees with me because I want to go against their navigation act. He has the minister's ear. The result: *Express* orders to close the port to foreign ships.' He sighed.

'That's why they sent the Royal Navy, Jonathan, not to help suppress the slave-trade but to suppress *our* trade, our lifeline.'

When Mr Farquhar called him by his Christian name, with such helplessness in his voice, Jonathan felt compelled to aid him, even though he disagreed vehemently with defying the secretary of state.

'Excuse me, sir,' he said, emboldened by Mr Farquhar's dismay. 'At the moment there must be several foreign ships bound for Mauritius. They have cargoes ordered by our merchants, British as well as French.'

'Dammit, Jonathan, of course there are! That's what I've been working on for all these years.'

'If you obey your instructions and close the port immediately, those colonists who have invested money in cargoes will be ruined.'

'Don't tell me what I already know.'

'I'm sorry, sir.' Jonathan waited while Mr Farquhar shook his head with exasperation, then he added, 'If colonists would be ruined, wouldn't that permit you to declare a grace period before putting your orders into effect?'

'By jove!' Mr Farquhar advanced on Jonathan and clapped his arm around his shoulder, hugging him. 'I didn't think you had it in you! Excellent idea, quite in line with the British government's thinking. Three months' grace, wouldn't you say? My dispatch will take that time to reach London so the Minister will have no opportunity to disagree with me.

'I'll be carrying out their policy with wisdom, minimizing its negative effects. I could get a knighthood for diplomacy!'

'Yes, sir,' said Jonathan, already forgetting that the idea had been his.

It was late when Governor Farquhar finished dictating his replies to the dispatches from London. Jonathan was hungry. He left the drafts on the desk of Mr Bateman, the acting chief clerk, so that he would arrange for their copying when he came on duty in the morning. He returned to Mr Farquhar's chamber, hoping to be dismissed for the evening.

'What entertainment is there tonight?' demanded Mr Farquhar unexpectedly. 'I'm in need of divertissement.'

Jonathan wanted to eat and go to bed. He doubted if he could find a slave to prepare him food at that hour. The dining-room in Massey's Hotel in the Chaussée, a few steps from Government House, was probably closed as well. He answered cautiously.

'Mistress Didcott has her veranda affair this evening –'

'So she does! Dreadful woman; such a social climber. Shall we honour her with our presence? She'll give poor Arthur Didcott no peace at all if we don't. She depends on the affair to give her status for the season.'

'She is highly regarded for her academy. She does

wonders refining the young ladies under her tuition.'

'Otherwise they'd be chasing my soldiers, would they?' Mr Farquhar laughed, his good humour restored. 'No, Jonathan, the young ladies do wonders for her. They are all well born and properly behaved. They give Mrs Didcott the cachet she craves.' He was thoughtful before speaking again.

'Old Arthur's a good sort, pillar of the club, there every night. He's the one who does wonders for the welfare of others. More than his wife with her wretched prejudices. Have you ever seen a Creole kiss her hand? She'd as lief smash his jaw if he tried.'

Jonathan flushed at the slur. That Mrs Didcott gave the French and Creoles short shrift was well known; it was a common attitude among the British settlers. Ordinary people struggling to make their living in the colony found it difficult to share the governor's magnanimity to their erstwhile enemies and social inferiors.

'You look glum, Mr Rendye. An evening with Mrs Didcott's young ladies will do you a power of good.'

'I'm not invited.'

'I'm inviting you.'

'Yes, sir.' Jonathan was embarrassed when Mr Farquhar took him by his elbow and guided him out of the room.

'I shall instruct Mistress Didcott to introduce you to her prize student. She longs to be a matchmaker, let her practise with you. I'm surprised you've escaped her machinations.'

Jonathan blushed. 'She prefers army officers or merchants to an impecunious clerk.'

Governor Farquhar withdrew his hand and shrugged his shoulders. 'Yes, perhaps you're right,' he said with a sigh of distaste, casting his eye over Jonathan in a manner which made him feel he disgraced him.

'You're nothing to boast about, I suppose.'

'No, sir,' said Jonathan as his neck began to prickle. 'I mean, yes.' He followed Mr Farquhar blindly down the steps and into the courtyard.

THREE

The Didcott residence lay off the street leading to the Champ de Mars. At daybreak every morning, the town's market was held in that street and even as Jonathan accompanied Governor Farquhar along its length, vendors of produce newly arrived from the country districts were squabbling for the best pitches.

In the light from the flambeau held aloft by a slave walking in front of them, Jonathan gazed on the natives in fascination. They were all colours; the black of a Mozambique negro, the brown of a Malabar Indian, the copper of a Malagash and the sallow complexion of a mulatto.

Governor Farquhar skirted around them as he picked his way along the uneven surface of the street. The vendors were typical of the mixture of races that inhabited Port Louis. They gave the town its resemblance to an Eastern bazaar.

There were twenty-five thousand inhabitants in Port Louis; only three thousand were Europeans. They lived, like the Didcotts, in the area adjoining the Champ de Mars, a level green plain about a mile in area. In the town's western suburb, called Camp Libre, lived the coloured people and freed slaves, while the eastern suburb, Camp Malabar, was the home of the Indians. Between the two quarters lived the Chinese.

The streets of the town were in a lamentable state despite the governor's efforts to raise funds by lottery to maintain them. There was not a single street lamp. Even so, as the Champ de Mars was a short distance from Government House, Mr Farquhar preferred to walk. He strode out purposefully while Jonathan hurried behind him, keeping an eye on the ground so he did not befoul his shoes with sewage.

The houses in the street were wooden, built side by side with no gap between. Some had stood for a hundred years and were in danger of collapsing, their ramshackle appearance contributing to the inhospitable atmosphere of the area. Jonathan scarcely breathed because of the stench of the street until they reached the breezy spaciousness of the Champ de Mars.

The plain extended in a gradual slope from the distant mountains that formed an amphitheatre around it. Many neat villas were built overlooking the plain, each house with a large veranda at its front and a parterre enclosed by a wall.

The Didcott residence was located away from the plain, close behind the end of the street they had just left. They were drawn to it by the sound of chattering coming from the veranda, and by its gay appearance with lanterns hung in the flamboyant tree and lights blazing out from open shutters.

Governor Farquhar brushed aside the slave guarding the entrance and walked confidently up the path onto the veranda. There was a flurry in the crowd and a space opened around him, the governor at one end and Mrs Didcott at the other. She looked at him sharply, the hairs on her upper lip quivering with delight when she realized who he was.

'Your Excellency!' she exclaimed, sinking to a curtsy. Jonathan, lurking behind the governor, was impressed by the grace with which she moved for such a large woman.

Mr Farquhar nodded and glanced around him with every sign of pleasure. 'Ah, Mistress Didcott,' he said, 'how I have looked forward to this evening! Your veranda affair ushers in the season like a swallow in England heralds summer. I applaud your selfless efforts to preserve British standards and see we celebrate in style.'

The governor allowed her to present her young ladies. Jonathan was embarrassed by the smoothness with which Mr Farquhar lied, never revealing a hint of his true feelings.

Jonathan himself stayed at the edge of the veranda where

he could survey the gathering. He was conscious of his hunger, a gnawing pain that prevented him from relaxing, although he would never feel completely at ease in such company. When he heard a droll, high-pitched voice delivering sallies that were greeted with roars of laughter, he grimaced. Mr Hook was entertaining the guests.

Mr Hook was the colony's accountant general and treasurer. He was paid a huge salary of two thousand pounds a year. He was Jonathan's age, a dandified dilettante who had attracted the patronage of the Prince of Wales because he wrote musical comedies. His presence in Mauritius was to escape his creditors. Jonathan resented him for his lack of ability and for becoming one of Mr Farquhar's intimates. He flinched at the shrill sound of his voice.

There were others of his ilk on the veranda. Although Chief Justice George Smith was well qualified for his post, his flagrant dalliance with coloured girls destroyed the respect Jonathan once had for him. The garrison commander, General Campbell, was another liability. His pack of hunting dogs had caused a rabies epidemic. He was foolish enough to believe, so he had boasted to Jonathan, that Mauritians were so docile they could be governed with four men and a corporal.

Jonathan considered the guests and was depressed by what he saw. Fortunately no one bothered to speak to him. He stood half-hidden by a screen of trellis-work made of Indian reed with some shrubbery growing in pots around it. As he observed his fellow Englishmen enjoying themselves, he wondered if they were all as duplicitous in their powerful positions as Governor Farquhar was. The prospect chilled him.

'Jonathan, what a surprise!'

The gushing of a woman's voice interrupted his thoughts and he turned in alarm. His cheek began to twitch as he tried to speak.

'Uh, eh ...' he stammered, feeling ashamed. 'Mrs ... Mrs ... uh ... Trenchard ...' He bowed stiffly.

'You used to call me Georgina,' the woman said, fluttering her eyelashes. 'You said it so sweetly.'

'Yes.' He could not think of anything else to say. The sudden sight of Georgina Buchanan, as he used to know her, was a shock. She had changed almost beyond recognition. In vain he looked for the svelte beauty he had once worshipped. She had broadened, toughened, and there was in her eyes a glint of malice where before a flirtatious twinkle used to shine.

'It's been a long time.'

'Yes,' he said again.

'Oh, Jonathan! You're gaping at me like a startled fish. Am I really so repulsive?'

'No. I'm sorry, I didn't –'

'You never did, Jonathan. Now you must call me Gina.' She reached for his hand and Jonathan flinched. She tapped him lightly on his cuff. 'Sometimes, my dear, I long for the old days. I declare, you haven't changed since you were my beau.'

He pulled at his nose unhappily.

'Don't be embarrassed, Jonathan. I'm not going to *expose* you.' Her eyes glimmered with a mischievousness that looked out of place in her bloated features. 'It's marriage to Ward that's done this to me. I'm still the same *underneath*.' She gestured at the formal gown she was wearing, making it quite clear what she meant. Her breasts seemed ready to burst out of her bodice.

Jonathan blushed at the innuendo.

'Dear me, Jonathan, neither of us are innocents now.'

'No. I mean yes.' He fidgetted, longing to escape from the woman. 'The governor's here,' he said lamely. 'I came with him. He might need me –'

'Nonsense. Robert Farquhar is quite capable of getting along without you, or so I've heard. I hear you're not as close to him as you were. Ward's pleased, and so am I.'

'Well –'

'Just because I haven't been to town for months doesn't mean I don't know the gossip.'

'I see.'

'Let's talk about you, Jonathan. Any romance in your life?'

'No!' His answer sounded like the croak of a man being strangled.

'Really?' Gina moved closer, forcing him up against the trellis-work.

'I don't have time.'

Gina's mouth was open, her lips parted in what she evidently imagined was an alluring smile. 'You must come to Black River to stay, Jonathan. Ward is so *involved* with his slaves. It gets very lonely. I'd *love* to see you. We could renew our friendship.'

'Yes.'

Gina's hand reached out and touched his chest, lingering too long. She fluttered her eyelashes again.

'Is Ward here?' he gasped.

Gina's face hardened and she withdrew her hand. 'Somewhere,' she said, her eyes wandering over the crowd of guests. She spotted Ward in conversation with Mrs Didcott. 'He's treating me abominably, Jonathan,' she whispered in a voice that was meant to win his sympathy. It sent a shiver down his spine.

'I'm sorry.'

'It's not *your* fault.' She tittered harshly. 'Do come! Ward won't even notice.'

He brushed at his forelock and felt a rash spreading under his stock. There was a lull as he tried to think of something to say. From the other end of the veranda came the sound of someone playing the guitar.

'I'll try,' he said, edging away.

'Good.' Gina's eyes narrowed. 'I'll be waiting.'

He nodded. 'The governor,' he said, stepping backwards and indicating that he had to leave. She smirked and turned her back on him, walking over to the crowd of guests with an exaggerated sway of her hips.

A voice began to sing softly the words of a song currently in vogue with the French. Jonathan was relaxed by it, although he was surprised to hear French sung on Mrs Didcott's veranda. He strained to listen to the tune above the hubbub of conversation, hoping that Gina would not return. When he lowered his head, he saw he was still alone.

He glanced at the backs of the guests. Gina was engaged in small talk with Theodore Hook. Hastily he stepped down off the veranda. At that moment the song came to an end.

Moving swiftly, he crossed the front of the house to its corner and glided down the side where it was dark. He sighed with relief at his escape.

He guessed the kitchen would be located at the back of the house. He was too shy to ask Mrs Didcott for something to eat; his hunger drove him to seek the food himself. Refreshment at these veranda affairs was restricted to *eau sucree* and beer although sometimes burgundy and water would be offered and even rum if the men were alone.

His stomach rumbled as he reached the rear of the house. He paused. There was a cabin a few paces away from the back door which he supposed was the kitchen. The door was fastened and it was in darkness. The only light was the faint candle glow shining through the cracks in the shutters of the house.

There was a rustle in the garden behind him. He froze, terrified of being discovered like a common prowler. A whiff of perfume tingled his nostrils before someone bumped into him. He put his hands up to defend himself, praying that it was not Gina.

A strange voice squealed with surprise. 'Let me go!'

Hastily he dropped his arms to his side and pressed himself against the wall of the house. 'I'm dreadfully sorry,' he said. 'I didn't mean to frighten you.'

'What *are* you doing?' The voice was that of a woman, husky with excitement yet confident despite the shock he had given her.

'Actually,' he said, swallowing his embarrassment, 'I was looking for the kitchen.'

'Why?'

'Why?' He pulled at his nose. 'Well, because I'm hungry.'

A tinkle of laughter greeted his confession.

'What's so funny?' he asked, feeling at a disadvantage because in the darkness he could not see his interrogator.

She was obviously not Gina and was too bold to be a servant. Yet her accent, with its charming lilt and hint of mischief, owed more to French influence than to English. She was probably Creole.

'I've been watching you since you arrived,' the mysterious Creole said. 'You hate this affair, don't you?'

'I assure you that's not true. I haven't had supper. I thought I could find the cook –'

'How very independent! You could have sent for something.' The woman moved away from him toward the back door and again he caught the scent of her perfume, a heady mixture of verbena, lime and the fragrance of vetiver.

'Come with me.'

'I really don't want to be any trouble.'

'You're not.' She opened the door. In the light that spilled around her as she climbed the steps into the house, he saw she was a girl in a white dress with black hair hanging in ringlets around her shoulders.

He stumbled after her, stepping into the house with the clumsiness of a country bumpkin.

'I'm sor –' he began to say before she cut him off with a giggle.

'You seem quite faint with hunger,' she said. 'Sit here.' She caught his arm and guided him to a chair beside a long dining table. It had been cleared of its wares; a haunch of cold venison was on the sideboard opposite.

He sat down and watched the girl carve off several slices from the joint with the assurance of a woman used to her way around the kitchen.

He gazed at her, uncertain whether he could trust himself to speak. Another hunger gnawed at him and he was ashamed of it. His eyes were caught by those ringlets bobbing above her shoulders as she carved energetically. He knew by instinct that her curls were real, not the product of a maid's labouring the whole afternoon with hot tongs. Such a contrast to Gina.

She turned to him and her friendly smile made him forget his nervousness.

'A glass of wine?' she asked as she laid the plate on the table in front of him.

'No, no, I don't really drink.'

'I recommend it,' she said. 'It's the only thing French that Mrs Didcott allows in the house.'

The girl took up a decanter and poured wine into a glass before he could protest. She offered it to him, so he took it to please her. She waited with her eyes on his until he raised the glass to his lips and sipped.

'I forgot the cutlery,' she said, breaking the spell. She spun around the room, the skirt of her dress billowing at her ankles. With another laugh she placed a knife and fork in front of him. 'Now eat.'

'I don't feel hungry any more,' he said guiltily. Her laughter made him smile.

'That's better,' she said. 'You looked too melancholy before.'

'I'm not given to frivolity.' It sounded pompous and he took up the knife and fork to disguise his embarrassment. He tried the venison; it was delicious. Within moments he was eating ravenously. He took another sip of wine and raised his eyes to look at the girl.

She seemed to have sensed his shyness and moved away while he was eating. She was standing by the door which was still open, gazing out into the night. Her face, in repose, was gentle, with delicate features and long dark lashes. Her cheeks glowed richly like a native rose. She was the opposite of English girls, who hid all day from the sun and the open air. Her figure was slender and graceful, with a hint of womanhood.

He was drawn to her eyes, sombre as she stared into the darkness. She felt the intensity of his gaze for she turned abruptly. Her cheeks, he was enchanted to see, deepened in colour.

'You must think me very bold,' she said, standing with her hands clasped daintily at her waist. She was breathing rapidly and he wondered why she was nervous.

'It is I who am bold,' he said, rising to his feet. 'Please forgive me. My intrusion –'

'No, you are a guest, you didn't intrude. I am the one. I'm forbidden to talk to you.'

'Why is that?'

'Mrs Didcott's instructions.'

'Ah,' he said, relieved to find a clue to her identity. 'You are one of her pupils. Oh dear, what have I done that you are obliged to avoid me?'

She looked at him as though she found him odd. 'Not you.' She shrugged. 'It's my background. I'm Creole, you see.'

'You *are* one of her pupils?'

'Only on sufferance. I'm Emma's companion. I'm allowed on the veranda to play the guitar, not as a guest.'

'We have something in common.' He moved towards her. 'Mrs Didcott didn't invite me either but I'd wager I'm enjoying myself more than any guest on the veranda.'

He was amazed at what he was saying. The girl had loosened his tongue and confused him so he was unable to think properly.

'How *charmant*!'

He wondered if she was mocking him by her use of the cliché that was fashionable among the Creoles. Her smile, though, was warm. She seemed oblivious of his greasy hair and too long a nose.

'Miz Nicole!'

A black face suddenly reared up beside the girl and Jonathan shrank back. The negress pushed her way into the room and stared at him for a long moment before she turned back to the girl. She said nothing.

'Fidou, this is Mr Rendye. He's very important at Government House.' There was silence. The girl continued. 'He was hungry so I brought him here for something to eat.' She paused again, then added in a rush, 'Please don't tell Mistress Didcott.'

Jonathan looked at the slave sternly.

Fidou's expression wavered from outrage to fear and he felt he could trace what was going through her mind as he watched her face. He sensed her acquiescence was important to Nicole (he would remember that name) so he spoke too.

'I'm sure this pretty maid is intelligent enough to know when a secret should be preserved?' He raised his eyebrow and was rewarded with a broad smile from the slave.

'Lor', sir,' Fidou said with a conspiratorial wink, 'Miz Nicole is my sister! Why should I tell tales to the Mistress 'bout how she entertainin' a man to victuals?' She laughed suggestively and Nicole blushed at her coarseness.

'*Charmant*,' said Jonathan, allowing himself half a smile to amuse the anxious Creole.

Nicole recovered her poise. 'You should return to the veranda, Mr Rendye.'

'What about you?'

'When you hear the guitar, you'll know I'm there.' She stood aside for him to walk down the steps back into the garden.

Fidou fussed around them preventing him from lingering. He bowed and left the dining-room in a daze, forgetting even to thank her for the meal and the wine. He was light-headed as he followed the path towards the parterre, where lanterns lit up the hibiscus flowers and the chatter of conversation drew him in.

He stepped warily onto the veranda, hoping to avoid another encounter with Gina. He did not want her to spoil the pleasant glow that remained from his meeting with Nicole.

'Say, Jonathan!' a man drawled. 'You here too? Agnes Didcott's standards must have dropped if she's got you on her list of eligible bachelors.'

From anyone else the insult would have caused Jonathan pain, but not from William Buchanan. He was the American commercial agent, the man who might have been his father-in-law but for Gina's preference for Ward Trenchard.

'I'm not that unfortunate,' he replied with more vigour than he usually showed. 'I came with His Excellency.'

'I thought you'd been relegated to the galley, Jonathan. We see you so seldom.'

Jonathan was used to Mr Buchanan's desperate insults. The man had slipped so heavily into debt, mostly to Ward, that he was incapable of a civil word for anybody. He was an American merchant who had married into a Creole family. Since his wife died and his only daughter, Gina, became mistress of the Black River plantation, his self-respect had declined as his desire for liquor increased.

Jonathan regarded his degeneration from his former respectability as a disgrace. It reminded him how lucky he was that Gina Buchanan had jilted him.

Mr Buchanan gripped his elbow suddenly. He staggered, pulling him away from the crowd. 'I hear there were dispatches this evening, son?' he whispered into his ear, inviting a reply.

'I believe so.'

'Nothing to tell me, Jonathan? Must have been important for the Royal Navy to bring them. Makes me wonder what your Governor is scheming now.'

'I dare say you'll be informed in due course.'

'Don't be so pompous, Jonathan. I guessed right – there is something afoot!'

'No, no, I –' He stopped speaking as his ear picked up the music from a guitar. No one else seemed to have heard it. The tune was an eighteenth-century love-song with enchanting lyrics. He listened, spellbound.

William Buchanan pulled back his head from whispering in his ear and stared at his glazed eyes. He snorted, then weaved over to where the music was being played by a young lady sitting behind a screen of miniature palm trees. He nodded to himself and returned to Jonathan's side.

'Who is she?' Jonathan demanded.

Mr Buchanan laid his hand on his shoulder. 'Nicole Genave.' He shook his head in mock pity.

'What's wrong?' Jonathan felt his legs weakening at the unspoken warning in Mr Buchanan's gesture. 'What is it?'

The American shrugged. His smirk implied that he would not tell Jonathan what he knew unless ... 'You have a secret to exchange, son?'

Jonathan was maddened to know more about Nicole. There was no harm in telling what he knew. It would be public knowledge soon.

'Mr Buchanan,' he said gravely. 'You would be advised not to order any foreign merchandise for delivery after August. Foreign ships are to be banned from using the port. British Government orders.'

'Ye gods!' The American swung around and leaped off the veranda. Jonathan chased after him.

'Where are you going?'

'To buy all the landed foreign cargoes I can find, of course. Before the price rises. I'll sell at a profit. Jonathan, this is the break I need to clear my debts.'

'The girl, Buchanan, who is she?'

'I told you. A Creole.'

'There's something else, isn't there?' Jonathan clung to his arm, pleading. 'You promised to tell me!'

'It's not important.'

'Then tell me.'

'She's no good, son. Her real name's not Genave.'

'What is it?'

'No one knows, not even her mother.'

'Why not?' Slowly Jonathan's hand slipped from Mr Buchanan's coat as he realized, with disgust, what the American was implying.

'Her mother was a whore. Everyone had her. She died three years ago of the pox. That's when Arthur Didcott took pity on Nicole. I expect she's opening her legs for him herself by now.'

Jonathan watched in dismay as Mr Buchanan crumpled into a heap at his feet. He lowered his hand, realizing with horror that it was *his* fist that had slammed into the American's jaw and knocked him out.

He kneeled down and buried his head in his hands, weeping as the solemn strains of a haunting guitar solo swelled into the night air.

FOUR

'What a scandal,' said Emma. 'Poor Mamma. She'll never live it down.'

Nicole kept silent. Fidou was in the room, fussily hanging up their dresses. Emma was sitting on the edge of her bed; Nicole was already in hers. She longed for Fidou to blow out the candles and leave them alone so she could snuggle up with her pillow and think of the extraordinary events of that night. Emma seemed determined to chatter.

'Simply everyone was there, even Ward Trenchard. He was prowling around like one of the general's rabid hounds. The whole of the garrison will know in the morning. I'll be the laughing stock. How will I dare show my face when the season begins?'

Nicole put her thoughts aside and turned to look at Emma. 'Does it matter just because two men fight? It can't affect you.'

'Oh, it can, Nicole. People might think it was because of me.'

Nicole sat up in surprise. 'Why?' Fidou was glancing at Emma scornfully too.

'Daddy told me to be nice to Mr Rendye. I simply couldn't be seen speaking to him. I thought he was a bit of a wet fish. You know how people talk. They might think he's my beau and hit Mr Buchanan because he insulted me.'

'He insults everyone.'

'That's what I mean.' Emma shook her head. 'It will be dreadful if no one comes near me because of it. Imagine having my season ruined before it even begins.'

Nicole found it difficult to humour Emma when she wanted to think of Jonathan Rendye herself. He *was* a bit of a wet fish; that was what intrigued her about him. 'How did it happen?' she asked.

Emma wailed. 'Mr Rendye chased Mr Buchanan into the garden and attacked him. Everyone saw it except you. Mamma's in tears. I must go to her and tell her it wasn't my fault.'

Nicole saw Fidou open her mouth and realized she was about to tell Emma to stop talking nonsense. 'Yes,' said Nicole before the slave had a chance to spoil everything. 'Go to her now. She's alone. Your father took Mr Buchanan home. She'd appreciate your comforting her. Tell her not to worry.'

Emma stood up, setting her jaw squarely. She was dressed in her night-robe, her straight hair falling loose around her shoulders. 'I will,' she said with a frown. 'You're so sensible, Nicole.'

'Stay with her as long as necessary. I shall go to sleep.' She watched Emma leave the room and sighed with relief. Fidou advanced towards her before she could turn away and pretend to be sleeping.

'You're one smart miz,' said Fidou with a cluck of her tongue.

'You won't tell anyone, will you?' Nicole put her hands on the slave's arms and pulled her down so she was sitting beside her on the bed. 'If Mistress Didcott knows Mr Rendye was with me in the dining-room ...'

Fidou looked undecided. She scratched her ear. 'You partial to that buckra?'

'Of course not! He was hungry, that's all. Perhaps the wine I gave him ...' She was puzzled. 'Fidou, why did he punch Mr Buchanan? He seems such a spineless sort of man.'

'There are things you and I don't know 'bout, miz.' Fidou leaned over as Nicole nestled down into the bed. She tucked the sheet in around her shoulders.

'Tell me?'

'Mr Rendye does have a reputation.'

'No! Is he a lecher?' She squirmed with excitement, then had to blink so Fidou would think she was tired and not frantic to know all about him.

'I was talkin' to Mr Buchanan's boy. He says that Mr

Rendye was sweet on his daughter.'

'Mrs Trenchard ... Gina?'

'The very same. Happens that Mr Rendye asked Mr Buchanan if he could marry Miss Gina and he agreed. Only she chose Ward Trenchard instead.'

Nicole frowned. She could not see a vulgar woman like Gina Trenchard being suited to such a sensitive person as Jonathan Rendye.

'That the reason they fight,' said Fidou emphatically. 'He still blue vexed with Mr Buchanan an' it all boiled up.'

'That's nons –' Nicole shut her mouth before her disagreement roused Fidou's curiosity.

'It the truth.' Fidou regarded her suspiciously. 'You sleep, miz,' she said, standing up. 'Too much excitement for a young lady today. What with the *accident* to Emma's hands and you consortin' with a desperate man in the mistress' dinin'-room ...'

Nicole smiled weakly, trying to look blameless.

Fidou was shaking her head. 'I knew your mam,' she said. 'You can't fool me with that look, Nicole.' Her smile was warm and understanding.

Nicole squeezed her hand. 'Good night,' she whispered, pleased to have an ally.

'Happy night rest.' Fidou padded softly around the room, snuffing out candles until only one remained, burning in its glass shade by Emma's bed. Nicole turned her face to the wall and nursed a pillow in her arms.

Her first thought as she closed her eyes was of Jonathan Rendye. Before she could dwell on him, the spectre of her mother raised by Fidou's remark chased him from her mind. It was because of her mother that Mrs Didcott kept her hidden on the veranda. If the guests saw her they might remember Belle Genave and her reputation.

Her own memories of her mother were different. She recalled a lady of striking beauty and frail health who died before she was thirty. She was adored by all who knew her, courted by the island's wealthiest men and treated like a lady. It was only since her death that Nicole heard the vile stories that so-called respectable people whispered about her. She would never believe them.

Her mother always had a kind word for everyone; how shocked she would be if she knew Nicole was suffering because of what people said about her. She had been determined that Nicole would grow up as a lady. She struggled to raise her, to give her the best, and in the end the effort killed her. People thought she was cunning, strong; they did not want to see the real woman, alone and afraid, behind the bright façade.

Her mother never mentioned her father. As a child, Nicole assumed he was a sailor always at sea which was why her mother lived alone. As she grew older, she understood. Only since she joined Mrs Didcott's household did she learn that her fatherless status and her mother's ingenuity for survival marked her as a social outcast, a girl born of shame. Her mother, dead, seemed to have more influence over her than when she was alive.

Nicole twisted in her bed, pummelling the pillow. She believed she knew the reason for Mr Rendye's odd behaviour that evening. He was intelligent, even if he was shy and disapproved of fashionable society. He probably asked Mr Buchanan about her. Who better? As the agent of the United States of America, he knew everything. He would have told Jonathan about her mother.

She sighed with disappointment. In her short life she had observed many men, her mother's friends, with the innocent eyes of childhood. Never had she met a man so tortured, so alone. In a way Jonathan was similar to her. She was intrigued.

She fell asleep before Emma returned. There was a smile of determination on her face as she dreamed.

Jonathan was ready for the summons when it came. He had been waiting all the morning, pacing his narrow room, first defiant and then trembling about what would be his fate. He assumed Mr Farquhar would have to send him home to England.

It would be ironical if he had to leave the island after

meeting a young lady who might become his friend. He shuffled along the corridor behind the slave, brushing back his hair anxiously.

When he entered the antechamber where the clerks were working, he kept his eyes firmly fixed on the door to Mr Farquhar's office. He was aware of the clerks eyeing him but he refused to give them the satisfaction of seeing how ashamed he was.

He walked with his head erect through the desks to where the acting chief clerk was holding the door like a gaoler. He was puzzled by the expression of polite regard on Mr Bateman's face as he ushered him into the governor's presence.

There were four people in the room, standing in a group around Mr Farquhar's desk. When he saw the naval uniforms and the stern faces, Jonathan panicked. It was the first inkling he had that he was to be court martialled. He heard Mr Bateman close the door behind him. He began to sweat and the hairs of his crotch tingled as though being pulled out one by one.

None of the men around the governor took any notice of him. Mr Farquhar himself nodded imperceptibly while one of the naval officers was talking. Jonathan faltered, understanding Mr Farquhar's glance to mean that he should wait until asked to speak. He listened to what was being said and wondered what bearing it had on his own case.

'The secretary of state for the colonies was very clear on that point,' the naval officer, a captain, concluded.

There was silence. Mr Farquhar looked crestfallen. Mr Barry, who was the chief secretary to the government, pursed his lips. Colonel Draper, Mr Farquhar's oldest friend and a gambling man who was a jack of all trades acting for any official who was on leave, sucked in air noisily. The captain looked askance at the sound.

'Well, Edward,' said Mr Farquhar, addressing Colonel Draper. 'Our friend Prinny has ignored us this time.'

The two naval men looked even more shocked.

Jonathan's confusion increased. What had striking Mr

Buchanan, even if he was the American agent, to do with the prince regent?

'Your Excellency,' said Colonel Draper in a sardonic tone that made Jonathan wince. 'Captain Curran has given us only a *verbal* account of developments.'

'I assure you, Colonel, that what I say is documented.'

'That's all right, Captain.' The governor waved him to silence. 'I wonder if you understand the situation you are so eager to confuse. In the treaty signed in Paris restoring the captured colonies to France, there was a specific exception made of the Isle de France *and its dependencies*. That is why we are here. The Isle de France is now Mauritius and it's British.'

'So are its dependencies,' added Colonel Draper.

Jonathan was bemused. He expected a reprimand. Instead he was a witness to incomprehensible affairs of state and not part of an inquiry into his own conduct. Mr Farquhar never did anything without an ulterior motive so he pushed aside his confusion and listened carefully. Perhaps his indiscretion was being overlooked because of this latest crisis?

The discussion concerned Madagascar, a vast island country lying between Mauritius and the African mainland. It was the source of the colony's slaves. These were the captives of whichever warring tribe was victorious in the frequent battles when one tried to gain territorial rights from another.

'Madagascar is a dependency of Mauritius,' said Mr Farquhar, banging his fist down on the top of his desk. 'It becomes a British possession by virtue of the treaty.'

'With respect, sir,' said Captain Curran. 'My instructions are to the opposite effect. Madagascar is to be considered within the French sphere of influence.'

'The devil it is! Do you know what that means?' Mr Farquhar jumped to his feet.

'Give Madagascar to the French and they will have a monopoly of the flesh trade. They'll be able to ship all the slaves they need to develop their island of Bourbon while Mauritius is left without any new slaves at all. We'll be worse off than we are now.'

'The slave-trade, Your Excellency, is banned.'

'Yes, yes,' said Mr Farquhar, spinning around on his heels and pacing the length of his office. 'You have your instructions, Captain, to catch slave-ships. My concern is the welfare of this colony and its inhabitants. How I do it is my responsibility.'

'Here is Lord Bathurst's communication,' said Captain Curran without wavering. 'It states that His Royal Highness the Prince Regent has been pleased to concur on the construction which has been put by the French government upon the details of the treaty.'

'It's official, Robert,' drawled Colonel Draper, flinging himself into a chair with a display of boredom. 'Prinny doesn't want you to have Madagascar.'

'We could have succeeded!' Mr Farquhar glared at the naval officers. 'I'm not giving up. Why should the French be handed an inexhaustible supply of slaves? They have not banned the trade, Captain.'

'Stop it yourself, Robert. Madagascar won't be any use to Bourbon if they can't get its niggers.' Colonel Draper chuckled at his jibe. Captain Curran shifted uncomfortably.

'By jove, Edward, you're right! I'll stop them trading with the French.'

'We have no authority to intercept French vessels, Your Excellency.'

'To hell with that, Captain Curran.'

'The captain means –'

'Mr Barry, I know very well what the captain means.'

Jonathan quivered at the blast of the governor's temper even though it was directed at the chief secretary. At such times as this it was prudent to let Mr Farquhar develop his thoughts without risking interruption.

'I'll stop the trade at its source! If the Madagascar chiefs won't sell slaves, the French won't get them.'

'Neither will we,' said Colonel Draper pointedly.

Mr Farquhar smiled at him in such a way that Jonathan was ashamed. He sensed trickery at work to deceive

Captain Curran from knowing the governor's real intention.

'That's exactly what I am directed to achieve, is it not, Captain?'

The officer was looking perplexed. 'How will you persuade the chiefs to stop selling slaves?' he asked innocently.

'Me?' said Mr Farquhar, his voice taking on an edge of scorn. 'That will be your task. You, and Mr Rendye here.'

Jonathan snapped to attention, blinking as the four men turned to stare at him.

Colonel Draper snorted. 'Send that boy to Madagascar and you'll never see him alive again. He's not a soldier. If the Hova capture him they'll pull him apart limb by limb and send you the pieces.'

Jonathan gasped. The others in the room evidently shared Colonel Draper's poor opinion of him, for they turned their backs and gazed out of the window to the Place d'Armes, beyond the courtyard.

Mr Barry coughed. 'If you proceed with this plan, Your Excellency, with whom would Mr Rendye negotiate? There are so many chiefs. They all sell slaves.'

'Radama.'

'He's a boy!'

'I agree. He's two years younger than Mr Rendye. He leads the Hovas.' Mr Farquhar's eyes were twinkling with excitement at the boldness of his plan. 'He's ambitious, he wants to be king. Very well, I will recognize him as king. The French never will. We'll treat with him on that footing.'

Colonel Draper slapped his thigh. 'Doubtless you'll offer him arms to beat the other tribes and really become king, only if he stops selling slaves?'

'Ah, Edward, you're ahead of me.'

'Nonsense, Robert. I'll wager you've had this planned for a long time.' Colonel Draper rose impatiently to his feet. 'You've sent Captain Lesage there already. I suppose that's to give Rendye some military support. God knows he'll need it, if you're serious. I doubt that Mr Rendye has either the tact or the guts to treat with a bloodthirsty savage.'

He stalked out of the room, glancing contemptuously at Jonathan.

Jonathan flushed and looked at Mr Farquhar. He noticed his mouth was twitching at Colonel Draper's rudeness in walking out in front of the others. He sensed it was his fault, because the Colonel disapproved of him.

'How soon can you sail, Captain?' Mr Farquhar demanded, re-asserting his authority over the men in the room.

'The ship needs repairing and my crew need leave. Our voyage out here took over four months.'

'Please arrange to sail as soon as possible. The negotiations could take some time. Put Mr Rendye ashore at Tamatave so he can meet Captain Lesage. Your duty is to catch slave traders. You'll find plenty there.'

The captain's shoulders stiffened. 'Yes, Your Excellency. He saluted and withdrew from the room, followed by his lieutenant. Mr Barry hovered at the desk.

'Dispatches, Mr Barry,' the governor said, before the chief secretary could comment. 'We must inform the secretary of state for the colonies what we are doing.'

Jonathan stepped forward, preparing to take notes from Mr Farquhar's dictation.

'No, no, Mr Rendye, you are relieved of this duty.' Mr Farquhar was grim faced. 'Stay to hear my report. The recording of it shall be done by a government writer instead.'

Mr Barry ushered in a clerk and Jonathan stood at the man's side. His dismay grew as he listened to what was expected of him. Beginning the dispatch by outlining the background to his proposal, Mr Farquhar went on to explain to the secretary of state that the Hova were the most numerous and industrious of the tribes in Madagascar.

'Their ruler,' he said slowly so the clerk could follow his words, 'is the most powerful, warlike and enlightened of the various chieftains. His army consists of forty thousand men. It is necessary to assist him to become the recognized sovereign of Madagascar so that, as paramount ruler, he will be an ally of the British. We must convince him of the benefits the prohibition of the exportation of his subjects as slaves would bring him and his country.'

He was gloating as he looked at Jonathan. 'You see what you have to do?'

He did not wait for Jonathan's reply but continued dictating. 'My desire is, by every amicable means, to cut off the one great source of slave supply. Hitherto attempts by Englishmen have failed, apparently from want of that delicacy and personal address so requisite in matters of this nature.'

The more Mr Farquhar dictated, the greater became Jonathan's feeling of inadequacy. The governor knew he possessed neither the bravery nor the initiative to succeed in this mission.

The realization stunned him. He stared at Mr Farquhar, no longer hearing the words he was uttering for the benefit of ministers in England. He was being sacrificed so that the governor could claim he had made an attempt to stamp out the slave-trade. Mr Farquhar expected him to fail, even depended on it!

Curiously, although he was the one who would be the victim of Mr Farquhar's scheme, Jonathan admired him for it. He was being removed because he was an embarrassment to Mr Farquhar in such a way that he would win honour for the governor, and for himself too.

'You have some doubts, Mr Rendye?'

They were alone in the room. The clerk had left without Jonathan noticing. He drew himself up to his full height and brushed back his hair, wiping the sweat off his brow with the palm of his hand.

If Mr Farquhar expected him to beg to be excused from the mission, he would be disappointed. Even though it meant death, and he was terrified of negroes, even the tame ones, he would do his duty. He should be thankful that he was being given a chance to leave Mauritius with honour.

'I understand what you require, sir.'

'Do you, Mr Rendye?' The governor's eye met his. 'Ah, yes, I believe you do.' He coughed. 'You may go.'

Jonathan reached the door and was holding the handle when he heard Mr Farquhar say, 'Jonathan?'

He turned. 'Sir?'

'Mr Buchanan presents his compliments to you. He says he was drunk last night at the veranda affair, and that's why he fell down at your feet –'

'Sir?' He gawked at the governor.

'Odd, isn't it? I could have sworn I saw you punch him. Of course, you wouldn't do a thing like that, would you?' He paused before adding, 'Such a pity. I'd like to think you'd punched him. He's a tiresome bugger. I'd willingly have knocked him out myself.' He grinned.

'Good luck, Jonathan. Bring back mv treaty. Don't let me down!'

FIVE

Massey's Hotel was the principle house of public entertainment in Port Louis and Jonathan found himself wandering despondently towards it that evening. There was also the Marengo Café, off the Rue Marengo, and the Grand Café, near the harbour, where Europeans congregated in the day. However, because of the state of the town's roads and the many private parties, those cafés were not patronized by people of quality at night.

Jonathan chose his acquaintances with care. He hid behind his position as a confidant of the governor as the reason for his reserve. Really, it was his lack of liking for people that prevented him from making friends. He went only to places where he would not be bothered by anyone, especially persons of ill repute.

Massey's Hotel had yet to acquire the notoriety of the Maison Despaux, a popular haunt of the Creole planters when they stayed in town. The hotel was a pleasant place, three stories high, with its hall and lower rooms floored with marble. The walls of the public rooms were covered with paper exhibiting large landscapes. The stairs and floors of the upper rooms were polished red and rubbed bright.

Here, for four dollars or twelve shillings a day, a traveller could have a bed with breakfast at nine o'clock and dinner at half past five at the table d'hote. The dinner was French style, consisting of a great variety of small dishes and concluding with coffee.

There were usually English residents to be found in the public rooms after dinner, and on his free evenings Jonathan liked to visit the hotel and sit quietly in a corner by himself. Occasionally he would be drawn into conversation, although he preferred to observe rather than participate. His habits were known and the English generally left him alone.

As he approached the entrance to the hotel, he was seized with a nervousness that set him trembling. He tried to ignore it and pushed open the door. Heads rose to gaze at him as he walked in. Someone said something and there was a snort of ribald laughter. He faltered, certain he was the object of attention because of the fracas at Mrs Didcott's. He blushed and turned back, leaving the hotel and walking rapidly away from it as catcalls echoed around his ears.

The moon was nearly full and he was able to see without a light. His customary fastidiousness was forgotten as he hurried along without worrying about the effects of the dirty streets on his shoes and trousers.

The town extended two ways like the top of a letter T, with the stem of the T being the distance from the harbour to the Champ de Mars, about a quarter of a mile. The left of the T was the west, where the mulattoes and free negroes lived, while the Malabars and Indians were on the right.

Mountains with gaunt peaks surrounded the town, channelling a breeze that blew down the valley and cooled it. The most notable peak, with a height of nearly three thousand feet, was called Pouce because of its strong resemblance to the summit of a human thumb.

The town's location was decided by its natural harbour. The prevailing winds were so strong that ships were usually obliged to anchor at the mouth and be warped in.

Jonathan was conscious of the town's limitations as he walked along aimlessly. He longed to lose himself, to go where no one knew him. The native quarters offered no solace. The only Europeans who visited the quarters were the lower class of soldier in search of whores. The thought of it made Jonathan shudder. He turned off instead in the direction of the Champ de Mars.

If he had a friend, Jonathan would have gone to see him. Even after six years of living on the island, he could not call anyone his friend. The island was small, thirty-five miles long by twenty-eight miles wide. There were no roads. A bachelor like Jonathan was confined to the town and its cafés, unless he visited the plantations.

The thought of the plantations reminded him of Black River and of Gina, who was its mistress after her marriage to Ward Trenchard. Gina had come close to being his friend. He spent entire evenings with her, sitting in the garden of her father's house adjoining the Champ de Mars. Their conversation was limited because he was too tongue-tied to answer Gina's brash attempts to draw him out.

At the time he was dazzled by her exuberance and beauty. He never really believed she would become his wife. The possibility arose because his connections with the governor would have made him a useful son-in-law for William Buchanan. Ward Trenchard, with his fortune made by selling seasoned slaves, turned out to be a better partner for Gina as well as a sounder proposition for Mr Buchanan.

Jonathan was surprised when he found he had walked without realizing it to Mr Buchanan's house. He hesitated by the gate. In the moonlight, standing at the edge of the circle of light thrown by the lanterns hanging on the veranda, he was visible from inside the house. He heard the dulcet tones of a woman's laughter and was fascinated by the sounds of happiness.

He had never known a woman. The thought of lying with

one intrigued him. He assumed that, in time, perhaps when he returned home to England, he would marry a respectable lady and raise a family. Now the peal of female laughter mocked him with the truth: he was never likely to marry nor return to England.

He stared at the house, marvelling at Mr Buchanan's lecherous ways that enabled him to have a wench to console him, even at his age. The man had no shame.

'Jonathan?'

The voice spoken softly at his side made him jump. He turned to see Mr Buchanan standing in the shadows regarding him quizzically. He held a cane in his hand and had returned from taking a stroll across the plain.

'I thought …' Jonathan looked towards the lights of the veranda and caught the sound of suggestive laughter again. 'I thought you were inside. With a wench. I was afraid to enter.'

'*Mi casa es tu casa*, Jonathan. My house is yours.' Mr Buchanan linked his arm under his elbow and guided him up the path. 'You are hearing the slaves amuse themselves.'

He reached the veranda and thumped on the floor with his cane. A middle-aged negro wearing a shirt and breeches, no shoes, opened the door and looked out.

'Burgundy and water,' said Mr Buchanan curtly, tossing his cane at the slave, who caught it and shuffled back into the interior of the house. 'Sit down, son.' He indicated a planter's chair, with its long arms and deep pitch that made it ideal for relaxing with feet hooked up over the arms when they were extended.

'I'm weary,' he said with a sigh. 'I think I've done it.'

Jonathan frowned and kept silent.

'Still vexed with me, are you?' Mr Buchanan chuckled lazily. 'We sure gave them something to gossip about last night. How the hell you knocked me cold, I don't know. Ain't no strength in you for that.'

'You lost your balance –'

'I was drunk, you mean. How else could I attend a veranda affair of earnest young ladies and the rogues the governor calls his advisers?'

Jonathan was stunned by Mr Buchanan's remark. It was an insult to Mr Farquhar but he knew it was true.

The arrival of the slave with a decanter of burgundy and a clay jug of cool water provided respite for him to collect his wits. Mr Buchanan showed no surprise at finding him lurking outside his house; it was Jonathan who was puzzled by it all.

He accepted the glass of wine and water from the slave and sipped it without thinking. He was usually abstemious. He associated drinking in the tropics as an advanced stage of degeneration, not far short of going native and living with a negro mistress. He glanced suspiciously at the American, wondering if there was a wench waiting for him inside the house.

'I'm indebted to you, Jonathan,' Mr Buchanan said, raising his glass in a toast. Jonathan nodded glumly without replying.

'Yes, I think I've done it now. I bought every foreign cargo I could find. Had to borrow money, of course. I'm having the goods transferred to my warehouse. I'll keep them until the port's closed, then I can set my own price. You did me a favour, son.'

'I did?'

'Sure! That's why I told Farquhar not to discipline you. Said I fell down myself and knocked my head on a stone. We're quits now.'

'You lied to protect me?'

'Of course, son. Drink up, I've no hard feelings.' He rubbed his jaw and grinned ruefully. 'I know how you felt. My tongue carried me away.'

'You lied about Nicole Genave as well?'

Buchanan frowned. 'Still thinking of her? Forget her, son. Go down to the Chaussée and get yourself an obliging wench. Black, brown or white, you can take your pick. Sometimes a man needs to drain himself in this climate. Gets too heated otherwise. It's no sin.'

Jonathan tensed, his hand gripping the glass until his knuckles showed white. He wanted to leave, but he still needed to know the truth. 'What you said about Arthur

Didcott and the lady, Miss Genave, that was a lie, wasn't it?'

'Of course, Jonathan!' Mr Buchanan leaned over and slapped his knee. 'You paid me for it already. Blood will out though, son. She's from bad stock, she –'

'I've heard enough!' He stood up. 'She's not a breeding slave. She's a charming white lady and I refuse to believe anything to the contrary just because she's Creole and not English.'

'Oh aye,' said Mr Buchanan, keeping a wary eye on Jonathan. 'Agnes Didcott's a strict teacher. She's moulded the girl well.'

'Did you know her before … when her mother was alive?'

'Yes.' He shut his mouth, reluctant to say more. 'Jonathan, believe me, have nothing to do with her. She's not of your class.'

'What do I care about that? I've only a few days left here. I'll never see her again anyway.'

Mr Buchanan got to his feet and put his arm around him to calm him down. He frowned. 'What do you mean?' He removed the empty glass from Jonathan's hand and placed it on the table.

The words came out in a rush. 'Mr Farquhar's sending me to Madagascar to treat with the Hovas.' Now that he was sharing the hopelessness of his mission with someone he felt better.

Mr Buchanan stared at him in disbelief. 'You? What the devil! By yourself?'

'I'm to liaise with Captain Lesage at Tamatave and then seek an audience with Radama.' He watched Mr Buchanan's expression as it changed to scorn. 'You don't think I'll succeed, do you? Colonel Draper says the Hova will kill me, piece by piece.'

'You poor bugger.'

There was a shriek of laughter from inside the house and Mr Buchanan moved towards the door. He opened it. 'Ranavola!' he called. 'Leave your husband alone and come here.'

Jonathan grimaced at the thought of having to meet Mr Buchanan's concubine. He was ashamed of his mistake when he saw the fat slave who waddled through the door and stood with her arms akimbo and her eyes twinkling.

'Yas, massa?' she laughed. 'Mah husban' troublin' me.' She gestured at the grey-haired houseboy who followed her onto the veranda.

'She's Hova,' said Mr Buchanan. 'A Malagash slave.' He addressed her. 'This gentleman is going to meet your countryman, Radama.'

The female's good humour vanished. She backed away into her husband's arms and stared at Jonathan with fear in her eyes. She muttered something in dialect, like a prayer.

'Well?' demanded Mr Buchanan.

'Sah,' said Ranavola. 'He a dead man. Don' let him go. Radama eats whites. If he survives the jungle swamps, Radama will cut out his liver and eat it whole.'

'I'm obliged to go,' said Jonathan with despair. 'It's Mr Farquhar's orders.'

'More like his sentence of death than orders, Jonathan. There's a ship sailing for Baltimore tonight. The master's an old friend. I can smuggle you aboard.'

Jonathan shook his head. He backed off the veranda into the night, deaf to Mr Buchanan's cries for him to stay. He was conscious only of the carefree laughter of the Hova woman and how it ceased when she gazed on him. Slaves were fey people; she had seen death in his future. He could do nothing to prevent it.

He walked blindly from Mr Buchanan's garden to the plain, its grassy surface springy under his feet. His mind was made up now. He would go as Mr Farquhar decreed; it would enable him to escape from the corruption and deceit that surrounded the governor.

He was relieved by his decision. No more would he have to refrain from speaking his mind. He would go to his fate stoically. He was scared; he was scared even of the dark that shrouded the Champ de Mars, but he would obey orders.

He stopped walking aimlessly into the depth of the plain and turned around to face the direction he had left. The hillside sparkled with the lights of lanterns blazing on the verandas of the cottages and villas overlooking the plain. It was an inspiring sight.

To the right of the hills, close to the street that led to Government House, was a cluster of houses. There were many lanterns flickering from them. He tried to make out the ones hanging on the veranda of Mrs Didcott's house.

He stared at them for a long time, lost in thought. Would he see Nicole again? He pictured her from the night before, in her simple white dress with her innocent smile.

She had known nothing about him, except that he was hungry. Yet she trusted him, befriended him despite his plain features, greasy hair and nervous mannerisms. Would an English girl have been so kind? He longed to see her again, just once, to discover if she really was as he remembered.

He felt rather than saw the threatening presence of someone approaching him. He moved swiftly but he was too late. A hand brushed against his arm, gripping it and detaining him.

A voice said gruffly from the darkness, 'I here, sir.'

He looked down. The person standing close to his side reached in height to his shoulder. He shook his arm free and tried to walk away. The person followed him like a shadow.

He wondered whether there were more of them ready to jump on him. He was angry at his stupidity in straying off the path. He kept his eyes on the lights where Nicole lived and walked on, feigning boldness.

He reached the path. The lanterns threw sufficient glow for him to see around him. He turned, expecting his pursuer to flee into the night. He saw only an urchin grinning at him with eyes that sparkled with mischief.

'You want something? Girl?' The youngster fluttered his hands in the air, making a shape as though caressing a woman and mimicking the grinding movement of copulation with his hips.

Jonathan looked away in disgust. He was offended at the

juxtaposition of the lad's obscene gestures and the image he had in his mind of Nicole. He strode out along the path and found himself confronted by the urchin again.

'You want boy?' the youngster asked hopefully. He pirouetted on the path and loosened his breeches. They dropped to his ankles and he bent over, offering Jonathan a view of his bare backside.

'Get out of my way!'

The boy pulled up his breeches and pranced beside him, quite unabashed. Jonathan ignored him and tried to pick out in the darkness the house where Nicole lived. He hoped the boy would get bored and go away.

'I'm sorry, sir,' the lad said brightly. 'Not my fault. You were on the plain. That's where men go when they want a companion. Can I do *anything* for you? Escort you to your hotel, run an errand?' His voice dropped. 'I haven't eaten today, sir, nor yesterday. A coin, sir?'

'Be gone with you!' Jonathan's anger was half-hearted. He believed he could see the Didcott house nestling behind the ones that marked the beginning of the street. He wished he had paid more attention to its location the previous night. He stopped and stared at it. The boy bumped into him. Jonathan touched his pocket in alarm.

'I'm not a thief.' The boy glanced at him with outrage. 'I could have picked your pocket while you stood dreaming on the plain. I kept the thieves away.'

'Did you?' Jonathan was distracted. The veranda of the house was hidden but there was a light in one of the upstairs rooms. He saw a figure move towards the window. He held his breath.

There was a flamboyant tree spreading its branches outside the window, obscuring part of his view. He moved to a better position. The outline of a girl was visible through the branches. She wore her hair in ringlets and was gazing out into the night.

Jonathan gasped. He clasped his hands around his chest and hugged himself. His body was sticky with sweat and he released it, opening his arms and extending them towards the house. 'Nicole,' he whispered.

'I tell her you here.'

'What?' He looked askance at the boy.

'I tell her you waiting for her.'

'No, no!' He caught the boy by his neck. 'You little devil. She must never know.'

'Why not?'

'Because.' His heart ached.

'That's stupid. She's looking for you.'

'How do you know?'

'Has she got another beau?' The boy wriggled free.

'Wait!' Jonathan tried to catch him. The boy dodged around his legs and popped up at his other side, laughing happily at the game.

'What do you mean, she's looking for me? I'm nothing to her.' His words were meant to convince himself. 'Do you know her?'

The boy pouted, his dark eyes studying Jonathan shrewdly. In the faint light from the lanterns the boy seemed to be a mulatto, a half breed. His shirt was torn and his hair, black and curly like a Malabar's, was tousled and dirty. He hopped from one bare foot to the other.

'Don't lie to me,' Jonathan said sternly. 'I want the truth.' He dived to catch the boy by his ear. He slipped aside with a laugh.

'Mistress Didcott has many young ladies. You ain't the first to stand here and moon.'

'I'm not mooning!'

'No?'

'She is an acquaintance, barely that.' He sighed. 'It must remain so.' He turned and walked away with reluctance. The boy followed.

'Don't you have a home to go to?' Jonathan shouted at him irritably. The youngster was disturbing his mood. He wanted to dream of how his life would be if Governor Farquhar still had confidence in him.

'I've no home,' said the boy breezily, pushing aside a beggar who loomed up out of the darkness to challenge Jonathan with his open palm. 'No friends.'

The kid's plaintive note shook Jonathan out of his

self-pity. 'Where are your parents?'

It was a middle-class English question and he knew he was being foolish to ask it. The boy had no parents, he was probably a runaway from a plantation. In a few days he would be rounded up, put in chains and set to work in the government slave gangs.

'Parents dead. I'll be dead soon.'

'Dead?' The word set Jonathan's heart thumping.

'Yes. No food.' He rolled his eyes and rubbed his stomach making a joke of it. Jonathan sensed his pain. He was reminded of how he had sought food the previous evening and Nicole fed him.

'Come with me!' He gripped the lad's shoulder with excitement. His despair vanished.

'Let me go,' the boy shouted. 'I've done nothing. Where are you taking me?'

'To eat!' Jonathan propelled the lad along the street towards Government House. 'By jove, I believe I'm hungry too. Let's see what we can find in the governor's kitchen, shall we, boy?'

He was unaccustomed to the feeling of generosity that swept through him. He felt a glow and floated over the pot holes, scarcely noticing the sleeping vendors with their baskets piled high with provisions to sell at daybreak.

He clung to the boy, not to keep him prisoner but to retain contact with him. He had discovered, after six years of lonely selfishness, a liking ... a need ... a love ... for his fellow human beings.

SIX

The young ladies of Mrs Didcott's academy led a sheltered existence. Six of them lived in the house, lodged there by parents who lived on plantations. The other three were escorted daily to and from the house by formidable negro chaperons who were conscientious in their duties. Mrs

Didcott ran her academy as a fortress, regarding Port Louis as enemy territory into which her young ladies were forbidden to venture without an escort.

Nicole was content with her life at the academy. Thanks to Arthur Didcott she had been rescued, at thirteen, from a fate that held no hope. He had brought her into his home against Mrs Didcott's wishes. Now that she was there, however, Mrs Didcott was determined that she would have no recollection of her former life. She was forbidden at first to leave the premises while Mrs Didcott exerted her full influence to make her a worthy companion for Emma.

Her success in moulding Nicole in the likeness of a young lady of quality was due to Nicole's eagerness to learn, although Mrs Didcott claimed the credit. Nicole listened to everything, did what she was told, copied the behaviour of the other girls and made every effort to fulfill the hopes Mrs Didcott held for her.

Mauritius was French territory when Nicole was born and remained so for the first ten years of her life. Her mother was of French descent but because she was born on the island she was known as a Creole.

Her mother encouraged her to speak English, sensing in that language an opportunity for advancement. So Nicole fitted in quickly at Mrs Didcott's. The continued exposure to English gave her a fluency that matched the ease with which she spoke French and Creole.

She even thought in English. She was wise enough, as she grew older and sensitive to the differences that existed between her and the other girls, to know she could never be English in outlook. It pleased her. She was becoming aware that her nature was more passionate, more serious, than Emma's and the other girls'.

She was accepting, too, her role as a companion and chaperon to Emma as she gained Mrs Didcott's trust to perform that part.

There were occasions when she was allowed out of the house to accompany Emma on a visit to friends or for the Sunday promenade on the Champ de Mars. It was the custom for ladies to stroll in the late afternoon, emerging like fireflies as the sun set.

No respectable woman, nor any with any aspirations to respectability, would be seen on the streets during the heat of the day. The sun was considered injurious to a lady's complexion and the fairer a skin, the nobler a lady deemed herself to be.

Nicole loved the open air. She obtained Mrs Didcott's consent to tend the garden and spent many hours trimming the bougainvillea and laying out hibiscus borders. It consumed her energy, added greatly to her happiness and gave her the rosy appearance of a country girl. With such a diversion she was unmindful of the restrictions placed on her by Mrs Didcott's regime.

From the window of the bedroom she shared with Emma, she could see the mountain peaks at the other side of the plain. Sometimes she gazed out at them idly. That morning she was surprised to find herself staring from the window with a new yearning.

'Do hurry, Nicole, you'll be late for prayers. You know how Mamma creates if we set a poor example to the girls.'

She smiled ruefully at Emma and tossed her head to chase away her confusion. 'I was watching the sunrise,' she offered as explanation.

'Day dreaming,' said Emma. 'You've been like it ever since Mamma's veranda affair.'

'Have I?' She brushed her hair impatiently, watching the curls bounce back as she smoothed them out.

'You know you have. What were you watching out of the window last night? The moon rise?'

Emma's harsh remark brought a flush to her cheeks. She finished preparing herself and smiled sweetly. 'I do hope your mother will let me accompany you to the balls and fêtes this season. I can wait with the duennas in an anteroom. I shan't disgrace you.'

'Of course you will come!' Emma hugged her. 'My dear, I will *need* you. How else can I hope to escape any man who's *forcing* his attentions on me?' She gasped with excitement and her eyes sparkled at the thought of it.

'Good.' Nicole sighed. 'I'm longing for the season to start.'

It did not occur to Emma to ask why but Nicole had her explanation ready. 'Don't you wish to go out sometimes, to walk the streets, to see the town, to visit the shops?'

'Of course I do. We shall be going for a picnic on Pouce when the weather's cooler.'

'I mean just strolling around the town, to the harbour, the Place d'Armes –'

'What a curious notion. Don't tell Mamma. She'll suspect you want to meet a secret *admirer*.'

Nicole caught her breath. She had very nearly said too much. She stood up. 'I was thinking of you, Emma. I have the garden to amuse me. I thought you might be bored in the house all day, now that you can't practise the guitar.'

'We have our lessons, dear. I can't let Mamma down.'

Nicole's confused thoughts gained some order when she visited the garden in the morning break. She had been unattentive during the lessons and the slash of Mrs Didcott's tawse across her knuckles had stung her to reality.

There was clearly no way she could see Mr Rendye again, at least until the season when she would be allowed out with Emma. Why should she crave to see him again anyway?

She was sensible enough to know she was not in love. This was not even infatuation. She sighed as she took the scent of the frangipani blossoms. She plucked one of the dainty pink buds and held it to her nose, breathing deeply.

She wanted to see Mr Rendye, she reasoned, because he was different. He was so unlike the usual kind of English man, he fascinated her. He was pathetic in a way; that made her angry.

'I goan tell the mistress you sickenin' for somethin'.' Fidou was standing at the door to the kitchen cabin with her eyes blazing accusingly. 'I been watchin' you, Nicole. You ain't done no prunin' nor nothin'. Just moochin'.'

Nicole shrugged her shoulders. 'I need your advice, Fidou.'

'What's that?' Fidou was instantly suspicious.

'Seriously, Fidou. Won't you walk with me?'

'I have my work to do,' the slave said grudgingly.

'Very well.' Nicole pouted and turned her back on her, knowing that curiosity would draw her out.

She was taking a risk in confiding in Fidou but she needed the slave's help. She smiled as she heard her shuffling behind her on the path. Taking her hand, she led her over to a seat hidden from the house by the shrubbery surrounding it.

'Do you remember Mr Rendye?' Nicole began, not waiting for Fidou's reply. 'I was wondering if I should send him a letter. To express my hope that he was not hurt at the –'

'Oh Lor',' said Fidou. 'I knew it.'

'Knew what?' Nicole blushed, steeling herself for the slave's rebuke.

'You ain't done thinkin' of that buckra?'

'He's a gentleman, Fidou. Show respect.'

'Oy, oy!' Fidou squeezed her hand with delight. 'He ain't much of a gentleman even though he white.'

Nicole ignored the criticism, convinced by her outburst that Fidou would be her ally. 'Will you take him a note? It's impossible for me to leave here. Perhaps he could call.'

Fidou suppressed her merriment and considered. 'I could take a note,' she said, then shook her head. 'No, I won't. It ain't wise. If he interested, he find a way to see you 'gain, you can be sure.'

'He's probably forgotten me already! I want him to know he can think of me as a friend.'

'Little point in that.' Fidou pulled away and stood up. 'Put the man out of your mind, miz. If he gives you a sign, you can rely on me to help. Otherwise I ain't doin' nothin'. You must show respect for yourself, not chase every lonely man you meet.'

'Mr Rendye doesn't have the confidence to give me a sign,' she said sorrowfully. 'He's too shy a man to make an approach without encouragement.'

'Then he ain't,' said Fidou decisively, 'the man for you!'

*

Late in the afternoon of the following day, Fidou was returning to Mrs Didcott's academy after running an errand for Emma. The girl needed a new ribbon to thread through the corsage of the dress she was planning to wear to service on Sunday.

Fidou dawdled her way along the street to the Champ de Mars, passing the time of day with her acquaintances. As one of the slaves of an important town establishment, she was regarded with envy by the free negroes who idled their time in the street without employment.

'Damn you, boy, leave me alone,' she snapped in Creole to the youth who sidled up to her, trying to attract her attention. She had been aware of his presence for several paces. 'I'm a respectable nigger.'

'I know that, Miss Fidou.'

Hearing her own name spoken so boldly, she glanced at the youth. He was clad in a clean shirt and new breeches; he was without shoes so she knew he was a slave. His colour was the cinnamon of a mixed breed, with locks of silky black dangling over his ears and forehead. She was attracted by his broad grin and the mischief that flashed in his eyes.

'How do you know me so good?' she demanded, slackening her pace. She declined to acknowledge the youth completely by stopping to talk. He dodged around two slaves carrying a pannier of bread and danced back to her side.

'My master told me your name,' he said in English.

She stopped at once. Any female slave who wanted to improve herself knew the easiest way was through a liaison with a white man. She dreamed of attracting the attention of those who visited Mrs Didcott's academy from time to time. None showed the slightest interest in her although she served them well and kept the top buttons of her bodice open so they could glimpse her buxom figure.

'Your master?' she said huskily, scarcely daring to believe her luck. 'What does he want?' Her eagerness gave her away and she smarted under the youth's cheeky smile.

'You.' He winked.

'Liar!' she said to cover the excitement rising in her breast.

'You shall see,' the youth said, indicating the Champ de Mars ahead. 'Will you spare a few minutes to make his acquaintance?'

'Like this?' Her hand flew to her *mouchoir*, the kerchief she wore knotted around her head. She tucked up the loose strands of hair and patted the back of her neck. Her dress was respectable, too respectable if she was to meet an admirer.

She would have to stand in a way that showed off her figure to full advantage, so the man could see the curve of her *derrière* and the fullness of her breasts. Negro men liked their women comely and she had no reason to believe a white man was any different.

'Follow me,' the youth urged.

She watched him force his way through the people thronging the street and hurried after him. She was trying to guess what manner of man his master was. If he was rich, his boy should be better accoutred, unless he was so rich he chose to hide it.

She glanced ahead to the groups of white men promenading across the plain, wondering which of them had summoned her.

The youth was waiting for her at the end of the street. 'My master asks if you can keep a secret?' His smile had gone and his eyes looked at her sternly.

'I'll box your ears,' she said, offended by his superiority. 'I ain't no tittle-tattle.'

'Good, because I have friends.' The boy smashed his fist into the palm of his hand and looked menacing. Fidou was mildly amused.

'So have I,' she replied, to put him in his place.

The youth jerked his head, indicating with his chin a group of men standing a few yards away. She saw a young French Creole, bearded and mustachioed, his hair smooth and very long. He was wearing a light green cravat, a puce-coloured coat with bright buttons of the latest Paris cast, and sky-blue trousers. She gasped.

Her hope that he was the man was dashed when the youth skirted around the group. He moved towards a forlorn gentleman who was twisting his hands in front of him and gazing in the direction of Mrs Didcott's house. He wore an ensemble of grey, his stock a lighter grey than his coat. His hair flopped into his eyes, his face was red, and he gave the appearance of being in considerable discomfort.

The youth tugged at his coat. The man looked startled, blinked and dug in his sleeve for a handkerchief which he used to dab at the sweat pouring down his cheeks. Fidou halted, staring at him in dismay.

The man was frowning as he walked over to her. 'Miss Fidou,' he said. 'Do please forgive this impertinence. I was persuaded by this lad here that you would be agreeable to taking a message for me.'

She laughed with relief. 'Lor'! I thought you wanted *me*! You gave me such a fright.'

The man pulled his large nose and looked embarrassed. Fidou wondered why Nicole was interested in him. He was dowdy, morose and slouched like a clerk. His language showed he was unused to dealing with people.

She saw him as one of life's misfits, an unfortunate Englishman who would be better off pushing a pen in a banker's office in London than standing on a humid afternoon in the Champ de Mars trying to plan an assignation.

'Where is the message, Mr Rendye?' she said briskly.

The Englishman seemed gratified that she remembered his name. 'I have nothing written,' he said. 'Is it too much of me to ask you to intercede on my behalf? Your mistress, Miss Nicole, was kind to me at the veranda affair –' He gulped himself to silence.

'What Mr Jonathan is trying to say,' interrupted the youth with an air of impatience, 'is that he wants to see Miss Nicole again. Can you arrange it? Would she agree?'

'Me?' Fidou sucked in her breath and took a step back. 'It's impossible! Mistress Didcott has the eyes of a vulture. Nothing escapes her notice. She'll surely question me about this meeting. She has her spies ... we're too near to her house.'

'Tell her I'm your brother,' said the youth.

'Hush, Verette!' The man bit his lip, then seemed to gain confidence. 'Can you tell me if Miss Nicole would be, well, receptive to my desire to see her again?'

'You can try …' Fidou was eager to be gone. 'I'll tell her I saw you.'

'Please do. I believe I have an idea. Perfectly respectable, I assure you. I will arrange something.'

His eyes glazed over and he turned back to face the house as Fidou, with a sigh of exasperation at his foolishness, hastily left him to return home.

Mrs Didcott walked at the head of her line of girls into the courtyard of Government House. The girls followed in pairs, with Nicole bringing up the rear with Fidou at her side. Several male slaves in livery acted as their escorts.

Mrs Didcott had been unable to hire sufficient carriages to take them on this visit and judged that an afternoon ramble with sufficient attendants to keep away trouble-makers would be safe.

The invitation to visit Government House and take tea with the governor had arrived unexpectedly. Mrs Didcott basked in the glory it brought her, telling the girls how honoured they were.

Nicole was in a state of tension until the day of the visit in case Mrs Didcott banned her from going. The invitation, which was delivered personally by Mr Rendye, was explicit that all the young ladies of the Academy together with any chaperons were to come.

Nicole had watched Jonathan's visit from the garden where she had a view through the window into the drawing-room. He did not see her. She saw him make an apology for his conduct at the veranda affair and was relieved by Mrs Didcott's gracious nodding of her head in acceptance of it.

She was on tenterhooks when Fidou told her of the encounter with Mr Rendye and his boy. She found it hard to believe that this visit to Government House was his way of creating an opportunity for them to meet.

'Good afternoon, sister,' said a voice at Nicole's side as she followed the others through the courtyard. She was puzzled to see a handsome coloured youth sweep low in a bow to Fidou. The youth bowed with less exaggeration to her.

'I am Verette,' he said swiftly, directing his remark at Nicole.

At the same time he was keeping his eyes open in case Mrs Didcott, who was in the process of being welcomed by the governor, should turn and see him.

'Mr Jonathan wants to speak with you,' he whispered. 'When you have tea with the governor, beg to be excused.' He moved away with a laugh and said loudly. 'See you again, sister.' He nodded at Mrs Didcott, who was watching him in astonishment, and sauntered off towards the slave quarters.

Nicole was conscious of the other girls staring at her. She shook her ringlets at them defiantly. 'Is he really your brother?' she asked Fidou when they were out of earshot of the others.

'Of course not,' Fidou answered sharply.

They were shown around the building by Mr Bateman, the acting chief clerk. He explained how Governor Farquhar was delighted to receive visits by school pupils and that this was not the first. His Excellency believed that it was important that young people should take an interest in how the colony was run.

Nicole was too excited to listen as the clerk droned on, conducting them through the ground-floor reception rooms. Her thoughts were on the forthcoming encounter with Jonathan.

She was intrigued as to why he had gone to such lengths to see her. Poor Fidou was quite distracted, her eyes darting from Mrs Didcott to Nicole and back again as though she feared something terrible would happen. At last they were ushered into the governor's drawing-room to take tea. Fidou was escorted elswhere by one of the house slaves. As she was led away, she cast a look of warning at Nicole, who ignored it.

Fortunately Mrs Didcott was so preoccupied with preening herself under the influence of the governor's charm, she was lax in the attention she paid her charges. When Nicole whispered in her ear that she simply must be allowed to leave the room, she waved her away instantly.

Nicole blushed as she withdrew and some of the girls tittered at her behind their hands. Emma glared with outrage for the shame she was causing them. A lady, she seemed to be saying, was not supposed to ask to use the lavatory when being received by the governor.

'Come, miss.' Verette was waiting outside the door. A footman closed it behind her. 'It's this way.' He hurried along the corridor, his bare feet making no sound on the carpet. He reached the end and opened the door into a small chamber. Jonathan Rendye walked uncertainly across the room towards her.

'Miss Genave … Miss Nicole!' he said, brushing furiously at his hair.

She was suddenly nervous and glanced behind her. The youth stood at the door smiling his encouragement.

'This is Verette,' Jonathan said lamely.

'Your slave?' she asked in the silence that hung between them. He was swaying from side to side, even more nervous than she was.

'Yes. No. I met him on the Champ de Mars. I was looking at your window.'

She gasped at his confusion, wondering what she could do to still his trembling.

'I brought him here with me. My servant, not slave. Mr Farquhar gave his consent. He reminds me of you.'

'Mr Farquhar does?' Nicole wished he would ask her to sit down.

'No. Verette does.' He coughed to hide his embarrassment. 'You helped me at that veranda affair so I repaid your kindness by helping him. Fed him, you see, like you did me. Bought him some clothes. When I leave …' His voice died away and he appeared alarmed at his own words.

'Are you going somewhere?' She gazed on him with

concern as he agonized over what to say next.

'Yes! Oh bother. Do forgive me. I meant to tell you in another way.' He took a step towards her and then moved back hastily as though afraid.

She smiled, hoping it would relax him. 'Tell me,' she said. 'It will be our secret.'

'Yes. A secret! Hah!' He frowned and pulled his nose. 'You must think me an awful bore. I'm presuming too much. I so wanted to see you again before I went.'

'Well, we don't have many minutes.' She longed to reach out and hold him, to tell him to pull himself together and be a man. What he had done in arranging this clandestine meeting took extraordinary nerve. Her heart was filled with admiration for him.

'Yes, only a little time.' He sighed and looked straight into her eyes. He seemed to be searching for some sign of hope.

'Would you like me to wait for you until you return?' She said it to make conversation without thinking of the implications.

His gloom vanished and he smiled. His features were transformed and he seemed so pleased that she was overwhelmed with a new regard for him. She took a step forward and met him as he came to her.

He placed his arms around her shoulders as a brother would. She held him gently at his waist.

'Nicole,' he said softly, his breath tingling her ear. 'I'll always remember you, whatever happens.'

'Jonathan.' She raised her face to his, waiting for his lips to close over hers in their first kiss.

'Master!' said Verette anxiously. 'Someone coming.'

His arms left her and he drew away. 'Go,' he said, 'before they see you with me.'

Verette hurried her out of the room. She felt suddenly bereft. She glanced along the corridor and saw Mrs Didcott and the girls emerging from the governor's suite. She looked back into the room before Verette closed the door.

Jonathan was standing by the window; the light was dim so she could not see his face. He seemed to be crying.

'Where is Mr Rendye going?' she asked Verette to keep the tears from her own eyes.

'Bless me, miss! He forgot to tell you?' He shook his head in amazement at Jonathan's foolishness. 'That's why he wanted to see you. He asked the governor to entertain all Mrs Didcott's ladies as his last request.'

'Last request?' Her tears dried and she looked at him with horror. 'Whatever for?'

'He's going to Madagascar, miss. No one expects to see him come back alive.'

Nicole faltered, aware of Mrs Didcott's eyes on her. She took a deep breath to save herself from swooning. She wanted to go to Jonathan and hold him, to try to inspire him with her strength. Now it was too late.

'Don't worry, Miss Nicole,' said Verette brightly. 'I'm going with him. I'll bring him back for you.'

SEVEN

There was no chance to see Jonathan again before he sailed. Fidou told Nicole how HMS *Tyne* left the harbour proudly, borne out by a stiff breeze. Verette was on deck to wave farewell, but Jonathan remained below.

'Probably seasick,' said Fidou with scorn.

Nicole looked up at her from the flower-bed where she was digging a hole with a small trowel. She said nothing, searching Fidou's face to see the reason for the slave's contempt. She picked up a flamboyant tree seedling and gently laid it in the hole, holding it steady while she filled the soil in around it.

'That's slave work.'

'Perhaps it is, Fidou.' Nicole stood up and smiled. 'I like to do it. Of course, I can't dig new borders but I can plant a tree. That's Jonathan's tree.'

'You'll soon forget him. He wasn't much anyway.'

'He is a sincere person, Fidou. I shall remember him

always.' She glanced at the seedling. 'Every day I will give this plant water. You'll see what a huge, strong tree it will become. It will give us shade.' She gestured towards the bench a few yards away in an arbour.

Fidou scowled and flounced away. Nicole could not blame her. The slave was ambitious for her as well as for herself. Although he had *carte blanche* at Government House, Jonathan was, in Fidou's eyes, inadequate for her.

Nicole smiled fondly at the tiny plant and wondered how fast it would grow. It seemed fragile, shocked at its transplanting from the seedlings at the base of the huge tree in front of the veranda. She hoped it would survive; flamboyants were hardy, despite this one's fragile appearance.

She strode through the garden, relishing the caress of the sun on her cheeks. Lessons were over for the day. Emma was in their chamber, trying on different gowns as she prepared for the first ball of the season. The thought of Emma's anxiety over what to wear contrasted with Nicole's sombre mood. Jonathan was gone. Instead of sadness she felt a sense of relief. It shocked her.

Only Fidou, and the boy Verette, knew of her meeting with Jonathan. His departure removed the need for clandestine meetings and deceit. She was happier because of that.

She reasoned with herself as she walked around the small garden. Fidou was right, Jonathan was not very impressive. She tried to thrust him out of her mind but the image of his solemn features and sudden, vibrant smile would not be pushed aside. She pursed her lips and took the trowel back to the garden shed, deciding to help Emma choose dresses instead of moping among the hibiscus and frangipani blossoms.

The first important ball of the season was being held by the Mauritius Turf Club. Colonel Draper founded the club in 1812. It immediately became popular, partly due to Colonel Draper's own connections. He had been educated at Eton, where he was a brilliant student. He was a page of honour to George III and a close friend of the Prince of

Wales, becoming ADC to him when he was made Prince Regent.

Colonel Draper was forty years old, a bachelor, and could command any post in the administration that he desired. He was the target of every match-making matron in Mauritius; all of them flocked to race meets in the Champ de Mars with their daughters in tow while their husbands were nagged into joining the Turf Club to become intimate acquaintances of the colonel.

Mrs Didcott was in the vanguard. She had been disappointed that Colonel Draper did not attend her veranda affair, but was mollified when she received invitations for herself and Emma to attend the Turf Club ball. That Arthur was a member of the committee and was the one who put her name on the list was irrelevant.

This was Emma's first season and Mrs Didcott was determined that Emma should be noticed by Colonel Draper and every bachelor who was eligible. There were plenty of them. Young English ladies were scarce and each could command a following of a score of officers, planters, merchants and officials.

All this was related breathlessly to Nicole by Emma, who was trying to explain the importance of the Turf Club ball. 'Without it,' she said, 'how can one hope to meet a man of any value.'

Nicole ignored the implication that because she was not invited, she would never meet a man of consequence. There was intense competition for husbands between the English débutantes and their Creole counterparts. Creole women were proud of captivating British hearts. The military habit appealed to them, particularly if they could take the very men who were their country's conquerors.

Nicole caught Emma's enthusiasm for the season. As the day of the Turf Club ball approached, she grew anxious about whether she would be allowed to attend. Mrs Didcott closed the academy for the season. Two of her pupils stayed on while those who were too young to come out returned to their houses in the country.

With no lessons to occupy them, Emma and the two girls

were in ecstacy with their preparations. There were frequent expeditions, with Fidou and Nicole and a male slave as escort, to the town to visit jewellers and milliners and dressmakers.

Port Louis was well supplied with the latest in fashionable clothes and accessories. The merchants stocked up in advance for the season, with shipments from France, England and India to give a stunning choice of baubles and fabrics.

There was so much to fascinate and occupy her that Nicole's thoughts seldom dwelt on Jonathan. She watered the seedling every day if there was no rain and she had time. She was pleased when it showed signs of taking root and buds appeared on its stem. She began to accept that she would never hear of Jonathan Rendye again.

The day before the ball she was summoned into Mrs Didcott's presence. To her surprise Arthur Didcott was in the drawing-room with his wife. Both of them looked serious. Mr Didcott turned his face away from her to stare out of the window when she stood meekly in front of Mrs Didcott. There was no tea being poured as there usually was during Mrs Didcott's cosy reprimands.

'Nicole!' The large lady's stentorian voice was more menacing than usual.

Immediately Nicole wondered what she had done. Mr Didcott held his hands clasped behind his back. She saw him opening and closing his fists uneasily. She lowered her eyes to the floor when Mrs Didcott began to speak.

'My girl, it's time for you to pull yourself together!'

Nicole stiffened obediently. Mrs Didcott paused; she seemed to have trouble getting the words out. Nicole peeped and saw she was glancing at her husband, who was deliberately ignoring her.

'Men!' Mrs Didcott said suddenly, the word bouncing back off the walls and reverberating around the room. 'They are everywhere! They want only one thing, to compromise a lady. I won't have it!'

Nicole raised her head a fraction and frowned. She desperately wanted to understand what Mrs Didcott was talking about. Could it be that somehow her secret meeting with Jonathan had been discovered?

'You must stop it, Nicole! That's your duty.'

'Yes, m'm.'

'I have persuaded Mrs Didcott,' said Mr Didcott turning away from the window with a lopsided smile that was supposed to make Nicole feel at ease. 'Your schooling is over now. You have learned well. I want you to remain here with us as Emma's chaperon for the season.'

'You must see a man never *touches* her, never takes her to an alcove alone, never gets *close* to her. You must see –'

'Yes, my dear.' Arthur Didcott's voice was soft, yet he was able to interrupt his wife with ease.

It made Nicole think that Mrs Didcott's harsh manner was really a bluff. Despite his self-effacing personality, it was her husband who controlled the marriage.

She was amazed as she realized it was always like that. How else could Mrs Didcott have accepted her into the house but for her husband's insistence? She understood suddenly that the strength of a man was not in his physical stature and bold mannerisms. It came from within, was something unseen until the moment it was needed.

'There are pitfalls for the unwary,' Mr Didcott was saying, looking at her benevolently.

'You are a wise girl, Nicole, far more experienced in *certain* ways than Emma or any of Mrs Didcott's young ladies. We both want you to watch over Emma and the others.' He paused, trying to remember their names.

Mrs Didcott cried out, 'Jane and Louise,' as if he were deaf. He grimaced.

'We took a risk giving you a home, Nicole. You've repaid our trust. We're proud of what you've become. Now we are entrusting our daughter and the daughters of friends of ours to you.'

'Remember, it's your duty, Nicole. To us!'

'Yes, m'm.' She bobbed a curtsy. 'Can I go to the ball too?'

'That's what Mr Didcott is saying! You won't be there to enjoy yourself, mind! I shall be watching you.'

Nicole sensed that what Mrs Didcott was consenting to went against her prejudices. She distrusted Nicole because she was Creole and because of her background. However, the Turf Club ball was not exculsive to British girls and there would be Creoles and French ladies there too. Nicole's presence would not cause a ripple of concern.

'I won't let you down, sir, m'm,' Nicole said, smiling gratefully. She drew away towards the door. She felt, at that instant, that she was on her way to becoming if not a woman of the world, at least a respectable lady of Mauritius.

The dancers swirled with precision around the ballroom floor. Nicole, sitting in the back row of chairs at the edge, watched with her eyes bright as the lines formed and parted. The chandeliers glittered, the gorgeous dresses dazzled and the men in their smart uniforms and breeches looked devastatingly handsome. She had never known such a wonderful time.

Emma, Jane and Louise were among the most popular girls at the ball. Men were constantly coming over to ask for dances. If they looked like they were going to speak to her, Nicole lowered her eyes demurely. She would not intrude on Emma's success.

Mrs Didcott was seated a few rows away with the other matrons. She was busily gossiping about every young man in sight, in the same manner as men did about horses on the race days.

The older men – Arthur Didcott, Colonel Draper, Governor Farquhar, Dr Telfair – were gathered with their cronies at the opposite end of the ballroom. When Nicole saw the governor she felt a pang of guilt about forgetting Jonathan. In the days of preparation for the ball she had overlooked watering the seedling too.

The orchestra played a rousing finish to a dance and the gentlemen escorted partners off the floor. There was much giggling and guffawing. Nicole cast her eyes over her three charges with pride.

'They are much better behaved than I am,' she thought to herself. 'I was very nearly kissed in the governor's mansion.' The memory brought a blush to her already rosy cheeks.

'By the devil! You're a pretty sight.'

She flinched, praying that the remark was not directed at her. A man moved into her line of vision so she was unable to see Emma and the other two. She shifted in her seat, hoping to peer around the man obstructing her view. She was dismayed when he moved as well.

'Sir,' she said primly, 'you are separating me from my friends.'

'I have been accused of worse than that.'

She stared up at his face. He was smiling arrogantly. She saw his confident eyes of green sparkling like emeralds as he appraised her. Her blush deepened.

The man's hair was blond, a mass of unruly curls. From his tanned complexion and strapping physique, she guessed he was a planter, a poor one, judging from the outdated quality of his clothes. The drawl of his voice marked him as a Creole.

'Please excuse me,' she said, standing up. 'I have my charges to attend to.'

She tried to move around him but he would not give way. She glanced frantically at Mrs Didcott in case she was being observed. The man caught her arm.

'What's the hurry, m'mselle?'

Now that she was on her feet she saw he was only a few inches taller than she was. It gave her courage and she returned his stare boldly. He was younger than Jonathan, more her age. His face was lean with a firm jaw that hinted at toughness in his personality. In the challenge of his eyes she thought she discerned a brooding spirit buffeted by tragedy and disappointment.

'By the devil!' he exclaimed excitedly. 'Do you see right inside me?' He released her in surprise.

'Please leave me.' She kept her voice low. 'I am chaperon to Mrs Didcott's young ladies. She will be distressed if she sees you detaining me.'

'Then I must seek the old dragon's permission to flirt. Where is she?'

Nicole was appalled. Heads were turning to look at them. If the man created a scene, Emma and Mrs Didcott would be disgraced. Suddenly she remembered how her mother had coped with unwanted advances.

'Let this be our secret,' she whispered in the man's ear. 'I will meet you later.'

He was astonished by her boldness and stepped away as though he suspected her of immorality. Then his eyes twinkled. 'You have a zesty sense of humour.'

Nicole glanced beyond him to where Emma was standing with Jane and Louise. Emma was looking outraged and signalled a warning with her fan. Nicole frowned, trying to explain with her eyes that it was not her wish to be accosted.

The man laughed at her distress and bowed with a flourish of insolence. 'Ward Trenchard at your service, m'mselle. I regret I did not meet you at Mistress Didcott's affair last month.'

Nicole snapped her fan open and fluttered it briskly. She noticed that the men who had been hovering around Emma hoping for a dance were regarding her with curiosity.

'Ward Trenchard!' she gasped aloud in a delayed reaction. The flush stole over her cheeks again. 'I was the guitar player. I'm Creole so Mrs Didcott did not allow me to be seen.'

'By the devil, what a notion! You are the most beautiful young lady in Mauritius. Everyone must see you! Shall we dance?'

'Oh no!' She withdrew, trying to put the chair between herself and Ward.

Everyone knew how evil he was. He was reputed to be as wicked as his late father, an American slave-trader. The scandal about his wife being caught with a black lover matched his own nefarious deeds.

'You are scared of me?' Ward's question challenged her.

She shook her head but before she could answer, Emma jostled her aside.

'Nicole, come away at once! She is my chaperone, Mr

Trenchard, and I have need of her.'

'Indeed?' Ward's eyebrow arched. 'I doubt she has need of you,' he said sardonically. He bowed to Nicole, deliberately ignoring Emma and her companions. 'We shall meet again, m'mselle, without the cabal.' It sounded like a threat as he turned and strode away.

Nicole watched him go, her heart fluttering as fast as her fan. The crowd of dancers parted to let him pass, impressed by his brusque swagger. She saw him join two ladies who were sitting side by side without speaking to each other.

The older one, with the trimness of a French lady of quality, was obviously his mother, Monique Trenchard. The other, blonde and overweight with a painted face and sour expression, was Gina, his wife, the girl who had jilted Jonathan.

Nicole had known Gina when she was younger. She was the envy of the town then with her lithesome figure and whisps of blonde hair billowing like spun gold from under her bonnet. She had an inspiring smile, sang beautifully and held the garrison's officers in thrall.

Whatever love Gina and Ward once shared, it was obvious that it had died. Gina seemed angry at what Ward was telling her. They both looked in her direction. Nicole blushed and raised her fan to shield her embarrassment, feeling ashamed at what he must be saying about her.

'He called us a cabal,' said Emma. 'What did he mean by that?'

Nicole was amused by the aptness of Ward's expression. 'Perhaps he thought the three of you were gathering to criticize him,' she suggested coyly.

'Well I'm glad Emma scared him off,' said Louise. 'It's obvious what he wanted.'

Nicole was genuinely surprised. 'What did he want?'

'You,' said Louise. 'He was looking at you in the wickedest way.'

'You loved it!' Emma scowled. 'He's the most notorious man in Mauritius, Nicole. How dare you encourage him!'

'It wasn't my fault,' she said, suddenly feeling unhappy and longing to leave.

The ball continued until the early hours of the morning. Nicole was asked for more dances than Emma but refused every one. The British officers had difficulty in understanding why she would not join in the fun.

As the ball progressed it seemed that Emma, Louise and Jane were her three chaperons instead of the other way round. The more Nicole tried to be discreet and unnoticed, the more men sought her out.

She remained conscious, throughout the evening, of one man's persistence. Whenever she raised her eyes, he was watching her, peering at her over the rim of his glass as he drank with Colonel Draper, or gazing at her from the seat opposite, where he sat with his mother.

Try as she might, Ward Trenchard was impossible to ignore. He was biding his time, with the arrogance of a man to whom nothing was denied. His wife, now quite exuberant, was dancing with all and sundry, shrieking with delight and believing herself to be the life and soul of the party. Ward showed no sign of concern over her outrageous behaviour.

'We must be going,' said Emma crossly. 'Unless you want to stay, Nicole?'

'Who would take her home?' Louise tittered.

'She'll have to pick up someone,' added Jane viciously. 'Like a whore.'

'She does it with a flicker of her eyelashes, have you noticed?'

'It's the way she shows off her ankles when she's seated,' said Jane. 'Men know the signals.'

Nicole laughed, pretending to enjoy the jokes at her expense, although she was puzzled by her friends' spitefulness. 'You've all danced so much, you've had such a success,' she said cheerfully. 'I'll tell Mrs Didcott you're ready to go.'

'Mamma's waiting for us. I haven't enjoyed this ball at all, have you?' Emma asked Louise. 'No one asked us to dance twice.'

'How could they when they saw Nicole with us?'

'Do you think she jinxed us?'

'No. But I suppose people think she's like her mother was.'

'Are you, Nicole?' Jane leered at her. 'Are you like your mother?'

Nicole bit her lip. She had been teased before about her past and shrugged it off. Tonight the taunts had more venom. She drew herself up, tossing her head so her ringlets shook. Her cheeks were flushed and her eyes flashed defiance.

From across the room Ward Trenchard watched her constantly.

'Why,' she asked, feigning indifference, 'is it of interest to you? Are you jealous because I have no doubts about my virtue?'

'Someone has!' Emma nodded across the room. 'See how Ward's ogling you. It's disgusting.' She gave a mock shudder. 'I'm insulted. Take me home, Nicole!' She tapped her on the shoulder with her fan.

Taking their cue, Louise dug her in the ribs with her fingers, while Jane banged against her hip with her reticule.

Nicole fought back the tears as her three so-called friends bustled her out of the ballroom. Mrs Didcott was waiting in the antechamber, her expression as dark as the night outside. Even Mr Didcott, at her side, looked pained. The presence of other mothers and daughters eyeing Nicole warily forced Mrs Didcott to control her indignation until they were clear of the Turf Club compound and walking across the Champ de Mars.

'To think,' Mrs Didcott exclaimed, slapping Nicole's backside with her hand, 'that after all the time and money we spent on you, you should repay us like that!'

Nicole was confused. 'What have I done?'

'Done, child? Ruined me, that's what!'

Nicole turned to Mr Didcott for help. 'I was discreet,' she said. 'I looked after Emma and the girls as I was supposed to do. I didn't dance although so many men asked me to. You saw!'

'I saw,' he said gravely. 'I also heard.'

'Heard what? I didn't speak to anyone unless they

addressed me first, and then I only replied to be polite.'

'What about Ward Trenchard?' asked Emma.

'You talked to him too.'

'I don't want to hear that man's name! He was asking questions about you, Nicole.' Mrs Didcott smacked her again. 'He's a married man!'

'I did nothing to encourage him. Please believe me.' Nicole was distraught, wondering if they had all gone mad. 'What did he say about me? He must have lied.'

Mr Didcott coughed. 'I won't repeat his words, Nicole. You've shocked me.' His voice was steeped in sadness.

'He had a bet!' Mrs Didcott was unable to be so discreet.

'A bet, Mamma? What about?'

'You're too young to know.'

'Mamma! I'm sixteen. Let me know so I can understand what a dreadful man he is. I did tell Nicole to have nothing to do with him, didn't I, Louise?'

'She was encouraging him.'

'That's enough!' Mrs Didcott pushed Nicole in front of her. 'He wagered one thousand pounds with Colonel Draper.'

'One thousand pounds!' Emma clutched Louise's hand. 'What for?'

'For Nicole. He bet Colonel Draper he will have her maidenhood before the end of the season. Imagine!' Mrs Didcott was close to hysterics.

'Everyone knows about the bet. I'm the laughing-stock of Port Louis.' She pummelled Nicole with her fists while the girls joined in, punching her breasts and thighs.

Mr Didcott walked away gloomily into the darkness.

The next morning, at daybreak, Nicole stole out of the chamber. She let herself out through the back door of the house into the garden. Slowly she walked along the path to the arbour where she had planted the flamboyant seedling.

It had gone. Someone had pulled it up, torn it into tiny pieces and scattered it over the path.

EIGHT

The stench of mouldering vegetation and fetid water filled Jonathan's nostrils as he stumbled, exhausted, along the path through the swamp. It was a warm, damp smell of decay that hung in the air like an invisible mist. Since wading ashore at Tamatave he had breathed nothing but that aroma of rotting jungle. It clung to him in the clammy heat and now his pores exuded it as a putrid odour.

His eyes were closing and he was almost fainting with nausea. A few more steps and he would willingly slip into the seething liquid mud on either side of the narrow trail. He envied Verette his agility in negotiating the quagmire; he also envied him his tiny button nose that prevented him inhaling the vast quantity of obnoxious smells that assailed Jonathan every time he breathed.

He was supposed to be marching with Captain Lesage and his escort of soldiers. They were already too far ahead for Jonathan to care. Verette was with him, he could just see him through the haze. Two natives accompanied him. Their swarthy features and barbaric grunts distressed him almost as much as the stifling smell.

He faltered and gasped; he tried to cry out for Verette but he felt himself slipping. He relaxed and lay with relief in a fitful stupor, his head lolling back in the thick, black mud.

He had arrived in Madagascar five weeks before on the *Tyne*. He was greeted at first with pleasure by Captain Bebe Lesage, until the captain read the instructions Jonathan had brought with him from Governor Farquhar.

Captain Lesage was stationed temporarily in Madagascar with soldiers of the Twenty-second Foot to obtain redress from the Hovas for the murder of a party of British officials three months earlier. He boasted of his success in extracting an offer of eight hundred oxen in compensation but he did nothing to allay Jonathan's misgivings at having to treat with Radama.

Bebe Lesage's attitude added to his concern. The captain was scornful and disinclined to believe Jonathan's instructions were more than a joke. He scandalized Jonathan by refusing to obey the order. Jonathan was forced to wait in Tamatave while the *Tyne* was sent back to Mauritius for clarification before Captain Lesage agreed to go into the mountains with him.

In the meantime Jonathan had to camp in a makeshift shelter in the damp wooden fort that was Lesage's headquarters. It added to his despondency. Lesage regarded him as a nuisance and left him alone. For solace he could only contemplate the low-lying swamp lands that had to be crossed before he could start the long climb into the mountains that contained Radama's stronghold.

Verette enjoyed the delay at Tamatave. He shrugged off the enervating atmosphere and used his time to gather intelligence. 'The Hovas are winning the war against the Saccalanas, who are the tribe friendly to the English,' he told Jonathan.

'Are the Hovas friendly?' Jonathan asked anxiously.

'Sometimes.' Verette ignored his groan of despair. 'There are over five million people in this country. It's vast. The swamp lands extend thirty miles into the interior. The hills rise to six thousand feet; that's three times the height of Pouce.'

Verette was irrepressible. He asked questions, met people and conducted himself with the enthusiasm Jonathan should have shown. From Verette's enquiries Jonathan learned the country was divided into two distinct races, one inhabiting the table land of the interior, the other the districts bordering the coast.

The coastal people, as Jonathan saw for himself, were negroid, especially in the shape of nose and skull. Their figures were lofty and Herculean, their complexion black and their hair bushy and dark. The Hovas, on the other hand, resembled Asiatics. They were copper in colour, with hair long and silky, and head and face in the European mould.

Jonathan drew some comfort from that. If they were European in appearance, he imagined they would be civilized in their conduct. Verette brightly contradicted him. The Hovas were vicious people, cruel when enraged and with no respect for human life.

The capital, where Radama lived, was known as Tananarivo, located in the highlands near the centre of the island. It was reputed to be remarkably healthy. The swamp surrounding it, however, was deadly to Europeans. It was a huge border that could not be avoided, caused by the coastal land and its rivers being at a lower level than the sea.

Verette said that beyond the swamps was a place of great beauty with luxuriant valleys, passes and ravines, awe-inspiring craters of extinct volcanoes, immense forests, savannas, rivers and lakes. The thought of its beauty meant nothing to Jonathan. First he had to survive the swamp.

Fighting for his breath in the midst of the seething, stinking mud, Jonathan doubted he would ever see open country again or breathe pure air. He was limp as strong arms pulled him to his feet. He tried to stand. He who was distraught if mud splashed on him from the wheels of a bullock-cart on the streets of Port Louis was covered from head to toe in slime.

'I'm not going to make it,' he croaked, succumbing to the weakness he was feeling.

He had spent one night in the swamps, huddled with Verette under a blanket on a grass mat spread beneath a mangrove tree. Sleep was impossible with the droning and biting of mosquitoes. His body was covered with sores that were festering where he scratched at them with muddy finger-nails.

'I'm finished.' His legs wobbled under him like a baby's.

'No, you ain't,' said Verette. 'I promised Miss Nicole I'd bring you back safely.'

The mention of Nicole roused him so that he stumbled a few more steps. It also anaesthetized him to the wretchedness he was feeling. In a daze he clung to Verette, nearly slipping from his grasp back into the waiting swamp.

Verette was ready. The natives, despite their savage appearance, were trained as bearers and escorts. One of them hoisted Jonathan onto his shoulders. He carried him like a sack of maize and trotted along the path so that Verette and the party made better progress. They carried Jonathan to a village in the middle of the swamp land where Captain Lesage was waiting.

Jonathan was vaguely aware of being laid on a mat in a grass hut, and of his face being bathed by Verette. When he tried to rise, he fell back, all strength drained from his limbs.

'Fever,' pronounced Captain Lesage as though it were a death sentence. He left him on the floor without a word of sympathy. Verette fanned the flies away from his face.

'What you want to get fever for when we just beginnin' the march?' Verette was cross. 'Cap'n Lesage vexed 'cause he have to negotiate with Radama. He goin' get blamed if he fail.'

Jonathan moaned. He had no energy to speak although he understood. He was ready to die, as Captain Lesage expected.

The fever raged unchecked through his body. At times he was delirious, dreaming he was at home in England in the chill of the autumn; other times he was lucid and concerned that Verette should rest and not worry about him. Night fell and there was only the light of the moon filtering through the grass thatch to illuminate the hut.

Jonathan roused himself as the moonlight exploded and filled the hut with a misty glow. He sniffed and was beset by the stench of the swamps, a smell so strong it was embracing him, claiming him. He wondered if this was death, when he looked up into a face of glittering bronze.

'An English?' a deep voice asked.

'Yes.' Verette scrambled to his feet and confronted the intruder, who was peering at Jonathan. The man held a spear in his hand and raised it above his head.

'Hey!' Verette shouted as he realized what the bronze man was going to do. He leaped at him, deflecting his arm as the spear thrust downwards. It glanced off Jonathan's leather belt and lodged in the earth.

'Get out of here.'

Verette's anger astonished the man and he drew back and regarded him disdainfully.

'Who are you to command me in my father's land?'

'Who are you to attack the imperial messenger of His Majesty the governor of Mauritius?'

Jonathan listened with disbelief to Verette's outburst. The exaggeration seemed to have an effect. The intruder squatted on his haunches at one side of Jonathan's limp body while Verette crouched at the other. The spear remained stuck in the earth between them.

Jonathan heard their conversation in gusts, like a wind blowing over him. Someone stood at the entrance to the hut with a flaming torch that lit up their faces.

He saw that the bronze sheen of the intruder was his naked flesh smeared with grease that gave off a sparkle in the torchlight. He was a young man, with the muscular physique of a warrior. His eyes, watching Verette intently from behind a mask of white paint, were intelligent.

'I give you leave,' the warrior said, 'to convince me why this white man should not die.'

Verette glanced at the spear, probably realizing for the first time the danger he was in. He did not let his fear show. 'You speak English with the tongue of a brave and clever chief,' he said smoothly..

Again the man looked astounded by Verette's behaviour. He expected him to beg for mercy. 'I learned from slave-traders,' he snapped, nodding at Jonathan. 'People like him.'

'Not like *Mr Jonathan*!' Verette's outrage was intimidating. 'My master is carrying a message from the

Prince Regent to your king to *stop* the slave-trade.'

'King? Who is my king?'

'King Radama. My master is a special envoy to his court.'

The native warrior laughed. Jonathan, hearing the sound from far away, thought it was the cackling of the devil.

'If he is a slave-trader, I will kill him,' the native said. 'If he is as you say, he is my friend. I have sworn to kill flesh traders. My people will be free.'

'That's what Mr Jonathan wants too. If King Radama bans the selling of your people to the white man, then there will be no trade in slaves. It is the King who has the power to stop it.'

'You speak wisely.'

Jonathan agreed, although he was unable to say so. He was impressed how Verette had absorbed the details of his mission. He showed more conviction about it than Jonathan could.

He shuddered when the fingers of the warrior began to prod his body.

'This man is not like the others,' the native pronounced. 'He is a weakling, unused to hardship. His clothes are those of a gentleman, not a slave-trader.'

'You see, I speak the truth,' said Verette. 'He is sick with fever. Will you help him? If he dies, he can't deliver his secret message.'

'Secret? What is that?'

'It is for the king's ears alone.'

'I am Ratsitatane,' said the warrior. 'I am Radama's kin and ally. You can tell me.'

'Only Mr Jonathan knows the secret. If he dies, it dies with him.'

'Ho!' Ratsitatane sat back on his haunches and appeared to be thinking.

He looked several times at Jonathan and at Verette. His features lost their menacing savagery. He was plainly curious about Jonathan's mission. He studied Verette's face for a long time. The youth stared back confidently.

The warrior was satisfied. He called to one of his men and gave him orders.

Minutes later the man returned, accompanied by an old woman wrapped in the hide of an animal that was not properly cured. Jonathan wrinkled his nose at the smell.

Ratsitatane spoke to the woman. She grunted and leaned over Jonathan. She began to mutter, smearing his brow and his chest with swamp mud she carried in a clay pot. He was too weak to protest. The stench overpowered him and he fainted.

When next he opened his eyes, Jonathan was flying. The tops of the trees drifted by his eyes, the sun was no longer hidden by jungle and the sky was clear. He breathed tentatively and took in the scent of pasture and a fast-running stream. He smelled the sweet fragrance of flowers and fruit. He was certain he was dead.

'At last!' a voice cried.

He looked around and saw Verette grinning at him, bobbing along at the same height. He was sitting in a chair, and when Jonathan looked down he saw that he was in a similar conveyance carried on the shoulders of eight copper-skinned soldiers.

He was surrounded by an army of men dressed in flowing robes of cotton cloth in a plaid pattern, worn like a Roman toga. They were armed with muskets, spears, and shields of buffalo hide. They danced around him as they advanced along the trail winding up the side of a hill beside a river.

'You saved me,' he whispered.

'Not me,' said Verette, laughing. 'Ratsitatane did.'

'Where is he?'

'With the king. We're going there now.'

'Captain Lesage?'

'He has the fever too. He's in a village with his soldiers.'

'We have none with us? No one to protect us?'

'Your secret does that.'

'I don't have a secret.'

Verette shrugged his shoulders and spread his hands in a

gesture of amusement. 'Then you must think of one at once.'

Radama received Jonathan sitting on a throne surrounded by his ministers and bodyguards. It was an impressive ceremony, with Jonathan being warmly welcomed by the king. At the time he did not realize the consternation he provoked by coming into the king's presence without an escort and without gifts. Both were with Captain Lesage in the swamp lands village where Lesage lay sick.

It was the first time that Radama had met a white man without an armed escort to protect him. The lack of presents puzzled him but he offered Jonathan provisions which Jonathan, in his innocence, politely declined.

'There are only two of us,' he said through the court interpreter. 'We don't want to cause any inconvenience. We prefer to eat with your soldiers rather than cook ourselves.'

Radama clapped his hands in surprise at the idea. Later Jonathan learned that white visitors insisted on preparing their own meals. His willingness to eat with the king's army created a greater impression on Radama than any gifts. It marked Jonathan as a singular man with the natural sympathy the Hovas appreciated.

For his part Jonathan found Radama a very ordinary young man after he had heard so much about him. He could not imagine him being guilty of the brutalities rumour suggested. He was Jonathan's height, with an athlete's build, yet he was very unprepossessing in appearance. Jonathan had expected him to look and act like Ward.

After the magnificent pride and physique of Ratsitatane, who really looked like a king, Radama was a disappointment. Jonathan judged him by his expressions as he did not understand what he said until it was translated. He noticed the king seemed impatient with his advisers and the formalities of court.

During that first audience two of the ministers began to argue in front of the king. Jonathan was shocked by their behaviour and he frowned, his glance meeting the king's. He recognized the king's expression as one he had often seen on Mr Farquhar's brow. He grinned with empathy, not considering the disrespect he was himself showing Radama.

The king rose abruptly from his throne. The ministers continued arguing, and even the soldiers took no notice of Radama. Only Jonathan and Verette bowed as he swept past them out of the court chamber.

Jonathan waited nervously, wondering what to do. It seemed the ministers were discussing his fate, one being in favour of his visit, the other one, judging by his mean looks, obviously against it. Ratsitatane watched from a corner, smirking arrogantly.

The interpreter beckoned Jonathan and Verette to follow him. They crossed the compound of the king's fort to a large mud and grass hut. A meal in dishes was laid out on a mat on the ground.

Although Jonathan was by nature finicky, he appreciated food however it was cooked. His nose was his guide. If it smelled good, he tasted it. His years in India and Mauritius, eating local delicacies prepared by native cooks, increased the range of dishes he relished. He had no qualms about eating with his fingers, something that British officers refused to do as they considered it barbarian.

After the rigours of the long journey, and his debilitating illness, the aroma of the food gave him an appetite. He was hungry and eager to eat. He plucked a piece of meat from one of the dishes and ate it with gusto.

Radama, who had been hiding in the shadows of the hut to see what Jonathan would do, emerged as he was smacking his lips.

'Forgive me, Your Majesty.' Jonathan was appalled by his gaffe. 'I thought … I mean, I assumed this was for us. I'm dreadfully sorry.' He bowed again, convinced that he and Verette would be punished.

'You said you would eat what we eat. I didn't believe you,' said Radama. 'You must forgive me for my doubts.'

He waved for Jonathan to be seated beside him. 'Shall we begin?'

Jonathan's training in dealing intimately with someone of authority, coupled with his natural humility, made an impression on the young king. Jonathan was aware of Radama studying him whenever the interpreter addressed him.

As the meal came to an end, the king offered him a woman for the night. Jonathan blushed scarlet and looked so shocked, Radama laughed.

'I will listen to your propositions tomorrow,' he said firmly. 'You are such an honest man, your face would not let you deceive me.'

When Captain Lesage recovered from his attack of fever and arrived at Tananarivo a few days later, he was greeted with full honours. His soldiers saluted in return by firing volleys.

Radama received him courteously but made it clear he was interested in listening to Jonathan, not to the Captain's official announcements. He insisted on talking with Jonathan alone. Only the interpreter and Verette were to be present. Captain Lesage protested; so did the king's ministers.

Radama joked about it. 'They don't trust us,' he said. 'Perhaps we will make an alliance with no profit for them.'

'Governor Farquhar has the same problem with his advisers,' said Jonathan sympathetically. 'They all want to use him to benefit themselves.'

Although he knew he should be discreet, there was something about Radama that provoked Jonathan to unwind. In their daily conversations he answered Radama's probing questions and was soon telling him about the machinations of Dr Telfair, the incompetence of the treasurer, Theodore Hook, and other details of his resentment with Mr Farquhar's officials.

Radama responded with indiscretions about his own ministers and with insights into Hova customs. Jonathan learned how Hovas regarded sacrifice as honourable. They kept no prisoners from battle but sold them as slaves to the

British and French. White men were killed if they caused offence. To Jonathan's relief the king assured him that he wanted to be a friend to the British.

'If only you could come to Mauritius,' Jonathan declared spontaneously. 'You could meet Governor Farquhar himself and see how he solves problems. He is a great man too.'

Jonathan was enjoying himself and almost forgot the purpose of his visit. Lesage was impatient for him to negotiate the treaty of friendship and sound out the king about banning the sale of slaves. Jonathan tried to explain to him that he needed more time to win the king's trust and to educate him to British ways.

Bebe Lesage was jealous of Jonathan's warm reception and annoyed that he was excluded from the talks. He had expected Jonathan to be sacrificed to a Hova god instead of being treated like a prince. For the sake of the mission he was obliged to check his own impatience and wait.

While Jonathan and Radama passed pleasant hours talking about their different countries, Verette was forming a friendship with the king's two brothers. The eldest, nicknamed Tiko, was fourteen. He took Verette on hunting expeditions to the interior, an activity Jonathan declined to join. Tiko and his brother, Manda, who was nine, sometimes attended the sessions between the king and Jonathan.

One afternoon, when the boys were bored, they joked about the size of Jonathan's nose. He got annoyed with their giggling and rebuked them firmly, without thinking. Radama stared in astonishment at the reprimand.

Jonathan immediately regretted losing his temper. If Radama felt insulted, the talks would fail.

There was an ominous silence in the hut. The interpreter was shocked speechless. Radama frowned and Jonathan hung his head in shame.

'My people need discipline,' the king observed quietly. 'Your soldiers are well drilled, they obey your captain; mine don't. Your governor's ministers do as he instructs; mine argue.

'Your counsellor,' he pointed to Verette, 'respects you; mine merely laugh. You can teach us many things. Will you stay in my kingdom?'

The invitation served to remind Jonathan of his duty. Having found himself so warmly welcomed, he was reluctant to give thought to returning to Mauritius.

'Your Majesty,' he said, unable to hide his regret. 'I must return to tell Governor Farquhar all I have learned from you.'

'Aha! Your intention is to spy on me, is it?' Radama pulled a knife from his belt. 'Very well.'

The blade of the knife glittered in the sunlight streaming into the hut. Verette tensed. Jonathan trembled, aware that neither Verette nor he could do anything if the king decided to kill them. Radama raised the knife into the air and pointed it at Jonathan's heart.

He eyed it anxiously. A feeling of disappointment welled up in his chest. His limbs were weak and he felt sick. At the very moment when he was encouraged to think he would return alive, Radama was making it clear that he would not. A simple thrust and he would be dead.

He bit his lip, annoyed with himself for being so careless that he had caused the king displeasure.

'Give me your arm,' Radama said coldly.

Jonathan complied without hesitation, though he was filled with fear and was trembling.

The king took his fingers in his own with an odd smile. 'Have you ever killed a man, Jonathan?' he asked to indicate what he intended to do.

'No.' Jonathan watched as the king rolled up his sleeve to his elbow and held his wrist tightly.

'I have, Jonathan, many times. I cut them here,' he drew the blade across the soft flesh at the crook of Jonathan's elbow, 'and leave them to bleed to death. It is very satisfying to inflict a lingering death. The one who is killed knows he is dying. He becomes amazingly peaceful. It is a gift to let someone die slowly.'

Jonathan shuddered. The knife sliced into his flesh. He waited to feel the pain and glanced at the cut in amazement as blood spurted from a vein in his forearm. He seemed to be watching the blood pumping from another's arm. It trickled down his wrist to the floor. There was a hiss as Tiko and Manda sighed together. Verette watched spellbound.

Radama eyed the blood with interest. 'You would not take long to die,' he said. He drew the knife down his own arm without flinching, cutting a gash larger than the one he had given Jonathan. He laughed at the shock in Jonathan's eyes. 'A Hova tradition,' he said casually.

He caught hold of Jonathan's arm and drew it towards him, holding it against his own arm. The blood mingled. He chanted energetically and then, to Jonathan's intense embarrassment, kissed him on both cheeks.

Jonathan wondered how long it would take him to die.

'Now,' said Radama with a smile, 'we are brothers.'

Jonathan's head spun and the pain in his arm brought tears to his eyes. He gulped, trying not to faint.

'Blood brothers?' he said, disgusted at the sight of his own blood dripping to the floor. 'In England ... we shake hands.' He extended his right hand and grasped the king's fingers with desperation.

'Good.' Radama smiled. 'Now we shall make the treaty of friendship you require and we can talk of why the British no longer want to buy my slaves.'

Jonathan looked in panic at Verette as he felt his legs buckling.

'These two,' said Radama, thinking he was looking at Tiko and Manda, 'are royal princes whom no outsider can reprimand. Now they are your brothers too, so you can chastize them as I would.'

Jonathan was too weak to speak. He was waiting to bleed to death.

'Yes, they are your brothers,' insisted Radama. 'If you cannot stay here, take them to Mauritius to learn your ways. Leave me a sergeant and men to train my soldiers.'

Jonathan tried to protest. Instead he sank forward into Radama's arms. The king smiled, shook his head in pity and signalled for his guards to carry him away.

NINE

The season that had begun so sweetly for Nicole with her meeting Jonathan turned sour after her encounter with Ward. Mrs Didcott decreed she was a bad influence on Emma and would not allow her to chaperone her to any of the season's festivities.

In vain, Nicole explained she had done nothing. She tried to reason with Emma but the girl she considered her friend proved otherwise. Emma seemed to delight in taunting her about Ward and what he had bet Colonel Draper he would do to her.

'He thinks you're a trollop,' she said. 'Everyone knows what Ward's like. No need to give yourself airs about him. I'd be ashamed if it were me!'

At night she cried herself to sleep, thinking of her lost friendship with Jonathan and how she would never see him again, and the thoughtlessness of Ward for maligning her with his drunken wager. Despite her misery she did not condemn him. She remembered the unhappiness she had seen deep in his emerald eyes. It was Emma and her mother who were to blame for seeing his remark as something worse than the stupid joke it really was.

She kept her feelings to herself and behaved with politeness to Emma. She helped her to dress for the parties and balls without jealousy. In actual fact she was relieved to be staying in the house when Emma was out. There was no chance of encountering Ward again if she stayed in her chamber.

A week after the Turf Club ball she was summoned to see Mrs Didcott in the drawing-room. Emma was there, her eyes glinting wickedly as she sat with exaggerated outrage on the edge of a chair.

Nicole smiled brightly at Emma and curtsied to Mrs Didcott. They both regarded her coldly. Mrs Didcott's face puffed up and turned purple with rage.

'How dare you!' she said, spluttering to let out the words. 'After all we've done for you! Oh, I will send you from this house, back to the gutter where you belong. Yes, I will. Wait till Mr Didcott hears of this.'

Nicole braced herself. 'Please, m'm, what are you talking about?'

'Hold your tongue, girl. You are not fit to address me.' For once, Mrs Didcott was at a loss for words. She stared savagely at Nicole, gripping the tawse in her hand.

Nicole tried to guess what could have caused this outburst. Perhaps Ward was at the ball Emma attended the night before. Maybe he was bragging about his senseless bet. What an odd man he was. Surely he knew she would suffer from the narrow-minded British settlers because of his remark.

She longed to protest her innocence but without knowing what she was accused of, she could not. She glanced at Emma. 'Is it something someone's said?' she asked softly.

'Said!' Mrs Didcott's shout almost launched her from the chair. 'How could you, girl?' She sniffed before answering her own question. 'I should have known. You will leave this house, oh yes.'

Nicole sighed. 'I've done nothing. I've spent every evening in the chamber when Emma was out. Fidou can vouch for that.'

'It's what you do in your chamber when Emma's there. What about last night?'

'Last night?' She looked at Emma in confusion, blushing as she remembered.

The night before she had been asleep when Emma returned. She had been dreaming that a man was holding her, pulling her towards him and roughly thrusting himself against her. With a shock of horror she had woken to discover that someone actually was holding her. She opened her eyes and was about to scream when a voice whispered close to her ear.

'Kiss me, kiss me!'

'Emma!' she had cried in alarm. 'What are you doing?' She twisted her head and felt the moistness of Emma's lips brushing against her cheek.

She peered frantically around the room. A single candle burned by the bed. Emma was under the sheet, groping with her hand to raise Nicole's night-dress.

'You're a Creole trollop, Nicole. Don't pretend you don't like it. Let me touch you there. Give me your hand. You can do it to me too.'

For a moment Nicole was too stunned to resist. Emma's hand clawed up the inside of her thigh and rubbed against her vagina. Although she was overwhelmed with dread, it was mixed with a strange feeling of warmth. She shuddered.

'Stop it!' she hissed as loud as she could without disturbing the rest of the household.

'Give me your hand, Nicole,' Emma gulped. 'Here!'

'No, I won't!' She pulled back to the side of the bed but was trapped against the wall. She brought her legs up to ward off Emma and her knee rubbed against Emma's crotch.

'You bloody whore!' Emma sighed with pain.

'I'm sorry.' Nicole was dazed. She lay back, not daring to move. Emma fell on her, pummelling her breasts with her fists. Gradually she calmed and her blows changed to rough caresses. Her hands slipped down between Nicole's legs. Nicole gasped at the shock as Emma's fingers opened her.

'That's sweet,' Emma murmured, pressing her lips onto Nicole's mouth. She was fondling herself in a frenzy.

'Stop it,' Nicole begged, frightened by the passion that Emma had roused in her. She struggled to ease herself out of the bed but every time she moved, Emma caught her. Suddenly Emma's body arched and, with a whimper of ecstacy, she plunged her fingers into Nicole, drooling with pleasure.

The silence as Mrs Didcott waited for an answer to her question was ominous. Nicole looked her straight in the eyes. 'Last night? I was asleep when Emma came home,' she said confidently.

'That's a lie!' Mrs Didcott shook the tawse in her face.

'You were doing something disgusting.'

'I wasn't!'

'Don't answer back. Emma saw you. You were touching yourself in a way no decent young lady ever does.'

'I was asleep. I wasn't doing anything.'

'It's not the first time, Mamma. I've seen her doing it before. Rubbing herself between her legs. You know.' Emma's eyes gleamed. 'She was whispering something. I think she was saying "Ward".'

'Oh!' Mrs Didcott clasped her hand to her brow and sat back in the chair. She thumped the tawse against her thigh. 'You wicked girl!' she cried when she regained her composure. 'How dare you bring your mother's evil into this house.'

Nicole closed her ears to Mrs Didcott's ranting. If she and Emma wanted to banish her from their house, there was nothing she could do. She was determined to remain calm, despite the lies and slander that were being used against her.

She turned and left the room. She could not understand what was wrong, for she knew she was blameless.

She never discovered what transpired between Mrs Didcott and her husband. Mr Didcott was too embarrassed to tell her. Anyway, she was not ordered from the house.

There was a room at the back of the building, adjoining the dining-room, where the slaves stored the table wares, a kind of scullery. She was told to leave the chamber she shared with Emma and sleep there. A pallet was placed for her on the floor and her chest was carried down from the upstairs chamber.

She was to take her meals alone and was forbidden to speak to the other girls unless responding to an order. She was placed in Fidou's charge while Mrs Didcott decided what to do with her. It was implied that she would be married off to a non-commissioned officer as soon as a willing one could be found.

Her attitude to these frightening developments was one of bemusement. She had always known her stay with the Didcott's was temporary and accepted the change in her fortune with resignation. It was the injustice that confused her. She was being condemned for nothing.

'That's the way it is,' said Fidou when Nicole confided in the slave. They were in the garden together, the only place where Nicole still found happiness.

'You're like me, only you're white,' said Fidou, helping Nicole to plant some bougainvillea cuttings. 'You have no life of your own.'

'Of course I have.' She frowned. 'When I leave here …'

'What you goan do?' Fidou laughed scornfully. 'You ain't hear what people sayin' 'bout you?'

Nicole placed the cuttings in the soil with determination. 'If people were fair they would say how fortunate I am.'

'Why?'

'Because Colonel Draper bet one thousand pounds that Ward would *not* succeed in his scandalous plan. The Colonel is known to back certainties.'

Fidou gazed at her with admiration. 'Why, lor', you always see the bright side.'

'I need to, Fidou. You don't believe that nonsense Emma made up, do you?'

Fidou winked. 'Makes no difference if I do. I ain't jealous.'

'Jealous?'

'No, I ain't. She does do it to me too.'

'Fidou! You must tell Mist –'

'Who? Ma Didcott? I'm a slave, Miz. Ain't no "right" for me, only wrong.'

'It will help me to prove I'm innocent.'

'Makes no diff'rence. They goan make you a slave even though you Creole. They despise you, 'specially 'cause your mam was a lovin' lady an' your father – Lor', no one know who your father be!' She chuckled merrily, digging at the earth with her strong fingers.

Nicole stood up and glanced at the bed counting the cuttings she and Fidou had planted. There were twenty of them. 'I don't want to be married off to a subaltern, or anyone! Woe is me!' she muttered with a sigh.

Fidou snorted. 'You're the most envied woman in Port

Louis. That's why Ma Didcott and Emma so spiteful.'

Nicole squinted with surprise. 'Me? Envied?'

'Of course. Every woman like to have Ward Trenchard hot in his pants for her. He the richest man in the colony. If you snare him, you can have everythin'. I'll be your slave, Nicole. He'll buy me for you.'

'Stop that talk!' She glared at Fidou. 'Ward's a married man.'

'So's Mr Didcott. That don't stop him lovin' a whore in the Chaussée. That's how he met your mam.'

Nicole's composure left her. She lashed out with her hand and caught Fidou with a stinging blow on her cheek. The slave reeled, a look of respect replacing the insolence in her eyes.

'Lor', miz,' she said happily, rubbing her cheek. 'So you do fancy Mas Ward in truth!'

Emma, together with Jane and Louise, danced the season away in a succession of balls, parties and intimate veranda affairs. Nicole heard about their activities from Fidou. Soon Emma found a regular beau, a major in the Fifty-sixth West Sussex regiment.

Nicole seemed to have been forgotten. No one bothered her as she pottered in the garden or spent hours in the kitchen with the cook, trying new recipes.

The bougainvillea cuttings sprouted tiny leaves. When she was alone she planted another flamboyant-tree seedling and was thrilled when it began to bud. She thought fondly of Jonathan although as the weeks passed and there was no news of HMS *Tyne* she accepted she had seen the last of him. She thought, too, of Ward Trenchard.

In her loneliest moments she admitted to herself that he was attractive. He was also moody and unpredictable and that was excitiing. She tried to ignore the gay time Emma was having with her major, yet there were moments when she longed to be free from her predicament and carried off in the arms of a strong, handsome man too.

That the man in her dreams had Ward's face was, she

reasoned, because she knew no other with his rugged good looks and arrogant charm, a dangerous combination for any young woman to day-dream over. She was piqued that he had not followed up his reckless wager by at least one attempt to see her. She longed to rebuff him. Could he be lacking the courage even to try? she wondered.

After several weeks of brooding, idling in the garden with only the birds and the flowers for company, and listening to slave gossip in the kitchen, Nicole was hungry for diversion. She questioned Fidou daily about her outings to Port Louis. Had the *Tyne* been sighted? Was the Master of Black River in town?

One morning, when the sky was overcast and it was cool in the garden where she was weeding a flower-bed, Mr Didcott sought her out. She was aware of him watching her for several minutes before he coughed to announce his presence. She rose slowly from the ground and wiped her muddy fingers on her apron.

'If you think I'm doing slave work, Mr Didcott,' she said before he could criticize her, 'it's because I like it. There's peace in a garden. The flowers don't lie.'

Mr Didcott half smiled. 'You remind me of your mother, Nicole. She was one with spirit.'

'I'm surprised to hear you mention her.'

Mr Didcott glanced anxiously around the garden in case someone overheard. There was only a slave in sight. 'You must not feel bitter, Nicole. It is not I who condemned your mother.'

'I am grateful to you. Who condemned me?'

'Why, no one!'

'Then why am I here?' She held up the soiled palms of her hands for him to see. 'Are these the hands expected of a young lady from Mrs Didcott's academy?'

'Nicole,' he said softly. 'Do you really want to go to those balls with all those boring young men?'

'Yes,' she said defiantly. 'I have done nothing. It's unfair.'

'Now you sound peevish like Emma.'

Nicole lowered her eyes, knowing that Mr Didcott was

right. 'I'd rather sound like my mother,' she said, her good humour restored. 'Forgive me.'

Mr Didcott strolled over to sit on the bench in the arbour. It was where she dreamed her days away. She found it odd to see him sit there and she stared at him, wondering what had moved him to make peace with her.

'Have you found me a subaltern?' she said, unable to keep the mockery from her voice. 'You have been good to me, Mr Didcott. Please stop it. Let me choose my own husband when I'm ready. I don't mind tending the flowers. I'm not languishing, really.' She laughed to show him she was happy.

Mr Didcott smiled. 'That's better,' he said. 'Just the sort of thing your mother would say. I never believed her, either.'

Nicole's heart missed a beat and surged with affection for him. She would have run over and kissed him but ... Instead she walked slowly to the bench and sat down beside him. 'What is it you have to tell me?' she asked, composing herself.

He took her hand in his, ignoring her muddy fingers, and squeezed. 'You're a good girl, Nicole. I've never doubted it.'

She looked away as she recalled that night in the Champ de Mars after the Turf Club ball and she heard him saying 'You've shocked me.' She waited until the memory clouded over so she could face him with forgiveness in her heart.

'Tonight,' he said, 'a palanquin will come for you. I've prepared Mrs Didcott. She will not be here. Take Fidou as your chaperon.'

'I don't want to marry someone I've never met!' she cried, tearing her hand from his grasp.

'This,' he said gravely, 'is not marriage.'

Nicole's instinct was to refuse to go. 'Lor', miz,' said Fidou as she brushed her hair, carefully patting her ringlets into place. 'You been so down in the dumps these past weeks. Don't you see how you have a sparkle in your eyes just thinkin' 'bout it?'

'Thinking of what?' she said, almost snapping. 'Mr

Didcott wouldn't say. Am I to be palanquined through Port Louis like some fancy lady of the night?'

Fidou giggled at her anger. 'Mr Didcott is an honourable man.'

'You said he has a mistress in the Chaussée.'

Fidou finished brushing her hair. 'Can you condemn him for wantin' to spare Mrs Didcott his desires?' She chuckled. 'She ain't no beauty with her moustache, is she?'

Nicole's temper was diffused by Fidou's remark. 'I still don't think it's honourable for me to ride out without knowing why.'

'I be with you.' Fidou smiled mysteriously.

At eight o'clock the palanquin was outside the house. There were eight slaves to carry it, and four others as torch bearers and escorts. Mrs Didcott was gone out with Emma and her major. Mr Didcott was not at home so Nicole was able to leave the house without fear that she would be stopped.

She squeezed with Fidou into the palanquin, clutching her as it was hoisted by its carrying poles onto the shoulders of the bearers. Each slave held a staff for support and they began to chant as they trotted out into the Champ de Mars and along the darkened street leading from it.

Nicole peeped out through the silk curtains to see where they were going. The darkness chilled her. One of the negro escorts grinned and she withdrew her head quickly. There was only one man in the colony who could afford an entourage of grandly dressed slaves and a palanquin of such magnificence.

'Tell them to halt,' she said with determination. 'I want to go back.'

'No, miz. It's too late for that.'

The palanquin swayed to a stop and they were lowered to the ground with a jolt. Nicole tried to jump out but Fidou restrained her with a firm grip on her wrist. 'The whole town goan know 'bout this if you run,' she whispered.

Nicole shivered, suddenly realizing that Fidou was in the plot as well as Mr Didcott. 'You know whose palanquin this is!' she exclaimed, feeling bitter at being duped.

Fidou grinned broadly, held her finger up to her lips warning her to be quiet and slipped out of the palanquin. She closed the curtains and left Nicole sitting alone in the darkness.

The curtains were gold and red. The flames of the torches held by the negro guards threw a glow into the interior. It was like being in a mobile prison. She sat rigid, listening to every sound, wondering how she could escape.

The slaves were murmuring among themselves. She reached for the curtain to peer out. Abruptly they stopped talking. Footsteps clattered down steps and strode across cobbles towards the palanquin.

She shrank back into the cushions, regretting her decision to come. She had guessed whose head she would see when the curtains were pulled apart.

Arthur Didcott, Fidou, they had both deceived her. Ward Trenchard could buy anyone, even them; he was a flesh trader. As she waited, the rumours she had heard about him brought a flush of anger to her cheeks. She rued the night she saw him at the ball.

She raised her hand, ready to slap his face the moment he put his head through the curtains.

'Miss Genave?'

The hesitant voice surprised her. She let her hand fly and it connected with the cheek of a large-nosed man before she could stop herself.

'Oh dear!' she gasped. 'I'm ... I'm sorry.'

The man retreated and the curtain fluttered to a close. Only then did she notice the royal crest of the governor woven in gold thread into the silk.

She pulled open the curtain. Jonathan Rendye was blinking and rubbing his cheek. He bowed deeply. Verette held the curtain and gestured to her to step out.

'Jonathan!' she said. 'I had no idea ...' She gazed around the courtyard of Government House. 'I thought –'

'I'm sure I deserved that,' he said. 'This was to be a surprise.' He offered his arm to escort her up the steps to the reception room, where the chandeliers were blazing.

'His Excellency is waiting for you.'

'When did you arrive? Thank the Lord you're safe.' She was overwhelmed and acutely embarrassed by the slap she had given him. 'What is this all about?'

In the moments while he led her to where the governor was waiting she had time only to notice that he was leaner than when he went away, and tanned. His hair still flopped on his brow and his suit was the same grey of a nondescript clerk.

He released her and she found herself facing the governor. She curtsied hurriedly as Mrs Didcott had taught her. She was vaguely aware of men in the room standing behind him, and of ladies seated on couches.

'Miss Genave,' said Mr Farquhar, his eyes welcoming her with a genuine kindness. 'I think you will like this little surprise. You know everyone here?' He indicated the people gathered around the room.

She gasped in astonishment.

'Mrs Didcott! Emma!' She gazed beyond them to where a man was standing with his arms folded, watching her with piercing green eyes. 'Ward Trenchard?' she breathed in awe.

'Yes,' said Mr Farquhar briskly. 'And Colonel Draper. The other gentlemen, with their ladies, are on my staff. You know Dr Telfair, Captain Lesage and, of course, Mr Rendye.'

'Nicole, you may sit here.' Mr Didcott stepped forward to lead her to the couch where Emma and her mother were waiting. They made a space for her between them.

Emma shyly patted her hand. Nicole was too perplexed to withdraw it.

The governor stood opposite her. 'Miss Genave,' he began grandly, then lowered his voice. 'My duties normally involve me in affairs of state. Sometimes I am enlisted to help people too. This little gathering is at the request of one of our most prominent citizens, Mr Trenchard.'

He gestured at Ward, coughed, and continued. 'He requested that all the people you see here tonight be present. He has explained to me his purpose and he has my support.'

The silence in the chamber was broken by Mrs Didcott blowing her nose. Mr Didcott looked away.

Ward, his eyes fixed on Nicole's, stepped forward. His face was ashen and a vein pulsed in his forehead. She felt sorry for him as she recognized the strain he was under.

'Miss Genave,' he began, then swallowed. 'His Excellency and I rarely agree on anything. However, on the matter of a lady's honour, there can be no disagreement. A few weeks ago I did you a disservice when I was in my cups. His Excellency invited your friends here so that they can witness my apology.'

Nicole listened with her mind in a turmoil. She glanced at Jonathan, who was standing alone in the shadows, almost hiding behind a pillar. Ward's eyes drew her gaze back to him.

'Because of a foolish wager with Colonel Draper here,' he continued, 'your good name has been besmirched. I have even learned that those you love have doubted you.' He looked sternly at Mrs Didcott, who was covering her face with her handkerchief.

'Colonel Draper had faith in you, and so have I, mademoiselle. I sincerely regret my wager and the slur it cast upon you. I ask you now,' he said, dropping forward to kneel on one knee, 'to accept my apology.'

Mrs Didcott burst into tears. Emma hid behind her fan.

Nicole pulled herself free from them and rose to her feet. 'No,' she said, facing Ward and bringing him to his feet. 'I will not forgive you.'

'Nicole!' Mrs Didcott's voice rasped around the room.

Nicole took no notice. She stared at Ward, enjoying the moment. 'There is nothing to forgive. Who knows, you might have won.' Her eyes twinkled. Mr Didcott stepped forward and took her arm with a smile.

'Just like your mother,' he exclaimed, shaking his head.

Ward frowned with confusion. Colonel Draper guffawed and his laughter relieved the tension in the room.

TEN

Jonathan had returned to Mauritius two hours before he had met Nicole at the Government House steps. As HMS *Tyne* was being warped in he had noticed the harbour's emptiness. The forest of masts that usually crowded it had gone.

In their place was a clear view across the sea to the palm trees of the Place d'Armes, the parade ground in front of Government House. The semicircle of mountain peaks, with Pouce predominant among the oddly shaped crags, formed a rugged backdrop to the town. It was a welcome sight for him.

As he gazed around the deserted harbour, he realized the ban on foreign ships had come into force during his absence. Jonathan was pleased that Mr Farquhar had kept his word and carried out the British government's orders. He was proud he had obeyed his own instructions to the letter. The two princes who stood at the ship's rail with him were proof of that.

Night had already fallen before he was able to leave the ship and escort Tiko and Manda to Government House. The boys were disappointed by the lack of a volley to herald their arrival. To console them Jonathan had to explain that they were on a private visit as his brothers, not as princes.

When he recalled Radama's blood-brother ceremony and his own fainting he was embarrassed. Fortunately the king had been understanding, even pleased because he reacted like a warm-hearted man instead of disguising his feelings to create the right impression.

Verette told him afterwards that King Radama had praised his naturalness and sincerity, giving that as the reason why he was treating with him. The king did not like Captain Lesage and kept him out of their negotiations.

Lesage was only brought in at Jonathan's insistence when the Treaty of Amity was finally drawn up. He was asked to sign it together with Jonathan.

Jonathan had been looking forward to a warm welcome from Mr Farquhar. He was discouraged when he was greeted by Mr Bateman, who said the governor was ensconced with Colonel Draper and Ward Trenchard. The princes were exhausted by the voyage so he had left them with a slave while he investigated what was happening.

Mr Bateman had told him of the scheme to surprise Nicole and restore her reputation in public. It made Jonathan decide to meet her and escort her from the palanquin himself. The slap on his cheek was his reward.

He had watched Ward's apology from the shadows of the governor's chambers, smarting at Nicole's slap and Mr Farquhar's offhand attitude towards him. He said nothing more to Nicole although he noticed her glancing in his direction.

When she left Government House with the Didcotts and Emma, he lurked on the veranda waiting for Mr Farquhar. His heart was heavy. He sensed that Ward, for all his apologizing, fully intended to win his bet and win Nicole.

Ward, Colonel Draper and Dr Telfair monopolized Mr Farquhar after Nicole had left. They talked of slavery and various schemes to bring benefits to the colony. Jonathan was tired. He longed to present the report of his success. In the end, weary of waiting for the governor to send for him, he left the veranda and went to his chamber.

He was still asleep when a slave roused him at ten o'clock next morning to say Mr Farquhar was waiting.

'I apologize for oversleep –'

Mr Farquhar waved him to silence. 'Captain Lesage has given me his report. He did very well to negotiate the treaty. A brilliant ploy to bring the princes here. I shall be commending him to the British government.'

'It wasn't Captain Les –'

'Do not interrupt, Mr Rendye. Your manners have suffered during your leave with the Hovas. Captain Lesage tells me you were down with fever for most of the time when you were in Tananarivo. I'm pleased to see the army doctor restored you to health.' There was a note of sarcasm in his voice.

Despair overwhelmed Jonathan as he listened to the governor. At Captain Lesage's insistence he had given him the treaty document for safekeeping. Now he had no proof that it was his triumph, not Bebe Lesage's. Mr Farquhar's willingness to believe what Lesage told him had deep roots. He had expected Jonathan to fail, even to die. His return was a dilemma.

'Captain Lesage is to sail again for Madagascar. He tells me there are women there who are willing to become brides to British soldiers. He will purchase some from King Radama.'

Jonathan stared with disbelief. 'The king is persuaded not to sell slaves!' he exclaimed.

Mr Farquhar glowered. 'Exactly. These are wives, Mr Rendye, not slaves. On his return I shall be appointing Captain Lesage to administer the Seychelles. He has shown extraordinary talent and capabilities.'

Jonathan was dumbfounded. His only witness to what he had achieved was Verette and the governor would not accept the word of a Creole half-caste against the claims of a captain of the Twenty-second Foot.

'I have replaced you with Dr Telfair,' the governor said. 'He is an excellent private secretary, stimulating company and is playing a positive part in the development of this colony.'

'He's a flesh trader!' Jonathan blurted out in disgust. 'Captain Curran captured the *Gustave* bound from Madagascar for Dr Telfair's plantation. There were sixty-four slaves on board in a wretched state.'

Mr Farquhar waved his hand nonchalantly. 'Obviously some misunderstanding. Some slaves have been landed in Port Louis and become Government property. Dr Telfair has kindly consented to house them on his plantation. He will make a contribution to Mr Hook's treasury to defray expenses.'

Jonathan nodded his head sadly. In the three months of

his absence Mr Farquhar had allowed himself to be manipulated by Telfair and Hook. He was flouting his own laws by a technicality.

Mr Farquhar sensed Jonathan's unspoken disapproval. He rose from his seat and paced up and down in front of the windows with their view of the harbour. 'What shall I do with you, Mr Rendye? You rather disgraced yourself by falling ill and leaving Captain Lesage to do all the negotiating.'

'That's not true, sir!' He stared at Mr Farquhar defiantly. 'I was with the king every day. It's Lesage who was ill. I won the king's confidence. He made me his blood brother!' Jonathan pulled back his sleeve, struggling to roll it up so Mr Farquhar could see the scar.

'Some pagan rite of no consequence!' Mr Farquhar shuddered at the sight of Jonathan's bare arm. 'Cover yourself at once.' He returned to his desk.

'Those two boys who Captain Lesage brought with him – for the time being I have no one to tutor them. They must be influenced in our ways, taught English, shown the season's festivities. Let them see how a Christian people live and behave.' He paused and looked at Jonathan doubtfully.

'Can I trust them to you, Mr Rendye? Can you tutor them until I find someone more suitable?'

Jonathan hid his resentment at his dismissal. He had been cheated. He bowed formally and withdrew from the governor's presence.

Nicole prepared eagerly for her first appearance at the race meet since her rehabilitation. The races were to begin at three o'clock and she and Emma were to be Colonel Draper's guests.

Mrs Didcott had willingly given her consent for her to attend. She regarded Nicole with a certain amount of awe since the meeting at Government House. It had shaken her that Governor Farquhar and the island's notables and their wives were concerned about Nicole's welfare.

Nicole herself was gratified by the turn of events. She had learned much from it. While she accepted Emma's renewed friendship and Mrs Didcott's condescension, her heart remembered the wounds they both had caused. She declined to stay with Emma in her chamber and continued to sleep in the former slave scullery. By day she preferred to spend her time with Fidou in the garden, tending the flowers instead of gossiping with Emma, Louise and Jane.

She was greatly intrigued by Ward's public apology and sensed the difficulty he experienced in making it. She saw no sign of shame in his manner and that made her wary of him. She feared their next encounter. On the other hand she was keen to see Jonathan again and learn of his adventures.

The whole population of Port Louis seemed to have congregated at the Champ de Mars. It took half an hour for her and Emma, followed by Fidou, to wend their way across the plain from the house to the governor's booth. Nicole was thrilled by the crowd although Emma dubbed it a common mob.

Colonel Draper saw them approaching and escorted them to seats next to Theodore Hook, the treasurer. Fidou waited outside. Mr Hook greeted them effusively, paying special attention to Nicole.

'Colonel Draper says you brought him luck!' he trilled. 'I shall bet only on the horses you choose.'

Nicole smiled to disguise her doubt. 'I know very little about horses.'

'Knowledge is not necessary, Miss Genave. Look at me,' he giggled. 'I know absolutely nothing about figures. I can barely count beyond my ten digits.' He held up his hands, heavy with glittering rings on every finger.

'Sir, you are the accountant general, the treasurer!'

'Yes, isn't it a scream! Now what do you fancy?'

The banter closed in on her from all sides. She soon tired of the flippancy and left it to Emma to keep up the smart chatter. She surveyed the crowd instead.

Booths had been erected for the British while the French ladies were seated in chairs ranged on the opposite side of the course. Behind them, several rows deep, were long lines of coloured females attired in the gayest manner. Their heads were uncovered, displaying a profusion of glossy black hair, braided, plaited and curled.

The variety of colour in the dresses of the females was dazzling. The men wore a range of costume, from the military uniforms of Europeans to the robes and turbans of Orientals. The crowd, the sight and the sound of the horses, the noise and bustle of people enjoying themselves, created an exciting clamour that took Nicole's breath away.

She raised her eyes from the plain and gazed at the gaunt mountains surrounding it. The solemn stillness with which they brooded over the scene calmed her. She turned her attention to the others in the tent.

Mr Farquhar was in earnest conversation with Dr Telfair. Judge Smith was eyeing a group of negro wenches under the pretext of looking at a horse. Captain Lesage was swaggering around the tent, receiving congratulations for his Madagascar venture. Nicole was relieved that Ward was not present.

Her attention was attracted by a boy who darted through the throng with lusty shouts of delight. He elbowed his way around Judge Smith, took no notice of Captain Lesage and headed straight for Mr Hook. The boy was the colour of gold. He wore a green silk coat that was too large for him and made him trip. He laughed as he fell in a heap at Nicole's feet.

She bent down to help him stand up. He shrugged off her hand until his eyes met hers. Then he paused for a moment and grinned mischievously. She was worried that the boy would be punished for entering the governor's tent.

'Who are you?' she whispered, returning his smile. 'I'll say you're with me.'

He studied her carefully before he spoke. 'Manda.'

'Manda, indeed?' She puzzled over the name. The boy poked out his tongue at Mr Hook, who pretended not to notice.

'I'm dreadfully sorry,' said a voice. She looked up with pleasure. It was Jonathan. His hair was dishevelled, his stock askew and he was flushed with the heat. He was panting. 'I don't know what's got into him.'

'He's yours?' she asked, surprised when he nodded.

'Well,' she said, holding the boy by his shoulders to stop him running off. 'Does he think he's a horse?'

'He's a Hova prince,' said Jonathan gloomily. 'I wish I could control him.'

'Is that so? Well, Prince Manda, why don't you sit here with me and watch the horses. There's going to be a race.' She made a space between herself and Mr Hook.

Another boy, dressed similarly in an ill-fitting coat and breeches that seemed to cause him discomfort, peeped around Jonathan's back. He said something in a tongue that Nicole had never heard. Manda answered with a snigger and tried to grab one of the rings off Mr Hook's hand.

'How can a mere man of figures figure against a Prince?' Mr Hook said, scrambling to his feet. 'Miss Genave, perhaps you will have better luck with Hovas than with horses.' He bowed. 'I shall leave you to their royal high spirits.'

'Oh dear,' said Emma, 'you've upset him.'

'Manda did that.' Jonathan sank into Mr Hook's seat with a sigh. 'It's been the same ever since they came ashore.'

The fury of the galloping horses racing around the track filled the air with earth and dust. Manda and his brother watched in awe as they sat wedged between Jonathan and Nicole. Glancing over their heads, Nicole was touched by Jonathan's expression. He was frowning, lost in thought, and looked quite helpless.

'Why do you have to care for them?' she asked, intending to offer sympathy.

'I think it's because Mr Farquhar is embarrassed by my presence.' He shook himself. 'Please, I shall burden you with my troubles. Thank you for trapping my little prince. He seems to like you.'

'Good.' She squeezed the boy's shoulder. 'I like him.'

'The Hovas are wonderful people. King Radama is a man of stature, young and yet wise and powerful. He became my friend. More than that we *trusted* each other. That's why he put his brothers in my care.'

Nicole noticed how Jonathan's lugubrious features brightened when he spoke. He was unaware of his surroundings and cared nothing for the people in the booth. The presence of the two princelings provided a wonderful opportunity for her to talk to him without attracting the attention of the gossip-mongers.

'I heard Captain Lesage,' she said, seizing on what she thought was troubling him, 'claim that he is the princes' patron.'

Jonathan's vivacity collapsed. He looked disgruntled and stared at her without speaking.

'Have I upset you?' she asked in a panic. 'I believe you, not him. Really.'

'It's all right.' He brushed at his hair with his hand. 'Duplicity and diplomacy are bedfellows in Mr Farquhar's court. I'm beginning to get used to it.'

The despair behind Jonathan's words upset her. 'I wish you'd tell me about it.'

He looked at her carefully. 'It would bore you.'

'Why? I longed for someone to talk with when I was in disgrace. That was through no fault of mine. Perhaps it's the same with you?'

'You're too kind. We must go.'

'Stay. Prince Manda is happy with me, aren't you?' The boy grinned up at her when she tugged his hand. There was a bustle of annoyance next to her. She turned and saw Emma glaring at her crossly.

'What are you bothering with those black boys for?' she snapped. 'You can meet so many *men* here.'

'Black men, Emma?'

'You're being facetious. *Marriageable* men! These nigger brats will keep them away.'

'I don't mind.'

'It's me I'm thinking about.'

'Where is your major?'

'He's been posted to the south. So he says.'

Nicole smiled sympathetically, although Emma's doubt told her the truth of the matter. The major had withdrawn from the campaign.

'You'll soon find another beau,' she said to encourage her. 'I'm content here if you want to mingle with the Governor's guests. Mr Rendye will look after me.'

Emma regarded him with contempt. 'Don't waste your time on him,' she hissed. 'He's only a clerk.'

Nicole hid her anger with a smile. She turned back to Jonathan when Emma had gone. 'At last,' she said. 'We are quite alone.' She giggled, suddenly aware of the huge crowd and the blabber of dozens of voices in the booth around her.

Jonathan saw the humour and relaxed enough to grin too. She was pleased. 'See,' she said, 'I'm too foolish to be anything but a good listener. Tell me about Madagascar.'

The afternoon slipped by. Jonathan talked animatedly about his trip. The young princes joined in when they grew bored in the intervals between races. They made a happy group together and people commented on it. Nicole ignored the glances cast in her direction and the remarks that she was supposed to overhear.

She was captivated by Jonathan's tales and touched by his respect for people she had thought of as savages.

'You come Tananarivo,' said Tiko gravely. 'Radama make you queen.'

She laughed until she saw that Jonathan was regarding her with an odd gleam in his eye. 'What's the matter?' she asked anxiously.

He tugged at his nose, began to speak, then stopped. 'The princes like you,' he said lamely and she wondered what was really on his mind.

The last race had finished. Jonathan had told her a lot but not what troubled him. Manda was pulling her hand and it prevented her questioning him further.

'What name?' the boy demanded.

'My name? Nicole.'

Manda and Tiko giggled as they tried to pronounce it.

'You have won the hearts of these two charming royal scamps, Miss Genave.'

'Your Excellency!' Nicole rose from her chair to curtsy but the governor waved her down.

'Rendye here finds them a chore. Takes a woman's touch, I suppose?'

'Mr Rendye and the princes have been telling me the most fascinating stories about his adventures in Madagascar.'

'Hmm.' The governor frowned. 'Don't believe all they tell you.' He spoke of the princes but managed to convey by his eyes that it was Jonathan who was not to be believed.

'I do,' she said. 'Mr Rendye said King Radama believed him because his face was too innocent to shield a lie.'

'Really?' The governor gazed beyond her to the crowd, plainly uninterested. He returned his glance to the princes. 'Have you enjoyed yourselves, boys?'

Manda hid behind Nicole while Tiko stared at him insolently. 'Say, "Yes, thank you, Your Excellency",' instructed Nicole, squeezing Tiko's arm. He did so with a bow.

'By jove!' the governor said, impressed.

'Perhaps the princes could visit me at Mrs Didcott's?' Nicole smiled. 'I would be pleased to assist in their tuition. Mr Rendye could bring them every morning.' She held her breath, praying that the governor would consent.

A glint of relief entered his eyes. 'What a splendid idea!' He leaned forward and patted Manda on his head. The boy clung to Nicole's skirt and stuck out his tongue. The governor straightened.

'I warn you, Miss Genave, these little savages are a handful. They have no respect.'

'Really, Your Excellency?' She smiled coyly. 'To them perhaps we are savages who have no respect.'

Tiko and Manda's unruly behaviour appalled Mrs Didcott. 'The tawse!' she told Nicole, waving it threateningly at the two boys. 'That's the only way to deal with them.'

'Never!' Nicole shepherded them away from her towards the garden. 'These are princes, brothers of a king who rules over a country of five million people.'

Mrs Didcott scoffed but Nicole knew she was impressed. It was what the neighbours thought that concerned her most. Two princes and the governor's aide calling at her establishment every day was an honour to be boasted about. Mrs Didcott even made Mr Rendye welcome, apparently deciding he was too uninteresting a man for his presence to compromise any of her young ladies.

Jonathan himself, for the first few visits, did nothing but sit in the shade of a flamboyant tree and keep a doleful eye on Nicole and the princes. She played games with them and, as she won their confidence, turned to simple instruction. They were bright children; she was able to draw them out easily and soon they were chattering away in a mixture of Hova and English, delighting in everything she showed and told them.

Fidou and Verette attended the garden classes. Nicole devised games and dramas to involve both of them. She overcame Jonathan's protests that he was not one for skylarking and persuaded him to take part as well. After a week of lessons Tiko and Manda calmed their exuberance while Jonathan seemed more at ease in their company, and with Nicole too.

She bid the princes farewell for the weekend. They had been invited by Ward to visit the Black River plantation. Jonathan was taking them, a prospect he viewed gloomily.

'You'll enjoy the change,' Nicole said to encourage him. She was intrigued and wished she was going too. 'It must be boring for you to sit in our garden and listen to me and the children chattering all day.'

'I'd rather that than adult cozenage!' he replied sadly.

Nicole watched him walk away from the house, following Verette and the princes, who were laughing as they dashed onto the plain. Fidou was standing beside her.

'That one foolish man,' she said.

'Verette? Why, what did he do to you?'

'You know I mean Mas Jonathan,' she said scornfully.

'Don't mock him, Fidou. He's very unhappy.'

'Lor', the whole town know that. He always has been. Brings it on himself, that why he foolish.'

'When credit for your achievements goes to others and your hopes are rebuffed, it's difficult to be happy.'

'Melancholy is his trade mark, miz.' Fidou's eyes sparkled. 'If he were to make an effort, he could change his luck.'

'It's something to do with him and the governor, I believe,' Nicole said, turning away now Jonathan was out of sight. She wanted to be alone to think. She would miss him, and the princes, during the three days they would be in the country.

She had hoped that by offering to instruct Tiko and Manda she would have an opportunity to get to know Jonathan better. The burden that weighed on his heart would be lighter if she could persuade him to share it with her. Perhaps next week ...

'What?' She was aware of Fidou having said something naughty.

'You heard.' Fidou smiled coyly.

'No, I did not.'

'I said he more in awe of you than he is of the governor.'

'That's ridiculous. I'm his friend.'

'Then why he nervous, always pullin' his nose and reddenin' when you look at him?'

'He's shy by nature, Fidou. It signifies nothing.'

'Oh no?' Fidou arched her eyebrow suggestively. 'I goan make that man stop pullin' his nose and pull somethin' else! You see if it rebuff or love he have in his heart.'

'Love?' she felt herself blushing and turned her face away. Fidou laughed triumphantly.

'Oy, oy, oy, Miz Nicole. You can't fool me.'

'Please, Fidou. You might do something rash.'

Fidou closed her eyes and hugged herself, swaying on the spot as though she were holding an imaginary man close to her bosom. 'Yes, I might,' she said, smiling coquettishly. 'He not much, but he better'n nothin', I s'pose.'

ELEVEN

When Fidou heard about the bet Ward made with Colonel Draper she had been thrilled. Of all the girls at Mrs Didcott's, she liked Nicole the best. She was the only one who spoke Creole and understood a little of slave ways. Fidou wanted her to have a man to bring her status. The bet made Nicole the talk of the town and did the same for Fidou.

Slaves in Port Louis fell into two groups. There were those rescued off slave ships and put in chain gangs by the government to work in the town and there were the house slaves. They were the privileged. There was a third category of slaves who were seen in Port Louis during their visits from the country districts with their masters or when they came to sell provisions. They were the plantation field-hands and did not mix with the town house slaves.

Fidou had as much freedom as she required. Generally house slaves in the town were born to their work. Many were the offspring of white masters and slave mothers. Fidou herself knew neither her mother nor her father. She had been bought by Mr Didcott from an impoverished French settler who was returning to France. He had acquired her as a girl of three from another slave holder.

She was proud of her position. Mrs Didcott was low in the social scale of the British but she was a respected lady and her pupils added cachet. Fidou had a high opinion of herself because of those young ladies. She loved to gossip about them. Whenever she visited the town on errands, she stopped to talk with her friends who were the house slaves of other whites.

The activities at Mrs Didcott's gave her considerable scope for gossip, and she was popular with the slaves because of it. Ward's bet about Nicole made her so popular even the Government House slaves stopped to talk to her about Nicole.

Just as the whites discussed the behaviour of their slaves when they met at veranda affairs, the slaves compared the doings of their masters and mistresses when they met at street corners. Nicole was regarded as *sympathique* by the slave community and the outcome of Ward's pursuit of her was awaited eagerly.

The meeting between Ward and Nicole at Government House, which Fidou witnessed from behind a serving door, was regarded by the slaves as a clever tactic. They knew Ward as a mean and conniving master. They feared him because of his reputation. Many of them had been Black River slaves themselves and remembered the whippings they had received on his plantation.

Fidou reported to all her friends on her daily perambulations through Port Louis that Ward had made no further approach. She was informed whenever he was in town and the house slaves waited impatiently for his next move. Ward, however, disappointed them. He did nothing.

Fidou was close to despair at his lack of action. She discussed the problem with Nita, her friend who was the slave of Theodore Hook. Nita was a few years older than she, black and bosomy; she was the second cook and chambermaid at Mr Hook's residence.

As treasurer, Mr Hook never stinted on his entertaining and the governor's set were daily visitors. This gave Nita a higher status than Fidou but they enjoyed each other's company and met every morning in the market street when they were doing their shopping.

'Lor',' said Fidou as she stood in the shade of the overhang of a large wooden balcony. 'My mistress come foolish.'

'With them Malagash princes?' Nita's eye roved over the crowd. She clasped her empty basket in front of her and sweated in the early morning heat.

'With Mr Rendye.'

'Whoo!' laughed Nita. 'She wastin' her time on that

buckra. He don' even stain his sheets at night. He dry up.'

'There!' said Fidou. 'What am I to do?'

'No word from Mas Ward?'

'Nothin'. More worse is she don't speak of Mas Ward 't all.'

Nita hitched up her bosom and let her face spread in a wide smile. 'If Ward out the runnin',' she said, 'it be your duty to shake Mr Rendye to life.'

'Me?'

'Yes, Fidou. Mayhap he only dry 'cause yo' ain' milk him yet?'

'I aint keen to lie with that buckra!' she said crossly.

'It ain' what yo' want, Fidou.' Nita's lips plopped open with scorn. 'If yo' don' do somethin', yuh mistress goan be an ol' maid. Ward 'gnorin' her an' Rendye too *makak*, like a monkey with a lazy prick. It yuh duty as a good house slave to 'range it.'

Nita's advice was sound and it presented Fidou with a problem. How to rouse Jonathan to take Nicole. It was becoming urgent.

The guest pavilion at Black River had been scrubbed and polished from ceiling to floor. It was months since it had been used as anything other than a place for Ward to pleasure himself with the plantation's females. The house slaves, under Ellen's stern eye, cleaned it enthusiastically. They remembered the days when townsfolk visited the plantation regularly. They hoped the opening up again of the pavilion to guests heralded a return to those happier times.

Jonathan was unaware of the slaves' thoughts as he surveyed the pavilion with approval. With its two rooms and large balcony, it was more luxurious than his miserable quarters at Government House. Tiko and Manda seemed to approve it too and they were soon making a great noise as they propelled each other on a coconut fibre mat over the highly polished floor.

'Hey up, boys,' said Ward, striding onto the balcony and

clapping his hands. 'Let's go for a ride to the river. Inspect the stock.'

The two young princes stopped playing and watched him in awe. Jonathan sighed with relief at the sudden silence. He did not know why Ward had bothered to invite Tiko and Manda to visit him, nor why Governor Farquhar had given his consent.

He was pleased nevertheless. The princes were too boisterous for him to handle alone. Even Verette had difficulty at times in keeping them under control. Ward, with his masterly manner, commanded their respect immediately.

'Say, "yes, sir",' said Verette, pinching Tiko's arm.

Tiko grinned as though he sensed a new game in the offing. 'Yes, sir!' Manda shyly said the same.

Ward looked impressed. 'Fine lads, eh?'

'Troublesome,' said Jonathan gloomily.

'Royal blood, though.' Ward clucked his tongue and gripped Tiko by his shoulders. He spun him around and passed his hands swiftly down his back, fondling his buttocks and thighs. Before Tiko could flinch, he shoved his hand in his crotch and squeezed. He ignored Tiko's yelp of pain and nodded with satisfaction.

'Balls dropped, by gad!' He seemed pleased. He cast his eye in steady appraisal over Verette. 'You look like a frisky colt.'

'Yes, sir,' said Verette, swelling with pride.

'He's my servant,' Jonathan protested, worried by Ward's actions without knowing why.

'Hmm.' Ward stroked his chin. 'Two for the price of one,' he murmured, offering no explanation for his conduct. 'Get them boys out of their togs,' he said to Verette. 'You too. Ain't right to see prime bucks dressed like eunuch fancies.'

'The princes are under my protection,' said Jonathan.

'Fat lot of good that will do them!' Ward laughed. 'Ol' Farquhar's lent them to me for the weekend. You, too, if you like. You want to choose a filly?'

'I beg your pardon?' Jonathan was appalled by Ward's

coarseness. He stared as Tiko and Manda happily pulled off their smart coats, waistcoats and silk shirts until they stood barefoot in their breeches in front of Ward. Verette joined in and flexed his muscles proudly as Ward tapped him on his chest.

'Follow me, boys. You can strip off those breeches at the river and I'll finger you.' He waved to Jonathan. 'I'm going to give these princelings a real education,' he said as he led them off the veranda.

Jonathan was stricken with misgivings. With the princes out of the way he ought to relax. There was nothing sinister in what Ward had in mind and the boys would be safe, even happier with Ward than with him. He was hurt when Verette went so eagerly. The lad was not bound to him by slavery but he had grown used to his company and would have preferred him to stay. He leaned on the balcony rail and gazed after the boys as they ran behind Ward, who was riding his horse down the trail to the river.

Gradually he became aware that he was himself under scrutiny. He turned and saw Gina watching him from the veranda of the mansion. It was too late to duck inside the cabin and pretend he had not seen her. He had been dreading this moment. Gina seemed to have kept their relationship a secret from Ward. He was nervous in case she planned to revive it.

'Jonathan!' Her strident voice shattered the peace of the afternoon. He saw Ward's housekeeper cuddle two youngsters, one white and one dark, who ran to her when they heard Gina's shout. One of them was Garnet, Gina's son, whom she loathed. The other was his playboy, Ellen's child, Randy.

'Won't you take tea with me, Jonathan?' Gina called, her cackle of laughter bouncing around the courtyard.

Jonathan smoothed back his hair and walked slowly across the flagstones to the mansion. A burly negro in a frilly shirt and skin-tight breeches held a chair for him opposite Gina. There were two cups and a teapot on the low table between them. Gina extended her hand and he raised it to his lips before sitting. The negro towered over him menacingly.

'Serve, Clovis,' said Gina, waving her hand at him nonchalantly. 'Take no notice of him. He's my pet. Isn't he adorable?'

Jonathan frowned, considering what to say. He saw the negro scowling at him as he poured the tea. 'Why, yes. I'm sure he is, er, adorable.'

'He's the only male Ward allows me,' Gina pouted, raising her cup to her lips. 'Because he's got no balls. Ward cut them off.' She drank thirstily.

Jonathan did not know where to look. He reached for his cup. There was no milk to add to the tea so he prepared to drink it plain, as it was. To his dismay, although the tea was cold, it burned his lips. He swallowed a mouthful and spluttered as it seared his throat. He let his cup fall back in the saucer with a clatter. Frantically he dabbed at his lips with his handkerchief.

'That tea,' he gasped. 'What is it?'

'Rum.' Gina looked at him as though he were odd. 'Perhaps Ward thinks you've got no balls and that's why he left us together?'

Clovis sniggered and moved to the back of the veranda, where he folded his arms across his massive chest and eyed Jonathan balefully.

'That nigger of yours,' Gina said casually. 'I haven't seen him before. When did you buy him?'

'I didn't.' Jonathan was pleased the subject had changed. There was something in the way Gina spoke and looked at him that made him even more nervous and uncomfortable than usual. 'He had no owner. He came to me the day after Mrs Didcott's veranda affair. He was living by his wits on the Champ de Mars. I gave him a home.'

'How charitable of you. He seems a spry young man.'

'Oh yes. Everyone likes him.'

'Indeed?' Gina gleamed. 'What age do you suppose he is?' Her voice sounded husky.

'About seventeen.'

'Really?'

There was silence. Jonathan glanced at Gina and saw her sitting with a dreamy look in her eyes. Her cup of rum was empty and she was licking her lips.

Jonathan became aware of a scuffling sound that at first he thought was part of a nightmare. He lay without moving, lodged in a dip in the coconut fibre mattress, too weary to comprehend what the noise meant. He guessed he had been asleep for more than an hour. His head ached from the rum forced on him at supper by Ward. Gina had remained in her chamber the whole evening and Jonathan had not seen her since her 'tea' party.

Yet in his bad dream the presence of a woman seemed so vivid, he was convinced her voice had woken him. He listened again. Tiko and Manda were asleep in the room next to his. Verette, who had escorted him to the pavilion when he found his feet too unsteady after Ward's rum, should be sleeping on the floor at the foot of his bed.

There was a lantern burning on the balcony but its glow was too dim for Jonathan to see clearly in the darkness of his room. His head was pounding with pain, and he could not be sure what the noise was. The scraping sound suggested a rat scampering along the rafters. He kept his eyes closed, assuming that the squeals he could hear were the cries of the rat.

Gradually the sounds assumed a rhythm distinct from the pounding of his head. He opened his eyes, straining to identify the noise. It was a regular thumping, accompanied by heavy breathing that was rising in crescendo. It was vaguely exciting and the sighing and crying began to rouse him. He raised himself up off the bed to see if Verette was all right.

As his eyes grew accustomed to the gloom, he was astonished to see that Verette was writhing and thrusting on the floor, apparently in the throes of passion. He peered intently and distinguished the shape of two bodies entwined. He stifled his cry of alarm and peeped over the edge of the bed, watching this odd sight with fascination.

The heat in the room was causing him to swell. For relief he pressed himself against the hard mattress, unconsciously moving up and down in time to Verette's thrusts.

He no longer knew if he was awake or asleep. A burning desire raged through him. He heard Verette's shout and a squeal of ecstacy from the girl coupled with him. He wanted to cry out too but something within still strained for release. He lay on the mattress panting. After a while he heard Verette speaking as though from a great distance.

'Go to my master,' he said.

'He don' wan' no slave chit.'

'Make him want you.'

'A white man?'

'Sure. You do it with Ward.'

Jonathan sensed the pressure of the girl climbing onto the mattress beside him. He pretended to be asleep. The tension was making him tremble; he longed for something to happen and was terrified that it might, and that it might not. His night-shirt had somehow become rucked up under his arms, leaving his body naked as he lay with his face buried in the pillow. A hand touched his hip; he jerked onto his side in surprise. He moaned as if in sleep.

'Do it,' Verette whispered.

For seconds Jonathan felt nothing, then gradually he was enveloped in velvet. The feeling was unbelievable; exquisite, torturing and pleasuring him at the same moment. His embarrassment at what the girl was doing dissolved into ecstacy. A demon seized control of him and caused him to thrust and plunge as though possessed. When the girl raised her head and slid on top of him, grasping him between her thighs, he was oblivious of everything except the need to submit and dominate together.

He made love the way he wrote dispatches, carefully and correctly. He was guided by the girl and followed her pace despite his urge to forge ahead. Perhaps it was his nervousness, or the girl's talent, that prolonged his passion. The cabin floor shook, the bed banged against the wall and then, finally, it was done.

He lay back on the mattress, the girl in his arms, overwhelmed by what this unexpected Black River affair had taught him.

A light flashed in his eyes. He opened them and was dismayed to see Tiko standing in the doorway holding a lantern. There was a young girl standing beside him with her arms around his waist. They were both naked.

'What ...' The words would not come, he was so drained of energy. 'What ... are you ... doing?' he managed to gasp at his second attempt.

Tiko grinned and rolled his eyes.

'Maybe he wants to ask you the same question,' said Verette with a chuckle. He took the girl lying with Jonathan by her hand and helped her climb off the bed. She was no more than sixteen, her ebony skin glistening with sweat in the lantern's glow.

'I don't understand ...' Jonathan struggled to pull down his nightshirt to cover himself. His loins ached as though he were still in her. 'Who are these girls?'

'Ward's fillies, for me and Tiko.'

'Tiko?' Jonathan groaned. 'He's too young.'

'Nonsense!'

The shout startled them all. Jonathan shrank, wishing the mattress would open up and swallow him. He stared at Ward, who was standing behind Tiko with his hand on the prince's shoulder.

'Tiko's young but his sap's flowing,' said Ward gruffly. 'With luck I'll get a whelp out of him. Royal breed, that'll be.'

'It's monstrous.' Jonathan sighed, suddenly not wanting to complain any more.

'It's bloody practical.' Ward squeezed Tiko's shoulder. 'That's why I invited the princes here.'

'Does Mr Farquhar know – about this?' Jonathan gestured lamely at the girls.

'Sure he does. Think of the political advantage to him if I manage to produce a kinsman to Radama born right here.'

'You've used Tiko! And me!'

Ward shrugged. 'You've used Betty by what I heard on the balcony. Still,' he added with a smile, 'if she gets me a whelp you'll have paid me her hire fee. Mixed breed fetch good prices.'

He chuckled heartily as he grabbed Betty by her wrist and pulled her after him out of the cabin. 'My turn now,' he said as Jonathan fell back on the bed.

When he returned from spending the weekend at Black River, Jonathan was in a subdued mood. He was cheerless at the best of times. As he sat on Mrs Didcott's veranda watching Nicole play with the princes, he seemed miserable and listless.

Fidou was enraged, not realizing that his attitude was caused by exhaustion, and by awe at what he had learned about himself. Remembering Nita's advice, she turned in desperation to Verette. Usually she ignored him because of his inferior status.

Verette was a runaway, a mulatto who fled from his plantation when the British invaded the island. Luckily for him, because he was only ten at the time, his absence went unnoticed in the general confusion.

Now, even though he slept on the Government House floor, he wore shoes and was Mr Rendye's servant, he was too recently a street urchin for Fidou to accept him as an equal.

'Boy!' she said to open the conversation. He was sitting on the kitchen step and rose quickly to his feet at her command. She liked that.

'Yes, Miss Fidou?' He stood on the grass in front of the cabin. His face was eager and his eyes bold, watching her in a way that could turn to impertinence if allowed.

She studied him for a moment, aware that he was taller than she was. She remained in the cabin to keep the advantage of the extra height its floor gave her.

His complexion was lighter than hers. His hair was the glossy kind of locks she would willingly have exchanged for the crinkly curls she kept hidden under her cap. Anyone who met him without knowing his past, seeing him neatly attired and with his winning smile, would assume he was better than he was.

'What do you want, Miss Fidou?' His eyes twinkled and he preened himself under her gaze.

She was surprised at the rush of blood to her cheeks that threatened to darken her features and betray her desire. She withdrew into the cabin, out of the sunlight. It was probably the subject she was going to discuss that made her so disturbed by the boy's frank stare.

'I need your help,' she said huskily.

'You ain't the first.' His meaning was clear and he swelled with pride and stuck his hands on his hips. 'Maybe I *help* you, maybe not.'

His cockiness amused her. She never considered him in that light before. Her preference was for darker, stronger bucks. She had a weakness for the muscular field hands who padded along the market street in their breech cloths and nothing else.

Of course, she dare not let them know; there was her position to protect. If she was involved with anyone less than a houseboy to a prominent family, she would be laughed at by the town's slave community.

'It's not me I'm thinking of.' She looked at him sternly to warn him she was serious. 'It's my mistress.'

Verette grinned. 'Mistress Nicole wants me?' He stepped back and gave her a quizzical look. 'I always say she a special lady.'

Fidou was shocked and let her anger show. 'Mistress Didcott right when she say men only think of one thing.' She glared at him. 'You wipe that silly smile of your face or I tan your backside.'

'What with?' He arched his eyebrow. 'Your hand? I have something better for you than my backside. Oh yes!'

She was exasperated because the conversation was not going the way she wanted. 'Listen, Verette,' she said, hoping he would stand still long enough for her to talk to him. She glanced around the kitchen cabin. It was empty. 'Come in here. We must talk – about your master and my mistress.'

He scratched his chin, nodding his understanding. Before stepping into the kitchen, he looked slyly up at the house to see if anyone was watching. Fidou noticed and quivered with excitement, despite her anger.

'Sit down,' she ordered, pointing to a bench where she could keep her eye on him. He did so, meekly.

'What about my master? What he done to Miss Nicole?'

'That's the problem,' said Fidou with relief that she was at last getting to the heart of the matter. 'He sits on the veranda starin' at her all the time. He don't even talk to her.'

'He's watching to see Tiko and Manda behave themselves.'

'He the one that need to *mis*behave.'

He grinned. 'What do you want him to do? I'll tell him.'

Fidou wished it were as simple as that. Good slaves could make their masters do what they wanted but Jonathan was a difficult case. 'Lor' knows!' she said. 'Why is he always so gloomy?'

'He's offended.' Verette sat back and stretched out his legs, placing his hands suggestively on his thighs. She tried to avoid looking at him but her eyes were drawn to the bulge in his breeches framed by his hands.

'I'll give you "*offended*",' she said tartly. 'He must do somethin'.'

'Like what?' He began to stroke his crotch, his eyes glinting.

'Tell her somethin',' she said, drawn towards him by his gaze. She sat down at his side on the bench.

'That he loves her?'

'Does he?'

'I don't know.' His hand reached out and touched her breast. He squeezed.

Pain sailed through her, leaving in its wake a warm desire. She swallowed, wanting to move away; she was held spellbound as his other hand slipped under her skirt and began to caress the inside of her thigh.

'He could do somethin',' she whispered.

She wanted to cry out to stop Verette. It was too late. His

fingers probed her and she throbbed at his touch. He was no longer a plain's urchin; he was a man whose ardour was stirring her own.

She closed her eyes to block out what was happening, unable to stop herself flowing to meet him as she lay back on the bench and opened her legs.

'That boy,' said Emma brusquely to Nicole as they stood on the veranda watching Jonathan, Verette and the two princes walking down the path from the house. 'Do you know anything about him?'

'Verette?' Nicole found Emma's question vaguely disturbing. 'He's Mr Rendye's man, very well mannered, obliging.'

'Hmm.' Emma pursed her lips in a meaningful manner that made Nicole wonder what she was thinking.

'Has he done anything wrong?'

Emma ignored the question. 'Good-looking colt, isn't he? Not as niggery as some slaves.'

'I suppose not.' Nicole dismissed the matter from her mind. She was engrossed in watching Jonathan. Even viewed from behind, walking with his shoulders hunched forward, he looked crestfallen.

'He was in the kitchen cabin with Fidou this morning. I saw him go in.'

'Really?' Nicole took no notice of the remark and missed the malicious glint of intrigue that entered Emma's eyes.

'Is he coming tomorrow?'

'Yes.' Nicole's spirits lifted at the prospect. She would ask Fidou and Verette to play with the children while she talked to Jonathan. She had waited long enough for him to tell her what was on his mind.

'Good,' said Emma, distracting her.

Nicole glanced at her idly as she swept off the veranda into the house. She wondered what Emma thought was good.

Jonathan and the princes were on time the next day.

Fidou and Verette obligingly took Tiko and Manda for a stroll around the garden, away from the orchid arbour, where Nicole invited Jonathan to sit with her.

He was alarmed by her closeness and moved slowly along the bench so there was a gap between them.

'Jonathan,' she said, clasping her hands demurely in her lap. 'I have been wanting to talk to you for a long time.'

'Yes?' He shifted uncomfortably.

'You could fight him.'

He looked blank.

'Governor Farquhar, Jonathan. He is treating you unfairly. Stand up to him. Demand rightful recognition for what you did in Madagascar.'

To her surprise he sat up with his back straight and his hands on his knees, staring at her pompously. 'I will not discuss government business, Miss Nicole.'

She tittered without thinking that he would find her rude.

'Miss Nicole,' he said, standing up. 'Please refrain from mocking His Excellency.'

'Good heavens, Jonathan, you're serious!'

'Most certainly I am.' He hovered over her, twisting his coat-tail in his hand. 'The government of this colony is not a laughing matter.'

'Sit down,' she begged him, puzzled by the strength of his reaction. 'Of course, it's not a laughing matter. Yet you are so dedicated to Governor Farquhar, surely you have a right to expect his support.'

He sat heavily on the bench and buried his face in his hands. His shoulders shook as he sobbed soundlessly into his palms.

Nicole wanted to put her arm around him. She was scared to do so in case he took offence. She waited patiently until he ceased to tremble.

'You'll feel better now,' she said. 'Tell me.'

'I'm so ashamed.' He kept his eyes on the ground, avoiding her. 'I've never done that before.'

'Perhaps you haven't had a friend like me before?'

He glanced at her gratefully. She felt her heart leap with pleasure now that he was responding to her concern.

'There are things happening, Nicole,' he said, taking her hands in his, 'that are against the wishes of the government of Great Britain. I know about them. That's why the governor wants me out of the way. Everyone else connives at what he is doing.'

'You could send a report to the Prince Regent.'

He withdrew his hands in horror at the suggestion. 'Oh, no, it would harm Mr Farquhar. That would be despicable after he has done so much for me. He believes he is working for the best interests of the colony.' He looked at her to see if she understood.

'For instance, he must ban the slave-trade yet he knows the settlers need slaves to grow sugar. The tax sugar earns helps to support the colony. Without slaves, no income. There are not enough slaves in Mauritius so they have to come from Madagascar. Dr Telfair and the settlers have persuaded him to turn a blind eye to the trade. It's not his fault.'

'Do you know who the slave-traders are?'

'Everybody does.'

'Make a complaint to Judge Smith.'

'That's useless. He owns a plantation himself. Every time a trader comes up for trial before him he sets him free on a technicality.' His eyes sparked with anger.

'All the officials are involved in double-dealing. Theodore Hook is swindling the treasury. Colonel Draper forgets to collect customs dues, Dr Telfair imports slaves with impunity ...'

'What about Ward Trenchard?' Nicole asked, trying to sound casual. 'Is he involved too?'

'He's not connected with the government.' Jonathan grimaced. 'He's refused to pay the commission Mr Farquhar levied for letting him import slaves. Now he's breeding his own. He wants the trade banned so he can sell his own stock at a huge profit.'

Nicole sat in silence, overawed by Jonathan's revelations. 'It's quite a roll of dishonour,' she said at last.

'I'm sorry. I shouldn't have told you.'

'I'm glad you did.'

'Those people are your friends.' He sounded mournful.

'You're my friend,' she said. 'They're acquaintances.'

'Am I really your friend?' He looked bewildered. 'Radama was a friend to me too. What will he think of me when he finds Captain Lesage wants to trick him?'

'He won't blame you.' She moved closer on the bench towards him. He stood up. She rose to her feet too.

'Shall we take a walk?' she said to calm him. 'Take my arm?' She tried to slip her hand under his elbow. He drew away with a glance of alarm.

'Mrs Didcott!' he warned. 'What will she think?'

'Does it matter?'

His mouth fell open and his hair flopped into his eyes. He seemed to have difficulty breathing. He gasped, shut his mouth, brushed back his hair and stared at her. 'Miss Nicole!' he said.

'Whatever is wrong?'

'Everything … I mean –' He gulped.

'Jonathan,' she said firmly, taking his arm. 'I only suggested a walk. Nothing more.'

'Oh well, yes, of course.'

'Do you think something more is implied?' she asked coyly, hoping he would at last understand how she felt about him.'

'Nicole!' voices called. Tiko and Manda chased around the corner of the house before Jonathan could answer her question. He drew away from her hastily. The boys rushed up and hugged her.

'Princes aren't ashamed to show their feelings, Jonathan,' she said softly. 'Perhaps we should learn from them. But, of course, they're savage.'

She took their hands in hers and ran off down the path with them, away from Jonathan. She wanted to show him her impatience at his refusal to see what was right under his extra-long and handsome nose.

TWELVE

Why, Jonathan wondered, was his dull, modest life suffering these complications?

'I'm not dense,' he told Verette. 'I know what's going on.'

He walked in silence, waiting for Verette to reply. Tiko and Manda were running ahead of them across the Champ de Mars, celebrating their release at the end of their lessons. Jonathan had been taking them to Mrs Didcott's house for four weeks. He tried, during that time, to be circumspect, aware that anything less would be a betrayal of the trust that Mr Farquhar placed in him.

'If you know that,' said Verette, 'and you're a man, you would know what to do.'

'Dash it, Verette!' Jonathan surprised himself with the vehemence of his own outburst. He coloured slightly and lowered his voice. 'Do you only judge what makes a man by his womanizing?'

'Some women do.' Verette smiled smugly.

Jonathan was taken aback. He studied Verette as he walked at his side. The youth had filled out in the five months he had been with him. His face was no longer pinched; now it had a leanness that, perhaps, some women would find attractive. His eyes were sharp and sparkling, forever scanning the prospect ahead, missing nothing, a habit developed during his years fending for himself. He exuded an independent air and moved with a swagger.

He wore a suit of Jonathan's he had appropriated for himself. He managed, by the addition of a colourful cravat and the panache with which he wore it, to give that drab outfit a touch of the exotic. It suited his complexion, complimenting his flowing locks, his dusky good looks, and emphasising his dark, flashing eyes.

White women watched him from under lowered lashes

as he passed, twirling their parasols in consternation when he glanced at them. The coloured Creole girls gazed on him boldly, their lips parting coquettishly with unspoken invitation.

He was more of a playboy than a slave; a fancy man. He had astutely taken advantage of his attachment to Jonathan and learned all he could. His brain was as lively as his eyes; he absorbed all he heard and conversed with confidence. To Jonathan he was a companion, not a slave nor a fancy. There was a bond between them, forged in Madagascar when Ratsitatane was going to kill them both.

He clapped Verette on his shoulder in a rare gesture of affection. 'Dash it!' he said again, which was the strongest oath he allowed himself to use. 'I wish I had your debonair style.'

Verette looked at him appreciatively. 'When you met me you thought I was a pickpocket.'

'My influence has obviously changed you for the better.' He smiled to himself and was surprised when Verette laughed with relief.

'That's it, Mr Jonathan! Treat yourself less seriously. Relax and enjoy your blessings. You have what men aspire to.'

Jonathan frowned with dismay at the intimacies his frivolous remark was leading to. 'What is that, pray?'

'The love of a beautiful woman.'

Jonathan halted. Ahead the mountains surrounding he plain were stark as sunlight played on them. The sky beyond was cloudless, a blue of such intensity he was dazzled by its sheen. He blinked and clenched his fists to re-assert the reason of a sensible, sober man to his thoughts.

'That's delusion,' he said flatly.

Verette shook his head. 'You may not recognize love, Mr Jonathan, being unused to it. I am an expert. Others agree with me.'

'What others?' He was shocked to hear that he was the subject of popular discussion.

'Fidou, for one. I dare say Miss Emma too, if she paused

long enough to think of someone other than herself for a change.'

'Do other people know?'

'Anyone with eyes and a nose for romance would know instantly.'

Verette's choice of word was unfortunate. Jonathan fingered his large nose unhappily. 'You're jesting. How can she be in love with me? I have the face and disposition of a donkey.'

'Yes, you have. Is that important?'

Verette's candour pleased him. He was sick of the hypocrisy of polite society, the flattery and complimenting of others on non-existent attributes. If what Verette said was true he must re-assess his conduct towards Nicole. It was a disastrous development.

'I'm sure you're mistaken,' he said. 'What possible reason can Miss Genave have for ...' he hesitated to cover his embarrassment, '... for being "in love" with me? I'm an outcast, my prospects are negligible, my future uncertain. I have no fortune, looks, charm, talent –'

'Reason is seldom involved in these matters,' interrupted Verette.

'She's infatuated, that's all,' Jonathan said desperately. 'She sees me every day, and no other man, so she's day-dreaming. She believes I'm more than I am. She was hurt by Ward's ungallant wager, that's why she's behaving in an odd manner.' He tugged out his handkerchief and wiped his neck where his stock was soaked with sweat.

'Indeed?' Verette sighed with a worldly indifference. 'So what are you going to do about it?'

'Do? My dear boy,' he said, making up his mind, 'I must do everything I possibly can to discourage her.'

'Why? She's chaste, beautiful, talented –'

'Dash it, that is why! She's everything I am not.'

Verette smirked. 'You are certainly no longer chaste.'

'Of course I am.' He blushed. 'That affair at Black River must be forgotten.'

'You can't forget it. Your loins quiver when you see Nicole. You long to crush her in your arms, to embrace her, to share love with her. You only feel what she feels.'

'Verette, I forbid you to talk to me in this manner!' He was deeply disturbed. 'Is it true?' he asked after they had walked several steps in silence. 'Do ladies feel this way too?'

'If you love them.'

'I'm sorry.' Jonathan grimaced. 'I didn't mean to get angry. I'm not the one for her, that's all. I must be guided by my head, not by the heat in my loins that Ward's slave roused.'

Verette shrugged. Tiko and Manda had stopped rushing over the savanna and were talking to a man dressed in brown who had been strolling across the plain. Jonathan recognized William Buchanan. It set him off again.

'I once did contemplate marriage, Verette,' he said to offer an explanation for his attitude towards Nicole. 'I was young and foolish then and assumed the feelings I had for the young lady were reciprocated. Now I see I was part of a business transaction. When a better deal presented itself, I was cast aside.

'No, no!' He held up his hand when Verette seemed about to interrupt. 'I'm not bitter, just wiser.'

'More foolish, more like. You know there's a difference between Buchanan's daughter, Gina, and Nicole Genave.'

'Maybe there is now. There wasn't then. Women change, don't they, Verette? Gina has what she married for – a son, wealth and a fine mansion. I had nothing to offer then, and I have less now.'

'Perhaps Miss Nicole wants nothing.'

He sighed, grateful that Mr Buchanan was approaching them so he could extricate himself from Verette's persistence. It was disquieting to discover his private feelings were common knowledge.

'Keep this conversation to yourself,' he warned. 'We owe it to Nicole to respect her.'

Verette nodded and his knowing smile made Jonathan think his consideration for Nicole's feelings had been misinterpreted. Mr Buchanan hailed him before he could explain it.

'I was hoping to meet you, Jonathan,' said Mr Buchanan, greeting him enthusiastically. 'I've been so busy since the port closed. Thanks to you.' He glanced cautiously at Verette.

'You can speak in front of him with confidence, Mr Buchanan,' said Jonathan with a slight edge to his voice for Verette's benefit. 'He is privy to my most intimate secrets.'

'So are all slaves if we did but know it, eh?' He patted Jonathan affectionately on his shoulder. 'Come to dinner! I've turned a fine profit because of your information. Know anything more?'

Jonathan brushed at his hair. 'Trade with Madagascar will cease –'

'What?' Mr Buchanan paused as he was about to hurry off to his house at the other side of the plain. 'That can't be true! Captain Lesage was very successful there. Farquhar is keen to annex the island for Great Britain. We'll trade goods for their cattle. It will be very profitable.'

'No,' said Jonathan, 'it won't. King Radama will ignore Lesage. In addition the British government has instructed Governor Farquhar to stop pursuing claims to Madagascar. I told the king that, which is why he signed the treaty I negotiated. Lesage was not involved.'

'By the devil!' Buchanan punched his hands together. 'So you've been slighted.' He looked at him closely. 'I believe you, Jonathan. How can I turn this to my advantage?'

'Don't order any trading goods. The other merchants will be stocking up in anticipation of a new market in Madagascar. They'll over-extend their credit and the market won't be there.'

'I declare!' said Mr Buchanan admiringly. 'You've got the makings of a smart young man of commerce behind that clerk's frown. I'm in your debt.' He hurried off, rubbing his hands together.

Verette smiled. 'The governor is trying to have the port re-opened, I hear,' he said slyly. 'The merchants are complaining, so is Dr Telfair. He's prepared a memorandum on Mr Farquhar's behalf to send to London.'

Jonathan was appalled. 'Mr Farquhar must be careful whom he trusts,' he said grimly. 'He could be heading for a fall.'

Verette's insistence that Nicole held romantic feelings for him made Jonathan chary. He yearned for the days when he led a simple existence as Governor Farquhar's factotum, unnoticed and unsung. He saw the irony in him attracting the attention of a young lady when he was in limbo, pushed aside by Governor Farquhar's associates and liable to even further humiliation.

To lessen the impact on Nicole of his inevitable fall from favour, he resolved to treat her curtly. He hoped she would grow out of what he regarded as a childish infatuation. He was remiss in encouraging her. She seemed to have taken his brooding when he was in her presence as a sign of passion that he was too shy to divulge.

He became resolute in his efforts to discourage her. During the lessons, when Nicole and the princes were in the garden, he would sit on the veranda; if they entered the house, he strolled through the garden. When contact was unavoidable, he was stiffly polite in a way that brooked no intimacy. A frigidity entered their dealings. He ignored Nicole's pouts of dismay and Fidou's glowering. He was determined.

Strangely his stern dealings with Nicole increased his own melancholy. He grew irritable, snapping at Verette and the princes when previously he would have borne their indiscretions in silence.

He watched Nicole secretively, growing jealous of Verette's easy familiarity with her and his growing friendship with Fidou. He observed Emma's apparent interest in Verette and the poise with which he responded to her. He was becoming resentful of the very people he cared for, and he could not understand why.

Tension gripped the morning lessons. Jonathan suspected his formal attitude to Nicole was the cause, especially when Verette constantly upbraided him about it.

'You want to make the lady *hate* you?' Verette demanded as they were returning from the Didcott residence.

'Yes!' Jonathan replied, ignoring his consternation.

One afternoon towards the end of September, Emma approached him as he sat on the veranda staring out at the path. He rose to his feet hurriedly, looking to see if Nicole was following her. She was not, so he returned Emma's greeting as cordially as his phlegmatic nature would allow.

'Would you like a glass of juice, Jonathan?' she asked.

'No, Miss Emma,' he said, frowning at her use of his Christian name.

'Forgive me for disturbing you.' She smiled and waited. He said nothing to put her at ease.

'We are having a small veranda affair on Wednesday, the twenty-fifth. Mamma is keen that you should come. Without Tiko and Manda, of course. She thinks you may need a break from chaperoning them.'

He coughed and avoided her eyes. 'I really can't accept, thank you.'

'Oh dear!' Emma's face registered her disappointment. 'I was looking forward to it. Your man, Verette, is helping us with the arrangements. He assured me you would be able to come.'

'Well, no ... I'm busy.'

'Mamma will feel you're ashamed of mixing with us socially.'

'Of course not!'

'Then you *will* come?'

'I ... er ...' He scratched his head. 'Very well, since you insist.'

Verette helped him to dress on the Wednesday evening although Jonathan reprimanded him for making a fuss. He wanted to look as drab and as unimportant as he felt, to blend in with the guests so he would not be observed.

Verette was determined otherwise. He gave him a new cravat to wear, a fetching silk one, wine red in colour, and pressed his coat until it was immaculate. He polished his shoes even brighter than Jonathan could do himself. He inspected every item of his clothing and supervised

Jonathan's dressing until he pronounced him perfect for the fête.

Jonathan was dismayed when he arrived at the Didcotts' with Verette as escort, to see only a small number of guests. There was Emma, Louise and Jane with three military men, Mr and Mrs Didcott and Nicole. Too late he realized he had been trapped.

Mr Didcott gripped him by his elbow and led him over to where Nicole was standing under the chandelier.

He pulled his nose, recalling with a flash of anger how Nicole had been banished to playing her guitar behind a screen when he first saw her. She was beautiful then. Now there was a deeper glow to her loveliness; a yearning, a desire that struck Jonathan dumb.

'Jonathan!' said Nicole brightly. 'What a relief not to have Tiko and Manda running around our legs. I do hope you'll enjoy yourself this evening. We have a special fruit punch.'

Fidou moved promptly to his side with a glass on a tray and offered it to him. He hesitated under her critical gaze.

'It's very refreshing,' said Nicole. 'Mrs Didcott adores it.' She lapsed into silence.

He gulped at his glass, frantic for something to say, yet not wanting to speak. His eyes drifted towards the ivory white flesh revealed through the lace corsage of her wine-red evening gown.

He was so used to seeing her in the garden in a sensible outdoor dress, he was stunned. Her ringlets glistened in the glow from the candles, accentuating the delicate lines of her neck and bare shoulders.

'I see your cravat matches my gown.' She smiled coyly. 'What a coincidence.'

'Yes.' He realized at once that it was not.

Verette and Fidou are behind this, he thought. Suddenly he suspected trickery everywhere. He glanced in a panic around the veranda. Mrs Didcott was talking to one of the officers. Louise and Jane were listening to the other two. Emma was at the door to the drawing-room, giggling behind her fan at Verette.

Jonathan felt his anger rising. He saw this veranda affair as a plot hatched by Emma and Mrs Didcott to force him to relax in his severe attitude towards Nicole. Emma's words when she invited him and said her mother would think he was ashamed gave him the clue. The cravat he had unwittingly worn, made from the same material as Nicole's immodest gown, proved it was an intrigue.

He swigged at his drink with deliberate rudeness and turned away from Nicole. 'It's stifling here,' he said, thrusting the empty glass at her. She took it in surprise.

'Jonathan –?'

He strode off the veranda. Instead of heading straight down the path to the Champs de Mars, perversity made him turn and stalk around the corner of the house in search of Fidou. He wanted her confirmation that the affair was planned solely to bring him and Nicole together. He was going to stop their meddling once and for all.

'Fidou!' He saw the slave standing at the back door. There was a breeze blowing down from the mountains. It gusted into his face when he rounded the protective wall of the house, and cooled his rage.

'Yes, Mas Jonathan?' Fidou waited expectantly, holding down her skirt with her hand as the wind tugged at it.

'Inside!' He indicated the door. 'I want to talk to you.'

He followed her into the dining-room. The guests were all on the veranda, so they had the room to themselves.

'You and Verette have gone too far,' he said as soon as he was in the room. He left the back door open so he could leave quickly.

'Mas Jonathan?' Fidou regarded him with surprise, startled by his tone and angered by it. It was a glance that said, 'Jonathan, are you all right?' and clearly implied that he wasn't.

'Damn it, Fidou!' he exclaimed, shocked by his own fury. 'Stop it! Leave me alone.'

'I don't understand –'

'Yes, you do. You and Verette and Emma. You're all trying to force me to woo Nicole. I won't, do you hear!' He leaned against the door jamb for support.

Fidou's eyes blazed. She grabbed a candelabrum from the dining-table and advanced on Jonathan, holding it up so the candle flickered close to his eyes.

'Are you blind, Mas Jonathan?' she shrieked, stung to action by his outburst. 'Miz Nicole *loves* you! Can't you see?' She waved the candelabrum in front of his eyes. He put his hands up to protect himself.

'Fidou!'

The softly spoken sound of her name caused Fidou to turn.

Jonathan peeped through his fingers and saw Nicole standing by the door to the drawing-room. She must have heard the foolish ranting. He was ashamed.

'Mr Jonathan is distressed, Fidou.' Nicole said gently. 'Leave him alone as he requests.'

Fidou swung around and faced Nicole with agitation. 'He knows, miz, he *knows* how he feels for you. Why doesn't he do somethin' to show you?'

'Calm yourself, Fidou. Mr Jonathan is very sensitive and I fear you're alarming him. Put down the candles. You might cause a fire.'

Jonathan witnessed the scene as though it were a tableau instead of something taking place around him, because of him.

Nicole was crossing the floor slowly, the candle-light reflecting the natural gloss of her hair where her ringlets caressed the delicate pallor of her bare shoulders. His throat dried as he gazed at her.

Fidou turned her back on Nicole and looked at him scornfully. 'Do something,' she urged, waving the branched candlestick carelessly, showering hot wax on the floor. 'Take her in your arms, hold her!'

'Fidou, that's enough! You are overwrought. Please give me the candelabrum. You should be attending to our guests.'

Her words sent Fidou berserk. She swung around, swooping towards Nicole with a wild shout. She thrust the candles at her; one dropped from the holder and fell onto the skirt of Nicole's dress. The flimsy organza caught alight, transforming the skirt into a crinoline of flames.

'Now you can save her!' cried Fidou with satisfaction. She flung the candelabrum away and stepped back towards the open door.

Jonathan was paralyzed. He watched horror-struck as the flames embraced Nicole.

On the floor a single candle was still alight. Its flame caught the hem of the curtain at the window. The breeze billowed in through the doorway and fanned the fire.

'Save her!' shrieked Fidou, her voice charged with a new panic.

Jonathan did nothing.

THIRTEEN

Someone hurtled through the drawing-room doorway and dived at Nicole, pushing her to the floor. It was Verette. He rolled onto Nicole's legs trying to smother the flames with his body, beating at them with his hands.

Jonathan gazed around him. The flames had a hold on the curtains, crawling along the pelmet and licking at the ceiling. He moved from the heat to the centre of the room. There was a bowl of fruit punch on the table. He lifted it and tipped its contents over Nicole and Verette, pieces of orange and pineapple showering onto them.

There was a scream from the doorway. Emma rushed into the room and pulled at Verette's shoulder, shrieking his name.

'He's not attacking her!' said Fidou, pulling at Emma's arm to drag her away.

The juice and Verette's bold action doused the flames. Jonathan stepped back, still holding the punch-bowl as Verette and Fidou helped Nicole to her feet.

'Verette, are you all right?' Emma flung herself at him, ignoring the flames spreading across the wall of the room. She put her arm around his neck.

'Of course I am.' Verette brushed her aside. 'Get out onto the veranda. Mr Didcott,' he called to where the others were crowding in the doorway. 'We need water. The house will burn ...'

There was confusion in the room. The back door was open and the breeze gusting through it buffeted the flames so they spread faster. The wall was wooden, as dry as kindling. Verette dashed out to the garden to see if he could find water. The guests followed to help him.

Emma erupted with hysterics and Mrs Didcott started to shriek at Nicole, demanding to know how the fire had begun. Nicole was dazed and unsteady, holding on to a dining-chair for support. The outer fringes of her dress were charred and one side of her skirt was in tatters up to her thigh. Jonathan averted his eyes.

It had all happened so quickly, he was unable to stir himself fast enough. The sight of Nicole's bare leg, and the heat of the fire behind him, brought him to her side.

She shook her head when he touched her arm, wanting to apologize.

'Help Emma,' she said softly.

He frowned, hesitating until he understood. 'Ah, yes ... Miss Emma,' he said, moving towards her. 'Er ... keep calm ... it will ... er be all right.'

He tugged at his nose, wondering what he should do. Nicole eased him aside and took Emma in her arms.

'What was Verette ... doing to you?' Emma gasped.

'Did he start the fire?', shouted Mrs Didcott.

'No, no.' Nicole spoke calmly, becoming more serene as the chaos increased. 'It was an accident. Fidou tripped, the candle caught in my dress.'

She drew Emma towards the door as she spoke and Mr Didcott let her pass. Mrs Didcott was torn between the fire and her desire to discover the truth. She followed Nicole.

Verette marshalled the slaves into a bucket brigade. Fidou ran to help them. Jonathan twisted around. The crackle of the flames was deafening. He moved toward the open door like a zombie. He was not afraid, nor was he a coward; he was numb, suspended in a state of shock by the fury his scruples had provoked.

He pushed past the slaves crowding in the room with buckets, pots and jugs of water. He saw no way the blaze could be contained. The flames were already in the ceiling, spreading along the joists to the opposite wall and burning through to the floor boards of the room above.

He strolled almost casually down the steps and onto the lawn, ignoring Verette's shout for him to go for help.

The flames themselves summoned people. The house was behind those at the end of the street, close to a phalanx of wooden cabins that stretched the length of the road right up to Government House.

The glow of the dining-room burning bright brought the neighbours running. The provision vendors arriving for morning market added to their number. A crowd began to gather in the garden, trampling the flowers, watching the blaze with ghoulish interest.

Like Jonathan, they did nothing. There was no large supply of water nearby, no well and no river. Soon every drop had been thrown on the flames in vain.

Someone alerted the fire brigade. The slaves who constituted the outfit, together with some of the garrison soldiers under a perspiring sergeant, hurried up with a cart loaded with two barrels of water. It was useless.

From the dining-room the fire climbed to the upper story, sped through the house across the ceilings and floors, and descended the walls to the drawing-room and veranda. The breeze encouraged it, tossing burning shingles from the roof to the ground, showering the onlookers with sparks.

Some pieces of flaming straw were carried away by the wind and landed on the roof of a cabin in the market street. A shout of horror drew the attention of the crowd to a new blaze.

The cabin in the middle of the row began to burn fiercely, its flames leaping into the night, spreading a glow along the street and bringing people running from as far away as the harbour. In this part of the town all the buildings were of wood, and packed closely together.

The inevitable soon happened. The fire, seeking more timber to devour, spread to the neighbouring cabins. Suddenly there were three of them aflame. The focus of the blaze changed from Mr Didcott's house, now completely engulfed by the fire, to the street. People were realizing the danger to their own homes. They left the garden and raced down the slopes in panic.

The cabins on either side of the three that were ablaze caught alight too. Jonathan gazed dumbfounded at the destruction his contrariness had caused.

My God, he thought unhappily, backing away from the sight. His heart raced. He stumbled against the stone bench of the orchid arbour and sat down with a sigh.

The fire was determined to spread. The only way it could be stopped would be to pull down houses in its path and create a gap. The inhabitants of the cabins were poor people; freed slaves, labourers, vendors. They had no leader and no one took the initiative needed to stop the blaze.

It spread to more cabins. It was no longer a question of watching the fire but of rescuing property from the houses in its path.

The town was in pandemonium, people running from one end of the street to the other, some fleeing with their possessions, others coming to help. In the darkness and confusion, belongings that were smouldering were saved from some of the houses and dumped at a distance from the blaze. The breeze was restless and sought out the embers nestling in straw mattresses and cotton pillows.

The sky brightened with a fresh fire in the Rue Royale, ignited from those embers and nurtured by the willing breeze. Within an hour of Fidou's challenge to Jonathan to save Nicole, the fire was advancing on the town in three directions at once. It flared towards the Place d'Armes, towards the sea and towards the Rue Desforges.

From the old wooden shacks it spread to the warehouses of the merchants, devouring in its terrible march the wealth accumulated over decades from commerce and industry.

Jonathan wept openly. Someone sitting on the bench beside him touched his arm. It was Nicole. Verette stood behind her.

'I am ashamed,' he gasped, tearing at his hair. 'Just because –'

'It wasn't your fault.' Nicole restrained him with her hand. She wore a blanket wrapped around her. Her face was smeared with soot and her ringlets were bedraggled. Her eyes, revealed in the light of the flames, were fiery like tempered steel as they reflected the blaze.

There was a new hardness forged into her spirit. He could feel it as she gripped his wrists. He lowered his hands and stared at her.

'It was,' he said softly. 'I could have stopped her.'

'There is a reason for everything, Jonathan.'

He shook his head. 'It doesn't make sense. The house, the town ...' He gazed at the line of fire that now extended the whole length of the street.

'It could reach Government House,' said Verette excitedly. His hair was scorched and his palms were raw and blistered.

'Yes.' Jonathan felt his sense of duty returning with the strength he was drawing from Nicole's touch. 'We must go. Mr Farquhar may need me.' He stood up and Nicole rose with him.

'I'm coming with you,' she said.

'No, Nicole.' He was humbled by her willingness to go with him. When she needed his help he had done nothing. 'Stay here with Emma, and Fidou. She needs you now.' He indicated where Fidou was crouched at the edge of the lawn wailing loudly. 'I know how she feels.'

'Will you be all right?'

'I take care of him,' said Verette with a shrug.

The hungry flames, roaring like a furnace, had consumed half the town. Between that and the other half stood Government House. Jonathan and Verette found Governor Farquhar in the courtyard directing soldiers to collect water in buckets. Across the street the wooden cabins were ablaze.

'Thank God you're here,' Mr Farquhar said sternly, pointing at Tiko and Manda, who were gambolling around the courtyard. They ran over and seized Jonathan by his hands, tugging him to join them.

'The house is safe at the front.' Mr Farquhar waved at the Place D'Armes, where people had formed a long line to carry water from the sea. 'The back where those cabins lie close to it looks dangerous. If they catch alight ...' He looked around anxiously.

'We could stop the blaze here. But if my house is caught in the vortex of the fire, no power on earth can save the whole city from being destroyed.'

'Look!' Verette pointed. Flames had begun to lick the corner of the roof.

Governor Farquhar backed away in horror. 'It's the end,' he said. 'Come, Mr Rendye, we must save our papers, the ledgers.' His orders were lost in the night air as he ran towards the house. Jonathan hesitated. Tiko and Manda clung to him.

'I'll take the princes,' Verette said, 'if the governor needs you.'

'Don't leave us!' Manda clutched his hand desperately.

Jonathan glanced down at him. 'I won't,' he said with a shrug.

'There's a soldier!' Tiko yelled with excitement as he pointed at the house.

Wearing a damp towel wrapped around the lower part of his face and holding a pail of water, a man could be seen climbing up to the roof. He made his way cautiously, at times holding the pail's handle by his teeth when he needed both hands to hold the walls of the house.

Governor Farquhar ran back to the courtyard for a better look. 'Who's that man?' he demanded.

'Sergeant Hastie, sir!' a soldier answered proudly. 'Fifty-sixth West Essex.'

'Brave chap!' The governor glanced meaningfully at Jonathan. 'If he stops the blaze the files will be safe. The city will be saved!'

They watched while the soldier crawled over the roof and splashed water on the flames, using it sparingly so each drop was effective. When his bucket was empty, he flung it down to the ground and unwound the towel from his face. He used it to beat at the flames.

'Someone take him more water!' Governor Farquhar's command fell on deaf ears among the soldiers.

Verette left Jonathan's side and disappeared into the darkness at the side of the house. The soldier edged back across the roof and began to climb down. The flames flared up on another part of the roof, ignited by sparks landing on the shingles after being blown there from across the street.

'Mr Rendye!' said the governor, beginning to panic. 'Help that man.'

'I can't, sir. The princes ...'

Mr Farquhar scurried away from him in disgust.

In the flickering light from the fire Verette could be seen handing the pail, refilled with water, to the sergeant. He climbed down while Hastie returned to the roof and repeated his methodic dousing of the flames. He spent hours on the roof aided by soldiers who took over from Verette out of shame. As a result Government House was saved and the fire was contained.

It took the whole night to bring the blaze under control. In the morning the sun shone on an incredible scene of destruction. A fifth of the capital was razed to the ground, over seven hundred houses destroyed. The damage was reckoned at more than eight million Spanish dollars.

The whole population of the town was plunged into a state of shock. Governor Farquhar and the garrison soldiers were the only ones spared the despair and apathy that seized the townsfolk. The soldiers had their hero in Sergeant Hastie to inspire them; Governor Farquhar had his extraordinary energy and the impetus of power to keep him going.

The governor organized the relief effort with a frantic zeal. Those who lost everything were rehoused and fed.

Slaves were brought in from the plantations to clear the debris and restore order to the town. Food and clothing stocks were distributed from the merchants' warehouses.

Finally, in a gesture that turned the disaster to the advantage of the colony, Governor Farquhar declared the port open to ships of all nations. It was a blatant defiance of his instructions from the British government.

Jonathan observed what Mr Farquhar was doing with mixed feelings. He admired his zealous spirit that galvanized the people to recover from their anguish. Yet he deplored Mr Farquhar's deliberate flouting of the orders of the secretary of state.

He wondered whether he should make his feelings known. The opportunity came when Mr Farquhar summoned him five days after the fire.

He was nervous as he was admitted to the governor's office by Mr Bateman. It was several weeks since he had been inside the room where he used to be a daily visitor. As he expected, the obsequious Dr Telfair was present as well as clerks and messengers dashing in and out with dispatches and orders to be signed.

An air of energy emanated from Mr Farquhar. Jonathan could feel it as he hovered by the door.

'Sir?' he said diffidently to draw Mr Farquhar's attention to his presence.

The governor had just dismissed a merchant with a promise to consider his claim for compensation. He lifted his head, saw Jonathan and glanced at Dr Telfair.

'Ah yes ...' he began in that tone of voice which warned of bad news. 'Mr Rendye.'

Jonathan stepped forward. A messenger pushed in front of him, placed a document on the governor's desk, waited while Mr Farquhar signed it and hurried out of the office. The governor seemed to relish the activity the disaster had caused.

'I understand you were present when the fire began?'

'Er, yes, sir.' Jonathan stammered at the unexpected question, forgetting his own criticism of the governor's conduct.

'There will be an enquiry, of course. I'd like to hear your version of events.'

Jonathan gaped at Mr Farquhar. How could he tell the truth?

'Speak up, man. I haven't got time to waste. I hear you saved Miss Genave's life by putting out the blaze when the fire caught her dress.'

'I did?'

'Miss Genave says it was an accident caused when her slave tripped. A candle caught the curtain alight. I want to know why the blaze spread to the street. Wasn't any effort made to extinguish it?'

Jonathan tried to recall what happened. 'There was a shortage of water ... the wind carried the sparks –'

'Just as I said, Charles.' Mr Farquhar turned to Dr Telfair standing at his side. 'We need water. We must pipe water from Dayot Canal into the eastern part of the town. Look at the west. Five public fountains there and not a single supply in the east. We need a new canal!'

'You are a visionary, Robert.' Dr Telfair smiled ingratiatingly.

'Thank the Lord for Sergeant Hastie.'

'He was sent by providence.'

Mr Farquhar looked Dr Telfair in the eye. 'Perhaps you are right.' He swung around. The glint of hope in his expression died as he contemplated Jonathan. 'Mr Rendye, I wonder who sent you?'

'Sir?'

'You have served me for a long time, perhaps too long. I'm afraid you're not up to it, Rendye. We have to rebuild. I need people like Sergeant Hastie around me. He's a giant physically with a gentle nature and a loyal heart.'

'He's a Cork man,' said Dr Telfair proudly, for he was also born in Ireland.

'I'm appointing him tutor to the two Hova princes. He will instruct them in accordance with my principles, rather more strictly than you and Miss Genave are capable of.'

'Tiko and Manda?' Jonathan was flabbergasted. 'They're mine! I brought them from Madagascar. King

Radama entrusted them to me.'

'They were entrusted to you because of your official status,' said Dr Telfair. 'His Excellency means that now you are dismissed from his service, you no longer have official status. We will need your quarters for Sergeant Hastie.'

Jonathan made no attempt to move or speak. He was staring at Mr Farquhar, waiting to hear his dismissal from the governor's own lips.

Mr Farquhar spoke at last. 'It's for the best, Rendye. I informed your aunt by letter some months ago. She agrees with me that if you are not happy here, and are no longer of the calibre I require, you should return to England.

'I understand she will find you something in the city more suited to your abilities than pioneering in Port Louis.'

Dr Telfair tried to wave him out of the governor's presence. 'That will be all, Rendye,' he hissed between clenched teeth.

Jonathan hesitated. He knew exactly how to unnerve the smug Dr Telfair. He knew so much about his corrupt dealings, he could make a lot of trouble if he was sent back to England against his will.

'Very well, Your Excellency.' He bowed to Mr Farquhar, deliberately ignoring Telfair. 'I must inform you I will report to the Secretary of State as soon as I arrive. I shall do so candidly since I am no longer on your staff.'

'Heh?' Mr Farquhar looked at him sharply.

'I am obliged to do so to explain my unexpected return. There are many matters on which I could give an account, possibly in clarification of your own reports.'

'Now wait a minute, Mr Rendye –'

'On the other hand ...' Jonathan paused, then added, 'If I have your permission I would prefer to stay in Mauritius.'

'What?' Mr Farquhar glared at him. 'There is nothing for you to do here.'

'Forgive me, sir. You have often said how the colony needs young British settlers. I am willing to become one.'

'This is no country for lazy pen pushers,' snapped Dr Telfair.

'Then perhaps I will explain to the secretary of state how you, Dr Telfair, have so many unregistered and newly arrived *black* settlers on your estate? It might be assumed that you are engaging in the slave-trade without, of course, the knowledge of the governor.'

Mr Farquhar steepled his fingers, gazing over the tips as he leaned back in his chair and contemplated Jonathan.

'I have to ask myself, Mr Rendye, if you are settler material. Do you have assets?'

'If my aunt knows I am keen to settle here in a private capacity instead of being returned to England against my will, she would give me her support.'

Mr Farquhar sighed, put down his hands and turned to Dr Telfair. 'Young Rendye's Aunt Hortense is a formidable lady, Charles. She has the ear of the Regent.'

'I didn't know that.' Dr Telfair paled.

'What would you do if you stayed, Mr Rendye?'

He remembered what William Buchanan had told him. 'I would go into partnership with a merchant and concentrate on importing the goods needed for rebuilding.'

'Dammit!' Mr Farquhar shook his head ruefully. He waved away Dr Telfair, who was trying to object.

'Have I underestimated you, Jonathan? Of course, we need you here where your talents can serve us better than in London.' He rose to his feet but did not offer his hand.

Jonathan nodded politely, did not bow, and turned on his heels. He walked out of the room a prouder man than when he entered. He was without a clue what he would do, or where he would find the financing. But he was free.

Book Two

ROLL OF DISHONOUR
1817–1818

Let him hang with a curse, this atrocious, pernicious,
Scoundrel who emptied the till at Mauritius.

Theodore Hook, 1825

FOURTEEN

Mr and Mrs Mango were carefully tended and watered. These were two large mango trees growing by a stream and had been whimsically named by Louise.

Nicole sat in the shade thrown by their branches over the lawn. She gazed, enraptured, beyond the stream to the bay far below. The sea shimmered a deep blue, contrasting with the light-green ribbons of the sugar-cane that waved on the slopes leading down to the shore.

Nicole had been reluctant to go when Louise invited Emma and herself to stay on her father's plantation at Tamarind. She wanted to remain in Port Louis. Mr Didcott insisted. With half of Port Louis destroyed they would fare better at Tamarind, a small community about twelve miles south of the capital.

In the excitement of the voyage by coastal schooner Nicole forgot her reluctance. Even Emma grew keen on the idea when she realized the season was curtailed and there would be no more balls and festivities. The three of them were accompanied by Fidou.

Jane had returned to her parents' home on the east coast. Mrs Didcott was vapourish after the shock of losing everything in the fire, so she remained in lodgings in Port Louis with her husband.

The freedom Nicole discovered on the Tamarind plantation was a heady experience. Mr Moult, Louise's father, was a dedicated planter who ran his estate with a gruelling efficiency. He worked in the fields beside his field hands from dawn until late at night. Sometimes he was absent from the house for days. Louise's mother was a mild-mannered woman whose time was taken up in domestic affairs, managing the female slaves in clothes making, laundering and housekeeping.

Because the Tamarind plantation house was small, the three girls were obliged to occupy Louise's tiny room. There was only one bed. After her first night squeezed between a restless Emma and a snoring Louise, Nicole chose the floor, where she slept fitfully each night on cushions.

There were no other inhabitants in the small house and Mrs Moult seemed overwhelmed by their presence. She reacted by leaving them to their own devices. They rose late, took a leisurely breakfast together prepared and served by Fidou and spent their time lazing on the plantation until dinner. Their initial delight at being free of Mrs Didcott's relentless disciplining changed within a week to frustration.

'I shall die an old maid if I stay here,' said Emma, rudely interrupting Nicole's contemplation of the seascape in Tamarind bay. She threw herself with a groan onto the grass at Nicole's feet.

'No one ever comes here. That's why Louise preferred to live in town with us.'

Nicole fingered her ringlets under her bonnet and blinked away her own thoughts. She smiled encouragingly at Emma. 'We are fortunate to be here. Hundreds of people in Port Louis are sleeping in the streets.'

'Creoles,' said Emma harshly, 'and blacks. We were the only ones who really suffered. What a stupid thing to do. Fidou should be whipped until the skin peels off her.'

Nicole blenched. 'It was an accident. She's been punished enough.'

'How? Mamma was too distraught even to lash her with the tawse.'

'Her conscience, Emma. It won't let her forget.'

'She doesn't have a conscience. She's black.'

'She's a woman like you and me.'

'I hope that I am better than her! She was doing things with Verette.' Emma's eye gleamed when she mentioned the youth's name. 'Ah me …' she sighed. 'When will I see that buck again?'

'Why do you want to?' Nicole asked the question to keep

the conversation flowing, without thinking that Emma would take offence.

'Hah! You should know! I saw him pawing at you on the floor.' Emma scrambled to her feet. 'You can forget about him, Nicole! He's interested in me, not you.'

'Indeed?' Nicole supposed it was plantation life that made Emma behave oddly. She had noticed Emma gloating at the slaves when they came near the house. She averted her eyes. Those half-naked men owned by Mr Moult were of no interest to her.

'Write to him,' Emma said suddenly, gripping her arm with excitement at her idea. 'Invite him here for a visit.'

'Verette?'

Emma pinched her. 'You're as dumb as Fidou! Jonathan Rendye, of course. He's *your* friend. He'll come here and he'll bring Verette.' She smiled coyly, then her eyes widened. 'He'll take me for a walk by the stream –'

'Verette is a very respectful young man.'

'Hah! You'd like him though.'

Nicole twisted on the grass, distracted by Emma's strange accusation. She was thinking of Jonathan, wondering what he was doing in Port Louis. She missed him, and Tiko and Manda. Perhaps he would bring them too.

'Yes,' she said, 'I will write. I'd like news of him and the princes.'

'When Verette comes, he's mine, remember.'

'I don't know what you mean.' She turned away, disturbed by Emma's intention and wanting to push it from her mind.

She returned her gaze to the stretch of coast below her. The plantation house was built on a small plateau that afforded a view of the cane fields. From her vantage point under Mr and Mrs Mango she could see where slaves were cutting the ripened canes for crushing.

The sugar mill was built in a thicket of trees beside the Tamarind River. The sweet aroma of cane juice being boiled hung over the plantation in a sickly cloud.

There was a tranquillity on the plantation that appealed

to Nicole. Doves and pigeons cooed in the distance and foraging birds chirped noisily in the trees around the lawn. Close by, a small stream gurgled as it raced over its stony bed to join the Tamarind River.

There was the occasional shout from Mr Moult telling his negroes to work harder. Sometimes the snap of a whip, like gun-fire, shattered the peace. She tried to forget it was a man, or a woman like her, who was being lashed. Stern treatment was necessary when slaves were lazy.

She spent many hours with Mr and Mrs Mango. At first she thought she would do some work in the garden. The memory of her cuttings and plants trampled and rooted up by the crowd who invaded her garden on the night of the fire deterred her.

She was thankful she was not a restless soul like Emma. She would like to have had something to do, perhaps help care for those made homeless by the fire. Yet while Mr Didcott still regarded her as his responsibility, she must do as he said. When she was occupied instructing the princes, instead of being Emma's companion, she gained an insight into her own capabilities.

Perhaps she could become a tutor, or a governess, to the children of an English family? It would be more satisfying than being at Emma's beck and call.

Her interest in Tiko and Manda sprung from her concern for Jonathan. She had discovered much about herself because of him. She sensed, without knowing why, that something had made Jonathan change in his attitude towards her. He no longer acted naturally; he behaved as though he were afraid of his own emotions.

Beyond the enormity of the fire there was the question of his deliberate coolness towards her. He had refused to declare his feelings for her when Fidou goaded him; yet he was the one who doused the fire.

She was puzzled by him. Because of his action, the burns on her legs were slight, the scars would heal completely in a few more months. The scars were all she had to remember him by in the lonely fastness of the Tamarind house.

She was uncertain if she would write to him as Emma

suggested. He was probably too busy, and too timid, to visit. She meant nothing to him, that was obvious. For her part she defined her feelings as similar to a sister's interest in an elder brother's well-being.

She laughed aloud when she pictured in her mind Jonathan's characteristic brushing at his forelock of hair. It always tumbled back over his brow the moment he released it.

From the corner of her eye, as she laughed, she caught sight of someone sauntering across the lawn from the house. She swallowed her laughter and gasped. The contrast in her vision of Jonathan and the man in the distance could not have been greater.

The man swaggered where Jonathan slouched, his dress was casual and flamboyant where Jonathan's clothes would be correct but dull. His complexion was the healthy golden tan of a planter, not the pallor of a city clerk.

Nicole tightened inside. The composure fostered by the Tamarind tranquillity cracked as she gazed at the man in his tight breeches and full shirt with puffed sleeves, open to the leather strap at his waist. She dared not raise her eyes beyond the scuffed leather walking boots that trod relentlessly over the grass towards her.

He began speaking before he reached her side. 'Mrs Moult said I would find you here. I walked over the hills from Black River. She says you mope too much, not like Emma and Louise, who are always in some kind of mischief.'

He halted in front of her, casting a shadow and blocking her view of the ocean.

She smoothed down her skirt modestly to cover her ankles. 'I am alone,' she said, keeping her eyes on the ground.

'From anyone else that would be an invitation.' Ward crouched beside her. She caught her breath at the sight of his unruly mane of blond hair and sparkling eyes so close to hers.

'From you, it's a challenge.'

'Is it?' She drew herself to an upright position, sitting

with her back straight as he settled down on the grass. He lolled forward on his arms and she found she was gazing down on him. He looked absurdly young and dashing.

'You are on your guard all the time. Ever since you met me. What have I done?'

'The wager –'

'I hoped you'd forgotten that.'

'It was an awakening for me.'

'You've changed.'

'Perhaps.' She relaxed a little. In the countryside, seeing him dressed as a planter, without the formalities of fashionable society, she found Ward less intimidating. He was younger than Jonathan, at ease and confident. Despite her nervousness she warmed to his presence.

'I hate the season,' he said. 'My wife makes me go. That's why I get drunk, I suppose. Can't stand Governor Farquhar either.'

'Oh?' She let him talk, studying his lean features, noticing the pain that lurked behind his wry smile. It intrigued her that he had sought her out after so many months.

'Hypocrites, they are. You're different. You're Creole, like me. I know your story. One day you'll break out of the mould they fashioned for you and you'll be yourself.'

She blushed at the truth.

'Damn,' he said. 'I've upset you already.' He pulled himself up so he was sitting on his haunches. 'That's my weakness. I should think carefully before I speak. Did I insult you?'

She was bemused by the question. 'You seem to assume a lot about me.'

'I'm a flesh trader, Nicole. Mr Moult raises cane, my main crop is slaves. I study their expressions to know what they're thinking. Little signs give me a clue to a person's character.'

'It sounds dangerous, you could be wrong.'

'Yes. I was wrong with you.'

'Are you right now?'

He stared at her. 'You're laughing at me!'

The idea seemed to delight him. He rolled over in the grass and stretched himself full length in front of her, resting his head on his hands. He looked up at the boughs of the mango trees, pretending to be unaware of the effect he was having on her.

She was fascinated. He seemed so relaxed, almost childlike. She was enchanted by the naturalness of his manner; it was trusting, as if they were friends of long standing. She wanted to embrace him but she kept her hands firmly clasped in her lap.

'I knew you were different,' he said, 'from the moment I saw you.' He stared at the branches. 'It's not your eyes, your hair or your beauty, all that can change as you grow older. It's you!'

She turned her head so this time her blush would be private. 'You flatter me,' she said, hoping he could not hear the pounding of her heart, for it sounded so loud to her.

'Why should I?' He lowered his eyes to face her. 'Nicole, I am a married man. Oh, I know what people say about my wife and it's all true. She does like black men, some women do, but I have my slave mistress, Ellen. Now, I ask you, what do I hope to gain by flattering you? I'm not trying to win that wager.'

She was appalled by his outburst and it showed in her face. He laughed.

'Are you cross because I'm frank with you?'

A feeling of pity engulfed her. She touched his shoulder. 'I never knew that about Gina. You poor man.'

'Poor?' He gazed at her incredulously. 'No one's ever said that about me.'

'You must be so unhappy. Your wife –'

'I'm not. We put on a brave face in public once a year. I have my consolations. Some of the whelps I'm raising in the slave pens are my own offspring.'

This time she kept her shock under control. She assumed he was teasing her to see what she would say. Of course she knew planters kept bed wenches and sometimes their mulatto children were sold as slaves. It was a tradition for which many plantation wives were grateful, since it saved them from their husband's too-frequent carnal attentions. What surprised her was Ward's candour.

'Why are you telling me these curious things?' she asked, holding her eyes steady on his.

He lowered his head. 'So you know the kind of man I am. It will save anguish later. Keep your romantic ideas for others. I'd like to be your friend, that's all. I owe you that much for the slur I cast on you at the Turf Club ball.'

'Really!' His arrogance stirred her. It seemed so long ago. 'Romance is far from my mind.'

'Mrs Moult thinks otherwise. She says you must have a beau in Port Louis to be dreaming so much. Every day you come here, she said.'

'It's a peaceful place. Usually.'

He chuckled. 'Now I see you have a shrew's tongue. Perfect! We'll have great arguments. You may even slap my face from time to time. I won't let it spoil our relationship.'

'You're insufferable.' She reached out to steady herself against the trunk of the tree as she rose to her feet.

'And you have a temper!' He rose up beside her. 'I'm glad to discover your serenity is only skin-deep.'

She was about to protest when she caught sight of the eagerness glinting in his eyes. She swallowed, gripping the tree trunk to bring her back to reality. If she grew cross with him, she realized, he would deem it a triumph. He was testing her for some squalid reason of his own.

She smiled, her eyes taking on a hardness that made him blink.

'I am not one of your slaves,' she said, 'who will play your games. You have a very poor opinion of me if you think I am.'

'You're right, Nicole.' He stepped backward awkwardly. 'Shall we walk around the garden?'

She wanted to refuse him; her curiosity drove her on. Now they were standing side by side she recognized the physical strength that made him an imposing figure. She guessed his reputation as a man of ruthlessness arose because of his ignorance of English manners rather than through a desire to offend.

She was uncertain if his offer of friendship was to be taken seriously or whether it was a ruse to lull her into accepting his company. She strolled away from him in the direction of a coppice dividing the edge of the lawn from the cane fields. He followed her.

'Do you like living here?'

'I miss being in Port Louis. I was tutoring Prince Tiko and Prince Manda. They were very *amusant*.'

'Sergeant Hastie has them now.'

She faltered in her stride, then recovered and continued walking to keep her doubts hidden from him. 'Who is he?' she asked, hoping she sounded casual.

'Some lackey of Robert Farquhar's.'

'What about Mr Rendye? He was the one who brought them from Madagascar.'

'Jonathan?' Ward laughed in a mocking tone that she found irritating. 'He's been sacked.'

'I don't believe it!' Her heart raced. She hated the way people sneered when they talked about Jonathan. Even Ward was doing it.

He was watching her with his eyebrow raised. 'Odd, isn't it? The young fogey's been with Mr Farquhar for ten years. His right-hand man when he first arrived. Something changed between them, I suppose.'

She sprang to Jonathan's defence, resenting the slighting even by implication. 'It could be Governor Farquhar who changed, not Jonathan.'

Ward grinned. 'Well, he's out of the ruling clique now so perhaps he won't be so prissy and pompous.'

'That's his shyness.' She caught her breath and stopped walking. 'What will he do? Has he gone back to England?'

'No, Nicole.' He was watching her shrewdly. 'It's rumoured he wants to stay in Mauritius. He'll soon weary of that. Without the governor's support he's being laughed out of the colony. No one takes him seriously.'

'I do.' The words slipped out of her mouth before she could stop them. 'I must go to Port Louis at once.' She turned to run up to the house.

Ward caught her arm and swung her into the coppice, holding her around her waist. She tried to resist but the firm hands that gripped her body were strangely reassuring. She hesitated.

His face was pressed close to hers. She saw the fine down above the shaving line on his cheek. His eyelashes were long and he was peering at her with a sardonic gleam. His hands held her loosely and she sensed she could break away if she wanted.

She let him kiss her on her neck. It was a gentle brush of his lips against her skin and she barely felt it. She raised her face to meet his, her lips moist.

He pushed her away with a chuckle. 'I'll take you to Port Louis to see him,' he said, 'if that's what you want.'

'Yes,' she breathed, smoothing down her dress. 'That's what I want.'

FIFTEEN

William Buchanan held his glass of burgundy and water up to the candle flame and squinted at the liquid. 'Like blood,' he said before he raised the glass to his lips and drank thirstily. 'Robert Farquhar's blood.'

Jonathan sat in a seat opposite him on the veranda of his house and stared gloomily at his own glass of wine. He disliked drinking for the way it deprived him of caution. He remembered how Mr Buchanan was a sober, well-respected gentleman until he suffered losses when trade was cut off in the war between Britain and America. Drink had changed him, made him talkative and careless.

'Don't you like Mr Farquhar?' Jonathan asked reprovingly.

'I worship him, Jonathan. That's why I drink his blood. Without ol' Farquhar my fortunes would be very low.' Mr Buchanan drained his glass. He looked at the decanter, saw it was empty and staggered to his feet.

'Basin!' he shouted. There was no reply. 'Damn boy foolin' with Ranavola,' he muttered, then shuffled off into the house to look for the slave.

Jonathan sipped warily at his glass. The dryness of the wine braced him. He leaned forward and tipped the rest of its contents over the edge of the veranda, flushing at his boldness. He sat back and stared out at the night.

He had been Mr Buchanan's house guest since leaving Government House two months before. He appreciated the American's kindness in giving him shelter. Massey's Hotel and the Maison Despaux were full with people made homeless by the fire. He had no friends to whom he could turn and when Mr Buchanan heard, he insisted he stay with him.

It was a satisfactory arrangement; the house was large and Jonathan had his own chamber. His host, in the tradition of the old settlers, refused to consider payment. He took his payment in company, in those evenings on the veranda when his tongue was loosened by wine and he needed a companion to talk with.

Sometimes he was maudlin and Jonathan had to suppress his yawns; other times his indiscretions gave him a new insight into the colony and how Mr Farquhar was regarded. Jonathan was ambivalent in his attitude. He blamed his ousting from the governor's side on others and was sensitive to criticism of Mr Farquhar.

'I'm relieved you approve of His Excellency,' said Jonathan pompously when Mr Buchanan returned. Basin followed him with a full decanter of wine and a jug of water. 'He's doing a splendid job setting the city to rights again.'

'Eh?' Mr Buchanan peered at him suspiciously while Basin filled his glass. 'Have another, Jonathan. You're too formal for me.'

Jonathan covered his glass with his hand and appealed to Basin with his eyes. The slave took no notice and prepared to empty the decanter over his hand.

'Very well,' he said with bad grace, holding out the glass. Basin poured in wine and added water. He sidled away into the depths of the house, taking the decanter with him.

'Farquhar's a fool.' Buchanan sipped his wine and watched Jonathan.

He shifted uncomfortably under his gaze, and at his words. 'You said you worship him.'

'I do, I do, but because he's a fool. His folly is going to make my fortune.'

'Because he closed the port?' Jonathan had heard the story so many times he was not keen for Mr Buchanan to repeat how he made a huge profit selling foreign goods when the other merchants had none.

'Because he opened it again! The fire was the excuse he needed. What luck it was for Mauritius. Commerce will be born again. Already we have French and American ships here in convoys. If I had more capital, I'd buy everything.'

Jonathan was puzzled. 'How does that make the governor a fool?'

'He's engaging the government in the import business. He's ordered supplies of food and clothing from India.'

'That's because people lost everything in the fire.'

'Quite right. He's selling off the food at fifty percent below what it costs.'

'That's good government. People are hungry, there's a famine.'

'Ah, the people ... Yes, they'll borrow, steal and beg to pay for food. But what is really happening? We merchants can buy from government at below cost and sell at a better profit than if we shipped the goods in ourselves. Now isn't that the work of a fool? I love him!'

'Is it true?'

'Ask Mr Barry.'

'The Chief Secretary?'

'The same. He and Major Waugh bought rice at three dollars a bag *on credit*. They resold to the military commissariat at four dollars twenty-one cents. If I had the finance, Jonathan, I'd be doing the same.'

He sipped his wine slowly as though waiting for Jonathan to announce his decision.

For weeks Jonathan had been considering where his

future lay. His talent for the cut and thrust of commerce was untried. The open doors he expected were closed when people knew he was no longer in the governor's employ.

He discovered that previously he had been tolerated because of his connections. Now he had nothing to offer, he was ignored.

He became despondent when no one offered him a position. He wrote to Aunt Hortense explaining his desire to remain in the colony and establish himself. He enquired if she would care to start him with a loan. It would take at least another four months before he received her reply.

Only Verette's loyalty stopped him succumbing to despair. The youth was amazing. He cajoled him into keeping up his spirits. He made him walk through the town daily, calling on acquaintances and businessmen as though he were a gentleman of leisure.

'Don't let people know you have nothing,' Verette said sternly. 'If they think you are down they'll make sure you stay down.'

Verette's maxims, developed during his own struggle for existence, helped Jonathan cling to what little self-respect he had. Mr Buchanan, who claimed he was only repaying Jonathan a favour for the profit he helped him make, provided extra support with his encouragement.

'Well, Jonathan,' said Mr Buchanan suddenly, 'I see you're thinking over my proposition. Can you raise some capital? We could do some very profitable business together.'

Jonathan sipped at his wine to gain time. The American was offering a small chance. His problem was how to take it. 'I'd like to do so,' he stammered, remembering Verette's advice: *never refuse an offer*.

'You could get a loan from the government, Jonathan, with your record.' Mr Buchanan smiled as though he could read his thoughts.

'Government officers borrow at six per cent. You could re-lend that at the legal colonial interest rate of nine per cent. Far better to invest it with me. We can make thirty per cent easily, even fifty if we capitalize on Farquhar's folly.'

He chuckled, twisting his empty glass in his hands.

Jonathan studied him surreptiously. He was dressed in a shabby, wine-stained coat. He had been the American commercial agent for fifteen years until his replacement earlier that year when his efficiency waned and his drinking waxed.

His appearance did not inspire confidence. His glance was shifty and his finances, judging by his table, were low. He was heavily in debt to his son-in-law, Ward.

'I'll think about it,' said Jonathan, draining his glass and quaking at the reckless feeling the wine induced.

For the next few weeks, while Mr Buchanan shuffled about the city setting up deals that never happened, Jonathan considered two aspects: raising money and what to do with it.

Verette's advice was to buy a cargo on his own, rent warehouse space and set himself up independent of William Buchanan.

'Use a failed man's experience,' cautioned Verette, 'not his reputation.'

On his daily perambulations around the town, always with his clothes neatly laundered and pressed by Verette, Jonathan became a familiar sight. The slaves saluted him respectfully because Verette had spread the rumour that he was soon to come into a fortune and would be opening a large establishment of his own. The news spread upwards from the slaves to their mistresses until it was common gossip.

He was puzzled to find some doors were re-opening. At Massey's Hotel, where he went to be seen every day, a young man by the name of George Allen struck up an acquaintance. Since he was a financial officer in the treasury, Jonathan encouraged the friendship. He was hoping that by doing so he might find a way to obtain a government loan.

George Allen was a nervous character prone to lapsing into long silences during which he twiddled his fingers and his lips moved soundlessly as though counting. He was a bachelor and addicted, he confided to Jonathan, to a mulatto whore with expensive tastes.

'On my stipend, Mr Rendye,' he said dolefully, 'it's difficult to give the wench all she wants.'

Jonathan, who was accustomed to receiving confidences, merely nodded without comment. Soon he was the recipient of all George Allen's secrets and grouses. He learned that the Chief Justice was deeply in debt to local merchants and that Dr Telfair and Captain Lesage had land ceded to them at one third of its value which they sold at once for a huge profit.

Theodore Hook, the treasurer, came in for George Allen's greatest condemnation. 'He pretends to know nothing about accounts,' he whispered in Jonathan's ear. 'It's a lie! He helps himself to cash and tells me to recipe the accounts. 'Make a little stew,' he says in his sing-song voice. 'You're a master chef, Mr Allen".'

'What do you do?' Jonathan tried to keep the shock out of his voice.

'I cook the books a little, like he says.' He paused, squinted at Jonathan and then said, 'I suppose you couldn't lend me a thousand dollars, old chap?'

The request, tagged on to the information about Theodore Hook's dishonesty, perplexed Jonathan. He remembered Verette's caution and said grandly, 'Mr Allen, that's an appealing proposition. Unfortunately I'm not in a position to do so at present.'

His own situation was parlous. He was running up an account at Massey's and saw no way to settle it. Verette urged him to be hopeful. The youth's optimism was infectious so Jonathan kept to the routine of daily visits to Massey's although he could not afford it.

One morning George Allen was in considerable distress. 'There was a fire,' he gushed in a louder voice than usual. 'In me office! I'd just took delivery of eleven thousand dollars in paper money and it all burnt up!'

Jonathan commiserated but everyone else sniggered knowingly. George Allen wore a hangdog expression for days, ignoring the taunts of the regulars at Massey's. Jonathan tried to encourage him by passing on Verette's advice that he should be stout-hearted and optimistic.

A court of enquiry was held under Colonel Dalrymple, the genial commanding officer of the Twenty-second Cheshire Regiment. George was acquitted of any blame or suspicion. There had been a fire and the money was missing. It was an act of God, decreed the colonel, adding, 'To quarrel with the results of which would be impious.'

Jonathan congratulated George on his acquittal when he saw him the next morning at Massey's.

George laughed and drew him aside. 'You were the only one to trust me,' he said in his customary whisper. 'Here's five thousand at ten per cent until your inheritance comes through.' He thrust a package at Jonathan, glancing sideways to see they were unobserved.

Jonathan pushed the package away in dismay.

'It's all right, Mr Rendye. I know your situation. Take it. I was lucky in a wager ... An act of God, you might say.'

Verette listened eagerly to Jonathan's account of George's offer as the two of them strolled across the Champ de Mars that afternoon. The sun was slanting over the plain, throwing long shadows on the grass. It picked out Mr Buchanan's villa, strikingly white in its embrace of foliage on the lower slope of the hillside.

Further down, Mr Didcott's home was still a charred ruin. Some of the cabins of the Champ de Mars were being rebuilt. The market was now held in the gardens by the Chaussée.

'Well,' said Verette brightly when Jonathan finished his story. 'Where's the money?'

'I didn't take it.'

Verette sighed. He knew Jonathan would not touch anything that had the slightest hint of impropriety about it. It was one of the reasons he liked the Englishman. He was gullible but incorruptible; just the person he needed to help him make his own fortune.

'Why not, Mr Jonathan? We need that money. I could parlay it to ten thousand.'

Jonathan looked horrified. 'What would be worse,

borrowing tainted money or giving it to you for some swindle?'

'The money's not tainted. George was officially acquitted. He earned it. Better you borrow it at ten per cent than some whore in the Chaussée spends it for him.'

Jonathan lapsed into a brooding silence while Verette sauntered at his side pondering what to do. He needed Jonathan not for some swindle but for legitimate schemes to make money. Although he was a free mulatto, he was unable to move in the circles where the deals were made. He could not sit inside Massey's Hotel hob-nobbing with government officials the way Jonathan could.

Verette was using Jonathan as his ears and eyes. When the opportunity came, he intended that the Englishman would be his key to open the doors to a fortune.

Verette had great faith in his own luck. When times were darkest, providence could be relied on to throw him something, even though it was only a crumb. He regarded his meeting with Jonathan as a crumb. The cake was to come.

His attention as he strolled by Jonathan's side was caught by a palanquin heading for William Buchanan's villa. When it was followed by a second and a third, his heart beat faster. Jonathan, still sunk in his own reverie, plodded on.

Verette grinned to himself. Descending from the first palanquin was Ward Trenchard, while from the second emerged Miss Emma and from the third came Miss Nicole and Fidou. Now he knew what was to be done.

He steered Jonathan around the plain for another lap, pretending to listen to his bouts of self-pitying conversation. He was making his own plans.

Mr Buchanan's house was large. Since there was no accommodation at the hotels, Nicole and Emma would certainly be invited to stay in the house. It suited his scheme perfectly.

When he judged the guests were settled, Verette suggested to Jonathan that they walk back to the house.

'Another evening to spend paying for our host's

hospitality,' groaned Jonathan with a sigh. He did not notice the empty palanquins being borne away from outside the house.

'Sometimes,' said Verette, scarcely able to contain his own excitement, 'there are surprises when we least expect them.'

'Another of your maxims?' Jonathan ruffled Verette's hair affectionately and strolled up the path to the villa.

Verette darted away to go to the slave quarters at the rear of the house.

'Fidou, my love!' he said in Creole, seizing the slave around her waist and hugging her before she could wriggle away. Ranavola, preparing supper over the fire in the kitchen, chortled delightedly at his joke. Basin frowned.

'I missed you!' Verette lied. 'How well you look. Country air agrees with you,' he said, squeezing her breast.

Fidou pulled away and glared at him suspiciously. 'Verette, I declare you grown more rascal than ever.'

'Mayhap, mayhap!' He pranced around the kitchen, his eyes twinkling. 'How did you persuade Emma to make this visit and bring you too?'

'Lor', Verette, Miz Emma don't need no persuadin'. Nicole hot to see Jonathan an' Emma, she sure talkin' 'bout you, boy!'

It was enough. Verette shrugged as though it were of no importance. 'Basin,' he said sternly. 'I'll serve the guests if you give me the decanter. You'll have too much to do by yourself with the extra guests.'

Ranavola and Fidou laughed together. 'We know what you want, boy,' Ranavola said. 'Nigger thrive on buckra thirst.'

Verette smoothed his hair and dusted his shoes. He was dressed as a black dandy, regarding himself as too superior to go barefoot. Basin disapproved of him but accepted his offer of help because he had to make up the beds in the guest-rooms.

Fidou said she would help Ranavola with the extra preparations for supper, so Verette was able to pursue his purpose without interference. He observed the five whites on the veranda and listened how the conversation was going.

William Buchanan was trying to interest Ward in a deal. Jonathan was staring open-mouthed from Ward to Nicole and back again, clearly in a state of shock at seeing them together.

Verette soon became aware of Emma's eyes following him as he moved around the veranda. He served her wine and water and winked so no one noticed.

Her breasts, he saw with satisfaction, quickened in their rise and fall. He said nothing but lingered by the doorway, out of sight of Ward and Mr Buchanan, where Emma could see him.

He lounged against a chair back, his breeches stretched tight across his thighs. Emma's eyes were drawn towards him. She blinked and looked again.

Yes, he smiled to himself, his plan would work.

He paid special attention to Emma when he served supper. The others were too preoccupied with their own affairs to notice. Mr Buchanan soldiered on through several glasses of wine to convince Ward about his scheme. Nicole attempted to draw Jonathan into conversation but he sat mute and embarrassed.

'I see what you're doin',' said Fidou when she cornered Verette as he returned to the kitchen. 'You makin' sweet eyes at Emma.'

He laughed. 'Save a space for me on your pallet, girl,' he said. 'Ain't no white lady with your talent for pleasurin'.'

Ranavola erupted with a shriek of delight. Fidou threw a plate at him as he darted out of the cabin to continue his plan of attack.

It seemed ages after supper before Emma and Nicole declared they were tired and would withdraw to leave the men on the veranda. Fidou escorted them upstairs to their rooms.

Ward was to share Jonathan's chamber in the opposite wing. Verette served the men more drinks, noting that Ward was still sober. Jonathan was flushed yet his glass of wine was untouched.

Jealousy, thought Verette, diagnosing Jonathan's condition with the eyes of an expert. He was pleased. If Jonathan saw he had a rival for Nicole's affections, he might stir himself to action.

'I'll do that,' he told Basin when he saw the slave was about to carry flasks of water upstairs to place in the guest chambers. 'You've climbed too many stairs tonight.'

The old man yielded his tray but regarded Verette suspiciously. 'You ain't white so don't play hanky-panky in Mas Buchanan's house,' he warned.

'I helpin' you!' Verette pretended to be shocked. He climbed the stairs two at a time. Fidou was on the landing. He gave her a flask.

'For Nicole,' he whispered, his eyes rolling with meaning. 'I'll be down soon.'

He waited until Fidou entered Nicole's room, then he knocked softly on the door to Emma's chamber.

'Come in,' she called.

He opened the door slowly, giving her time to see it was him, not Fidou. *This was the test.* If Emma took the flask and dismissed him, he would have to try another tactic.

'Water, Miss Emma?' he asked, noting the flush that stole over her cheeks as he extended the tray.

'Thank you.' She rose from the bed, where she had sat to remove her shoes. She crossed the floor in her stockings. She was an inch shorter than him. Her perfume of verbena and lime, a smell he associated with white ladies when mingled with their natural odour of pickles, wafted over him.

He stepped inside the room, closed the door and waited.

SIXTEEN

'You are very kind.' Emma took the flask from Verette's hand, her fingers touching his. She giggled, slightly hysterical about the closed door and his reluctance to go.

The two glasses of wine she drank at supper had made her light-headed.

Her body surged with passion as Verette's eyes seemed to undress her. She fought back the desire to hug him.

'You may go,' she said, clasping the flask to her bosom. Its neck lay between her breasts. She fondled it nervously.

He was startled by her command. He arched his eyebrow and smiled at her suggestively.

Emma gripped the flask. She had often imagined a moment like this in the lustful dreams that bedevilled her sleep. She edged back towards the bed.

'I come later,' he said, reaching out his hand and touching her breast. He caressed it and she closed her eyes, longing for him.

Suddenly he stopped. She opened her eyes; he was gone.

In a daze she placed the flask of water on the bedside table. She moved across the room slowly, shedding her clothes and letting them fall carelessly to the floor until she was naked. She touched her nipple where his fingers had touched. A wave of desire swelled in her bosom. She fell on the bed with a moan.

Emma's lust for womanhood consumed her waking thoughts as well as filling her fantasies when she slept. She desired above all else to know a man, to feel his secret strength inside her and to achieve fulfilment through him. It was a hunger that grew, over the years, assuaged occasionally by frantic coupling with Fidou.

Fidou's dexterity with her fingers both delighted and frustrated her. She thrilled to the waves of passion the girl's touch set off, yet the chasm of yearning only deepened after each encounter.

With the onset of the season, Emma had looked forward to meeting men who would relieve her of that feeling. To her dismay her desire increased as she realized it would never be satisfied.

She was aware that an unmarried woman who wanted a man in that way was a scandal. If she gave into her desire she would be the gossip of society. Worse, she would never find a good husband as men demanded that their brides be virgin. In a small society like Port Louis there was no way she could satisfy her craving without ruining her reputation, her prospects and her mother's good name.

Eventually Emma decided that there were two options open to her: either to have a husband or a lover no one would know about. The major she met at one of the season's balls was viewed by her as a possible husband.

She was patient with him, understanding his reluctance to proceed beyond a gentle kiss behind the bougainvillea bushes in her mother's garden. In the end her craving forced her to reveal her willingness to go further. The major took fright and stopped calling.

She was on edge for days in case he gossiped to the officers in his mess. Fortunately he was a gentleman and she emerged unsallied from the affair. It taught her the necessity for discretion. She concealed her passion, consoling herself with Fidou's firm caresses instead.

No one, not even the other girls, suspected what she was doing with Fidou. There was nothing more natural than for a slave to move freely in and out of her room. Slaves were invisible to whites; their presence was so familiar that they performed their duties unnoticed. It gave Emma an idea.

If she was to have a lover no one would know about, a slave was the only choice. Verette was a godsend. He was not a slave, yet he was accepted in her mother's household without comment. His dark good looks, cheerful manner and availability added to his appeal.

She approached him with extreme caution. Although it was a planter tradition inherited from the French for white men to have coloured mistresses, she had never heard of a white lady having a black lover. That did not deter her, only made Verette seem ideal since no one could possibly suspect. To her relief he responded eagerly to her initiative.

Her flirting increased gradually and he showed no alarm; in fact he seemed to encourage her. He postured enticingly when he knew she was watching and blew her silly romantic kisses across the veranda when no one else could see.

Emma nearly revealed her interest in him with her outburst of jealousy when she saw him on top of Nicole on the night of the fire. The chaos of that night saved her from suspicion.

At the thought of him she rolled over onto her back on the bed and hugged herself, squeezing her breasts. She had not seen Verette for weeks although he was often in her mind. The slaves at the Tamarind plantation were hulking, gormless brutes. It thrilled her to see their black skins glistening with sweat and the size of their near-naked bodies, and she was in awe of them.

She recognized she was becoming desperate for Verette. Fidou was inadequate to satisfy her demands and Nicole – proud, prissy Nicole – was inviolable. So when Ward invited Nicole to visit Port Louis with him, she insisted on coming too. Her long wait for an opportunity to be alone with Verette was at last coming to an end.

She lay with her legs apart and ran her hand gently up the inside of her thigh. She pressed her fingers against the moistness of her flesh as she thought of him. She hoped he would be tender but with a brutality she would remember for ever.

Her fingers slipped inside and she squirmed as she imagined his hardness forcing into her, bringing her to the peak of love-making. Then she would be, yes, a woman.

She stopped in time and removed her hand, gasping at the surging and quivering of her body. She panted. A single candle burned in the room behind a glass shade. She concentrated on the flame until the passion subsided. Only a few more minutes to wait, she told herself. The reality made her sit up in the bed and stare at the door.

How would she receive him? Naked like a slave wench or in a demure night-dress? Reclining in the bed or posed alluringly in a chair? At the window?

She wanted to urinate. She clambered off the bed and reached under it for the chamber-pot. She pulled it out and squatted over it, sighing with relief.

The door opened. She raised her eyes in dismay as Verette sneaked in and shut the door behind him. She tried to stand but the flow would not stop. The only sound was the splashing of the stream of urine into the porcelain pot.

He was feasting his eyes on her, leering sardonically. Suddenly the room was in darkness and she was able to finish. He had snuffed out the candle, a gesture which showed her how considerate he was. She rose to her feet and carefully pushed the pot out of the way under the bed. She clasped the carved wooden bedpost to steady herself.

'Why didn't you knock?' she demanded, realizing too late that they were not the romantic words she had planned to use to greet him.

'Should I wake everybody?' he asked mockingly.

In her single glimpse of him before he had doused the candle, she saw he was bare chested like a field slave and wore only his breeches. His colour was a burnished gold and his chest had whorls of downy hair spreading between his nipples. His body was not as heavy and muscular as the negroes she loved to watch cutting the sugar cane at Tamarind. He was slender and youthful.

His hand placed without warning on her hip made her jump. 'Can you see in the dark?' she gasped.

'Like a cat,' he said, pulling her towards him.

She released the bedpost and wrapped her arms around his waist. Her lips tingled and she waited expectantly for his kiss. Instead she felt his fingers caressing the side of her thigh. She quivered with longing.

'Kiss me,' she breathed.

His lips brushed against her throat. She pulled away, put her hands on his cheeks and held him while she pressed her mouth against his. She parted her lips and strained to feel his tongue driving inside her. He moved away.

'Where are you?' she asked in panic. There was a creak from the boards of the bed. She fumbled in the darkness, desperate to find where he was lying.

'I can't see you,' she said, her body aching to be close to his.

She touched his leg, running her hand up to his knee. He was still wearing his breeches. She hastened to lie down on the bed beside him. In the darkness, with the shutters closed, it was impossible to see him. By touch she realized that he was stretched out with his head resting on her pillow. He seemed to be offering his body to her to see what she would do.

This was not the fantasy of her dreams; she expected him to make love to her. Yet her eagernesss and curiosity drove her on. She massaged his chest gently, letting her hand slip farther and farther down his torso, touching first his navel and then the buckle of his belt. In circular motions she descended lower until she was rubbing her palm over his crotch, feeling him rising to meet her under the fabric of his breeches.

'Verette,' she said huskily, flinging herself on top of him and kissing his face. An urgency swept through her. She ached for him to take her in his arms and crush her underneath him. He twisted his head away.

'Verette,' she whispered again, hunting his ear with her lips. 'I'm yours. I want you, Verette, so much.' She guided his hand down her thigh.

'Here!' She thrust herself on him, wishing he would stop teasing her and do what he came to do.

His hand hung limply between her legs. She rolled her hips and squeezed her thighs together, trying to trap him. Wave after wave of desire gushed through her.

His fingers moved and she trembled, poised to respond to the slightest touch. Suddenly he chuckled, pulled his hand away and gripped her by her shoulders.

'What's wrong?' she gasped, her ardour sinking at the abrupt change in his manner.

'Nothing.' He sounded casual.

Even in the dark she felt his eyes were on her, studying her face. 'I'm not like other women,' she said, trying to guess his doubts. 'I really do want you. I always have. Please, Verette, don't you want me too?'

His silence worried her. His hands still held her by her shoulders. She shuddered. His finger reached up and softly traced a line down her cheek, under her chin and down the divide between her breasts. Its pressure increased as it traversed her taut stomach and came to rest between her legs. The finger was stiff and taunted her.

'Please,' she gasped again, on the verge of distraction.

'I've been thinking,' he said, pulling his hand away and releasing her.

She reached for him but he had rolled to the side of the bed. She floundered until her hands made contact with his chest. 'Yes, yes,' she said eagerly. 'What?'

'I would treat you like a lady, buy you jewels and dresses, be a real man to you.'

'You shall,' she said breathlessly.

'I need money to do that.'

She laid her head on his chest, placing her hand over his crotch, stroking him adoringly. She would convince him she wanted him as he was, no matter that he was a penniless black Creole.

'That's not important,' she said softly.

He moved away with a jerk and she fell back to the mattress. 'It is to me,' he said. 'If I had my own business, I could be worthy of you.'

'You are worthy of me, Verette. I want you now, as you are. I don't care if you have nothing.'

'I do.' He was sitting on the edge of the bed. 'I'm ambitious, Emma. If you help me I could do so much.'

'Help you?' She reached for him again. He caught her hand and squeezed it.

'Yes,' he said, raising it to his lips and kissing it.

'How?' The brush of his lips on her fingers set her quaking again. *If only he would seize her, crush her, take her …*

'Ten thousand dollars should do it. There's a cargo of rice coming from India. I can buy it at less than cost, double the money and return your stake within a month.' He kissed the inside of her wrist, gliding his lips up her arm to the soft flesh on the underside of her elbow. He drew in the flesh and kissed her noisily.

She held her breath, reluctant to speak in case he stopped. His locks were brushing against her bosom. She thrust her breasts at him, hurting for him to caress her there with his mouth.

'Well,' he said sharply, 'can you get it?'

She was alone on the mattress. He was standing beside the bed. 'I ...' she sighed deeply, the pain of frustration throbbed in her head.

'Ten thousand,' he repeated.

'I don't know.' She found it difficult to think.

'I'll come, I'll do what you want ...' he said, walking away so softly she only realized he had gone when his voice uttered from the doorway, ' ... when you have the money.'

The creak of the bed boards roused Jonathan. He was drifting into sleep, his mind filled with a vision of Nicole sitting on the veranda asking questions he was too tongue-tied to answer. He raised his head from his pillow and listened anxiously.

He and Ward had climbed the stairs together to the chamber. He had been embarrassed about sharing his bed with Ward but since he was a guest too, he could not decline.

Ward had removed his boots and his shirt and flung himself on top of the bed with a grunt. Jonathan undressed carefully, laying out his clothes neatly on a chair for Verette to collect in the morning. He put on his night-shirt before removing his trousers.

Ward was snoring softly by the time he was ready for bed. He eased himself under the covers, fearful of disturbing him. It took him ages to compose his mind for sleep as he contemplated the unexpected arrival of Nicole with Ward.

She was emphatic that Ward came as her escort and that the sole purpose of her visit was to see him. The innocence of her smile when she spoke made him feel guilty at doubting her. Yet he could not help wondering what was the connection between her and Ward.

He listened in the darkness. Ward's snoring had ceased. There was a gentle release of pressure on the coconut fibre mattress and the bed board creaked again. He stared into the gloom.

The window shutters had been opened at Ward's

insistence and he could make out the dim shape of Ward tiptoeing across the room. He held his breath and watched as he slipped out of the door.

Jonathan was filled with foreboding. He sat up, fighting back the dread that was making him sick with worry. The crack of a floorboard resounded in the silence as Ward made his way along the passage linking one wing of the house with the other. It confirmed his fear. He clasped his head in his hands, pressing the heels of his palms into his eyes to still the tears.

Ward was going to Nicole's chamber. He undoubtedly intended to fulfill the prophecy he had made at the Turf Club ball.

A rage replaced the sickening despair that trembled in Jonathan's breast. He thrust back the covers and leaped from the bed. It was scandalous of Ward to take advantage of a young lady in the house of his own father-in-law.

He would not allow it. Nicole was a trusting, innocent girl. He knew he was no match for Ward's superior strength but he would do everything in his power to stop Nicole from being violated.

His rage made him blind. He staggered in the darkness to the door and pulled it open. A lantern burned in the passage, throwing grim shadows along its length to the other side of the house, where another burned. He began to stride angrily down the corridor until caution suggested he should tread more lightly. If the slaves were aroused and spread word of this scandal, poor Nicole's reputation would never recover.

He slowed in his progress and peered into the gloom, wondering which of the doors was Nicole's. He listened carefully; there was no sound except from the rumbling of William Buchanan's drunken snores from the master bedroom.

Jonathan's rage simmered and bubbled with doubt. What if Nicole was waiting for Ward to visit her. Was she already his mistress?

The possibility made his legs weak. That such innocence should be tainted by the skilled lechery of a slave-trader was heinous. What defence did Nicole have against Ward's glib tongue and smooth charm?

'By God!' Jonathan murmured. 'I won't have it!'

He seized the handle of the door nearest him and pushed it open. The room was in darkness and he stopped on the threshold, his nose twitching to scent out what his eyes could not see. There was the silence of fear in the room, as though its occupants were holding their breath. He sniffed. His nostrils took in the aroma that was uniquely Nicole.

He listened, waiting for the tell-tale sounds that would tell him Ward was in the room with her. He muttered under his breath at his stupidity in not carrying a lantern so he could see who was in the room.

'Who's there?' a voice demanded timidly.

'Nicole!' he cried out. 'I'll save you!'

'Jonathan?'

There was a rustle of skirts in the room and he felt her hand gently touch his arm. He grasped it and held it firmly. 'Are you all right?' he said hoarsely.

'Of course I am. What about you? Are you sleep walking?'

'No, no.' He began to feel hot. 'I thought Ward was here.'

'And you came to rescue me?' Her laughter made him feel ashamed. He drew back to the passageway.

'No,' she said soothingly. 'Stay a while. I wasn't asleep.'

'Stay?' He was astonished.

'Yes. I want to talk to you. In private.'

'What will people think?'

'Who's to know?'

He paused. His eyes were becoming accustomed to the dim glow thrown by the lantern at the end of the passage. He saw Nicole was in her night-dress, a full-skirted garment that covered her from neck to toe. Her hair was loose, the ringlets falling around her shoulders. They bounced as she moved away from him to open the shutters of the window.

The moon's soft light enhanced the glow in the room until he could see her clearly silhouetted against the darkness. He left the door open and moved towards her in a daze.

'Sit there,' she said, halting him at the chair beside the bed. He slumped into it gratefully, dismayed by the pulsating desire that had propelled him to her.

'Ward?' he said in confusion. 'He'll see us together.'

'I hope he does.' She smiled. 'It was sweet of you to think of me in peril from him.'

'Where is he?'

'That's none of my business,' she said scornfully. 'Probably with Fidou.'

Gradually it dawned on him how foolish he was. He began to get to his feet, holding his hands in front of him to hide his erection under his night-shirt.

'No, sit, Jonathan. I want you to tell me about yourself. What are you going to do now the governor's dismissed you?'

He considered the question, unable to answer. She was waiting patiently. The silence, and the dim light, reassured him. He felt at ease with her despite his condition. He pretended he accepted the situation as naturally as she did.

Gradually he found himself telling her his story, from the bluff he used on Mr Farquhar to gain permission to stay in the colony to the rumours Verette started to make people believe he had prospects of wealth so they would not spurn him. The only thing he kept back was the Black River affair, which had changed his life.

'What do you *want* to do?' she asked.

He dared not say he wanted to throw her on the bed and make love to her. Instead he mumbled about wanting to become a merchant and his lack of finance to do so. Finally, overawed by her innocence, he blurted out his respect and regard for her.

'Jonathan!' she said brightly, drawing his hands into hers and pulling him to his feet. 'There must be a way to get the capital. I'll see how I can help.'

He had been speaking for over an hour. Her touch caused him to leap with desire. He tensed, standing rigid, pleading with his eyes for her to release him.

Innocently she raised her face to his and kissed him on his cheek. 'Good night, Jonathan,' she said, leading him to the door. 'Go to your room. I'll think of what's to be done.'

He gasped when he reached the brightness of the passage, praying she would not look down. He raised his fingers to his cheek, touching the place where her lips had touched. He stared at the door as it closed.

A blow struck him between his shoulder blades. He jumped with fright at being caught coming from her room. He twisted in vain to escape the arm that circled around his neck, trapping him in a tight embrace.

'Jonathan!' a voice chuckled. It was Verette, steering him along the corridor back to his room. 'Now I see you're a man at last!'

SEVENTEEN

Ward's business in Port Louis was completed the next day and Nicole and Emma were obliged to return with him to Tamarind. Before she left town, Nicole tried to speak with Jonathan but he avoided her. Knowing his moods, his pride and his shyness, she understood. It made her determined to find a way to help him succeed.

She thought of him often after her return to Tamarind. There was nothing else to do. Emma was strangely withdrawn, her usual vivacity dulled by the heat. Winter was over and the days in the country were dauntingly hot when there was no breeze to liven them up.

She would like to have discussed Jonathan's plight with someone. She had never felt close to Louise and doubted that she would understand. Emma, in the right mood, could have been a good listener but she was so preoccupied with problems of her own, Nicole deemed it best not to try. That left Fidou. Unfortunately the slave was insufferable since she had been bedded by Ward at Mr Buchanan's house and so Nicole was deliberately cool towards her.

She sat for hours in the shade of Mr and Mrs Mango's great boughs, listening to the stream and gazing out over the cleared fields to the surf surging on the beach of Tamarind Bay below. Lines of slaves trudged across the cane stubble, hoeing it in the hot sun while Mr Moult fussed behind them with his whip. She watched the slaves without seeing them, wondering what she could do for Jonathan.

At times she asked herself why she cared. He was like a big baby. He was so lost in Port Louis. He was running up bills he could not pay for the sake of appearances. His dream of establishing himself in commerce was futile; he lacked the capital. Eventually he was bound to return to England. She would miss him.

She sat up and stared at the sea. *Yes, she would miss him.* It would mean the system – Governor Farquhar and his Prince Regent clique – had won. Jonathan was the only honest man in that set; the rest were profiteering at the expense of the Creoles.

When Nicole thought of the Creoles, she thought of her mother. She had been abused in the same way as Jonathan by the island's colonizers, both French and English. It made her livid to think about it.

She wondered what her mother would have done. The answer made her feel even hotter than the sun blazing down on the cane fields. Belle Genave's way to raise money was simple – with her body. Nicole rocked backwards and forwards in the grass, her hands clamped around her knees. Her mother had the courage; would she?

Her heart raced. The idea was so bold, it thrilled her. Ward was the wealthiest man in the island. He liked her. The pretence of friendship, like brother and sister, was only a ploy to gain her confidence. Sooner or later, she knew, he would try to seduce her. Up to then she had dreaded the moment but if she could turn it to her advantage?

She gasped again, stood up, swung around with excitement and walked towards the stream. She kneeled down beside it and cupped water in her hands. She splashed it over her face to cool her down. Her ringlets stuck to her cheeks and she brushed them aside. She smiled to herself at her unladylike behaviour. It was her unladylike thoughts that were more ominous.

Ward was an attractive man. What frightened her was his experience. What would he think of her? Would she be good enough for him?

She tried to remember her mother, the little comments she muttered about her lovers. She pitied some, despised others. She never felt inferior to them; that was her strength. *A man is a baby*, she did say. *Suckle him and he's yours*.

Nicole paused as the sun's rays shone on her through the trees beside the stream. The English would say that what she was thinking was a sin, yet they all sinned if it was. For Creoles there was nothing sinful about making love with an attractive man, even if he was married.

'Oh!' exclaimed Emma sulkily, bursting through the foliage into the glade. 'I didn't know you were here.'

'It's so hot today,' Nicole answered to cover her own confusion. 'I was bathing my face.'

'That's why you look so red!' Emma pouted. 'Do Creoles feel the heat too?'

Nicole kept her peace but Emma's remark was not meant to insult her for she turned around and said, 'Shall I tell you a secret?'

'If you like.' Nicole was surprised by her overture of friendship.

'If you look down the stream,' Emma said, 'just between the bamboo that's growing by the bend, guess what you can see.'

She shook her head, puzzled by the excitement in Emma's eyes.

'Sometimes,' she said, lowering her voice, 'the negroes bathe there! I've seen them slip off their loincloths and stand up quite naked splashing water over themselves.'

Nicole frowned at this odd secret but pretended to be impressed. 'Aren't you scared they'll see you?'

'Why should I be?' Emma sniffed. 'There's one boy, he

has the most beautiful body. He's blacker than the others and he seems more refined. He comes down here very often. I think he steals away from his gang when Mr Moult isn't watching.'

'Emma,' said Nicole anxiously. 'He is a field-hand. Why are you interested in him?'

'I'm not *interested* in him, just curious.' She put her head on one side and smiled dreamily. 'A field slave isn't pretentious, not ambitious. He'd do as he's told, don't you think?'

'I suppose so.'

'His name is Brutus. Isn't that beautiful?'

'How do you know?'

'I asked Mr Moult.'

'You didn't!' Nicole was appalled. It was one thing to admire a slave's physique in a general way. To express an interest in a particular one would provoke concern.

'He was most obliging. He told me Brutus is a young buck he bought from Ward. He likes talking about his slaves, most men do.' She paused, then added scornfully, 'That's all they know about. You'll keep my secret, won't you?'

'Yes.' Nicole was puzzled. 'Have you spoken to him?'

'I've said hello.'

'What did he do?'

'He was so frightened, poor thing, he just ran away. Makes a change from an uppity slave like Verette.'

'Verette's not a slave.'

'He should be! He's too impudent.'

'I thought you liked him. You used to speak about him such a lot.'

'Well, I don't now!' Emma looked as though she was about to say more and then she changed her mind. 'I like a man to be respectful.' She gazed down the stream. 'I'm sure Brutus would be perfect.'

Ward was a frequent visitor to the Tamarind plantation. He explained to Nicole that it was because of the business he and Mr Moult were doing together. He held a mortgage on Mr Moult's sugar crop in exchange for slaves he had sold him. Nicole listened keenly to all he told her when they sat together on the piazza in front of the Tamarind house.

Usually they were joined by Emma and Louise. Visitors were rare and they were all eager to gossip. Ward obliged, although his knowledge of the latest scandal was too sparse for Emma's liking. After one of his visits she confessed to Nicole that she did not care for Ward at all.

'He's a bumpkin,' she said. 'He may be rich but he's like all the other slave-holders. Only knows about niggers and cane. No conversation.'

'He's very kind to me.'

'That's only because he wants to get under your skirt.'

'Emma!' Nicole flushed. 'He's always the perfect gentleman.'

'Then why does he come here so often? Do you think it's to see Brutus and the other slaves he sold to Mr Moult?'

'He says he comes on business.'

'You're the only business he wants to negotiate here.'

'I'm sure you're mistaken.' Nicole wondered if she was. It was important for her plan that what Emma said should be true.

She paid special attention to Ward's remarks when he visited, seeking an opportunity to let him know she was keen on him. It was difficult to say anything when Emma was present. It was due to Emma's fascination with Brutus, an obsession Nicole disapproved of, that her chance finally came.

Late that afternoon, when Ward had finished taking tea with Mrs Moult and was preparing to leave, Emma suddenly rose from her chair and asked to be excused. Nicole watched her hurry off in the direction of the stream. It was nearly sunset and the slaves were drifting away from the fields after their day's work. She guessed Emma was going to look for Brutus.

Mrs Moult took her leave and was followed into the house by Louise, leaving Nicole and Ward alone. Nicole seized the opportunity to broach the idea she had been thinking of for days.

'Ward,' she began coyly, 'may I ask you an impertinent question?'

'You may ask if you dare.' His eyes glimmered with amusement. 'Providing I'm not obliged to answer.'

'It's about money,' she said, smiling her sweetest. 'Everyone says you are the wealthiest man in the colony. Are you really?'

'Perhaps,' he answered, glancing at her warily.

She realized she would have to be cunning. 'I was curious,' she said. 'Mr Moult owes you money and Emma says you have mortgages on other estates too. Is that what you like to do, loan people money?'

He laughed and rose from his chair. 'At high interest rates, of course! Why do you ask?' He was holding out his hand to help her up.

She took it immediately, smiling and tossing her head so her ringlets swirled. 'It's very immoral, isn't it?'

She clung to his arm as he walked to the edge of the piazza. The path to Black River passed through the Tamarind plantation. There was no proper road so only a sure-footed horse or an energetic walker like Ward could use it. Most visitors to the coastal plantations travelled by schooner, anchoring in the bays that indented the coast.

'Immoral?' He chuckled. 'Is it your English schooling that gives you that strange notion?'

'I hear you demand usurious rates of interest and ruinous security. *That's* immoral.'

'Hey,' he said, breaking his hold on her and stepping away in mock alarm. 'You girls discuss the strangest matters. Since when have you been so interested in my business affairs?'

'I'm sorry for offending you. I said it was impertinent.' She moved to his side coquettishly so he would take her arm again.

'It's a beautiful sunset, isn't it?' She touched his elbow then slipped her hand under it.

He frowned, confused by her change of conversation.

Her ruse worked for he glanced out to sea, where the sun was poised like a blazing cannon-ball to drop beneath the waves. She tightened her grip on his arm.

'It's very romantic.'

'Yes,' he drawled.

She flushed at her boldness because he obviously understood what she implied. 'I'd like to walk some of the way with you,' she said. 'It gets boring here alone with Emma and Louise.'

'You're not afraid of the slaves?'

'Why should I be?'

'They could attack you.'

'Surely not.'

'If you tease them.'

'Tease? I never speak to them.'

'They are close to animals, Nicole. Worse than that, they are men. When a man is roused by a woman, he is liable to do violent things.'

She smiled to herself. 'Things he'll regret?'

'The woman regrets if she loses her virtue.'

'Then the man must pay.'

'Yes ...' He was thoughtful as they walked side by side in silence. The sound of birds arguing as they flew homewards and the shouts of slaves from the quarters by the river did not disrupt Nicole's concentration. She was desperate that he should understand what she was hinting at.

'I had a negro who was prime,' he said with a sigh. 'A woman teased him until he no longer knew right from wrong. I caught him lying with her.'

'What did you do?'

'I gelded him.'

Nicole caught her breath until she realized Ward was warning her about Emma and the slave she fancied, not referring to herself and him. She tried again.

'If I were a man, and a woman loved me very much, I'd risk everything for that love.'

'Ah, Nicole,' he said, embracing her briefly. 'It's because you're a woman you think that way. A man won't risk losing his manhood, however much he cares for a woman.'

'Who would geld a *free* man?'

He released her with a laugh. 'Why, only the woman herself!'

Nicole paused and looked around her in confusion, feeling he had got the better of her.

The path was rising up the hillside, away from the cane fields and into the trees of the forest that surrounded the Tamarind plantation. The sun had set while they were speaking. The branches of the trees were entwined overhead, shutting out the daylight and leaving only a subdued haze in the grove.

There was a fallen tree by the side of the path. Pretending she was weary with the climb, she sat down on it, careful to arrange her skirt so it revealed a glimpse of her ankle. She was wearing a bonnet tied under her chin with a pink ribbon. She released it, removed the bonnet and shook out her ringlets.

'That's better,' she said with a smile. 'Won't you sit beside me for a few minutes?'

'It will be dark soon. You shouldn't delay.'

'I know my way to the house.' She stared up at him. 'I know a lot of things.'

He sighed and flung himself rudely down at her side. His brows were furrowed and an unpleasant gleam entered his eye. 'Why are you doing this?' he demanded.

She looked at him archly. 'What?'

Suddenly his hands were on her, squeezing her shoulders roughly as he pulled her towards him. He kissed her with a violence that made her eyes water with pain, bruising her lips. He forced her mouth against his, keeping his hand at the back of her neck when she tried to wrench away.

She tasted blood as her lips smashed against his. She beat her fists against his chest. His strength overwhelmed her.

As suddenly as it began, she was released. She stared at him, gasping for breath. Blood trickled into her mouth and she swallowed quickly, hoping he would not notice. She blinked back her tears.

'Well?' he demanded without any sign of warmth in his voice. 'Is that what you want?' He glared at her.

'Ward,' she whispered, desperate to collect her wits. 'Would you do me a favour?'

'Ah,' he said, 'now I see what a bitch you are.'

The contempt in his voice shocked her. She blushed. 'I'm not,' she said. 'It's for a friend.'

'What is?'

'A loan.' She was relieved that she had managed to ask at last. She looked at him expectantly.

His eyes were hard and his lips curled in a sneer. The young man she found so attractive only minutes before, when they were flirting blithely on the piazza, was unrecognizable in this harsh-featured bully who glared at her. She drew back as his hand reached for her bodice.

'Nicole!' His voice grated on her ears with the pain of a whip slashing into slave flesh. His fingers caught in the gap between the fasteners of her high-neck dress. He tugged at the corsage, ripping it apart.

'No,' she said, forcing herself to move towards him. 'Not like that, Ward.' She put up her hand to stroke his face.

He raised his fist and knocked her hand aside. His eyes flared with anger.

She smiled, praying that if she could hide her fear, she could subdue him. 'You don't have to fight me,' she said. 'I want it too.'

'Shut up!' He leaped to his feet and stood arrogantly in front of her. Her eyes were level with the bulge in his breeches. She lowered her gaze to the ground.

'You can stand up,' he said, 'and walk down the path back to the house. I shall never see you again!'

'No!' she cried out before she could stop herself.

'By the devil, Nicole! Do you know what you're doing?'

'Yes.' She bit her lip to keep up her courage.

'Very well!' He punched his fist into his palm decisively. 'Take off your dress!'

She glanced up at him, unable to speak. His hair flopped forward on his brow and he was sweating. It reminded her of Jonathan. She was doing this for *him*.

'If you like,' she said, appearing composed despite the terror that gripped her. Her hands were shaking as she began to unfasten her bodice. She took a deep breath and managed to control the trembling.

'Come on, come on!' he said, slapping his hand against his thigh. He might have been speaking to a slave wench; his voice was devoid of feeling.

The dress was unfastened and she stepped out of it. She picked it up and looked around for somewhere to hang it, using the normal gestures of the dressing-room to keep her fear under control. He snatched it from her hands and flung it to the ground.

'Petticoat, chemise, the rest!' he barked, waving at her impatiently. 'I inspect my wenches before I mount them. White women wear too many damn clothes.'

She had never imagined she would have to stand naked in front of him. In the darkness of the forest glade, with his arm around her and her skirt raised, she was prepared to suffer for Jonathan's sake. Now her scheme had become more than that; he was crucifying her. *So be it.*

She stood naked before him, her eyes lowered.

'Hah!' he said derisively. 'So that's what you're so proud of. I've seen better dugs on a buck nigger. Your conny's flat and your hips too narrow. Couldn't get a whelp out of you 'less I prize it out with a paddle.'

Although she realized that he was deliberately humiliating her for his own reasons, she blushed, unable to control the signs that revealed her weakness. It made her angry. She raised her head to challenge him.

'Try me!' she said with a glare of scorn.

His sneer faltered. 'By the devil, I will!' He sat down on the tree trunk to remove his boots.

As she stood over him and watched him frantically undressing, she lost her fear. She was exhilarated by the sense of power that surged through her. Here was a man, the wealthiest on the island, grovelling at her feet to pull down his breeches and enter her. It was he who was humiliated, not her.

She backed away as he walked towards her. He pulled off

his shirt and was as naked as she was. His penis pulsed out in front of him at a crooked angle. It was the first time she had seen one and she glanced at it with curiosity.

'Here's a rod!' he said, clasping it and thrusting it at her. 'You'll remember this, wench!'

He punched her in the chest, making her lose her balance. As she fell to the ground she realized she had become part of his fantasy. He was treating her like a slave to cover the reality of what he was doing. The knowledge gave her strength.

She lay with her legs open, waiting for him. He climbed on her, a snarl of scorn escaping from his lips. He spread her roughly with his fingers and the pain struck her. She bit her lip to stop crying out, longing for him to kiss her, to show some affection.

She tried to pretend that she was the slave wench he wanted her to be. She raised her hips, linking her ankles together behind his buttocks. But when he forced himself into her, she screamed. She couldn't help it.

The scream calmed his rage. Her eyes were closed tightly as she felt the tremor of his body subside. His ruthless lunging became a long tender thrust. She surrendered herself to the agony of his penetration.

There was no love; she felt no joy, no climax. After a few minutes he shuddered, turned his head so his unshaved cheek bruised her breasts, and kicked up his heels. Then he was still.

She opened her eyes and gazed up at the trees. The sky was darkening. She felt the dampness of the grass and smelled the crushed vegetation. She gasped at the renewed pain when he pulled away viciously. She looked up at him.

He was staring at her in horror. His thighs were smeared with her blood.

She smiled, knowing she had trapped him. 'About that loan,' she panted. 'You'll give it to me?'

The horror left his eyes and he laughed evilly. He stood up and squatted over her with his legs apart. He pulled at his penis. A jet of urine shot out and splashed onto her stomach, trickling down to mingle with the blood at her crotch.

She screamed and rolled over to escape. He continued to shower her shoulders and buttocks with urine.

When he finished, he picked up his breeches and fished in his pockets. 'Here,' he said, pulling out a handful of coins and tossing them at her. 'Four dollars was all your mother ever charged.'

EIGHTEEN

From the window of her chamber, which gave a view of the lantern-lit courtyard in front of the Black River mansion and, in the day time, of the slaves toiling in the fields of sugar-cane that rolled down to the sea, Gina espied Ward. His unusual gait as he emerged from the darkness of the path through the forest from Tamarind attracted her attention. He was not swaggering nor striding out with his customary bounce. He was shambling, like a man defeated.

'Look at the master,' said Gina, her voice edged with curiosity as well as contempt.

Clovis, who was sitting in a chair in the corner of the room winding a skein of wool into a ball, rose quickly to his feet. He peered over Gina's shoulder, his nearness comforting her, as it always did.

'He seems subdued tonight.'

Clovis nodded his agreement, his eyes narrowing with hatred.

'Go downstairs,' Gina said. 'Watch him for a while and tell me what he does.' She sensed Clovis leave her and heard his bare feet pad softly across the floor. He could merge into the night so that even Ward, who had trained himself to be alert and sniff out any slave who lurked in the darkness, would not know he was there. Clovis was Gina's eyes; he informed her of everything Ward did while she remained alone in her chamber pretending indifference.

She sighed as she saw her husband pull himself wearily

onto the veranda and disappear from view. Despite the scorn with which she treated him when they were together, and his own cavalier attitude towards her, she retained an intense interest in him. The change in his mood indicated by his erratic progress across the courtyard intrigued her.

Of course she hated Ward. There was no alternative after what he had done to Clovis, and the ridicule to which he had exposed her. It had taken her two seasons to be accepted, and then only grudgingly because of Ward's wealth, back into society. The colony's gossips concocted gruesome tales about her, crediting her with an entire stable of slave lovers. In reality, since the night Ward caught her with Clovis, she had none.

But for the comfort and companionship of Clovis, she would have gone mad. After Ward castrated the boy, she and Ward's mother nursed him back to life, helped by the unguents of the slaves, and Ellen's prowess as an obeah woman. He had taken a long time to respond. She imagined that even now he, who was once so proud of his virility, was racked by shame at his condition.

She had taken him into her chamber and he lived with her, sharing her bed and her life. Ward said nothing. It was part of his punishment. He let her have Clovis knowing he was no longer a man. What he did not know, but Gina did, was that Clovis, when he was ready, would kill him.

Gina nurtured his hatred of Ward, through the slave seeking the vengeance she wanted for herself. When they lay together at night and he fumbled with his fingers to stir in her the excitement his limp body was unable to achieve, she whispered Ward's name in his ear, reminding him constantly who had robbed him of his manhood.

Gina spent long evenings in her chamber plotting vengeance. She had no intention of leaving Ward. To release him would be too kind. She was prepared to bide her time, waiting until his son, Garnet, grew to be a young man. Through him, and through Clovis, she would take her revenge.

By day, when she grew tired of the ladylike pursuits of sewing with Monique, Ward's mother, or knitting or embroidery, she would wander the plantation paths, watching the slaves. Their bodies, with muscles rippling in the sun as they cut cane or hoed the ratoons, fascinated her. The men wore breech cloths casually draped around their loins that only emphasized the contrast of their hard bodies with Clovis's neutered state.

Without a man, a real man, Gina suffered. That was Ward's intention. How she had enjoyed the Turf Club ball. She was the life and soul of the party, just as she was before her marriage when the garrison's officers queued to dance with her. She realized then, in the company of dashing young men, just how much life with Ward had embittered her.

She poured herself another rum from the decanter, added a little water and stared out into the night as she sipped it. She was accustomed to the rum's fieriness, it helped dull the ache. It would not be so bad, she thought, if she did indulge in the debaucheries that were rumoured about her. Perhaps if she were to have a liaison with someone she could cope better with her lot.

At the Turf Club ball, and at the other parties she attended during the season, she had flirted with several personable young men. None seemed, however, to have the wildness that originally attracted her to Ward. She had even considered Jonathan but found when he came to Black River with the Malagash princes that he was as lack-lustre as she remembered him. On the other hand his man Verette was clearly of different mettle.

Gina drained the rum, recalling with a shiver as it coursed through her how Verette had tantalized her during his visit. What he lacked in physique when compared with Ward's field slaves he made up in attractiveness. His face was rugged and handsome, made more alluring by his dark flashing eyes and the deep gold hue of his skin. His boldness intrigued her; like Ward, he was intimidated by no one.

She had observed him carefully during his stay on the plantation. She gave him no sign of her interest but he seemed to sense it. He was naturally a lady's man and flattered her on every occasion, making her feel particularly feminine, even vulnerable, when he stared at her from under his long lashes. Beside him Clovis seemed uncouth. She was bound to Clovis through habit. He was, as she had told Jonathan, her pet.

The door to the chamber creaked open and she turned, holding out her empty glass. Clovis took it and filled it without a word.

'Well?' she asked sharply.

Clovis shrugged. 'He sittin' 'lone on the 'randa,' he said in a voice that was so soft it was like a high-pitched whisper. It contrasted with his massive size, a constant reminder of his neuterdom.

She found the news disturbing. Rarely was Ward still for more than a moment. She returned to the window to watch, expecting him to cross the courtyard to join the wench she had seen entering his cabin earlier. Clovis brought her a chair and she sat where she had a clear view of the cabin, lit up by lanterns that burned throughout the night to convince the slaves of their master's omnipresence.

Clovis was curled up asleep at the foot of her bed when she finally left the window. Ward remained on the veranda. It puzzled her that he had not gone to his bed wench. Any change in his normal routine could be a threat to her own plans.

The next day Ward's mood was the same. He was lost in thought. He grunted when she spoke to him, instead of engaging with vigour in his customary discharge of invective at her and those slaves who riled him. He spent the day, as he had the night, slumped in his chair, his feet slung up on the veranda railing. The house slaves found his silence more intimidating than his rages. So did Gina.

When his reflective mood continued throughout the week, Gina questioned Ellen about it. Both the housekeeper and Ward's personal slave boy, Dell, were as puzzled as she was. By intuition, she recognized a new weakness in Ward. She decided to test it.

'Ward,' she challenged rudely, interrupting his meditation. 'You've failed, haven't you?' She was holding a full glass of rum in her hand, drawing courage from having something to do while she set about provoking him. Clovis, she knew, was close at hand should Ward turn violent.

'Failed?' He stared at her, the vivid green of his eyes sparking with anger at the word. 'I don't *fail*.'

'I've noticed,' she said, arranging herself comfortably in a chair beside his on the veranda, 'that you don't go calling any more at Tamarind.'

'Tamarind?' His lips tightened.

'Yes, Ward.' Gina smiled her sweetest. 'Has the Genave girl rebuffed you?'

'No, she hasn't!' His fingers gripped the wooden arm of his chair.

'I know when you're lying, Ward. You had such hopes for that little miss, didn't you? What did you tell me? That you could have her with ease?' She waited for Ward to reply. He scowled but said nothing.

'You see, I was right. Not even one of Mrs Didcott's young ladies, even if she is Creole and the daughter of a whore, wants you. That's why you're so moody, isn't it?'

The sweetness of her smile changed to malice and her eyes glinted with evil glee at the triumph she had scored over him.

Ward looked crushed. His knuckles turned white under the pressure of gripping the chair arm. His eyes stared back at her. She was momentarily surprised to see them devoid of hatred until she realized they were moist with sorrow. She was elated. It was even better than she had hoped. Ward was obviously weeping for his failure.

'Well,' she said, rising to her feet. 'I hope you feel satisfied now. What I said was true, wasn't it?'

'You can leave me,' he said, slowly and calmly. 'I will escort you to Port Louis. You can return to your father. I'm sure you'll enjoy his company, getting drunk together. Mr Rendye will no doubt be charmed to have you as a fellow guest.'

She was stunned by his reaction; it was more than she expected. It did not occur to her to wonder why he was sending her away, or for how long. 'I'll go,' she said. 'But I am still your wife, Ward Trenchard.'

'As long as it pleases me,' he said, slumping back in his chair and staring down the path in the direction of Tamarind Plantation.

Verette's buoyancy was wavering; Jonathan sensed the youth's lack of confidence in the future. For months they had been existing on credit and a dream. It was Verette's exuberance that encouraged Jonathan to continue the masquerade of being on the verge of receiving a large inheritance.

'My aunt will reply soon to my request,' Jonathan said when they sat whispering together on William Buchanan's veranda. Mr Buchanan was at his warehouse.

'You say that every day, Jonathan!' Verette drew away crossly and strode across the veranda deck.

Jonathan stared at him. Subtle changes had taken place in Verette over the months. He was still an engaging companion with a smile that won the confidence of white people, especially women. He was constantly in demand as an extra helper at veranda affairs and Jonathan was impressed by his popularity. Hiring out slaves was a common practice in Mauritius although in Verette's case he kept the hire fee for himself.

It was the frustration that lurked behind his ready smile that was a new feature of Verette's personality. The two had become very close in the months since Jonathan's fall from grace. Jonathan was attuned to Verette's moods, reflecting his temperament in his own outlook. He hoped Verette was not swapping his optimism for the gloom and despair he himself felt.

'After Nicole and Emma were here,' said Verette, halting in front of him and flinging his arms in the air in a reckless gesture, 'I expected something to happen.'

'You were mistaken. I told you Nicole and I talked in her chamber that night, nothing more.'

'Nicole?' Verette's mouth hardened in a scowl.

'Hey up, Verette!' Jonathan rose from his seat anxiously. 'What's wrong?'

Verette slipped away from his embrace. 'Not Nicole! I expected *Emma* to help us. She tricked me.'

'Why should Em –'

'Forget it, Jonathan!' He scowled again. 'There was a ship from England this morning. The mail's all been distributed.'

'I know.' Jonathan was glum. 'Nothing from Aunt Hortense.'

'People are beginning to talk. I've heard them behind your back. You should have taken George Allen's loan.'

'No! I have my principles.' It was odd that Verette's doubts were causing Jonathan to be more hopeful. 'Mr Buchanan said he's been offered a cargo of trade goods on credit. He wants me to help him with the inventory.'

'A boy could do that.'

'I must do something. Sitting in Massey's all morning won't get me anywhere.'

'It could if you wanted.'

Jonathan refused to be dismayed by Verette's attitude. 'I can't even go back to England because I owe so much to Massey's and the shopkeepers. Aunt will help!'

'When? That's all I ask, when?'

'I'll write to her again.'

Verette shook his head with exasperation. 'My luck seems to have run out, Jonathan. Usually I find someone to rescue me at the worst moments. I appear successful yet I'm really worse off than I've ever been. Living in this house, moving in fine society, a suit of clothes, shoes ... All the Creoles think I'm worth a packet. I was better off when I was a pimp on the plain.'

Jonathan was shocked. 'I'll find something. You're not going back to that way of life. It's degrading.'

'It's all I'm fit for, if I think of it,' Verette said with a rueful grin. 'Although I'm not very good at that.'

Jonathan tried to distract him by changing the subject. 'The new garrison commander looked in at Massey's this morning. General Hall. George says he's a stickler for discipline.'

Verette grunted.

'He's Mr Farquhar's age. Major General Gage John Hall. If appearances are a true indication, he'll brook no nonsense. He inspected Massey's regulars like they were foot soldiers.'

Verette's eyes flickered with interest. 'Did you speak to him?'

'None of us dared. He looked straight through me. Even Theodore Hook was silent until he'd gone, then he made some remark about there being no fun in an empty Hall.'

Jonathan frowned as he repeated Hook's rudeness, then he continued. 'They say General Hall's been sent here because of the anti-English demonstration at Plaine Magnien.'

'That was over two years ago.' Verette was scornful.

'It takes time for the British government to act. The Bonarpartist corsair, Perrot, was expelled by Governor Farquhar for leading that demonstration. He went to Britain to protest and was told he could return here.'

Verette brightened. 'The British government overruled your precious Mr Farquhar?'

'Yes.' Jonathan was thoughtful. 'Strange, isn't it?'

The sparkle returned to Verette's eyes. 'I think you should meet General Hall.'

'Whatever for? He won't sponsor me.'

'After the governor,' said Verette, tapping the side of his nose, 'the garrison commander is the most important man here. It would do you no harm to have him as your friend.'

Jonathan snorted. He was familiar with Verette's tactics and had learned to see through his scheming. 'You mean the general would be useful to *you*,' he said.

Gina alighted from the palanquin and gazed with anticipation at the house where she was raised. Her pleasure increased when she saw instead of her father sitting on the veranda, Jonathan there with Verette. The two men broke off their discussion when they saw her. The expression on Jonathan's face was a mixture of alarm and dismay.

Verette seemed delighted. He leaped off the veranda and danced down the path, beaming as if this were the happiest moment of his life. His welcome thrilled her and she let him know it with a lingering glance that swept over his handsome features and slowly traversed the length of his body.

'Madame Trenchard!' said Verette with an exaggerated flourish and a deep bow. He took her hand as though he were an English gentleman instead of a Creole mulatto and kissed it roguishly. The palanquin boys hooted with derision. His manner changed abruptly and he snarled a curse in Creole that quietened them and made Gina blush.

'Forgive me,' he said with a smile so appealing she would have forgiven him anything. 'I quite forgot you spoke Creole.' From an Englishman the remark would have been intended as an insult; from him it was a special compliment.

Verette proved himself every bit as endearing as she had imagined. She was delighted to discover her tension and quick temper dissolved through his company.

She was glad she had left Clovis at Black River and had brought no slaves to attend her. She had explained to Clovis she wanted him to stay at the plantation so he could tell her all that Ward did while she was away. Actually she was tired of him hanging around her heels like a snuffling puppy. Now the prospect of a liaison with Verette was becoming more than a fantasy as he reacted just the way she wished.

Mr Buchanan viewed her arrival at his house with less enthusiasm. 'You must have the guest chamber,' her father pronounced when he returned from the town for dinner. 'Jonathan has your old quarters and since he is likely to be here longer than you, he cannot be asked to give them up. Your stay is only temporary, I assume?'

'Yes,' she answered with a rueful grin at Verette. He was hovering at the doorway, listening openly to their conversation.

'Ward hasn't thrown you out?'

'Why should be do that?'

'Hmm.' Mr Buchanan grunted. 'Ward's a devious man. Like his father. Pretends to be simple, but he ain't.'

'I can handle him,' said Gina emphatically. 'I shall return when I'm ready.'

'The house is going to be full.' Mr Buchanan despaired. 'Money doesn't grow on trees here, like it does at Black River.'

'I have money,' Gina touched her reticule, observing as she did so that Verette drew closer. 'Despite his faults, Ward does not restrict me. He is too proud. I have an allowance that enables me to make my own investments.'

'Indeed?' Mr Buchanan straightened in his chair and looked around for Basin to fill his decanter. Verette stepped forward with it. 'I have a little scheme you might want –'

'Can we talk some other time, Papa?' Gina gestured at Jonathan, who was slouched in his chair, watching her warily. 'This is a family reunion. It is years since Jonathan and I sat in this dining-room.'

Gina knew exactly what she wanted. He was standing seven feet away holding the decanter. She was determined not to spoil her pleasure by hurrying it. Prolonging the anticipation was part of the fun. She flirted mildly with Jonathan, enjoying his discomfort. Her father watched with amusement, his mind concentrating on the wealth she might have to invest in one of his projects.

Three days were spent in this leisurely fashion. She skilfully avoided direct discussions with her father about business, and toyed with Jonathan so he was on tenterhooks about what she might do next. Having indicated to Verette a measure of interest in him, she intended to wait for him to make the approach. There would be a price to pay, she knew.

Under his daily showering of compliments, she felt again the vivacity of being a young lady of beauty and charm. The looking-glass revealed that her feelings fooled her. It was touching, and worth it, that Verette saw the real person beneath her ravaged appearance.

Verette's remarks grew more pointed each day. He

mentioned her beauty and her money in the same breath. She did nothing to discourage him – she craved his compliments and felt girlish at being desired, whatever the reason.

She relied on him to be discreet so that her father, whose dependence on the decanter outclassed her own and made him blind to everything after six in the evening, suspected nothing. She regarded Jonathan as too dim-witted to guess what she and Verette were doing.

His initial approach came the evening of the fourth day. When there was a knock on her chamber door and she expected Basin to enter with her flask of water, Verette strode in instead. She pretended to be startled, taking the flask from his tray and clasping it to her bosom to still the pounding of her heart.

'Basin too tired to climb the stairs,' Verette said casually. 'You don't mind me being in your chamber, do you?'

'Why should I?' She parted her lips in a dazzling smile.

'Some women might be afraid.'

'Of what?'

Verette lowered his eyes and she was pleased she had intimidated him. The door was open onto the passageway and the lantern added its glow to the candles alight in the room.

'Tell me, Verette.' She pouted. 'Should I be afraid of you?'

'If you are afraid of love, Miss Gina.'

He sounded so genuine, the emotion in his voice made her skin tingle. She placed the water flask on the bedside table and put her hands out to touch his shoulders. It was enough. He seized her in his arms and pressed his lips against hers. Her resolve to resist him, at least for a token few moments, vanished. His tongue found its way through her lips and she returned his kiss eagerly.

She was charged with excitement at the feel of his robust, vibrant body in her arms. She ran her fingers across his shoulders, down his side and over his buttocks in unconscious imitation of Ward inspecting a slave. She thrilled at the strength of him in her hands.

He was caressing her with a fervour that set her yearning to shed her clothes and lead him over to the bed. His lips crept down her cheek, nibbling at her ear. She cried out breathlessly at the tension shivering through her. He gnawed at her neck and she squirmed in his powerful embrace.

'The door …' she gulped when she opened her eyes and caught sight of the passage. 'Someone might come.'

He drew away slowly. 'Do you want me?' he asked.

'Oh, darling …' was all she could say, putting out her hands to hold him around his waist.

He gave an odd smile, pulled away from her grasp and strolled over to the door. He turned and stood beside it, his breeches rigid. 'Really?'

'Yes, yes.'

He smirked. 'I'm a poor boy,' he said. 'You're a rich woman. Perhaps you could help me?' He rubbed his crotch.

Gina sighed impatiently. 'Shut the damn door and come here.'

The deed was done. He turned the key in the lock and, stripping off his cravat and shirt and flinging them to the floor, walked over to her with his arms outstretched.

Jonathan raised his eyes from the book he had been reading. William Buchanan was striding up the path to the veranda. His face, usually slack and rosy with wine at that hour, was alert with determination.

'Our host looks pleased tonight,' he said to Verette. 'Get to your feet and call Basin.'

Instead of moving, Verette glanced at him lazily from the depths of his chair. Jonathan shrugged, knowing it was useless to tell Verette what to do. He was not a slave. Since Gina's visit, Verette had become very difficult. Jonathan chose not to question him about what occurred during Gina's stay in the house. His suspicions told him all.

From the fifth day of her visit, Verette had begun to show an independence. His depression changed overnight to outright optimism. He again took care of his appearance, strutting about in the new stocks and breeches which, he boasted, Gina had bought for him.

When Jonathan cautioned him about paying too close attention to her, he replied cryptically, rolling his eyes and mimicking a slave, 'It goan be a'right, Mas Jon'than.'

Then suddenly Gina left. She told her father it was time to return to Black River in case Ward got lonely. She gave no explanation to Jonathan for her unexpected departure. The scandal that had been brewing as word of her involvement with Verette was passed from one house to another, dissipated before it became society gossip. No damage was done.

Since Verette's optimism did not wane when Gina left, Jonathan wondered if he had misjudged him with his suspicions about his conduct.

He turned away from contemplating Verette, who looked like an indolent playboy as he sprawled in the chair, and stared again at Mr Buchanan.

His host jumped from the path onto the veranda and snapped his fingers at Verette. The gesture astonished them both.

'Get out of there, boy!' Mr Buchanan said in a voice that seemed remarkably sober. 'Tell Basin to bring the decanter and glasses for the three of us.'

Verette blinked as Mr Buchanan's apparent wrath became good humoured.

'Well, son,' he began as he sat with a sigh of pride in the chair Verette had vacated. 'I've done it!'

Jonathan smiled politely, brushing his hair from his eyes. Often Mr Buchanan brought tales of business deals pulled off, only to return the next day with news of their collapse. Either his partners reneged, the ship was diverted or someone cheated him. The failure was never his fault.

Sometimes Jonathan wondered if the old man was bluffing, in the same manner as he was, living on imaginary expectations. The sole asset of Buchanan and Company was an empty warehouse by the harbour. It was mortgaged for a loan he had taken from Ward.

Basin shuffled around with the decanter. Jonathan refused a drink. Verette stood at the end of the veranda to listen. Mr Buchanan seemed inclined to keep them in suspense about what it was he had done. He sipped his wine slowly and only the twinkle in his eye betrayed his excitement.

'Sometimes, Jonathan,' he said, smacking his lips, 'times are hard. Yet we never know what the next packet of mail will bring, eh, son?'

Only when he was drunk and sentimental did Mr Buchanan call him son. Whatever had happened that day, it certainly made the old man well-disposed towards him. Jonathan sat up straight and looked intelligent.

'I can't tell you the details now,' Mr Buchanan said airily. 'By the way, that inventory I asked you to check. I'll get a boy to do it.'

'That's not necessary. I'm willing. Clerk's work is my forte.'

'Nonsense! You're destined for better things, Jonathan. Oh sure!' He chuckled into his glass, drained it and held it out for Basin to fill. 'By the way, ol' Farquhar wants to see you tomorrow.'

'The governor! Why?'

'Can't say, can't say.'

'He probably wants me to leave the colony.' Jonathan was relieved. If he was expelled, the decision what to do was taken from him. Mr Farquhar knew he could not establish himself the way he promised. He would be sent home in disgrace.

'If you're leaving,' said Verette, interrupting his thoughts, 'take me with you. As your servant.'

'A clerk in the City of London can't afford to keep a servant. That's what I'll be.'

William Buchanan guffawed so loudly Jonathan was offended. 'You'd better look smart for tomorrow, son,' he said. 'Robert believes you're wealthy. Hah!'

'That confounded rumour.' Jonathan scowled at Verette. 'I'm going for a walk!' He hurried off the veranda before Mr Buchanan could stop him.

He was depressed by the old man's *bonhomie*, assuming it was put on just for his benefit. He was indebted to Mr Buchanan for his hospitality but he was in no mood for his jibes.

I'm a failure, he thought. William Buchanan's kindness, Verette's loyalty and Nicole's friendship were all wasted on him. The sooner he left for England the better.

It would be autumn when he would arrive in London. It was his favourite time. As he ambled across the plain he recalled an afternoon at his aunt's house when he stood at her window overlooking the London square where she lived. The leaves on the trees in the centre of the square were warm rust colours, gold and copper, highlighted by the dying sun. A man worked leisurely under the trees, sweeping the fallen leaves into heaps.

He could almost smell the smoke from the gardener's bonfire as it drifted across the square, adding to the magic of the scene, making it completely English. He liked the air when it was crisp and misty and the sun glowed pale like a Mauritius moon.

It was that same afternoon at his aunt's soirée that the Prince of Wales promised Mr Farquhar the governorship of Mauritius. How young and naive he had been then.

His aunt's words as she had scolded him for keeping out of the illustrious company came back to him. 'You must not denigrate yourself. My goodness! Are you still shy at your age!'

'A littie shyness, Aunt,' he had replied. 'But mostly modesty.'

'Modesty, Jonathan?' Aunt Hortense had queried, sounding scornful. 'That won't take you far. You must let people be aware of your presence.'

His aunt had been right, he had not gone far; he was several months' voyage by sea from England but he was still the same insecure, dull and unsuccessful man he was when he left. No wonder he liked the English autumn; it was a dismal, grey time of the year when the countryside shed its beauty, its flamboyance. How like himself.

He walked the Champ de Mars until after nightfall.

Occasionally the thought of suicide entered his mind. He dismissed it as futile, knowing he would never have the courage to do anything so drastic. He would take whatever punishment fate dealt him. Verette would find a more enterprising gull for his schemes; Nicole would soon forget him, if she had not done so already.

He returned to Mr Buchanan's mansion when the veranda was deserted. Undisturbed by Verette, he went to his chamber. He slept better that night than he had for weeks, knowing that on the morrow he could at last be himself; an abject failure and incompetent.

The next morning Verette seemed to sense his mood. The youth was curt to the point of rudeness when he helped him dress, offering him his clothes gracelessly. He drank his coffee alone on the veranda.

Mr Buchanan had already left for the town and his day's wangling. Mr Farquhar's habit was to begin the day early, so at nine o'clock Jonathan started to walk to Government House. Verette followed sullenly.

Jonathan refused to be provoked by Verette's gloom. Instead he gazed at the street in detail, seeing it for the last time as he had never seen it before. Some of the burnt-out cabins were being replaced with stone buildings. If he had the money, he thought to himself with amazement at his optimism, he would buy the vacant lots and build shops with living quarters above them. People needed homes not more imported luxury goods.

He entered Government House through the back entrance leading to the clerks' office. He avoided the eyes of his former colleagues, feeling they were laughing at him. Mr Bateman, the acting chief clerk, greeted him in his customary supercilious fashion and bid him wait on a bench. For ten minutes Jonathan studied the ceiling and composed a speech of apology.

Verette was hob-nobbing with the clerks; the sniggers that came from the group at the other side of the room were all Jonathan expected.

Mr Bateman beckoned him without a word. Governor Farquhar was at his desk. He stood up when Jonathan entered and came around it with his hand extended. Jonathan took it shyly and found himself being led to the armchairs set by the French windows overlooking the Place d'Armes.

He was aware of Dr Telfair being present in the room. To his surprise William Buchanan stepped out of the shadows and winked at him.

'Dear boy,' said Mr Farquhar, 'you're looking well.'

Jonathan cringed at the lie. From his knowledge of Mr Farquhar, he knew this was his way of putting him at ease. He brushed back his hair and stared warily about him before sitting down in the chair as instructed.

Mr Farquhar snapped his fingers and Dr Telfair handed him a document. 'I am pleased to tell you, Jonathan, that I have been instrumental in making some arrangements on your behalf.'

'When do I leave?' he asked flatly, hoping to save Mr Farquhar the chore of being considerate to his feelings.

Mr Farquhar faltered for a moment, then leaned across and handed Jonathan the documents. 'Whenever you like,' he said. 'Business first. These are the title deeds to Mr Buchanan's commercial premises and his house. They are conveyed to you.

'You are now the beneficial owner of Buchanan and Company. Would you care to sign the receipt?' He snapped his fingers again and Dr Telfair brought forward a ledger.

'I don't understand.'

Mr Farquhar laughed. 'I can see it's a surprise. I don't know how William kept the secret from you.'

'Damned difficult, Robert.' Mr Buchanan grinned broadly. 'I had to keep out of his way so I didn't give him a clue.'

Jonathan tugged his nose in his confusion. Dr Telfair was leaning over him with a ledger and a pen. He took it in a daze and signed trustingly.

'By the devil, I'm glad it's over!' said Buchanan. 'I can retire now, go back to Boston. I'm grateful to you, Robert.'

Mr Farquhar spread his hands magnanimously. 'You

will find your new business is in good standing, Jonathan. Free of debts. You should have no trouble getting credit when necessary. Now what was it you said about leaving?'

'I thought ... dash it!' He sat up. 'Is this true?'

Mr Farquhar joined in the laughter. Only Dr Telfair remained dour faced. 'It certainly is.'

'Who has provided the money?' Then it dawned on him. 'Aunt Hortense! You're acting on her instructions.'

'There has been a communication from her,' said Mr Farquhar cagily. 'I'm delighted you can stand on your own feet now, Jonathan. I hope you've forgotten any harsh thoughts you may have had of me?'

'Of course, Your Excellency, I never –'

'And of Dr Telfair and my other officials?'

'Yes, yes.'

'Good. By the way, Sergeant Hastie has been successful in Madagascar and a treaty to stop the shipping of slaves has been negotiated. King Radama wishes you well, as do the princes Tiko and Manda.'

Jonathan flushed with embarrassment.

Governor Farquhar continued. 'Very soon I shall be returning to England. Yes, Jonathan, it is I who am leaving, not you. Dr Telfair will be accompanying me on leave.' His expression hardened, making Jonathan wonder what had gone wrong.

'While I am in England, I'll be taking the opportunity to answer some complaints made about my administration. Minor matters. Perrot is one. My order expelling the Bonapartist corsair was revoked, damn it! There have been questions about the slave trade by ignorant people who don't understand my methods.'

Jonathan was only half-listening.

'General Hall will be my successor. I expect to return in eighteen months. I've instructed the general that all my officers in charge of departments are obedient, active, intelligent and zealous. He should find no fault with them nor, I trust, with you, Jonathan.' Mr Farquhar stood and offered his hand.

'You will give him your cooperation now you're

independent, won't you?'

'Of course, sir.' Jonathan shook Mr Farquhar's hand and bowed himself out of the room, clutching the documents to his chest.

Many times he had seen petitioners leave Mr Farquhar's office in similar postures of gratitude. The governor's method was to make potential malcontents feel indebted to him. It was beyond Jonathan how Mr Farquhar had persuaded his aunt to set him up so generously. It was an ideal solution for all concerned. Jonathan's lips were sealed and he would be a loyal supporter of General Hall's regime.

'What's this? he enquired when he walked down the front steps of the mansion and found Verette waiting for him, holding open the silk curtain of a palanquin. Eight slaves milled around with their sticks, ready to carry the contraption.

'Your transport!' Verette was beaming. 'When the roads are repaired, you'll have your own carriage.'

'You knew about this?' He waved the title deeds at him.

Verette smiled cryptically, implying that he knew much more than he would say. 'I said it goan be all right,' he murmured, rolling his eyes. 'Get in and the boys will take you to Massey's. I've ordered champagne from the cellar and din –'

'Damn you!' Jonathan trembled at his own violent language. He gripped his fists so Verette would not notice his trembling. 'Dismiss this palanquin at once. I shall walk, as I always do.'

'The crowd at Massey's will be impressed.'

'I'm not going to Massey's. Cancel that champagne and don't presume to speak or think for me! There is work to be done. You can come with me, or leave. As you wish.'

He walked straight out of the courtyard in the direction of the harbour. His legs were shaking yet he had a feeling of triumph, of standing up for himself.

Verette was trotting at his side in an instant. 'Where are you going?' he demanded, pouting at being rebuffed.

'To my warehouse,' he said, relishing the word. 'If you

can write, *boy*, we'll carry out an inventory.'

'All right.'

Jonathan swung around to face him. Verette lowered his gaze. 'Yes, *master*,' he said with a twinkle in his eyes.

NINETEEN

Jonathan had the Midas touch. No one, least of all himself, suspected that he, a former factotum, would change so dramatically. To his acquaintances in Massey's he showed no more initiative than usual. He still listened with a gormless expression to the chatter in the lounge and still picked his way fussily along the pot-holed streets, wiping the sweat from his brow with a silk handkerchief.

Indeed, Jonathan did not consciously change at all. He applied in his takeover of William Buchanan's business the same modest principles of diligence and honesty that had governed his work for Mr Farquhar. He had a clerk's brain and a keen eye for tally and detail. It was, he believed, his conscientiousness that helped his new business succeed.

His first opportunity came with the contents of the warehouse. It was not empty as he supposed but packed from floor to ceiling with bales of cloth and clothing. Mr Buchanan apologized for it when he gave Jonathan the inventory.

'I picked it all up cheaply,' he said, 'before I knew you would take over the business.'

'Anything bought from the government?' Jonathan asked anxiously. He was determined not to deal in goods acquired deviously through crooked civil servants.

'My own speculation,' Mr Buchanan explained. 'An old contract. Damned if anything here will sell for high prices! It's not for the fashionable set.'

Jonathan took Mr Buchanan at his word and with Verette began to check the goods. The items puzzled him. There were four hundred pairs of strong duck trousers, four hundred striped cotton shirts and fifty worsted Guernsey frocks. There were bales of madras handkerchiefs, woollen forage caps and jackets of thick woollen cloth. He found piles of blankets, flannel frocks, five hundred suits of English manufacture, and bales bursting with bolts of Indian blue and white cloth.

'That,' said Verette, airing his knowledge, 'is for shirts, petticoats and trousers.'

'Woollen clothes!' Jonathan groaned. 'In the tropics?'

'Slave clothes,' Verette said with satisfaction.

'Slaves?' It was ridiculous. 'Who's going to buy this clobber? Five hundred flannel suits! Slaves don't have money and the British won't wear them. Aunt Hortense has rewarded me with a sure loss in my first venture.' Gloomily he fingered a bolt of coarse calico. He shuddered.

In contrast Verette was beaming. 'The slaves won't buy but the slave holders will. Clothing is issued twice a year to slaves, on New Year's Day and at the beginning of July. It's cold in the hills in the winter and the slaves love wool. There are over sixty thousand of them here. When the word is known what you have for sale, you'll be beseiged by planters.'

Verette, as usual, was right. Ward Trenchard was Jonathan's first customer. They met by accident at Massey's and Jonathan told him hesitantly how his aunt had sponsored him.

'Glad to hear it,' drawled Ward with a patronizing smile. 'A woman came to your rescue, eh?'

Jonathan was too overwhelmed by his good fortune to see the insult. 'Mr Buchanan paid off his debts to you and the title is clear now.'

'So I've been told.' Ward yawned.

Jonathan hesitated again. 'I happen to have some slave outfits,' he said, expecting Ward to laugh. 'Forgive me for mentioning it. Nothing special, five hundred English suits, Guernsey frocks and so on. Would you be interested?'

Ward's glance was full of contempt. 'Not much of a salesman, are you?'

'I'm sorry. I shouldn't have troubled you.'

'What's your price on the suits?'

Jonathan stammered out the price he had calculated, based on the invoice figure and a small commission. He held his breath, dreading that Ward would find his price too high.

'What's wrong with them?' Ward demanded.

'Nothing. Excellent quality, according to my man, Verette.'

'Then why are you selling so cheap?'

'Oh dear, am I? I thought I'd added a fair profit.'

'Fair!' Ward laughed in his face. 'You're supposed to be a merchant now, Jonathan. There's no fairness in commerce. I'll give you a tip.' He leaned over and lowered his voice.

'No one will respect you if you beg. Listen to Verette. He's a wily lad and will serve you well if you give him his head. I know niggers, Jonathan, and I know trading. Add twenty per cent to your prices and I'll take those suits.'

'Add twenty per cent?' It didn't make sense.

'Sure! For contingencies – fire, cyclone, pilferage. You'll still clear your stock in two days. Believe me. If I buy from you, the other slave holders will follow.'

Jonathan intended to ask Ward if he had seen Nicole, but in the excitement of concluding his first business deal he forgot. For the next few days he was caught up in making invoices for the sales and in serving customers. The planters wanted credit and he found himself relying on Verette's recommendation whether to give it or not. It was Verette who told him to add interest on the unpaid bills.

The first week was hectic and all thoughts of informing Nicole of his good fortune were chased from his mind. Despite his resolve to curb Verette's tendency to boss him, he was soon acting on Verette's advice, as Ward suggested. Verette hired slaves to be porters and found willing free negroes to work as checkers and in other positions of responsibility.

If Jonathan had stopped to consider, he might have queried the ease with which his business was being established. His belief in his own integrity was sufficient for him. Verette scouted around to find merchandise – he gained information on the cargoes of merchantmen before they were sighted – and urged Jonathan what to buy. Only when he was satisfied that there was no graft involved did he authorize Verette to negotiate.

Verette's policy was to concentrate on goods that could be sold quickly. Jonathan watched in amazement as, on paper, his fortune increased rapidly in less than six weeks.

He was fortunate that Ward Trenchard was a regular purchaser because his business was in cash, not credit, and it gave him working capital. He was soon taking a longer-term view of his enterprise and planned with Verette what to order for delivery six months ahead.

Jonathan's success, although he was unaware of it, was a sensation in Port Louis. He remained meticulous in his dealings and bookwork, content with spending long hours at his desk in the warehouse, with an occasional break for refreshment at Massey's. Verette provided the energy for expansion.

Soon two more warehouses were rented to store the cargoes he bought. Turnover increased week by week, while the other merchants complained of sluggish business. Jonathan, and Verette, seemed to have the knack of acquiring goods at low prices just before there was a demand that enabled them to sell at a good profit.

His activities attracted the attention of the garrison commander, General Gage John Hall. Without warning, just as he was preparing to close up one evening in mid November, the general marched into the warehouse. Although he was alarmed when the general ordered him to dismiss his helpers so they could have a private conversation, he was obliged to obey instantly.

General Hall was an imposing figure. He was tall and as cold a personality as Mr Farquhar was charming. He first saw active service as a lad of eighteen under the Duke of York in Flanders. He was promoted major general in 1813 and had come to Mauritius from the Cape of Good Hope. He was an uncompromising military man and the habitués of Massey's said his intention was surely to become a field marshall.

Jonathan was astonished that the general, who was to replace Mr Farquhar as governor, should trouble to visit him. He offered him his own chair, the only one, in his cubby-hole office, but the general refused. Instead he paced around the warehouse peering at the bundles and crates and grunting suspiciously.

Eventually he led Jonathan back to his office, leaned on his desk and stared at him for at least a minute without speaking. Jonathan was hot under his collar and mopped his brow, wondering what he had done wrong.

'You have a good reputation, Rendye,' the general snapped. 'Yet Mr Farquhar speaks well of you and that makes me suspicious.'

'Sir?' Jonathan was aghast at the insult to Mr Farquhar.

'I find the attitude among officials here is "Praise me and I'll praise you, defend me and I'll defend you". You were praised, Rendye, but dismissed. Now that's curious.' His light blue eyes were unwavering as he waited for Jonathan's response.

'I served Mr Farquhar well, General. I am unambitious. Mr Farquhar feels I am not of the calibre he needs for his administration.'

'What do you think, Rendye?'

'I'm sure he's right. Dr Telfair and the others are more visionary than I am.'

'Perhaps they are not so honest?'

The line of questioning dismayed Jonathan and he shuffled his feet uneasily. General Hall was leaning against his desk, toying with a sheaf of bills of lading. He glanced through them idly.

'Mr Barry, the chief secretary to government no less, authorised the sale of famine supplies of rice from India at fifty per cent loss and then authorized a loan to Major Waugh so he could buy on credit. Have you ever been involved in such dealings, Rendye?'

'No, sir!' The accusation made him angry and he stared back at General Hall without flinching.

'Last week His Excellency gave Mr Barry a concession on twenty-six arpents of land in the suburbs of Port Louis. I find the commissary of justice, Chief Judge George Smith, is also a recipient of the governor's largess. Dr Telfair had ninety-five arpents in the Champ de Mars –'

'Why are you telling me this, General?' Jonathan sensed a trap was being laid for him. 'I have no connection with government. I am a private citizen now.'

'Ah, yes.' General Hall sucked his teeth. 'A very successful one after months of penury. Is it coincidence that your fortunes should improve so miraculously a few weeks before His Excellency goes on leave? I ask myself if you have been rewarded for your cooperation in the same way that the others have.'

'That's preposterous!' He wanted to throw the distrustful general out of the warehouse. He was not one of his soldiers nor a civil servant afraid to lose his sinecure. 'I resent your allegations. My Aunt Hortense has sponsored me.'

General Hall seemed to relax. 'Mr Rendye, you have convinced me. I have seen your premises and inspected your stores, talked to your acquaintances. I would like to think you are a man to be trusted.'

'Of course, I am. Mr Farquhar always did –'

'Yet he dismissed you! Have you been unhappy with the way the governor carries out his orders? Did you disapprove of his advisers?'

Jonathan could only gasp at the accuracy of the general's guess.

'I thought so, Mr Rendye. Your face reveals a lot.' He put down the sheaf of papers and stood up. 'I am pleased to make your acquaintance, young man,' he said, extending his hand. Jonathan took it gingerly and found himself being crushed by the general's handshake.

'I have a most difficult and unpopular game to play. I expect to meet intrigue on every side because I will not assent to public plunder nor suffer French interest to prosper at the expense of Great Britain.'

'You have my support, sir.' Jonathan massaged his hand

when General Hall released it.

'I never doubted that.' He permitted himself a small smile. 'Do you speak French?''

'I read and understand. My pronunciation is not the best.'

'I have no French.' The general seemed proud. 'For twenty-five years of my life, France has been at war with England. France is our natural enemy. I cannot trust the loyalty of these Creoles, ex-French subjects, to their new English allegiance. They still long for French goods, French law and the French language. Mauritius is British, Mr Rendye. You will support me in that.'

'Most certainly.'

'Import only British goods?'

'Yes.'

'Then you will have government contracts whenever possible. I look forward to your calling on me at Government House.'

Jonathan stared into the darkness of his office long after General Hall left, trying in vain to fathom the purpose of his visit.

News of Jonathan's success as a merchant reached the Tamarind plantation although it was not Ward who brought the gossip. His visits to the plantation had ceased, which gave Emma an excuse to taunt Nicole.

'All your beaux have abandoned you, Nicole.' Emma gloated as Nicole turned a trowel over in the soil of a small flower-bed she had made near Mr and Mrs Mango. 'Don't tell me you don't care! I always know when you're unhappy.'

'Do you?' Nicole dug listlessly without raising her head to defy her.

'You plant flowers, cuttings, just as you did when we lived in Port Louis. You're such a simple soul, Nicole. Anyone can read your mind.'

She waited, longing for Nicole to break down in tears or say something she would regret. She hated her for her complaisance and the patient way she waited out the days at the Tamarind plantation.

'I think it's lovely to see flowers grow, to help cuttings become trees. Look, this frangipani branch has buds on it already.' Nicole pointed to a cutting, no more than a stick that she had planted two weeks before.

Emma regarded it sullenly. She raised her skirt and lashed out her foot, kicking at the cutting and uprooting it. 'I don't know why you bother,' she said crossly, waiting for Nicole's reaction.

She was delighted when Nicole sighed, laid down her trowel and sat back on her haunches. She saw the dark shadows under Nicole's eyes and was pleased by them. Emma did not know the reason for Nicole's unhappiness but with a sound instinct to wound, she continued her attack.

'Ward obviously wearied of your silly ways.' She smirked, then added, 'You deceived yourself if you thought he'd be interested in you. And what about that insufferable bore, Jonathan Rendye? He's never visited here nor written to you. Now he's made a success of Mr Buchanan's business, he's completely forgotten about you.'

Emma was gratified when Nicole reached for her handkerchief and sniffed into it.

'My dear,' she said sarcastically, 'is that a tear? Water your flowers with it!'

She stamped on the frangipani cutting with the heel of her shoe, smashing the buds into the soil. She was thrilled by the sight of Nicole falling to her knees, reduced to tears. That would teach her a lesson, she thought as she swept away towards the coppice by the stream.

A lesson for what? Emma's conscience asked the question but she ignored it. She found Nicole unbearably smug and no fun to be with at all. She really had become a drudge since Ward stopped calling.

She herself did not care for Ward but his visits brought relief from the boring life of Tamarind and she enjoyed them. She blamed Nicole although she did not understand why.

Emma fought boredom by teasing Nicole, by taking Fidou to the forest and doing things with her in the undergrowth where nobody could see, and by her game with Mr Moult's ebony black slave, Brutus.

Brutus represented what she wanted from a man. She longed for him to take her and make her a woman. Since the British officers she fancied thought only whores lay with men, and Verette demanded money, she was distraught that she would never experience the thrill of being held in a strong man's arms and feel him enter her, until she was married.

She wanted to try it, just once, before she let her parents find her a husband. Having been spurned by the avaricious Verette, she needed to make sure of her new choice lest she make the same mistake again.

Her yearning for Verette had been so great that perhaps, if she had the money, she would have rewarded him. At least it would have guaranteed his silence. For days after she left Mr Buchanan's house in Port Louis and returned to Tamarind, she regretted the lost opportunity. Then she became more aware of Brutus.

When she strolled past him as he toiled in the fields, she was aware of his hungry gaze. Each thrust of his body as he attacked the cane with his cutlass seemed directed at her. He never smiled and his eyes glinted with an animal desire.

She studied his routine, worked out the times he went to the river and, as if by coincidence, contrived to be there at the same moment. Over the weeks she established a rapport with him. Neither spoke. He splashed in the river or lolled on the bank with the sun filtering through the leaves of the bamboo trees and mottling his body with shadows. She sat in the shade of a secluded glade on the opposite bank and blatantly feasted her eyes on him.

It was nearly sunset when she left Nicole snivelling over her broken frangipani cutting. Her victory over her made Emma bold. She resolved to seek out Brutus and challenge him too. She hurried along the tangled path through the undergrowth, each twig that snagged her dress adding to her impatience to find him. She wanted him, now!

It was his habit to bathe in the river at sunset. She was breathless with excitement as she parted the bushes. To her joy, he was there, standing in the middle of the river's race, splashing water over his body.

He was divine to look at with his mirror-black skin, tiny ears and deep, lustful eyes. His physique, despite his strength, reminded her of a foal rather than a stag. He exuded a docility that made her ache to take him in her arms.

She gazed at him entranced, dreaming of the thrill of possessing him. It would be like taming a savage animal. When he moved it was with an animal grace and a savage disregard for her. He knew she was there but he pretended indifference. It was a game they were playing and both, Emma sensed, were aware of the outcome. She was being tamed too.

She sank down on a tree stump and watched him. She was trembling with passion. She raised her skirt to her knees and as her hand brushed against her thigh, she stiffened. If only it would be his hands that touched her. She closed her eyes, stroking herself gently, then with greater strength as the fury seized her. She cried out his name.

A shadow fell across her face, blocking out the sun. She opened her eyes with a start. He was standing in front of her. His blue calico breech cloth was swollen, his mouth was open and his eyes were narrow with lust. With a blush of shame, she removed her hand and raised it to her bosom.

The sun caught his body, emphasizing the ebony of his smooth skin. Droplets of water sparkled on his body like diamonds on black velvet. His breech cloth was soaked and clung to him, revealing the firm outline of his muscles and thighs. He shook himself like a wild beast, showering her with spray.

She tensed and lowered her eyes, her heart leaping at his closeness. At last, she thought, her time had come. She could not control the throbbing of her body and the remorseless urge that surged through her. She smiled, slowly raising her eyes from his feet to his ankles and shins. His skin was wet and shiny. She saw his knees and his thighs, then she paused, blushed and looked again. He was naked, his breech cloth tossed aside into the undergrowth.

She slid gently off the tree stump onto the ground and lay on the grass. She reached up with her hands, beckoning him. He looked huge, like a giant as tall as the trees that shielded them both from prying eyes.

He kneeled beside her. He was grunting, and his eyes were glazed.

She put out her hand and touched his thigh. She was awed by the magnificence of his body, almost terrified of it. Her fingers shook.

He quivered at her touch, and whinnied.

She smiled at her mastery over him. 'Come,' she whispered, drawing her skirt up to her waist.

She wore neither petticoat nor drawers. Her thighs were ivory white. She gazed up at him, pleading with her eyes, overwhelmed that at long last she was to possess him.

His hands mauled her roughly, pushing aside the folds of her skirt. His fingers probed her.

She winced at his touch, expecting him to be gentle, like Fidou was. She squirmed but his hands held her firmly. She opened her arms and clasped his shoulders, preparing herself for the brush of his lips on her mouth.

Instead she was lifted up and flipped over onto her stomach before she could struggle free. Her face was pressed into the grass. Her nose was grazed by a stone and it hurt, bringing tears to her eyes.

'What are you doing?' she managed to gasp before he clambered on top of her, forcing her down so she could not move. Her fantasy was shattered, the moment of bliss that she expected and dreamed of for so long was changing to agony. Her eyes were filled with tears of pain and outrage.

'Stop it! Stop it!' she cried.

He grunted and pushed himself between her legs.

She shuddered. His arm pressed her head into the grass. His other hand jabbed at her vagina, rubbing viciously, gripping her so the only way she could move was with her back towards him.

He stabbed between her buttocks and a shock of horror ripped through her. It should not be like this!

She squirmed, desperately trying to wriggle free. She was clamped to the ground by his weight as he plunged up and down on top of her.

She shrieked with pain, but no one heard.

He was thrashing against her. Suddenly, with a burst of pain that destroyed her desire, he tore into her, splitting open her backside. She fainted as the blood flowed.

The last sound in her ears, instead of whispered words of love, was his loud and angry roar of hatred.

TWENTY

On 19 November 1817 Major General Gage John Hall succeeded Robert Townsend Farquhar as Governor of Mauritius. The entire British population of note was invited to the swearing-in ceremony at Government House, including the heads of all departments. Arthur and Agnes Didcott were among the invitees, to Mrs Didcott's enormous satisfaction, and Emma was summoned from Tamarind Plantation to attend as well.

She arrived, accompanied by Nicole, on a coastal vessel the day before the ceremony. The two young ladies were palanquined to the lodgings where Mr and Mrs Didcott were temporarily accommodated. Their arrival was reported to Verette by one of his informers who worked in the harbour.

Jonathan was busy with his ledgers when Verette sauntered into the cubby-hole in the warehouse, which he proudly called his office.

'Yes, yes?' he said, continuing to read. He was inundated with paper work and hated to be disturbed for frivolous banter even by Verette. 'I hope it's important.'

'Mayhap.'

Jonathan glanced up and saw Verette grinning smugly. 'Damn it, man!' he said, placing his pen down angrily on the desk. 'Can't you see, I'm busy.'

Immediately he regretted his outburst. Verette's face was crestfallen, his stock expression when he was reprimanded but nevertheless it reminded Jonathan it was foolish to lose his temper.

'I've been making out an order to send to the Cape,' he said to mollify him. He was amused by Verette's switch from a sulky grimace to keen interest.

'What for? You haven't told me.'

'I'm telling you now. Building materials, nails, screws, hammers, saws ... tools and so forth.'

'All the merchants have building materials. They ordered in quantity after the fire. Now there's a glut.'

Jonathan was not put out by Verette's scorn. 'It's for us, for the company.'

'What are we going to build?'

'That's what I want to discuss with you, Verette.' Jonathan smiled confidentially, using a technique he learned from Mr Farquhar to involve subordinates in decision making, although the decision was already made. 'You know those vacant lots in the Chaussée?'

'Where the whores' houses were before the fire? Of course I do.'

'What do you think will happen to them?'

'I don't know.' Verette shrugged, conveying his disapproval.

'The market has been shifted to the gardens opposite the Chaussée. A great many people go there every day.'

'There's a lot of business done in the Chaussée,' Verette agreed, pausing and looking at Jonathan with a canny expression. 'I see your idea! Build houses to rent to the whores.'

'And to merchants, shopkeepers, whatever –'

Verette interrupted him. 'Why are you ordering building materials when you don't know yet who owns the lots?'

Jonathan coughed to hide his pleasure at having done

something without Verette's knowledge. 'The company owns them. They were mortgaged to Augustus Blaize on behalf of Ward. He told me about it so I bought them. I worked out the deal –'

'You've done a deal with Ward!' Verette was scandalized.

'Why not? It's an excellent proposition. He said I was doing him and his agent a favour by taking the lots off his hands. I didn't say what I wanted them for, of course.' He was offended by the way Verette was shaking his head in ridicule.

'You're not the only one who can make deals.'

'It would be better if I was. The Chaussée!' Verette threw up his arms in scorn.

'Let me remind you, this is my company! I thought you'd approve.'

Verette calmed down. 'Maybe I do.' He grinned. 'You surprised me, that's all.' He turned to go as Jonathan picked up his ledger.

'Dam'me, I've got a surprise for you.'

'Yes?' sighed Jonathan. He wanted to get on with his work.

'Emma and Nicole are in town. They've come for the swearing-in ceremony tomorrow morning.'

The news made Jonathan's heart leap. He lay down the ledger and gazed full at Verette. 'What must she think of me? I've never written.'

'You've been busy.'

'Where are they staying?'

'With Emma's parents.'

'Why not at our house? Mr Buchanan wouldn't mind. He's sailing for Boston soon anyway. I'll have the house to myself then.'

Verette grinned. 'Aye, and that's when you'll need a wife.'

'A wife …' The thought stunned him. 'That's for a lusty buck like you, Verette. I'm not the marrying kind.'

'You're not the whoring kind, I'll agree. So you *must* be the marrying kind.'

Jonathan was distracted by his remarks even after

Verette left. He was unable to work so he closed up the warehouse. Instead of going to Massey's, he took a different road home, one that went through the Chaussée. He was convinced his building scheme would succeed.

He was relieved Verette approved although he did not want him to know he depended on his advice and judgement. Verette had become virtually his junior partner, yet little more than a year before he was a barefooted plain's brat.

Ward had been right, Jonathan mused. His success had come when he gave Verette his head, the way he suggested. Why not make him a partner officially? It would cause a minor stir but free coloureds were accepted in business. That was a legacy of the French, who had none of the harsh class strictures of the British. If Verette was his partner, he would feel more at ease in his dealings with him.

Jonathan halted and gazed around the charred houses of the whores' quarters in the Chaussée. With the flowers and plants in the town garden opposite it was a pleasant place. He wondered idly if Nicole's mother had lived in this area.

He felt a pang of guilt for thinking of Nicole because of her mother's profession. He owed her an apology for neglecting to write when his luck changed. The thought troubled him and he strolled home preoccupied with regret at his poor manners.

The next day, at Government House, he scanned the crowd eagerly for a glimpse of Nicole. It was an odd feeling being in the house that was so familiar and yet he no longer had any connection there. Mr Farquhar and his staff had gone. General Hall had replaced some civilian clerks, the French ones, with soldiers. His ADC was Captain Freeman.

Jonathan looked in vain for Nicole during the oath taking. Mrs Didcott with her ample frame was easy to see. He glanced twice at the young lady with her before he realized she was Emma. The change in her puzzled him and he studied her carefully to see what it was.

The mischief in Emma's eyes was gone. Her face had a serious, haunted mien. Perhaps her hair-style caused the difference? She wore her blonde tresses drawn back from her forehead, sculpted into a creation that made her look older than she was.

As he surveyed the faces in the gathering, he realized there were no French or Creoles there. He recalled Mr Farquhar's first reception, where there were more Creoles present than English. It had been Mr Farquhar's intention then to impress the local population with British fairness. General Hall distrusted Creoles so they had not been invited. He felt ashamed because it meant Nicole was banned too.

It was soon apparent that the new governor was using the ceremony to make his views known to the British. Although Mr Farquhar had said the general was only a temporary governor and would make no changes, he had left the colony for only two hours before General Hall was declaring otherwise.

The guests were treated to a harangue as though they were soldiers on the Place d'Armes parade ground, instead of being given the refreshments they expected.

'Justice,' proclaimed General Hall, sweeping his gaze sternly over the fashionably dressed throng, 'will be impartially administered to all classes of this country without distinction of Nation, Rank or Fortune.'

It sounded like a threat to Jonathan. He glanced at Judge Smith and saw he was scowling, irritated by this indirect criticism of his professional conduct. Some officials were openly yawning. Theodore Hook was engaged in a loud, high-pitched conversation with a flourish of giggles, deliberately trying to embarrass the governor.

General Hall must have noticed but he continued in the same vein without hesitation. His speech exhorted them all to uphold British traditions. It was clearly intended as a warning to the French settlers and those Creoles who still believed in a French renaissance. The general vowed to stamp out corruption in terms that implied that Mr Farquhar was responsible for it.

He concluded his speech emphatically. 'I request of all honest inhabitants that honest cooperation which it is no less their duty than their interest to afford me!'

There was no applause. The governor strode through the crowd, with his wife following on Captain Freeman's arm. The gathering found to its dismay that it was dismissed.

'No refreshments!' squawked Mr Hook in a voice intended to carry to the governor's ear. 'A whore entertains more lavishly than a Hall.'

'Ah yes,' the general whispered in retaliation as he passed close to Jonathan. 'But this Hall cannot be bought ... like a whore.'

In the courtyard of Government House, where palanquins and carriages waited and the escorts loafed, Nicole stood demurely with Verette. He was taller than she remembered him, and was dressed like a dandy. With him at her side she was drawing glances of envy from the female slaves awaiting their mistresses.

'They're coming now,' said Verette after peeking through the open windows into the reception room. 'The Governor's finished his pep talk.'

Nicole tensed. What would Jonathan think of her? Had Ward told him anything? Men boasted about their conquest of women when they were drinking together. That's all she was now, one of Ward's discarded conquests. Even if Jonathan did not know, he was sensitive and would see the change in her.

She had tried to disguise the pallor of her complexion with rouge where before her cheeks were naturally rosy. The shadows under her eyes lightened with a touch of powder. She was dressed modestly, and hoped no one could guess at the shame she hid by her high corsage and flowing skirts. She willed herself to be in high spirits so Jonathan would think she was an agreeable companion.

Her breath quickened when she saw him. He was on the steps trying to ease through to where Mrs Didcott and Emma were standing. He was hesitating, dodging around groups of chattering people and worming his way with effusive apologies through the crowd.

She walked towards Emma, her eyes searching for his; he was too preoccupied to notice her.

'Mrs Didcott ...' she heard him say softly. 'Mrs Didcott?' She saw his face brighten when Mrs Didcott turned and greeted him.

'Mr Rendye! What a pleasure! I've heard so much about your success in commerce. You've become quite wealthy, I understand.'

'Oh no,' he said. 'A small investment.'

'You must meet Emma.' Mrs Didcott looked annoyed when she saw Nicole had joined them. 'Emma!' she commanded. 'Say how d'you do to Mr Rendye. He's the talk of the town these days.'

Emma lowered her eyes and kept her hands clasped in front of her. Mrs Didcott banged her with her reticule. 'Fie, child!' she scolded. 'Have you become a nun since you've been staying at Tamarind?'

Nicole was sorry for Emma. Since her experience with Brutus she was prone to moods of despair. She had told no one what happened and Nicole could only guess. She no longer went to the glade by the river. Instead she moped all day under Mr and Mrs Mango while Nicole busied herself in the garden. She did not speak of Brutus and Nicole refrained from asking.

'A nun?' said Emma suddenly. 'They would not have me.'

'Far too attractive to be shut away in a convent,' Jonathan said as though he understood her embarrassment.

'Yes, isn't she?' Mrs Didcott sounded pleased. 'You have prospects now, Mr Rendye?'

The lack of tact in her enquiry did not seem to offend Jonathan. He brushed the question aside and turned to Nicole. She caught her breath as he bowed at her.

'It's a delight to see you again, Miss Genave.'

'She looks peaky, does she not?' Mrs Didcott was furious, trying to draw Jonathan's attention back to Emma. Nicole did not mind.

'As beautiful as ever!' exclaimed Jonathan, then lapsed

into silence, apparently lost for words.

'Why don't you and Emma walk with us. Nicole can talk to your boy.'

'Boy?' Jonathan blanched. 'Verette is my partner in Buchanan and Company.'

'Good show!' said Arthur shaking Verette's hand. Mrs Didcott took refuge under her parasol. Emma walked with her, leaving Nicole and Jonathan together while Arthur walked along with Verette.

Nicole waited for Jonathan to speak. She was touched by his pleasure at seeing her because it seemed completely genuine. He could not have heard anything. He looked the same to her. He was bathed in perspiration as usual and employed his handkerchief to mop himself dry. His suit of grey was replaced by one of brown, suitable for a hard-working merchant. He opened and shut his mouth several times before speaking.

'You must think me a dreadful bore.'

The statement surprised her. 'Why should I?'

'I wanted to write, to tell you. You know, you were so helpful that night when I thought Ward was in your chamber.'

Hearing Ward's name caused her to blush. Was it accidental that Jonathan had spoken of him? Fortunately he seemed too wrapped up in his own embarrassment to notice hers.

He might be successful in business, she realized, but he was still the same nervous and confused Jonathan. She listened to him gabbling, tying himself into knots as he tried to apologize. She could stand it no longer.

'Jonathan,' she said with a firmness that surprised both of them. 'Don't apologize! You're an important man now. I never expected you to think of me.'

'But I do, Nicole! Won't you, and Emma, come to an at-home one evening? A quiet veranda affair. Mr Buchanan is retiring to live in Boston. I'll be alone in the house.'

'I don't think we could,' she said with a sigh.

'Bring Mrs Didcott if you must,' he said, misunderstanding her reluctance. 'Good heavens! I owe her hospitality for the night I came to her affair and met you.'

'You must ask her. Perhaps, if she agrees ...'

In her heart Nicole hoped Mrs Didcott would decline the invitation. She felt unworthy of Jonathan since her attempt to get a loan from Ward to help him had led to her disgrace.

She sensed that Jonathan, despite his simple ways, was destined to be more than an ordinary merchant. It would be better if they never met again.

The encounter with Nicole buoyed Jonathan's spirits. He planned the veranda affair with enthusiasm. William Buchanan conveniently left the house to sail for Boston a few days before the date set for the party. Jonathan retained Basin and Ranavola, buying their titles. He was looking forward to the affair so he was dismayed when he received a visit at his warehouse from Arthur Didcott on the morning of the party.

'Mrs Didcott,' Arthur explained sadly, 'has the vapours. We won't be able to come tonight.'

'Perhaps Nicole – and Emma – could come alone?' he asked too eagerly. Arthur regarded him with the cold eye of propriety.

'Mrs Didcott would not approve.'

'Dash it! How unfortunate. Can I visit you at home?'

'We are in lodgings.' Arthur seemed to be struggling to say something.

'I like you, Jonathan,' he said after some hesitation. 'So do Emma and Nicole. There's some reason, I don't know what, that makes them shy of company. Naturally, Mrs Didcott is matchmaking, you being a bachelor. Emma will have none of it. She refuses to visit you because of the talk –'

'Very well.' He was relieved. It was Nicole he wanted to see again, not Emma. 'Tell Mrs Didcott, please, that I am a confirmed bachelor! Perhaps Emma would be pleased to hear that too.'

'Maybe another evening?'

'Yes,' said Jonathan, ushering him out of his cubicle office. 'Another evening.'

He had not realized how close he was to being inveigled into an embarrassing situation. He thanked fate for Mrs Didcott's vapours, at the same time being grateful to Emma for refusing to be part of an intrigue that he had never intended. Somehow he would see Nicole without the Didcotts in attendance.

The opportunity, when it came, was unexpected. It was late one Sunday afternoon, the favourite time for the townsfolk to flock to the Champ de Mars and be seen in the latest fashions. Ladies strolled in groups, wielding their parasols and fluttering their eyelashes at the cluster of dashing young army officers who sauntered close to them.

It was an entertaining parade which Jonathan could see from his veranda. He was leaning on the balustrade idly watching the brief encounters of the meandering groups when he became aware of two ladies in afternoon gowns and a man in an army tunic detaching themselves from the throng and heading towards his house. He hastened down the path through the parterre to meet them.

'Nicole!' he exclaimed, then glanced with misgiving at the man with her.

'This is Sergeant Hastie,' said Nicole breathlessly. She looked over her shoulder. 'He has to talk to you at once.'

'Of course.' He led the way back to the house, trying to guess the reason for the visit. Nicole seemed reserved and nervous, Emma withdrawn, even reluctant to speak to him.

'Is there something wrong?' he asked.

No one answered until they were seated in the shade of the veranda. Jonathan instructed Basin to bring some refreshments and turned to Nicole.

'We did not want to come,' she said directly.

'Mother would misinterpret my visit,' added Emma. She flushed and lowered her eyes to the floor.

'I hope you are not ashamed to be seen with me,' he said anxiously. 'There's no threat to your virtue, I assure you.'

'Don't joke about such matters, Jonathan!'

Nicole's unexpected outburst quietened him. He noticed

for the first time how drawn she was. Her ringlets were lank as though she no longer took care of her appearance. He wondered what was troubling her. When he looked at Emma he sensed the same lack of ease.

'Miss Genave insisted I should see you,' said the sergeant, breaking the strained silence. 'I arrived a week ago from Tananarivo.'

'He was with Tiko and Manda.' Nicole's eyes brightened when she mentioned the two princes. Their names brought back to Jonathan the rapture of those days when he used to watch her playing with them.

'How are they both? And King Radama?'

'They are well, Mr Rendye,' the sergeant said gravely. 'I fear they will not remain so for long.'

'That's why I brought Sergeant Hastie here.' Nicole spoke as if she wanted Jonathan to be clear that there was no other reason for her visit. It struck him as odd.

'Mr Farquhar told me you were successful in treating with the King to end the slave-trade,' he said to Hastie.

'I was. Devil's own job convincing his people. Radama's kept his word, though. Now he wants the British government to keep theirs.'

'What do you mean?' Jonathan frowned at the criticism in Hastie's remark.

'The terms of the treaty are simple. For prohibiting the exportation of his subjects as slaves, the king is to receive yearly the equivalent of what the sale earns him. There's a list of specific items such as a thousand dollars in gold, a hundred muskets, four hundred jackets, shirts, trousers, boots, capes and a dozen sergeant's swords like mine.'

'No difficulty in that, surely.' said Jonathan. 'I have most of those items in my warehouse. Mr Farquhar did agree, didn't he?'

'He did, but General Hall won't.'

'Why not? He can't change a treaty.'

'He says Radama has broken it. The navy intercepted a shipment of slaves from Madagascar. I told him that was not a breach because the slaves were sold before the treaty was signed.'

'That's understandable.'

'Not to General Hall. He is determined. In vain I argued that if we don't pay what was promised to King Radama, British faith will be destroyed in Madagascar.'

'Well put, Hastie. What did the General say?'

'He was scornful. He said there's no respect for British faith among a passel of savages. He called the treaty trash and nonsense.'

Jonathan brushed at his hair in anger. 'King Radama is an honourable man. How can he call him savage?'

'That's his word,' said the sergeant, his brow furrowed with anxiety.

'This is terrible.' Jonathan rose to his feet. He remembered Ratsitatane nursing him back to health, the King's desire to learn everything about the British, the trust Tiko and Manda placed in him and Nicole. He gripped the balustrade and gazed down across the Champs de Mars over the roofs of the town towards Government House.

A hand slipped under his arm and squeezed. 'I don't like to ask your help, Jonathan,' Nicole said timidly. 'You did so much for Mr Farquhar when you were in Madagascar and he never thanked you for it. General Hall's going to undo it all. Tiko and Manda will think I, we, all of us, have abandoned them. Is there anything you can do?'

'Me?' He turned and looked at her in astonishment. 'Me? What can I do? General Hall has his own advisers.'

'He might listen to you.' There were tears in her eyes. 'You could try, Jonathan.'

He tugged his nose as excitement surged through him. 'By the devil!' he said, gripping her shoulders. 'You're right. I could try. The General asked me to call on him. I think I know what would make him change his mind ...'

'Oh, Jonathan!' She gazed up at him gratefully through her tears.

He was startled to feel her trembling so he drew her into his arms and hugged her reassuringly.

'Everything will be all right,' he said. He had the oddest feeling that Nicole was crying for more than the broken treaty.

'I promise,' he added, his nose tingling at her perfume and his body soaring as he held her close. 'Trust me.'

TWENTY ONE

Nicole fired Jonathan with rather more determination than was prudent. As he sat in the anteroom waiting to be summoned into the governor's presence, the courage that inspired him when she was appealing for help withered away. It was the sight of Nicole with Sergeant Hastie that had driven him to make his rash promise. He wanted to show her that he could succeed where Hastie had failed.

He looked around the room hoping to see a familiar face. The new governor had replaced every one of the clerks with military men. Even Mr Bateman was nowhere to be seen.

The thoroughness with which Governor Hall had changed the tenor of the colony's administration made Jonathan nervous at what he was proposing. In the days when Mr Farquhar governed as a gentleman, it was possible to ask for a favour. General Hall's military efficiency was more intimidating.

The door of the governor's suite snapped open and Captain Freeman stared at Jonathan as though he expected him to leap to attention. He rose uncertainly and shambled after him into the governor's office, his self-confidence lowered by the glares of the officers assembled in the room. He never liked military men since his days with Mr Farquhar when they openly despised him because of his closeness to the governor.

'Mr Rendye, sir!' Captain Freeman announced so a whole parade ground of soldiers could hear.

The governor continued to sign documents while Jonathan shifted uncomfortably from one foot to another in front of his desk. He remembered with nostalgia the days when Mr Farquhar would do everything to make his visitors feel at ease.

Abruptly General Hall finished his signing session, thrust the quill at an orderly and stood up. The officers in the room tensed. The governor dismissed them with an impatient wave of his hand and they trooped dutifully out of the room. When only Captain Freeman and a writer, seated discreetly in a corner taking notes, remained, he greeted Jonathan with a curt nod.

Jonathan felt his skin prickling under his breeches and he dashed at his brow with a wild gesture to flick back his hair. He felt churlish, slovenly and out of place as he lowered his eyes under the governor's probing stare. Nicole would laugh at him if she could see him now, he thought.

'Your request for an interview intrigues me, Mr Rendye,' General Hall said, returning to his seat without offering Jonathan the chance to be seated too. 'Perhaps you have heard of my enquiries?'

'No, sir ...' He squeaked with nerves so his reply sounded like a bleat. There was silence in the room which made him even more conscious of the unfavourable impression he was creating.

'I've come ...' he began, then took a gulp of air and rushed on boldly, '... about King Radama.'

General Hall jerked back in his chair in surprise. His reaction made Jonathan conscious of his audacity in seeking to interfere. It had seemed easy when Nicole was appealing to him. Now, he wondered, could he actually achieve anything?

'*King* Radama?' General Hall sneered. 'That barbarous chief is not a king.'

The insult to his friend goaded Jonathan. 'He's the only one who commands the loyalty of the other chiefs in Madagascar,' he said angrily. 'I know him to be an honest man who keeps his word, even if his customs are not ours.'

'You are right. An Englishman can be trusted to keep his word, Mr Rendye. A savage, without British traditions, is a savage and must be treated as such.' General Hall's sneer became a glower of contempt. 'I am surprised you concern yourself with such unimportant matters.'

'Mr Rendye accompanied Captain Lesage in the first delegation that treated with Radamà,' Captain Freeman reminded the governor.

'Ah yes …' General Hall leaned back in his chair. 'What a preposterous exercise that was.'

'Governor Farquhar sought to cut off the slave-trade at its source,' said Jonathan defensively. 'The king has agreed.'

'So he can get his hands on British munitions to take more captives to sell to traders to ship to our shores!' General Hall looked up from his desk.

'Mr Rendye, I am not a gullible man. My duty is to stop the slave-trade, as it was Governor Farquhar's. My methods differ. I can allow no conniving at the trade under the façade of political expediency. My way is to stop it here, by prosecuting the traders in human flesh, not by a worthless treaty with a savage potentate.'

'The king will be alienated if the treaty is broken.'

'It is he who has broken it, Mr Rendye! I have a list of the shiploads of slaves sent from Madagascar in the last three months, when the trading was supposed to have ceased.'

'They were sold before the –'

'Enough! The Madagascar establishment last year cost over seventy thousand dollars, mainly in salaries and gifts. The slave-trade, however, continues. Even government officers are connected with the very trade they are supposed to discourage and terminate. Perhaps you know about that?'

'I …' The general's accusation made Jonathan hesitate, seeking to choose his words carefully. He had no interest in slavery but he was offended by the criticism of Mr Farquhar.

'Governor Farquhar,' he said firmly, 'was against the slave-trade.'

'So am I, Mr Rendye, as the planters will soon discover. Slave-traders will be prosecuted, despite Judge Smith's reluctance. My officers will seize slaves they believe to have been landed recently and, hence, illegally. They will be confiscated. The risks of the slave-trade will continue even after the slaves have been got to the estates.'

Jonathan regarded him with horror. It was obvious the general did not have the slightest concern for the people of the colony. There would be an uprising if soldiers invaded plantations and took away slaves from their owners.

He understood now that Mr Farquhar was right in his laxness in enforcing unpopular laws. General Hall's determination to do what he was ordered by his superiors in Westminster would lead to conflict.

'The planters won't like that,' Jonathan commented without thinking that the general would find him impertinent. 'There will be difficulties –'

'One expects difficulties to be interposed proportionate to one's zeal and activity for the public good,' the general said pompously. 'Executive authority is hampered by all these French forms and delays of law calculated to favour the slave traffic. Damn the French!'

'Sir?' Jonathan was baffled.

'I can speak freely in front of you, Mr Rendye.' The general pounded the desk top. 'There are too many Frenchmen here. There have been four hundred arrivals from France in the past three years.'

'The colony needs settlers.'

'Not of that calibre. British settlers! Fair minded men who obey British laws not flout them at every opportunity. We don't want agitators like Perrot who returned with four thousand guns. He's only waiting his chance ...'

Jonathan gaped in disbelief and General Hall shook his head sadly.

'Who knows,' he said, keeping his eye on Jonathan, 'if Governor Farquhar was aware of the intrigue and abuses hostile to his government that were perpetrated in his name. Look at the functionaries of justice. They are deeply involved in the slave-trade. They interpose their abilities and professional knowledge to defend the slave-traders, not punish them!'

'I didn't know ... I'm sure Governor Farquhar didn't

know –'

'Indeed?'

General Hall waved him to a chair and Jonathan sat in it gratefully. He was disturbed because he knew there was some truth in the general's remarks. He found himself speaking without thinking.

'It wasn't Governor Farquhar's doing,' he said, mopping his brow. 'He is a sincere man. It was the others.'

'Others?' General Hall's eyes glinted.

'Dr Telfair, Colonel Draper, Major Waugh ... Theodore Hook, too,' added Jonathan unhappily. 'He's Mr Farquhar's brother-in-law and the governor had to tolerate him because the prince regent himself sent him here. Mr Farquhar is not to blame.'

'You are very loyal to him.'

'I know him.'

'What do you know of Dr Telfair?'

The menace in General Hall's voice alerted Jonathan. He stared back at him, seeing the light blue eyes ablaze with a zeal that he could not defy. His months as a merchant had given him a taste for bargaining; he waited for the General's impatience to get the better of him.

'I know of Dr Telfair's manipulating the laws of this country to his advantage,' he said softly. 'Captain Lesage is a swindler, Colonel Draper performs his duties partially. I could tell you a lot.'

'Mr Rendye,' the general rose from his seat and walked over to him. 'It is your duty to do so.'

'King Radama would feel it's our duty to pay him the equivalent obliged by the treaty.'

General Hall halted, stiffening to attention. 'That has nothing to do with it!'

'I think it has.' Jonathan scrambled out of his seat as the general loomed over him.

'Forgive me, sir. I thought you might be disposed to reconsider your attitude. The king can be trusted, as can I.' He bowed.

'Perhaps,' the general said slowly, 'you and I should have a private meeting? I am always willing to listen to advice from someone who knows so much.'

'What will you do about King Radama?'

'I have not decided.' His stern face relaxed with the briefest of smiles and he extended his hand.

Jonathan, wary of the strength in the general's grip, winced as he took it.

'We shall see,' the general said, leading him out to his private suite.

It was several days before Jonathan was able to see Nicole again. She had expressly forbidden him to call at the lodgings where she and Emma were staying with the Didcotts. 'It will encourage gossip,' she explained and he was obliged to obey.

Instead he sent a message with Verette and his patience was rewarded when, as dusk was descending, a closed carriage escorted by Verette drew up to the warehouse.

It parked close to the building. Verette looked both ways, waiting until the road was clear, before opening the carriage doors. The occupants descended and stepped hurriedly into the warehouse without being seen by passersby.

Jonathan was delighted that Nicole had come although Emma's presence was annoying to them both. He sensed, but could not determine the reason for it, the uncharacteristic reserve of both women.

'I am honoured,' he said, trying to put them at ease, 'to have you here. You will be unobserved, my men are discreet.' He gestured to where his negroes were tallying goods. 'I'm sorry my office is small.'

'Pray don't inconvenience yourself on my account,' said Nicole formally. 'We cannot stay for more than a few minutes.'

'We told mother we were driving to the Champ de Mars,' Emma said. 'She was most impressed with the carriage.'

'I hired it,' said Verette with a grin. 'It's not the company's. Jonathan doesn't believe in spending on such necessities.'

'It's a luxury,' Jonathan protested, anxious to justify himself to Nicole lest she think him a cheapskate. 'There are so few streets where carriages can pass, and none in the country districts. A carriage is not a necessity when I can walk.'

'Without its privacy,' said Nicole with a coy smile at Verette, 'we couldn't come here. You know how people talk.'

'Is visiting me going to cause you disgrace?' Jonathan asked in an attempt at humour. Nicole flushed and he yearned to put his arm around her and tell her not to be so ashamed. He wondered what it was she had done that changed her liveliness to timidity.

'Miss Nicole thinks she is unworthy of you, Jonathan,' said Verette tactlessly.

'That's a foolish notion.'

'Is it?' Nicole's brown eyes opened wide. He felt confused when he saw the questioning look in them as though she were beseeching him to explain some insoluble problem.

'Sit down, sit down,' he urged, indicating his chair and hoping to cover his embarrassment with a display of activity.

'I'll show Miss Emma around the warehouse,' said Verette. 'If she has no objections.'

Emma started, glanced at Nicole in panic, and then turned her eyes on Verette. She hesitated and Jonathan tried to guess what objection she had to his partner.

'That,' she said, making an obvious effort to swallow her distaste, 'is unnecessary. I shall wait by the door. You need not concern yourself with me.'

Jonathan signalled to Verette to look after her, at the same time frowning to warn him not to offend her in any way. He was curious about the reason for Emma's new vulnerability. She had lost the brusqueness that marked her as Agnes Didcott's daughter. Verette would have to work hard to charm her.

He turned back to Nicole and caught her studying him shyly. Her glance before she lowered her eyes caused the sweat to ooze on his brow. He wiped it away self-consciously.

'I've done what you asked me,' he said with a rush of pride. 'Governor Hall is to reconsider his abrogation of the treaty with King Radama.'

'You believed him?'

He was stung by the doubt in her question. 'I gave him some information he needed,' he added crossly. 'He must keep to his side of the bargain.'

'Oh, Jonathan!' She pressed her hand to her bosom and looked at him with pity in her eyes. 'Surely it occurred to you that General Hall is different from Mr Farquhar.'

'Yes.' He pulled his nose, wondering what he had done wrong.

'His attitude to King Radama shows he cannot be trusted at all,' she said. 'Perhaps you were unwise to believe him.'

'Nonsense!' He tried to wave away the suspicion that she roused.

For an hour the General had listened while he told him everything he knew about the officials in Governor Farquhar's clique. He spared none of them, emboldened by his resentment at the way they dislodged him from Mr Farquhar's side, and lulled into indiscretion by General Hall's encouragement.

The possibility that the General would change his mind about Radama, as Nicole wanted, spurred him on.

'Jonathan ...' Nicole looked sad. 'Thank you for trying. Sergeant Hastie appreciates what you did.'

The mention of the soldier's name made him stare at her closely, wondering what was the connection between them. 'I did it for you,' he said, letting his irritation show. 'Not for Sergeant Hastie.'

'I am grateful, Jonathan. It is unfortunate that the General is not a man of his word.'

'Why do you malign him, Nicole?'

'This morning the General informed Sergeant Hastie that his services are no longer required. He is recalling every British subject from Madagascar. All contact with that island is to cease.'

There was a stillness in his cubicle office that made Jonathan aware of the sounds around him. From outside there was the muffled noise of carriages and bullock-carts creaking over the cobbles of the street, and the shouts of boys chasing after them. In the warehouse his clerks were calling bale numbers and their contents to one another in low undertones.

From the doorway, where she sat hidden in shadow so she could not be spied from the street, Emma was reprimanding Verette in a scandalized voice.

Jonathan eavesdropped, fighting back the reality of what Nicole's news meant.

'Fie, Verette!' Emma was saying, giggling nervously. 'I am not a Creole flibbertigibbet whose head can be turned by your chatter.'

'It's true,' said Verette with mock gallantry. 'I've heard many an officer express a desire to meet you. They find that your apparent aloofness is a challenge. I tell them you are really gay and warm hearted and would welcome their attentions.'

'How dare you discuss me in public.'

'I don't.' Verette sounded shocked. 'Only in the very best private circles. I can arrange an introduction to –'

'No!' Emma's outrage was tinged with a note of regret. 'My mother warned me about the men in this colony and she was right. I'll thank you to conduct yourself with propriety when I am mentioned.'

'Emma!' Verette's voice sounded so scornful it brought Jonathan's attention back to his own problem. He stole a glance at Nicole and saw she was watching him with eyes full of concern.

'I've been a fool,' he said, wiping his hand over his brow and pushing back his hair with a gesture of defeat. He smoothed it down until his lank locks stuck to his scalp. 'I believed the general would change his mind. I told him many things about Dr Telfair, Colonel Draper –'

'Things he has a right to know, Jonathan. Don't denigrate yourself.'

'Huh?' He looked at her curiously. 'My aunt told me that once.'

'She was an astute lady.'

'You know her? No, of course, you don't.'

'Do I need to? I can see your weaknesses, Jonathan, as well as she can.'

'So can everyone else, judging by the mistake I made in trusting General Hall. He used me, didn't he? I wanted him to know that it isn't Mr Farquhar who's behind the roll of dishonour as you once called it.'

Nicole flushed. 'I spoke with the callowness of youth then.'

'Are you different now?' He spluttered at his own rudeness. 'I mean, you're still so young and beautiful. There's an innocence in your eyes that's angelic.'

'Stop it, Jonathan!' She rose from the seat and her expression hardened. 'You do not know me. I have done things, terrible things, that make me unworthy to be alone with you. Verette was right.'

He was dismayed by her outburst and gaped at her without moving.

'You are a good man, Jonathan, and I respect you for it. You try to serve your friends. I should be honoured to be your friend but I am not the virtuous young lady you take me for. I didn't want to see you again but Sergeant Hastie begged me to ask you to intercede on his behalf. Thank you for what you tried to do.'

He saw her blink and noticed her eyes were moist as she swept past him, calling loudly to Emma.

'We must go, Emma, for your mother not to suspect.'

'By the devil!' said Jonathan, astonished. He bounded after her.

'What is this? It is I who am at fault. You have done nothing wrong!'

He wanted to seize her in his arms but Emma's frown and Verette's grin checked him. He clenched his fists and held his hands impotently at his side.

'We are going,' said Emma. 'Our carriage?' She turned to Verette with a faint smile on her lips.

His eyes twinkled in response. 'It's here,' he said, opening the warehouse door. He stood to one side while Nicole and Emma hurried out.

Jonathan swallowed his protest at their rapid departure, gazing after the carriage with his mind in a turmoil of mixed emotions. He had failed Nicole and she was repaying him by saying she was not good enough for him. It was ridiculous. How like a woman, he mused, to take the blame on herself when he was the one who was at fault.

'You have won her heart, Jonathan!' Verette slapped him on his shoulder. 'She's yours any time you care to say the word. I wish Emma were so agreeable.'

He reeled from the blow, and from the stupidity of Verette's remark. 'Have you nothing to do?' he demanded, tearing his eyes away from the coach as it rounded the corner back into the Chaussée. 'I have had enough of your pimpish ways.'

'Then why is Nicole crying?'

'Something in her eye, I suppose.'

'You're the one in her eye.'

'You misunderstand her. She said she won't see me again.'

'That proves I'm right!' Verette laughed and clapped his hands together. 'She's a Creole. She thinks you don't want her.'

'I don't! Not like you mean. As a friend, yes. What have I done to upset her?'

'Nothing, Jonathan.' Verette nodded his head wisely and led the way back to the cubby-hole office. 'Someone must have said something to her. Probably Mrs Didcott. That lady would like you to marry Emma so she'd try to warn off Nicole by reminding her of her background, of her mother –'

'Shut up!' Jonathan gripped the side of his desk in despair. 'Dammit, Verette, I didn't mean to shout, or to swear either. I don't know what's come over me lately. Can it be true about her mother? She's so pure, gentle, kind.'

'If you want to see her again,' said Verette, 'you'll have to prove to Nicole that she's not what she thinks she is.'

He sighed and turned back to the ledger on his desk. 'How can I do that?' He was dismayed by the futility of even trying. 'Sometimes I think I was better off when I had nothing. She was happy enough with me then.'

'Yes.' Verette murmured so suggestively, the tone of his voice alarmed Jonathan.

'You're mistaken about me and Nicole. She means nothing to me,' he said emphatically. He opened the ledger and stared at the figures that danced before his eyes.

Verette smiled knowingly and slipped out of the cubicle.

It was dark in the street off the Chaussée when Verette knocked three times on the door of the ramshackle cabin. He glanced up and down the street, standing to one side as the door opened so that the dim glow from the candle inside the house would not reveal him. No one was about at that hour; if anyone had seen him, they would see nothing unusual in a dandified Creole knocking on the door of a Chaussée brothel.

An old woman opened the door an inch and peered at him suspiciously before allowing him enough space to enter. He stepped in quickly and the door was closed behind him. The cabin consisted of one room with a dilapidated bed in pride of place in the centre. A stained sheet covered the worn mattress.

The old woman wheezed to herself as she waddled across the mud floor to the door at the other side of the cabin. She seemed reluctant to go. Verette watched her, refusing to look at the woman who was standing in the darkened corner of the room waiting for him to embrace her.

'Take your time, granny,' he said jokingly. 'Sit out there in the moonlight until I call. We won't be all night.'

'You paid for an hour.' The old woman hesitated, shrugged her shoulders and stepped out into the night. Verette strode over and fastened the back door.

'I thought you were never coming.'

He glanced at the woman in the corner. 'I was busy.'

'You know it's difficult for me to come here. I expected you sooner.'

He was determined not to apologize. He walked over and put his arm around the woman, hoping to silence her criticism. He flinched when she hugged him fiercely, holding up her lips to be kissed.

'Gina,' he said, 'I'm tired.'

'What about me? I may be disguised as a whore but I deserve better treatment. I had to walk through the streets from Massey's without a light so no one would recognize me.'

In the flickering candle glow he saw Gina's puffy face, her complexion blotched with rum, her eyes hard and her sulky pout. He saw no disguise.

'We haven't got much time,' she said, gripping his wrist and pulling him towards the bed.

Verette swallowed his disgust and followed.

At first it had been easy. When she was staying at Mr Buchanan's house, the sense of daring at taking his pleasure with the wife of Ward Trenchard made their love-making an exciting challenge. It was understood she would reward him.

He told her about his ambition to become a prosperous merchant. He regarded the change in Jonathan's fortune, and thus his own, soon after his brief liaison with Gina as evidence that she had kept her word, even if Jonathan believed the money came from his aunt.

Out of gratitude he agreed to see Gina again on her occasional visits to Port Louis although he harboured no affection for her. He saw the liaison as a business arrangement. He arranged for her to meet him in this old whore's shack so that no one would guess her identity. He performed stoutly, satisfied her and collected expensive presents – jewellery, clothes, snuff boxes – in return.

To his dismay Gina's visits to the town became regular. She summoned him to meet her several times a month. What began as a carefree encounter to help advance himself was becoming a nuisance.

'Gina,' he said, standing beside the bed.

'No time for talk. Come here.' She reached over to unfasten his breeches.

'I can't,' he said.

'Why not?'

He thought desperately, 'I've ... I'm sick!' he said, pleased with the brilliance of his lie.

'There?' She prodded him in his crotch.

'Yes. If I lie with you, you'll get it too. So will Ward, from you.'

'Ward!' She laughed with scorn. 'He doesn't make love to me anymore, Verette. Lord, I think he's become a eunuch. He's mooning about something. He doesn't even have a bed wench any more.'

'You're not angry with me?'

Her sigh reverberated around the tiny room. She looked so dejected, he felt sorry for her. He sat beside her on the bed and put his arm around her shoulders. She snuggled against him, causing him anguish at how he was deceiving her.

'It's for the best,' he said brightly. 'We might be discovered.'

She shrugged and pulled away from him. 'You can't fool me, Verette, with your silly story. I'm surprised you tolerated me for so long. You're a good boy. You'll make some Creole girl very happy. I shall miss you.'

'Miss me?' He had the feeling Gina was getting the better of him. 'Won't I see you again?'

'No, Verette.' She smiled to herself and stood up. 'I wondered how you'd break it off. Thanks for sparing my feelings. It shows you really did care for me, at least a little. It wasn't just for the money, was it?'

He stared at her. 'No,' he said, a tear coming to his eye. 'It wasn't.'

TWENTY TWO

The year of General Gage John Hall's administration was seen by the settlers as a time of disaster for Mauritius. His campaign against corruption among the ruling clique meant little to the ordinary merchant, planter or Creole. Each official's fall from grace was merely a source of scandal in the lobby at Massey's and in the drawing-rooms of the town's hostesses.

The menace to the survival of the settlers was the general's insistence on enforcing the laws that were inimical, in the minds of the inhabitants, to their well-being. As well as his determination to stem the influx of slaves without which the plantations could not function, he was a stickler for regulations.

The secretary of state had agreed to allow the ports to remain open until the first day of March 1818. Europe was at peace so this resulted in foreign vessels thronging the harbour and the warehouses were crammed with goods.

As the date for the closure of the port approached, the merchants petitioned the governor to allow the port to remain open indefinitely. General Hall was adamant. The port was to close. It was in anticipation of this that Jonathan ordered only British cargoes. He had summed up the contentious nature of the general and knew the man was incapable of compromise.

As a result Jonathan was more prepared than any of the other merchants for the port's closure. His prudence helped him survive a calamity that was not General Hall's making. For the settlers it seemed that providence was intervening when, the day before the port was to be closed to all but British ships, disaster struck.

Nicole, with the foresight of a lonely young lady given to musing, felt it in the air.

For days as the end of February approached, she was

restless; she slept fitfully, moped unable to read or attend to the lodging-house's tiny garden, and allowed Emma's perpetual nagging to get on her nerves. She was resentful of Mrs Didcott's fussing, had no appetite and suffered from an inexplicable melancholy.

Despite Mrs Didcott's protests on the last day of February, she went for a walk to the Place d'Armes alone. She sat there on a bench under the royal palm trees that were nearly as tall as Government House. The vast open square used by the military as a parade-ground was flanked by warehouses on opposite sides, with Government House at one end and the ocean at the other.

She was obsessed by the sea's appearance; its restlessness matched her own. For hours she stared at it, unaware of passing time, only conscious of the awful energy the waves contained as they dashed on the shore. The harbour was packed with vessels of all nations, bobbing uneasily at their moorings while boats hurried to ferry their cargoes ashore before the port's closure.

The weather was worsening. The sky was ominous with clouds scudding across it as though chased by some dreadful predator. Fluffy white clouds were followed by grey streaks that gradually swelled until they filled the whole sky. Dark, menacing shapes loomed up from behind the jagged range of peaks surrounding the town, and crested the mountains, heralding an early dusk.

All around her there was commotion. Bullock-carts loaded with goods lurched over the cobbles and into the muddy side streets, whipped along by half-naked Malabars as emaciated as their beasts. Gangs of slaves trotted along the waterfront with crates on their heads, followed by perspiring Creoles anxiously checking that none of their cargoes were lost.

In the urgency of unloading all the goods and storing them in the warehouses before the deadline expired, everyone was heedless of the darkening sky and the closeness of the atmosphere.

The abrupt change in the weather from the sun's brightness to a threatened storm eased Nicole's depression.

She blamed her mood on Port Louis. If she were at Tamarind she would be able to find something to occupy herself. In town she was aware of the disapproval of the English colonists. They never said anything and treated her cordially if they met her when she was out walking with Emma, but she knew what they were thinking.

Her mother was a whore who sold herself for four dollars a time! Ward's words were imprinted on her mind. Worse was that she seemed destined to follow her mother's ways. She was no longer a virgin. No man, whether English, French or Creole, would marry her. Her future was bleak.

The sight of Jonathan scurrying across the square, his head bowed as he walked against the breeze, disturbed her. He looked so frail, the tail of his coat fluttering and his hair billowing wildly in the wind.

She admired him for his determination to prove to everyone that he was not the miserable nonentity he thought himself. She deeply regretted not being part of his success. Had Ward agreed to help him, she might be married to Jonathan at that moment.

She recoiled at the idea. It was precisely because she was not good enough for marriage to him, or to any man, that she avoided him. Several times he sent messages through Verette that he wanted to see her. Emma taunted her by saying that Jonathan intended to make her his Creole mistress.

From time to time she saw him, sometimes on the veranda of his house gazing at the Champ de Mars, or like this blustery afternoon as he hurried across the square, too absorbed in his business affairs to notice her.

The speculation of Mrs Didcott and her friends could find little reason for Jonathan's phenomenal success. He was expanding, building business premises in the Chaussée, and granite-block houses in the road to the Champ de Mars. He never relaxed, driving himself like a man deranged. It was rumoured he had already made enough profit to pay back his aunt's loan.

Naturally Jonathan was an object of interest to all the

town's matrons with eligible daughters. Mrs Didcott was in despair that Emma showed no desire to cultivate his friendship. She urged her to take walks in the Place d'Armes, where she was sure to meet him. Emma refused.

Her reserved attitude puzzled Nicole as much as it dismayed Mrs Didcott. Nicole knew Emma's uncharacteristic self-restraint would crack.

Perhaps, mused Nicole, Emma *would* be suitable for Jonathan, Even as she thought of it, she dismissed the idea from her mind with a shrug of horror. Emma would bully Jonathan to distraction. He did not have the sangfroid of Mr Didcott, who coped with his wife's tantrums with stolid composure. In Mrs Didcott, Nicole could see Emma twenty years hence. She pitied the man she would marry. By all means Jonathan must be spared that.

She watched him fight his way against the breeze to round a corner towards the customs house. For all his success he still conducted himself with the parsimony of a clerk. When she saw him like that she longed to take him by his shoulders and shake him into being a man.

He was so easily discouraged. After she refused his invitations, he no longer sent her messages. Although she could never accept, she would have liked to know he had the gumption to continue to pursue her.

She sighed at her own inconsistency. She wished she could put him out of her mind completely. He was not handsome, cultured or suave. He was gawky and clumsy, the opposite to what a young lady was supposed to seek for a husband.

When a woman married Jonathan it would be for his connections and his prosperity. She would have to close her eyes to his long nose, his greasy hair, his shambling gait, his hunched shoulders, and think only of the fortune he would bring her.

For Nicole it was Jonathan's shortcomings that attracted her. She saw beyond his irregular looks and nervous manner to the kind, caring man within. He needed an understanding woman to encourage and reassure him when he made the kind of mistake that he had when he confided in General Hall.

It was Jonathan's information that set off the General's purge. One by one officials were suspended from their duties. Chief Judge George Smith was said by Hall to have 'counter-acted and embarrassed every act of my administration, by professional subtilty and vindictive counsel'. How the scandal mongers clucked their tongues when they heard that.

Even Theodore Hook, who considered himself immune, was questioned by a commission of enquiry over the loss of twelve thousand pounds from the treasury. George Allen, Jonathan's friend, gave evidence against him. Although Hook protested vehemently, he was unable to give a satisfactory explanation and was placed under arrest.

The humiliation of the man who delighted Port Louis society for six years was complete when he had been taken under military escort to a ship in the harbour a few days previously, and sent back to London in disgrace. General Hall condemned him publicly for 'the most daring embezzlement of public money which ever came within my knowledge'.

Nicole guessed at the misery Jonathan was feeling at the outcome of his exposures to Governor Hall. She ought to comfort him. He had no one to whom he could turn except Verette.

She gazed at the sky, heavy with gloom and premature dusk. The sun was blocked out and the wind seemed to be rising. If she waited she might see Jonathan returning. They could speak, she would accompany him to his house ...

Rain was about to fall. She could stay no longer in the square. She was pleased. If she allowed herself to become involved with him, he would never forgive her when he discovered what she had done with Ward. It would destroy him, for no man likes to know his wife has lain with another.

The wind was growing blustery. She glanced up in alarm at the palm tree above the bench where she was sitting. If one of the branches came crashing down she could be injured. Other people had noticed the weather's change. Men and women were hurrying anxiously along the streets.

The overhanging balconies of the newly built houses with their granite-block lower floors and wooden upper stories offered some shelter. People huddled under them as the rain began to fall in large drops.

Nicole clasped her bonnet to her head. She pushed against the wind into the street leading from the Place towards the lodging-house. Shutters were being slammed and doors bolted.

She was exhilarated by the frenzy of activity. Her gloomy mood lifted. She paused, wondering why she was hurrying.

The wind buffeted her, pulling her skirt around her legs so it billowed out like a sail. She laughed as she had to hold on to a post supporting an overhead balcony to stop herself from being blown down the street.

A wave of rain gusted into her face and her bonnet was swept off her head, straining at the ribbons that bound it to her neck. Mischievously she loosened the ribbon holding it under her chin and watched as it was borne away in the breeze like a kite. Her ringlets fanned around her face, smothering her eyes, then streaming out behind her when she turned into the wind.

The flurries of rain drenched her. Instead of seeking shelter she clung to the post and faced it, enjoying the water smashing her skin. She let go of her parasol and it fell to the ground, where it joined the debris flying along the street in the wind's blast.

People were shouting at her from doorways to take cover. She paid them no heed, revelling in the purification of the stinging rain and the cuffs from the violent wind.

Cyclones in Mauritius were not common. Every year there were storms and the heaviest rainfall was from January to March, which were also the hottest months. The last cyclone to devastate the island was forty years before. She was not worried by the wind's increasing velocity and the darkening sky, although by now she could barely see the other side of the street.

With the onset of the storm and the lifting of her despair, she was seized with a demonic desire to let go, not only of the post but of all the restraints gathered from Mrs

Didcott's upbringing of her as a pseudo-respectable young lady.

She felt at one with the wind. If she released her hold on the post she would be lifted into the air like her bonnet was. How perfect to float away in the gale until the wind dropped and she drifted down to a new life in another island where no one knew her and no one cared about what she was or what she did.

Whether it was because of the wind or her capricious mood, she never knew. Somehow her fingers slipped from their fragile grip on the post. She found herself, not floating as she expected, but flung into the mud of the street, where torrents of water, sewage and debris swirled around her. She floundered, struggling to rise as the wind howled, tugging at her skirts and hair. Shutters banged against brick walls and the air was filled with thatch, flying shingles and other objects torn from buildings and sent spinning into the air.

The chill of the muddy water and the stench from the gutter in the centre of the street shocked her to reality. She struggled to her knees and saw how her dress was ruined, her shoes gone and her hair soaked. Her ringlets were damp strands that she tried to brush from her eyes. Another gust of wind slapped her. She fell down face first into the mud.

The other people in the street were too preoccupied protecting themselves to bother with her. They rushed into houses and all doors were closed firmly as they huddled behind them, fearful of the wrath of the storm. She raised her face from the mud and peered around. The rain dashed into her eyes and she strained to see in the dark for someone to save her. The street was deserted.

If she could reach the sidewalk, she could cling to a post until there was a lull in the wind. These storms were brief, angry phenomenons. She was not frightened, only ashamed to be crawling on her hands and knees in the filth of Port Louis's main street.

Suddenly she was light-headed and it did not matter any more. The sewer was where she belonged. She deserved to be abused; it was a penance from which she would emerge purified. If only that were true, she thought with a giggle as water splashed into her face.

She almost reached the sidewalk when there was the sound of splintering and a noise more terrifying than she had ever heard. In the darkness she could not see what was rushing towards her but she felt its threat. She flung herself back into the gutter, lying still in its dip, as with a roar the entire balcony of a house smashed into the street, inches from her head.

People screamed. She lay in the mud in a daze, choking at the stench, wondering if she was going to die. Someone was pulling at her arm. She rose slowly to her knees, but wished she could stay there in the mud.

Strong hands pulled her to her feet and an arm held her under her breasts, supporting her. She wanted to tell her rescuers to leave her but somehow the words would not come. Some men surrounded her, forcing her to walk while the wind bashed into them, whipping her breath away and making movement impossible.

She was jerked off her feet and dragged by the men out of the street. A door was opened and she was bundled inside a building as the wind rose and blew out the candles in the room. The door slammed shut behind her.

She slid to the floor in the darkness and covered her face with her hands. Gradually she realized the buffeting of the wind had stopped, there was no rain smacking her cheeks. Instead there was the eerie howling of the gale as the wind whistled around the stout walls of the building and the loud clatter of debris hitting the street.

A candle was lit in the room and a glass shade placed around it to shield it from the draught. In the dim light, before the man holding the candle shone it on her, she saw she was in a large store-room. Sacks and bales of clothing were piled up to the ceiling. She shifted to a sitting position as the man with the candle walked towards her.

He was as dishevelled as she was. His hair dripped with water as it hung limply over his ears. His coat was sodden and shapeless; his breeches stuck to his thighs. His shoes squelched with water. He stood over her.

In the gloom she was reminded of Ward and the night he had stood in a similar stance and flung money in her face.

The man extended his hand to help her up. She shrank from it.

'Are you hurt?' he asked anxiously.

The voice struck her with a greater force than the wind outside. This wasn't a dream. She shivered and fell prostrate on the cold stone floor. She covered her head with her arms. She wriggled to shake off the hands that caressed her shoulders. Someone placed a dry flour sack around her. She heard voices but refused to raise her head.

'She's in shock.' The voice was practical in its deep timbre, as though nothing could unsettle its user. 'There's brandy in here somewhere.'

'No.' The dour tones of her rescuer caused her to squirm with shame. 'Don't open a whole case just to get one tot.'

'We could be here all night.'

'Then we must remain alert.'

'This building will withstand the worst cyclone. We strengthened it only last month.'

'Are the other warehouses secure?'

'Yes. And all the cargoes stored.'

Nicole listened with disbelief to the conversation. Curiously, because the two men seemed to have forgotten her, she was less nervous. If she kept quiet and in the shadow, maybe they would not realize her identity.

'Make up a bed with empty flour sacks,' the man ordered. 'She'll be better if she can sleep. Whatever was she doing out there?'

'She's been sitting in the Place d'Armes all afternoon.' Verette spoke cheerfully. 'Waiting for you, Jonathan, I suppose.'

'No!' The denial slipped from her lips before she could stop it. She scrambled to her feet, flinging the flour sack to the ground.

'Nicole!' Jonathan gaped at her, his lower jaw falling slack.

'Don't get excited,' cautioned Verette.

'You knew ...' she said, feeling the tears welling up in her eyes. 'You rescued me because you knew.'

'Verette did,' said Jonathan, his voice kind but edged with worry. 'He saw you outside. I thought you would drown.'

'Better I had!' The tears burst out.

He placed his arms around her and pulled her to him.

'No,' she sobbed, 'don't touch me! I'm unclean.'

'After wallowing in the town sewer,' said Verette with a laugh, 'what do you expect?'

She choked back her tears, resenting his attitude. 'You wouldn't understand,' she said crossly. 'Mind your own business.'

'See the thanks I get?' Verette shrugged and walked towards the door. 'I'm going to check the other warehouses. The wind's dropped.'

Jonathan shouted at him to stay but the noise as he forced open the door drowned his voice. Nicole prized herself from his arms.

'Let me go too,' she said, running to the door. It slammed in her face before she could reach it. She turned and stared at Jonathan.

'It's all right,' he said, looking baffled at the crazed expression on her face. 'You'll be safe here. It's snug enough. This store was built to withstand cyclones.'

He hesitated and she saw his eyes change, a fear suddenly reflected in them.

'Oh, Nicole!' He sounded shocked. 'Nothing will happen, I assure you. You'll not be compromised. I'm not like that.'

'Hah!' she said, feeling that demon in her spark into life. 'How do you know what I am like?' She stalked into the centre of the warehouse floor and pointed to a pile of flour bags.

'That looks more comfortable than the ground. I've made love on the grass so a heap of *sour flacks* is a luxury.' She was shaking, so out of control she could not speak properly.

'Nicole, calm down. You're distraught. I'll protect you, I

promise.' Jonathan wiped the hair out of his eyes. The gesture made her laugh hysterically.

'You are so innocent, Jonathan,' she uttered when she saw him staring at her with concern. 'You expect only good in everyone.'

He hurried over with a flour bag. 'Put this around you,' he said, frowning. 'It will keep you warm. Don't worry. You don't know what you're saying. It doesn't matter.'

'Yes, it does, Jonathan. It matters a lot. Do *you* understand what I'm saying? I've made love on the ground, in the forest at Tamarind, just like a whore. I can do it here too!' She pulled him down onto the heap of flour sacks, clinging to his shoulders.

He slipped away from her grasp and struggled so he was on his knees at her side. His cravat was loose and his hair flopped into his eyes. He smiled at her comfortingly.

'Why don't you rest, Nicole. I don't mind what you've done. I don't believe it.'

She lunged at him, grasping his cravat and pulling him by it until he toppled off balance and fell onto the sacks beside her.

'Don't speak, Jonathan,' she said, flinging herself on him.

She pressed her lips over his mouth to make sure he obeyed.

Book Three

MAN OF CONSEQUENCE 1818–1822

Oo kee oo?
(Who are you?)

TWENTY THREE

The cyclone of 1818 was as severe as that of 1773. If it had lasted a few hours longer the whole of Port Louis would have been a heap of ruins. Nearly all the ships in the harbour were cast ashore and severely damaged. Eight of them sank.

General Gage John Hall showed how obnoxious and unsympathetic a governor he was when he refused the pleas of the local merchants to allow the port to remain open to foreign trade so that relief could be brought from India. He believed the merchants would enrich themselves from relief supplies as they had done after the fire of 1816.

He told the merchants and planters who petitioned him that they should reckon on storms and calculate their profits accordingly. For the merchants and the townsfolk, the cyclone brought disaster. To Jonathan it brought fortune, and heartbreak.

He woke on the morning of 1 March to a cavernous darkness. The shrieking of the wind battering the walls of the warehouse helped him recall where he was. The presence of Nicole beside him, sleeping with her head nestling in the crook of his arm, confirmed his dream was a scandalous reality.

At first he had refused to believe what Nicole was trying to tell him, attributing it to her shocked state after being rescued from the cyclone's fury. Even her passionate demand for comfort could be a result of her distress. He had tried to calm her, holding her tenderly while withdrawing his face from her childish attempts to kiss him.

The intensity of her craving alarmed him when she

refused to be satisfied with a brotherly cuddle and heartening words. He was an undemonstrative man, steeled against passion as something unreliable. He was accustomed to formal relationships. The gradual realization that Nicole wanted more from him than he had ever given any woman in his life frightened him.

He was, by breeding and inclination, a gentleman regardless of his unimportant station in society. His impulse was to extricate himself from Nicole's demanding arms and plead misunderstanding. He tried.

She would have none of it. Her lips found his own again while her fingers caressed the back of his neck. He opened his mouth to gasp at the feeling surging through him and found himself tasting her tongue.

He tried to drive it out, with the result that his own tongue became lodged in her mouth. She sucked with a desperation that plunged him into an exquisite agony. The more he tried to withdraw, the greater grew her demand.

She swarmed over him, her hands rousing feelings of ecstacy that pushed him beyond logical reason. Soon, by instinct alone, he was responding, heedless of the consequence.

Under her guidance he took her. It was a flash of lightning, a howling of the storm, a raging gale, a tidal wave that swamped him. He lay exhausted and confused, feeling elated yet guilty until the balm of sleep calmed his conscience.

Now, as he felt her stirring beside him, Jonathan knew there was only one course open to him.

'Nicole ...' he whispered, shaking her awake. 'The storm is dying. I want to take you home.'

For an answer she wrapped her arm around his waist. It was then he became aware that he was naked, and so was she. He recalled with a tinge of shame the frenzy with which they had undressed each other, the delight they shared exploring with trembling fingers the secrets of their bodies. His loins sprang to life and he tried to hold her from him.

'I want to stay here. With you.' She breathed softly in his

ear, tracing a circle around his nipple with her finger.

His body quivered under her touch and he moaned a protest which she smothered with a lazy kiss. He lay back, not daring to believe it was happening again. It was. Yet this time their love-making was leisurely, with the assurance of knowledge.

They lay in each other's arms in silence while the dying wind feebly rattled the shutters. Dawn gradually became visible through chinks in the window frames. They could hear the startled cries of people venturing into the street. Jonathan hugged Nicole, profoundly aware that henceforth his life was transformed.

'I love you,' he whispered.

'No!' She pulled away from his arms, shattering the intimacy that had induced him to reveal his feelings. 'No, no!'

'I do!' He sat up and reached for her, puzzled that she was recoiling from him. 'We must be married this morning.'

In the dim light that was filtering in from the outside he saw she was feeling around their bed of flour sacks for her clothes. He felt sorry for her when he thought of the explaining she would have to do to satisfy Mrs Didcott.

'We can be married privately, immediately. I can arrange it. Then you won't have to be ashamed to face Mrs Didcott. You'll be my wife.'

'No, Jonathan.' Her voice was calmer now. She was sitting on her haunches, like a slave wench, and touched him gently on his shoulder.

He was surprised that this was the same frightened girl who clung to him for comfort as the storm raged the night before. She sounded confident, aware of her future.

'I won't be your wife. I shall tell them the truth. I was caught in the storm. I sheltered in your warehouse.'

'But this?' He gestured helplessly to the rumpled heap of flour bags that had been their bed.

'This means you were very sweet. It will be our secret, of course.' She touched the tip of his nose with her finger.

'I thought you would want me to marry you. It's the

proper thing. After what we did. Dash it! You know ...'

'Jonathan!' Her voice was husky. 'You're such an honourable man. One day I hope you meet a woman worthy of you.'

'I have, you!'

'You don't know what I'm like. You're confused, Jonathan. When you think about it, you'll see I'm right.' She paused, then added coolly, 'Could you open a shutter so I can see? My dress is here somewhere.'

'Listen to me, Nicole!' He stood up, became aware of his own nakedness and tried to cover himself with his hand. He groaned helplessly.

Nicole's laugh reflected a sadness. 'Put a flour sack around you,' she said. 'And please open a shutter.'

He fumbled his way towards the window, conscious of the weight between his legs and his reluctance to leave the pleasure Nicole had given him. Her words did not make sense. He wanted her as his wife. He thought that she would want him as her husband. Why else had she allowed him to make love to her?

Cautiously he opened the shutter. The wind had dropped, but he had to hold the shutter with his hand to stop it banging. He peeped out. People were already filling the street, surveying the damage. He was amazed at how many houses were roofless.

He thought of the consignment of building tools and materials that had arrived the week before from the Cape. He could sell them now at a handsome profit. Anxiously he wondered if his new property in the Chaussée had been damaged.

'You can look now,' a voice said behind him.

He turned in surprise. For a few moments he had forgotten Nicole. She was fastening her dress. A shaft of light fell on her face. She was biting her lip. He realized then that although she was trying to be nonchalant, her true feelings were different. He let the shutter blow closed so people could not see inside.

'What will you do?' he asked, yearning for her.

'I told you. Go home.'

'What about us?'

She pouted.

'I must see you again! This afternoon. Come to my house for tea. We shall talk.'

'Jonathan, you must grow up and be a man. What happened, happened. That's all there is to it. You will continue your life and I'll continue mine. My mother was a whore too, you know.'

'Nicole!' He was so shocked he ran across the store-room to hold her. The flour sack fell off and he crouched down quickly before she saw his nakedness.

'Look at you,' she said mockingly. 'If I were not a whore, you would never approach me like that.'

'Please understand!' He edged behind a stack of bales and peeped around them. 'Stay, Nicole. I want to marry you!'

'Keep your voice down,' she cautioned, moving towards the door. She was brushing at her hair with her hand, trying to untangle the twisted strands that remained of her ringlets.

'Thank you for saving me, Jonathan,' she said, her eyes glinting with meaning. 'From the storm ... and from myself.'

She opened the door and slipped out before he could run across to stop her.

When Verette reported that the lodging-house where the Didcotts lived had been destroyed, Jonathan's reaction was immediate. 'Invite them to stay with us!' he declared, refusing to be swayed by Verette's protests.

He had been fortunate in the cyclone; all his warehouses had withstood the blasts and the Buchanan house, which he had recently renovated, was also unscathed. Most of the town's merchants had suffered and they were envious of him for his good fortune. Jonathan was proud of his foresight. The first three months of each year were treacherous and he had prepared accordingly. It was providence, not luck.

Mrs Didcott was overwhelmed by his invitation to stay and she accepted at once. Together with her husband and Emma she presented herself at his home in the afternoon. As they descended from the palanquins and he eyed the bullock-carts bringing their possessions salvaged from the cyclone's wrath, he began to doubt the wisdom of his spontaneous offer of hospitality.

'At least,' he said to Verette standing at his side, 'I shall be able to see Nicole every day. She will be under the same roof.'

Verette regarded him queerly and moved away to welcome the Didcotts with an exaggerated bow. Emma ignored him with equal exaggeration. Mrs Didcott was fanning herself in the heat, Mr Didcott was grim faced and Emma peeped sulkily under the frills of her bonnet.

After he greeted them and told them how welcome they were, Jonathan asked, feigning an interest that was purely politeness, 'Is Nicole joining you later?'

Mr Didcott, sharing in the pretence of discussing something of little importance, murmured, 'No, she isn't.'

'We thought ... in your house ... too many of us,' said Mrs Didcott between pauses for breath.

'She's gone to Mahebourg.' Emma's tone was spiteful and her eyes shone triumphantly. 'Mamma sent her there!'

'To stay with friends,' said Mrs Didcott from behind her fan. 'It was her wish to go.'

'The Duncans have a plantation and a big family,' Mr Didcott explained. 'Nicole will be nanny to their children. She did want to leave Port Louis. It is an admirable arrangement.'

'Admirable,' repeated Mrs Didcott emphatically, while Jonathan could only stare at her in dismay.

Verette saved his embarrassment by conducting the Didcotts to their rooms. It was Jonathan's plan that Emma and Nicole would have the rooms they occupied before. He was stunned by the thought that Nicole would not be in the house after all. *Why not?* he asked himself in despair. Surely she understood how he felt about her?

That evening, after supper, when Mrs Didcott had

retired and Arthur had slipped off into the town, Jonathan approached Emma. She was sitting in the drawing-room, reading by the faint light of a lamp.

He did wonder what her mother would think about her being alone with him. Yet his eagerness to learn more of Nicole and the reason for her sudden departure was too great for him to suspect that a trap was being laid.

'You might find it lonely here,' he said, standing by the door to the veranda. 'With so many people seeking refuge in the country districts ... and being without Nicole.'

He could not help blushing slightly when he mentioned her name. His loins still throbbed from their loving the night before; his mind was still dazed.

Emma put down her book. Her smile was baleful. 'I'm glad she's gone! She was too tiresome. I had no friends because of her.'

'Really!' He was deaf to the venom in her words.

'Men were beginning to think I'm like her. Mamma says she's become a bad sort. I'm better off without her near me.'

He was appalled. 'I'm sure Mrs Didcott is mistaken about Nicole.'

'Oh no! She was getting quite a reputation.' Emma lowered her voice so that Jonathan was obliged to enter the room and stand close to her.

He averted his eyes from her *décolletage* although he noticed her bosom was heaving provocatively.

'She was like her mother, flirting with every man she met. It's a relief she wanted to go to Mahebourg.'

'Did she really want to go?' He could not help frowning. If what Emma said was true it would explain Nicole's behaviour. He resolved to ask Verette.

Emma nodded and her mouth parted with the tip of her tongue protruding in a way that some men would have taken as an invitation. Jonathan moved away rapidly.

'Basin will escort you to your chamber,' he said, feeling the heat rising around his collar. 'I retire early. Treat my house as your own.' He nodded himself out of the room.

The next weeks were hectic ones for Jonathan so he did

not have to take conscious steps to avoid being left alone with Emma. He returned late at night and left early in the morning. The Didcotts followed their own lazy routine.

Sometimes he met the three of them at dinner. They discussed current events. Emma made it plain she was regaining her high spirits. He began to suspect she was showing too enthusiastic an interest in him.

He became absorbed in his work. He wrote five times to Nicole and received no reply. Through Verette's network of contacts – that kept him better informed about the island than Governor Hall was – he learned that Nicole was well treated and happy with the Duncan family.

Despite his disquiet at General Hall's betrayal of him over King Radama, Jonathan came to admire the man for his intransigence. He knew his duty and carried out his orders without succumbing to the machinations that spoiled Mr Farquhar's regime. Because he was one of the few British settlers who did not condemn him, Jonathan was admitted to the decreasing coterie of men the Governor trusted.

Jonathan sensed this privilege was due to his position with Mr Farquhar and to his current independence. By nature and training he was someone those in authority could rely on. He valued his return to the administration's inner circle. It also consumed more of his time so the moments he would otherwise have wasted yearning for Nicole were spent watching General Hall battling his enemies.

These were led by Judge Smith and Mr Barry, the chief secretary, who never went near General Hall after the governor stopped the practice of government officials being given low interest loans.

Mr Barry sent his complaints direct to Mr Farquhar in England, writing:

> 'You must move heaven and earth to get General Hall out instantly, not an hour is to be lost. The colonists feel that their very existence is threatened ... They are in the power of one in whose bosom there is

a deep-rooted prejudice and rancorous antipathy and aversion towards all that bear the name of Frenchmen and colonist ... They may very shortly be goaded into pitiful indiscretions; martial law will be proclaimed, the slaves will rise up in arms and good night to all.'

During his months of suspension from office Judge George Smith set himself up as a rival power, head of a party openly hostile to Hall. Thrice the governor had to complain about Smith holding competing 'official' receptions.

On the king's birthday Smith's large party diverted merchants and inhabitants from Government House. Mr and Mrs Didcott, and Emma, out of loyalty to Jonathan attended the formal reception although Mrs Didcott longed to be at Judge Smith's to hear the latest scandal about their hated governor.

On the prince regent's birthday Judge Smith held an opposition dinner for forty people and on 20 August Smith and the law officers gave a dinner to 'displaced functionaries and their sympathizers'. Jonathan observed that the very contraband merchants that the governor was seeking to prosecute were the guests of honour.

Jonathan tried to warn General Hall that his opposition to the prince regent's protégés in Mauritius would lead to difficulties for him. He knew Mr Farquhar would not rest if his favourites were disgraced, or his own schemes abandoned.

The combined censure of Colonel Draper and Mr Farquhar, together with the local opposition, was too much for General Hall. He was recalled, just as Jonathan predicted.

He left Mauritius in December, complaining bitterly to Jonathan: 'I leave this colony beset and goaded on every side by the insults and clamour of the triumphant faction.'

Jonathan could only nod his head in agreement.

'There is a consolation,' General Hall boasted bravely as he bid Jonathan farewell. 'I can ask myself whether the applause or the censure of such a community is most likely to reflect disgrace or honour on my character.'

Jonathan's own character was unsullied by his association with the General, such was the universal relief at his departure. Judge Smith threw a party that lasted the whole night. Mr and Mrs Didcott and Emma attended, at last able to indulge openly in criticism of the hated general. Verette persuaded Jonathan to attend too. He strolled among the crowd unnoticed, frowning at the jubilation.

Judge Smith erected a gallows at his gateway in what he called 'Hall's dishonour'. He publicly embraced Frenchmen, slave-traders, and his latest coloured mistress beneath it.

The French and Creoles shared the British pleasure at Hall's departure. It was rumoured among them that it signalled a change in British policy towards the colony. Slave-trading, never successfully stamped out, would be allowed to continue with official blessing and the port would be re-opened.

Jonathan listened to the rumours, heeded Verette's advice and prepared for all eventualities.

General Hall was replaced by the easygoing Colonel Dalrymple for two months and then by General Darling, who, as acting governor, was as ineffectual as his delightful name implied. A second serious cyclone soon after General Darling's appointment only added to Jonathan's prosperity when he was able to cater for the losses it caused.

The cyclone marked a year of Mr and Mrs Didcott's residence in his house. Since he had no one to share his life with, Jonathan bore their presence philosophically. The household was ruled by Mrs Didcott, who vented her temper on the implaccable Basin and Ranavola, and on the hired slaves whom Verette found to serve her.

Jonathan spent most of his time, both day and night, in his warehouses, or with Verette in the premises they had built in the Chaussée.

He was amazed that the months passed so rapidly. The memory of Nicole was ever fresh in his mind. For months he racked his brain to see how he could woo her. He was distracted by Verette's reports of her happiness.

She was living in isolation on the Duncan plantation, tutoring the children. By all accounts she yearned neither for Jonathan nor the social life of Port Louis. Her apparent contentment made him shy. She obviously wanted to forget him.

The fault was his for taking advantage of her during the storm when she was frightened. The months, and his reluctance to believe bad about anyone, clouded the reality of her brazen seduction of him.

In a way Jonathan was content too. He had enjoyed one night of happiness, which was more than he had ever expected. He was blessed with good fortune in his enterprises. At times he wondered if there was an unknown partner helping him, so effortless was his success. If Nicole was happy, then he was prepared to leave her as she wished. He would be satisfied with his own life without her.

He was aware that his aloofness and steady retreat into crusty and confirmed bachelorhood was a challenge to the young women of the town, especially to Emma and her match-making mother. Verette joked about Emma constantly, saying she was destined to become an old maid.

'By the devil, Jonathan!' he said one evening when they sat in the bar-room in the Chaussée, which was one of their Company holdings. 'You must put that wench out of her misery.'

He was embarrassed by Verette's bluntness. 'I was not aware she is miserable,' he said dourly. 'She has suitors.'

'Mamma Didcott chases them away. She's set her sights on you.'

'Emma has?' He was appalled.

'Mamma Didcott has. I doubt that Emma cares so long as she has a man to roger her before she dies.'

'I'm certainly not the one.' Jonathan was shocked by Verette's coarseness.

'You're to blame for encouraging her to think you are.'

'That's preposterous.' He set down his glass of seltzer and stared at Verette in dismay.

'Mamma Didcott sees it differently. She claims it's only a

matter of time before you propose. You're an honourable man, she says, and will do the right thing by marrying Emma. That's the only reason she allows her daughter to remain under your roof.'

Jonathan groaned. 'Is this how I am repaid for my hospitality? We must find another house for them at once. I never knew –'

'Yes you did, Jonathan! Emma's presence keeps the others away. You'll marry her when you're ready.'

He rose to his feet in a daze. 'Dammit!' he said, spilling the seltzer in his confusion. 'Is that what you're scheming?'

Verette grinned broadly. 'I don't have to scheme, you've done it yourself. Everyone's waiting for you to be a man and make Emma your wife.'

'A man?' He glared at him, his temper rising. He saw Verette's startled expression at his raised voice, but was unable to stop himself shouting.

'If I am to be a man, I'll do what *I* want!' He turned on his heels and strode out of the room.

Verette's frown of amazement changed to a smirk of triumph and he nodded wisely to himself.

TWENTY FOUR

Jonathan's temper cooled during his restless walk along the darkened streets of Port Louis. He was angered that people assumed he would marry Emma yet that idea had never occurred to him. It showed him how blind he was through his obsession with work. Now he could understand why Emma sat alone on the veranda when he returned at night, as though waiting for him.

It was vital that he explain to Emma and her mother that marriage was out of the question. How, when they were his guests? He had invited them to stay because he expected Nicole to come with them. When she did not, it was impossible to tell them to go.

He needed an excuse to ask Mr Didcott to take his wife and daughter elsewhere. As he ambled along the footpath of the Champs de Mars he considered all the properties he owned to see what he could offer the Didcotts instead of his own home.

His buildings in the Chaussée were rented by merchants and shopkeepers; some were cafés and brothels. The houses he had built on the Champ de Mars were intended for Creoles. Neither districts would suit the fastidious Mrs Didcott.

It made him wonder if he should build some villas on the slopes surrounding the plain. It was a popular residential area for those English officials and merchants whose business obliged them to live in Port Louis year-round. In his mind he began to choose sites and to calculate construction costs, the rental he could charge and the return on his capital.

By the time he reached the plain, his worry about Emma was forgotten in the excitement of his new plan. He would discuss it with Ward, who had become a keen adviser in his projects. Planters such as Ward could be interested in renting the villas for the season.

Verette would have his own views too. The chief obstacle would be getting the land concessions, and that would require the consent of Sir Ralph Darling, as acting governor. He was an affable, if unimaginative man, whose sole desire was to preserve order until Mr Farquhar returned from England.

If necessary, Jonathan thought, he could write to Mr Farquhar himself. Ill health was delaying the governor's return to Mauritius. He had successfully rebutted the various criticisms of his administration, thanks to his close association with the Prince Regent.

Jonathan's aunt was his source of information on the London scene, and he reciprocated with progress reports on the business she had bought for him. He was surprised that she never conveyed her pleasure at being repaid in full, with interest. He assumed this was due to money being an indelicate subject for a lady to discuss, so he did not raise the matter himself.

He dealt with Augustus Blaize, who was Ward's agent and whom Mr Farquhar had recommended as intermediary. His aunt, he was sure, would approve of him building some villas for rental. She could help him gain Mr Farquhar's support for the venture.

Despite the dark there was a faint light on the plain from a half moon. He strolled into the centre, deep in thought. He was no longer nervous about walking the plain alone at night. It did not occur to him to feel anything but confident.

He stood silently in the dark, gazing in the direction of the far hills and picturing where he would build his villas. It occured to him then that he had met Verette in almost the same spot. He had been dreaming of Nicole that night. The sudden thought of her filled him with consternation. In those days he was nothing and she treated him kindly; now that he was a prosperous businessman, she hid from him on the other side of the island.

He could not understand why. Her attitude clouded the memory of their night together. Had he been wrong? He offered her marriage yet she refused him. Was she just pretending to love him that night?

A shadow drifted closer to him in the darkness and a voice rasped close to his ear. 'Happy time, master? Only four dollars.'

'Go away,' he said gruffly, annoyed with himself for allowing his thoughts to distract him from his calculations.

'I'm clean, master. No one gives loving like me.'

'Be off!' He wished he had a cane to shake in the whore's face. 'I shall tell Verette you troubled me.' There was a gasp and the woman hurried away. It made him think.

Nicole had behaved like a whore that night. *What was it she said?* He could not remember. He was the one to blame for her self-imposed exile. He would have to be patient until she chose to return.

It was a symptom of his new-found arrogance that he assumed Nicole would return to Port Louis some day. It did not occur to him that, caring for the Duncan children, she had discovered a use for her talents. Instead he contrasted her exile with Emma's persistent presence.

He turned to face his house on the hillside and saw lanterns still glowing on the veranda. Emma would be waiting, reclining on the *chaise longue* pretending to read a book as she did every night. If he returned late she would give up the vigil and go to her room. If he returned early when Mrs Didcott was with her, her mother would leave the veranda so they were alone together.

He was determined not to be snared by the trap they had been waiting to spring on him since the day they moved in. He would start the next morning on his plans to build a villa at the opposite side of the plain. He would let Arthur Didcott have it at a nominal rent. Mrs Didcott and Emma would leave and he would be free of the fear of marriage.

Now he was aware of the Didcotts' scheming, thanks to Verette's tip off, he felt less distant towards Emma than usual. He strolled up the path to his house, where he could see her seated on the veranda, keen to speak to her.

'Good night, Emma!' he said, stepping on the veranda briskly. She jerked up her head and blinked at him.

'You frightened me,' she said morosely.

'I'm sorry.' He hesitated at the rebuff, then added, 'I thought you were waiting for me.'

'Waiting?' She yawned without bothering to cover her mouth with her hand. 'That's an odd idea.' She swept away the strands of hair from her face with a gesture of weariness.

'You're here nearly every night when I come home.'

'Because I want to be! It's so stuffy inside. I love the breeze blowing in off the plain. I watch the promenaders. When it's dark the flames of the torches intrigue me and I wonder who's meeting whom.'

She glanced down at her empty hands in surprise. 'And there's my book, of course.' She reached for it, grimaced ruefully and held it up.

The monotony of her existence dismayed him. She was a lively, attractive young woman confined through no fault of her own to a dull life in a stranger's house with only her overpowering mother for company. Her languor, he realized when he saw her forlorn grin, was not of her chosing; he was the one to blame. She was a guest in his house; it was his duty to be more considerate, at least to treat her sociably instead of trying to sneak past her every night.

'Forgive me, Emma,' he said, sitting down in a chair opposite her. 'I've been a fool.'

'Have you?' She looked at him without interest.

'I've been so involved with my work, I never considered you.'

'Why should you do that?' She was frowning now but he was determined to explain himself fully and failed to notice.

'You are staying in my house. I should have paid you more heed. You must be bored here by yourself every evening.'

She glanced at him as though she found his remark odd. 'It's a relief to sit here by myself. I abhor men who constantly pester one. The season is the bore, not my own company.'

He withdrew in confusion, sitting back in the chair and putting his hands on his knee. 'It is not my intention to pry, Emma. Shall I go?'

'You are stupid, Jonathan.' She smirked and swung her legs off the *chaise longue* so she was facing him. 'For goodness' sake, stop touching your hair. If you don't want it to flop in your eyes, cut it short.'

He stared at her. No one in his life, except his aunt, had ever spoken to him like that. 'I'm sorry,' he said meekly.

'There's nothing to be sorry for. You're always apologizing.'

'Am I?' He tried to brush at his hair again, saw her frown and placed his hand firmly on his knee.

'You're not weary of living here?' he said, groping for the thread of the conversation he had started.

She sighed. 'It would be lovely to go to England. I was young when I left, it seems a dream. Life in this colony is too restricting for a young lady.'

'I was referring to this house,' said Jonathan. 'Wouldn't you prefer one of your own, with your own slaves, own furniture, able to live as you wish?' He was carried away with the thought of the house he would build the Didcotts and missed the knowing glint that entered her eye.

'Jonathan,' she said breathlessly, putting her hand out to touch his. 'Do you mean it?'

'I certainly do. It never occurred to me before. That's where I've been a fool. So engrossed in my business, I never saw what was right under my nose.' He glasped her hand in his excitement. 'If you agree, I'll seek the governor's consent tomorrow!'

'Is that necessary?' The puzzlement in her voice should have alerted him, but it did not.

'Oh yes!' He squeezed her fingers enthusiastically. 'These things have to be done properly. It saves complications later.'

'I suppose it does. When do you have in mind?'

'It could take a year.'

'So long? Why not this season?'

'Ah, Emma!' He paused, raised her hand to his chest and looked at her compassionately. 'I know the strain you are under, living here with me in this manner. Try to be patient a few more months until I have arranged everything.'

She sighed, banishing her reluctance. 'I accept. Mamma will be relieved.'

'It will be a wonderful home,' he enthused, delighted at how easily she had been persuaded. 'You can choose how you want it designed, where you'd like your bedroom ...'

He was unaware that her hand was in his. He stopped speaking as his eye caught hers. There was a glimmer of triumph in them.

She lowered her eyelashes, fluttering them coyly just as Mrs Didcott bustled onto the veranda.

'I *knew* I could hear voices,' she said with a glance at Emma. She was swathed from neck to toe in a voluminous night-gown. A cotton cap on her head hid some of the curlers that enmeshed her hair. Her face was blotchy with scrubbing. She gleamed at Jonathan when her eye fell on his hand holding Emma's.

'Mamma,' said Emma coyly. 'Jonathan's asked me to live with him.'

'Thank heaven!' Mrs Didcott threw up her hands with relief. 'It's about time, young man,' she said, recovering her natural querulousness. 'How the girl has suffered. It's been a scandal with the two of you under the same roof and no one knowing your intentions. Have you asked Mr Didcott's permission?'

Jonathan was stunned and groped for the energy to protest. He was gasping for breath as he opened his mouth to speak.

'I thought not!' said Mrs Didcott sternly. 'Really, young people today have no sense of tradition. I suppose because we're beholden to you for hospitality, you think you can ignore convention?'

'No, Mrs Didcott.' He shook his head, removing his hand from Emma's and standing up. 'I haven't *proposed.* It's all a mist –'

'He's been describing the house I'll have, Mamma. It sounds nice. He says he'll ask the Governor's permission tomorrow. Will Father agree?'

Mrs Didcott sniffed. 'He has no alternative when I tell him what I've seen.'

Again Jonathan was shocked speechless. He stared from Mrs Didcott to Emma. Only then did he notice Emma's corsage was unlaced and her skirt rucked up to her thighs. It was obvious what her mother thought, especially as he had been holding her hand. He brushed at his hair furiously.

'Jonathan!' Emma's rebuke stopped him. He blinked at her helplessly.

'You'll make a perfect couple,' Mrs Didcott was saying, clapping her hands.

Jonathan tried to speak, but he couldn't. Mrs Didcot swept forward, put her arm around Emma and drew her to her feet.

'Come with me, child. It's not proper for you to spend

time alone with him now. People *will* talk.' She hustled her off the veranda with a withering glance at Jonathan.

It was then, he realized later in the cheerless atmosphere of his own chamber, that he should have protested, explaining it was a misunderstanding and asked their forgiveness. Now it was too late. He flung himself on top of his bed, not bothering to undress, and cried himself to sleep.

The date for the wedding was set for November. To his astonishment Jonathan was the toast of the town. He gradually came to think that marriage was not such a bad idea after all. He was going ahead with his project to build villas on the slopes overlooking the plain. He planned that he and Emma would live in one of them. Removed from the nagging tongue of Mrs Didcott, he expected Emma to blossom into a supportive wife who would be an asset.

She was regarded with grudging respect by the town's bachelors. Her youthful high spirits were remembered by some. However, it was by her frosty behaviour since her return to Port Louis from Tamarind that she was judged. Jonathan ignored the comments in Massey's about his freedom ending with marriage. Now the decision was made, he was relieved.

'You'll regret it, *garçon*!' Ward Trenchard chided him when they met in the Café Marengo for one of their occasional business discussions.

Jonathan shrugged his shoulders glumly, preferring to talk about his villa project.

'I'm serious,' Ward said. 'The woman has no heart. Like her mother.'

'You are speaking of my fiancée,' Jonathan reminded him coolly.

'Hah! A devil's toss to that!' Ward shook his head. His arrogance was intimidating. Jonathan sipped at his coffee to calm his anger. It was pointless to argue with Ward.

'What about Nicole?' Ward asked sharply, catching Jonathan off guard so he choked, spluttering coffee onto the table top. He mopped it up hastily, blushing with embarrassment.

His question was the one Jonathan hoped to avoid. That it was Ward who asked it seemed unimportant for it only echoed what was on his own mind. 'I shall write to her,' he said despairingly. 'I hear she's very happy at Mahebourg.'

'Playin' with children!' Ward scoffed. 'With her hot blood there's only one thing she wants to play with.'

'That's slanderous!' Jonathan jumped to his feet and his chair toppled backward with a loud clatter. The other patrons in the café eyed him with interest. 'I demand an apology.'

'Hah!' Ward motioned to him to sit down. 'No woman's worth quarrellin' over.'

'You've no right to say what you did.'

'How do you know that, Jonathan? It's Emma you're marryin' not Nicole. Why do you want to defend her name instead of Emma's?'

Jonathan gulped, aware of the eyes watching him keenly. He picked up his chair and returned to the table. 'Forgive me, I'm not myself.'

'Yes, you are, *garçon*!' Ward winked. 'Think on it. Now what's this new scheme of yours?'

Although Ward with his cavalier attitude made light of his insult of Nicole, Jonathan could not forget it. While he explained his project he glanced suspiciously at Ward wondering what game the man was playing.

Had he deliberately provoked him to think of Nicole? If so, his success was complete. He thought of nothing else.

He had intended to write to her and explain but his courage failed him. Every time he tried, he doubted again the wisdom of his proposed marriage. If offended him that the action of informing Nicole should undermine his decision. That the decision was not his no longer concerned him. The marriage was a practical one and, as Verette said, was inevitable.

The day grew nearer and he still did not inform Nicole. He worked in a daze, blocking out thoughts of her from his mind. He was scrupulously correct and polite with Emma as though any indication of emotion on his part would jeopardize the union. He moved out of his own house and camped in a chamber above his new bureau in the Chaussée.

Since the closing of the port the year before only British ships were allowed in the harbour. Trade was slack and many goods were impossible to obtain. Every vessel was unloaded as soon as it arrived although quarantine regulations were sometimes enforced to protect the colony from epidemics.

A ship, the *Topaz*, arrived from Manila in late October with a cargo of general merchandise and foodstuffs. Mrs Didcott learned from Verette that its manifest included fine exotic silks, so she resolved to have them for her wedding outfit. As some of the ship's crew were ill with dysentery the off-loading of the cargo was delayed for quarantine. This infuriated Mrs Didcott.

'I need that silk urgently,' she told Jonathan. 'How else will my dress be ready in time? The wedding's only two weeks hence.'

Jonathan, distracted by her presence in his bureau, told her wearily that there was nothing he could do about it. 'Only Governor Darling can waive the quarantine regulation,' he said. 'You'll have the silk next week, when the crew recover.'

He underestimated the determination of his future mother-in-law. She appealed directly to Sir Ralph Darling. The governor, cowered by her formidable attack on his pettifogging restrictions, allowed the *Topaz* to discharge its cargo.

Within days it was no longer Mrs Didcott's temper that concerned Sir Ralph. The cargo the *Topaz* carried was a deadly one: cholera.

It spread through the town as swiftly as the fire of 1816. Some of the crew, whose infection was mild enough to enable them to go ashore, carried the pestilence to the waterfront cafés. After five days hundreds of the townsfolk were collapsing with sudden diarrhea. Within hours they were dying.

There was panic. All who were able to leave Port Louis hastened to do so. Verette chartered a schooner to take

Jonathan and the Didcotts to the Tamarind plantation. It was thought that there, isolated from the source of the disease in the town, they would be safe.

In less than two days after the alarm was given, Port Louis lost its gay bustle and became gloomy and desolate. The only people to be seen in the streets were scavenger slaves carrying corpses to a hasty and unceremonious burial.

Jonathan chafed at being forced into exile. Verette's insistence drove him to it, although Verette himself stayed behind to look after the Company's interests.

Jonathan felt that in a way he was to blame for the dreadful calamity. Over a hundred people had died since the *Topaz* discharged its cargo. Mrs Didcott got her silks; the bolts of cloth lay on her dressmaker's floor in a pool of vomit. The dressmaker herself was one of the first victims.

At Tamarind, Mr Moult welcomed their party with reluctance. It was the cane-cutting season and he eyed each of them, gloomily wondering if they had brought the cholera with them. Mrs Didcott took to bed with an attack of the vapours to be fussed over by Mrs Moult. Arthur joined Mr Moult in a bottle of rum while Emma wandered to the garden. Jonathan followed her and found her sitting under a pair of mango trees.

'We'll be safe here,' he said, lowering himself with difficulty to sit on the grass beside her. He was hesitant about removing his coat in her presence and sweated in the heat. 'It should pass over in a few days.'

'I hope so.'

He noticed she was subdued, but it did not worry him. He was used to her moods. 'We might have to delay the wedding,' he said warily.

'Yes.' She did not sound disappointed. She wasn't even looking at him. Her eyes were on the cane field a few yards distant.

He followed her glance and saw a negro, a huge, half-naked buck whose black skin gleamed in the sunlight, lower his arm casually and chop a cane stalk off at its roots. He flung the cane on the ground and gripped the next one in his massive hand. The strength of his effortless swift movements impressed Jonathan and he could appreciate Emma's fascination with him.

'That must be one of Ward's Black River breed,' he said. 'He prides himself on selling the best slaves.'

'Buy him!' It was a command. 'For my wedding present.'

'What?' He wasn't sure if she was serious.

'He'll be useful about the house. He'll protect me when you're not at home.'

'Verette can do that.'

'He isn't coming to live with us!' she said emphatically.

'Oh, no ... I suppose not.'

'You'll buy him?' She turned her eyes back to gaze at the negro.

'If you insist.'

'I do,' she said. 'His name's Brutus. I want him.'

He sighed, shrugging his shoulders at the funny ways of women. Perhaps the buck's presence would be useful. They would need a yard boy and the negro could also be the night-watchman. Emma, he decided, was right.

He slept fitfully that night and fretted throughout the following day. Plantation life did not agree with him. The sun sought out his nose and speedily burned it a bright red. His coat was drenched with sweat under his armpits, and his trousers stuck to his thighs in the heat. Emma, who complained of a stomach cramp, spent the whole day lying listlessly on a couch on the veranda.

Jonathan's misgivings about Emma's health began the following afternoon. The cramp in her stomach grew worse. She refused to eat but drank vast quantities of water. He had to help her to hold the glass because she was so weak. He spent the afternoon sitting with her. She watched the slave, Brutus, working in the cane without speaking.

Suddenly she uttered a great sigh. A stream of vomit emerged effortlessly from her mouth and fell to the floor. Jonathan stared at it. Emma gazed at him with fear in her eyes.

'Something you've eaten,' he said.

She shook her head sadly. 'I feel so cold.'

He ran for a blanket, calling for a slave to clean up the mess. The house was empty apart from Mrs Didcott and Mrs Moult upstairs in their chamber. He came back to see that the puddle of vomit on the floor had grown. There were stains of diarrhea on Emma's skirt.

Emma was lying limply on her back, unable to stanch the vomit when it trickled from her mouth. He covered her with the blanket and left her again to find a lantern as it was getting dark.

Mr Moult was at the mill-house supervising the sugar boiling. Mrs Moult was sitting with Mrs Didcott and could not leave her because she was vomiting too. Arthur Didcott had disappeared. Jonathan found a lantern in the drawing-room and returned with it to the veranda. He feared the worst. If they had brought the cholera to Tamarind with them, there would be no escape.

He hung the lantern on a hook at the end of the veranda. As he did so, he caught sight of a shadow moving in the garden at the edge of its rim of light. *One of the slaves*, he thought, hurrying back to Emma. He touched her brow. It was clammy. Her skin, usually so clear, was a dull blue in colour and wrinkled.

He took out his handkerchief and gently wiped away the vomit from her lips. The house slaves had vanished and he was obliged to tend her himself. He peered around anxiously. Once again he sensed a movement in the tangle of bougainvillea bushes that grew beside the veranda.

'If only Verette were here,' he muttered aloud.

Emma moaned. He touched her brow again. 'What is it?' he said, moving away as vomit seeped out of her mouth and splashed on his hands.

'Wa ... water,' she croaked, her eyes half closed.

'Oh dear!' He glanced around again. 'I'll have to get that myself. I'll need the lantern.' He unhooked it and dashed back into the house.

The onset of cholera is sudden. Death, in most cases, comes within hours. Emma had picked up the germ in Port Louis and been sickening with it since their arrival. Mrs Didcott probably had it too. Death was not inevitable, but rare was the victim who survived when the diarrhea and vomiting began.

His preoccupation with Emma's plight confused him. The clay water cooler was empty, and so was the filter. He wandered about the kitchen aimlessly, uncertain what he should do. *Water, yes.*

He was in a daze, unsettled by the absence of slaves to help him. Water must be outside, he decided. In a well? In the stream? In a water cask? He did not know.

He stepped out cautiously into the pitch darkness of the plantation to search.

In the blackness of the moonless night Brutus moved swiftly. He had the eyes of a jungle cat and he knew his prey. When he saw the white man carry the lantern into the house, he slipped from his hiding-place behind the bourgainvillea and stepped silently onto the veranda.

The woman was lying on the couch on her back, her head turned to one side and her legs open.

He stood over her, listening for her breathing. He heard nothing and lowered his ear to her mouth. He heard the soft gasp of the death rattle gurgling in her throat.

He smiled and removed his loin cloth, using it to wipe the vomit away from her lips.

She was moist. He thrust her legs apart and forced himself into her. He grunted, rubbing his mouth against her own. She was dead.

Vengefully he plunged into her, ejaculating into her lifeless body.

TWENTY FIVE

When the cholera epidemic ended six months later, twelve thousand people were dead. Its tentacles stretched over the whole island, aided by the inhabitants carrying the disease with them as they fled to the plantations from Port Louis.

In Mahebourg, Nicole escaped. Mr Duncan, for the sake

of his children, refused to take any of the refugees. Nicole was scrupulous in ensuring cleanliness among the household slaves. Her care saved them all.

Mahebourg was the main village on the south-eastern side of the island, over thirty miles from Port Louis through the mountains. It was a hazardous journey that had to be undertaken by palanquin or on foot because of the conditions of the road.

The building of the settlement began in 1805 under the French. It was named after a famous governor, Mahé de Labourdonnais, who changed the island in the eighteenth century from a trading post to a prosperous French colony.

It had become an important centre over the years of its existence, due to its proximity to the natural harbour of Grand Port. The Duncan plantation, with its acres of sugar-cane growing on the gentle slopes of the aptly named Montagne des Creoles, was a few miles north of the town. Visitors were rare and its isolation suited Nicole perfectly.

She had progressed from being a nanny to the five Duncan children to managing the whole household. Mrs Duncan, a Scots lass only a few years older than Nicole, was engaged with Calvinistic dedication in bearing her husband a new child every year.

The high sense of morality and adherence to the strict rules laid down by Mr Duncan appealed to Nicole. She did her work well, loved the children and in turn was loved by them and respected by the slaves who served under her in the house.

Fidou, who had been bought by Mr Duncan at Nicole's request, did not enjoy life on the plantation. She was appalled by the daily prayers led by Mr Duncan and by the upright behaviour of his slaves. She yearned for the seamier side of Port Louis, where she had her friends and was not subject to the strictures of the pious Mr Duncan.

Nicole was impressed by the way Fidou kept informed about events in the town. Slaves passed messages by word of mouth so the news that reached the plantation was rich in embellishment.

When Nicole heard through Fidou about Jonathan's

proposed marriage to Emma, she doubted it was true, especially when no letter arrived from him to tell her. The rumour persisted and Mr Duncan confirmed its truth. Nicole's despair, she was ashamed to admit, was only relieved when Fidou reported Emma's death from cholera.

'What about Jonathan?' Nicole demanded anxiously when Fidou brought her the news. 'Is he sick too?' If he was, she would have to go to him. He would be so helpless.

'He returned to Port Louis,' said Fidou, proud of her knowledge. 'Emma an' Mrs Didcott buried at Tamarind. You remember that slave Brutus?'

'The one Emma was fond of?' Nicole shuddered at her recollection of the gigantic, heathenish brute.

'Mas Jonathan bought him from Mr Moult. He take him to Port Louis.'

'How strange. He must be terrified of the boy.'

'I hear Emma died in the nigger's arms.'

'Poor Emma.'

Nicole wept that night over their deaths, and with gratitude for Jonathan's lucky escape.

Life on the Duncan plantation followed a rigid routine. Nicole was constantly occupied. She went to her bed in a tiny room adjoining the children's nursery only when the last house slave had gone to the quarters. She rose with the dawn to supervise the lighting of the fire and the making of coffee before the early-morning prayers that started the day.

She passed the months inspired by her work and those daily devotions with the Duncans. She refused to think of Jonathan. She was not angry with him. There was a room in her mind which, if she cared to open it, contained memories of the innocent times they had shared. That was past.

She drew her strength now from God. She believed herself blessed to have found a family who depended on her and gave her the chance to forget her sins.

She was no longer the same person. The change in her had created a gulf between herself and Fidou. She could not help it. When she remonstrated with Fidou about her yearning for the old life, the slave was scornful, rolling her eyes and muttering, *some day you change*, as though it were a prophecy.

To Nicole's dismay the unexpected arrival of Verette was all that it took to shake her new-found faith.

She was glancing out of the window of the nursery at the spectacular landscape of mountains and sea when she saw Verette striding up the path to the mansion. She blinked, unable to believe that it was him.

The children clamoured to know who was the 'grandly dressed gentleman'. She loved them for their innocence. A black man in Mauritius, however elegant his clothes and manners, was not a gentleman in the eyes of the British.

The years since she had seen Verette vanished when she came face to face with him in the kitchen. He rose to his feet and bowed gallantly.

'You haven't changed at all,' she gasped, ignoring his fine outfit and thickened waistline.

'You have,' he replied bluntly. The twinkle in his eye lightened his criticism. 'You look older, more a woman. And more beautiful.'

His flattery unnerved her, setting off a flow of emotions she wished to forget. She was suddenly tongue-tied and was grateful that Fidou's chattering made it unnecessary for her to reply.

'What you doin' here?' Fidou demanded, gazing at him in rapture.

'Business.' Verette shrugged, then added, 'In Mahebourg. The Company's expanding. The road is to be improved so Jonathan decided we should have a branch here.'

Nicole pursed her lips to control the shakiness in her voice. 'How is he?' she asked hesitantly.

Her feigned nonchalance did not deceive Verette. He glanced at her from under his long lashes as if to say, *Why are you pretending you don't care?*

'He survives,' he said with studied casualness. 'No time for fêtes or females, of course, although the season is underway now Governor Farquhar has returned.'

Fidou's eyes blazed. 'There must be parties every night –'

'Such a social whirl! The port is open again to ships of all nations, the shops are crammed with merchandise and commerce is flourishing. You would love it!' He was answering Fidou although his words were obviously intended for Nicole.

She turned her head to avoid the glitter of excitement in his eyes. It might have fascinated her before, but she was not going to be drawn into it again. She had found fulfillment with the Duncans. Verette's arrival was a threat, and it annoyed her.

'You won't be staying here for long?' she asked hopefully. 'We lead very dull lives.'

'So I notice.' Again his eyes stared at her meaningfully.

'We are happy this way,' she said with a note of defiance in her voice in case he misunderstood. 'I must go to the children,' she added, avoiding his eyes and making a hasty exit.

Her duties occupied her for the rest of the day. She was aware of Verette's presence either in the kitchen joking with Fidou or, in the afternoon, on the veranda talking business with Mr Duncan.

She realized Verette was a skilled negotiator from what she overheard. Mr Duncan, with his canny ways, was a match for him. Evidently, they reached a satisfactory agreement on the importation of clothing and tools for the slaves, for Mr Duncan clapped Verette on his shoulder and invited him to stay the night.

The look in Fidou's eyes when she heard he was staying made Nicole's heart flutter. It was clear what was going to happen and she was startled by it, even disgusted.

Alone in her nursery room that night she wondered why Verette's visit was disturbing her. She shrank from imagining Verette and Fidou on the kitchen floor together, but she could not keep it out of her mind. It forced her to open the door of her memories, and brought back the pleasure she had found that night on the warehouse floor in Jonathan's arms.

It was her enjoyment of their love-making then that had

frightened her. She resolved never to do it again. The passion he roused in her was overwhelming. If she succumbed to it she feared she would become like her mother. By remaining far away from Jonathan, by forgetting him, she was safe.

In a way she envied Fidou for enjoying with Verette that pleasure she denied herself. She trembled as she lay on the bed, struggling to sleep. If she lost her faith, her envy could change to resentment. She would become bitter, a lonely spinster sour at the world.

To her shame she dreamed that night of Jonathan. She awoke in the morning with her body afire with longing for him.

Fidou's announcement that she wanted to return to Port Louis with Verette was a relief. Nicole associated Fidou with her old life. After Verette's visit, and what obviously took place between them, it would be an embarrassment if she remained in the house.

'He won't marry you,' she warned Fidou, hoping to point out to her the error of her ungodly ways. 'Free blacks always marry women lighter than themselves.'

Fidou stared at her in amazement before she burst out laughing. 'Lor', Nicole,' she said between cackles. 'I don't want marry-age. Mas' Jonathan done send for me.'

'Jonathan?' Her pulse quickened.

'Verette says he needs a housekeeper. Basin and Ranavola are too old. He and Mr Didcott can't manage for themselves.'

'I didn't know Mr Didcott is living with them.'

'You didn't listen to half what Verette tell you yesterday. You were dreamin'. Mr Didcott join his Company as head bookkeeper.'

'I see.' She hummed a nursery rhyme to herself and pretended to inspect the kitchen shelves for dust.

'You don't mind if I go, do you? Mr Duncan agree to sell me. Verette arrange it last night.'

'Did he?'

'It will be wonderful to be in Port Louis 'gain now the season on. I goan see my friends. They'll be race meetin's at the Turf Club. Judge Smith has his parties, he been reinstated, you know, an' ...'

Nicole closed her ears to Fidou's prattling. The more she heard, the more she was troubled. With the ousted officials returned to power by Governor Farquhar, Jonathan would be feeling remorse at having informed on them to General Hall. He was such a nervous, private person, he probably longed for someone to share his doubts with. He would need someone to bolster his confidence.

'Look after him,' she said suddenly, halting Fidou's chattering.

'Mas Jonathan? Lor', that's why he buyin' me.' She looked coy. 'You should come too, Nicole.'

'No!' She drew away from Fidou's touch, placing her coffee cup firmly down on the kitchen table to emphasize her resoluteness. 'I have a duty here. Mrs Duncan will have another baby soon. She needs me.'

'Perhaps Mas Jonathan need you too?'

'You're talking nonsense!' Nicole paused, blinked rapidly so Fidou would not see the tears that were springing to her eyes, and headed out of the kitchen. 'I must go to the children,' she said softly.

At the door she gripped the doorjamb, sniffed and turned back to Fidou. 'Don't let me hear one bad report about you, my girl! Mr Rendye has enough problems without you adding to them.'

'Yes, he has,' said Fidou pointedly. 'It be very lonely for him without a wife by his side.'

Jonathan suspected he was being watched. The feeling disturbed him most at night. His only relaxation was when he sat on the veranda, staring out over the garden to the darkened Champ de Mars. He recognized then the tranquillity Emma must have drawn from her lonely evenings on the *chaise longue*. The sultry night, heavy with the perfume of night flowers, brought a balm after the fervour of a hectic day.

Yet it was on the veranda at night when no one bothered

him that he was disturbed instead by an odd sensation. He experienced it for several weeks before deciding it was as though someone unseen was seeking his attention.

After Emma's death he did not grieve. He had returned immediately to Port Louis, taking the slave Brutus with him, and resumed his work. Emma's hold on him had not been strong so without her presence he began to forget her. He was not superstitious yet since his sense of being watched persisted whenever he was on the veranda where she used to sit, he began to wonder if it was caused by her ghost.

Night after night, as he sipped the herb tea served with devotion by Fidou, he gazed out into the darkness. He could actually feel the presence hovering around him. One evening it was so strong, as though it were about to pounce, he shouted for Fidou to come quickly.

'Lor', what is it, massa?' she cried as she hurried to the veranda from the drawing-room.

He was gripping the arms of his chair, his eyes wide with fright as he stared into the night. He heard her, but he could not answer. There was something out there, something beckoning him. Fidou touched him lightly on his shoulder. His heart leapt with fear and he shot out of his chair.

'Massa,' said Fidou evenly. 'Calm yourself. It only me.'

'Yes.' He frowned at her, puzzled by the concern in her eyes. 'Yes. Forgive me. I was thinking.'

'You called me.'

'So I did.' He was confused. He listened. The night's creaks and caws, the boughs whispering in the breeze, the shouts of people on the plain, sounded normal. He scratched his forehead – he no longer wore his hair long in front – as the feeling of being watched left him. He felt comfortable with Fidou at his side.

'You worryin' too much, Mas Jonathan. D'you want me sit with you 'while?'

She was speaking as she would to a child. He returned to his chair without answering. She sat opposite him and began to natter about the prices of vegetables in the market. He half listened, keeping his senses atune for the return of the presence. The sensation had passed and gradually he became absorbed in what Fidou was saying.

It was Verette who had suggested buying her. His advice, as usual, was sound. Fidou behaved as though she had been trained her whole life just to serve him. She adjusted rapidly to his moods and routine and catered without obvious effort for him, Mr Didcott and Verette. She had two maids and a serving boy whose names he had never bothered to ask, to help her. Brutus tended the garden and slept on the veranda as watcher,

He had come to value Fidou, not only for the way she anticipated his needs and respected his desire to be alone, but also for the link she represented with Nicole. He was eager to know all he could about Nicole but was diffident when he asked Fidou. The slave ignored his hesitation and poured out tales of Nicole: how she lived, the work she did, even the prayers she said morning and night. Through Fidou he saw Nicole as she was now, a dedicated and admired woman of virtue. He longed to see her, and dreaded it.

'What was that?' he asked Fidou, returning his attention to what she was saying.

'I know you ain't listenin'.' She stood up in a huff.

'I was. Your voice is comforting. Please stay.'

'Here I am tellin' you 'bout Miss Nicole an' the children an' you treatin' me like I's some tittle-tattle from the market.'

'I'm sorry.' He sighed. 'I don't seem to be myself these days.'

'You ain't,' she said emphatically. 'I tell Verette so a'ready!'

'Sometimes I think Emma's ghost is watching me.'

'Lor', you goin' out your mind?'

'I hope not.' He waved the idea aside. 'What were you saying about Nicole?'

'I know you buck up when I mention her. She loves those Duncan children. She need some of her own.'

He was shocked. 'You mustn't say that about your betters.'

'Why not? I woman too. I know how she feel.'

'But you're a slave. You're black.'

'I got a conny between my legs, ain't I?' Fidou rubbed herself and grinned mischievously. Jonathan was appalled by her coarseness.

'It ain't natural for a young lady to stay by herself, no more than it is for a man,' Fidou added, beaming at him.

He regarded her nervously, wondering if this was an invitation. Her gesture brought back the memory of his brief affair at Black River with one of Ward's slave wenches. Compared with the magic he discovered later with Nicole in the cyclone, it seemed such an animal act. To be reminded of what he had done then made him ashamed.

'I believe white people aren't quite the same,' he said, gazing out across the garden to avoid her eyes. 'Physically yes, but we have different attitudes.'

'What attitude you like, I like,' she said. 'If you need Fidou, call me, Mas Jonathan. I serve you anywise.'

'You're very kind,' he said, responding with his customary politeness when offered something.

'My pleasure, I'm sure,' she said huffily. She retreated from the veranda, leaving Jonathan feeling guilty at offending her, instead of outraged at her insolence.

Brutus scratched his crotch as he squatted under the flamboyant tree and watched Fidou disappear into the house. Mas Jonathan sat back in his chair shaking his head.

Brutus stared at him, as he did every night. He was drawn to this strange buckra in the way a cat is fascinated by the bird he stalks. Like a cat, Brutus knew if the bird flew away it would return. He could wait.

He had been surprised when Jonathan bought him from Mr Moult. He was puzzled by his new work. There was no cane to cut and people strolled in fancy clothes on the plain where sugar-cane should be growing.

When Fidou arrived to live in the house, he understood

why Jonathan had brought him there. Another bird had returned. If he waited long enough the third female, Emma's friend, would fly down too.

Brutus was a simple man. He did the work he was ordered to do without complaint, as long as he was fed regularly and could bathe when it was hot, sleep when he was tired, and rut when he was roused.

He constructed a grass shelter for himself in the garden. There was a canal nearby where he bathed every evening. There was plenty of shade and his work was easy. He never felt hot like he did at Tamarind when he needed to cool off at the river three times a day.

He soon discovered females who wanted him. Every night after Jonathan retired to his chamber, he visited one of them, taking her on the floor of her master's house or on the sidewalk of a darkened street. At times he roamed the Champ de Mars and lay with lively lads in the grass.

His life in Port Louis was no different from the round of rutting he followed in the slave quarters of Tamarind. It was the life to which he had been condemned by his captors.

Brutus did not remember much of the freedom of when he was raised in the savannas of a vast, hot country. He knew only that he was captured and sent in the bowels of a pitching vessel across the sea to this land where white men owned him.

He had the whip scars on his buttocks from the beatings he was given until he learned to obey the white man without protest. Each stroke branded into his skin marked his pledge to his ancestors that one day he would take his revenge.

As he squatted under the flamboyant tree in the darkness, he stared constantly at Jonathan on the veranda. The white man seemed disturbed. He was peering out into the dark of the garden with fear on his face. It disgusted Brutus. A man who feared the dark was a weakling.

Each night as he watched Jonathan, he observed his every move and gesture. He was trying to understand how such a runt of a man had power. This master was different from slave holders. He was scared of his own shadow, he spent his time with papers and ledgers instead of strutting in the sun displaying his strength. Yet he controlled people and was respected by them. Obviously this master possessed a secret.

Brutus wanted to learn that secret so that, when he killed him and ate his liver, it would be his.

TWENTY SIX

The two men eyed each other warily. Governor Farquhar was the first to speak.

'I'm flattered you have time for me, Jonathan,' he said, striding across the room and holding out his hand. 'Won't you come and sit here by the window. Like we used to do, eh, in the old days.'

Jonathan let the governor speak, knowing it was not like the old days at all. Twice he had refused Mr Farquhar's invitation to visit. He was reluctant to renew the acquaintance and open up old wounds. He was also nervous about meeting Dr Telfair and the other reinstated officials he had denounced to General Hall.

He was surprised to find that Mr Farquhar was alone and, judging by his stream of chatter, was a little nervous too. It put Jonathan on his guard.

'You and I, Jonathan,' said Mr Farquhar, leading him to a chair and beaming when he sat, 'know each other too well to let small differences of opinion spoil our friendship.'

Jonathan watched him without speaking. The governor had aged. His hair was thinning and turning grey at his temples; he looked pale and had put on weight. Yet he still exuded an energy, an enthusiasm it was hard to resist. It was his colonialist's spirit, a boyish charm calculated to galvanize natives into action.

Knowing the effect he was trying to achieve, Jonathan sat

with his lugubrious features unresponsive to Mr Farquhar's forced heartiness.

'Come now, Jonathan, why so gloomy? We haven't seen each other for nearly three years.' He leaned forward and alarmed Jonathan by slapping him on his knee.

'No hard feelings, eh, Jonathan? You've done well since we parted. Who would have believed it! Your aunt's very pleased.'

'Why hasn't she acknowledged that I repaid her loan in full?' The bluntness of his question seemed to shake Mr Farquhar.

'You sent her the money!' He sounded as though he was about to upbraid him for stupidity.

Jonathan fidgeted, wondering why he was being made to feel ashamed for paying his debts. 'I paid Augustus Blaize as her agent, to foward to her.'

'Ah, good!' Mr Farquhar relaxed.

'She never thanked me. It wasn't easy.'

'I'm sure it wasn't, Jonathan. You've done very well. You're the kind of settler this colony needs. You learned your lessons from me, I suppose.'

Jonathan kept silent.

'You're too sensible a person to hold a grudge, Jonathan.' Mr Farquhar wiped his finger around his collar. It was a new mannerism. Jonathan guessed from it that he must have had searching questions to answer when he was in England.

'I have a confession to make.' The governor was waiting for him to drop his resentful expression. He shifted uncomfortably in his chair when Jonathan did not.

'Yes,' said Mr Farquhar slowly, clasping his hands together and releasing them. He repeated the gesture. 'A confession. Perhaps you have guessed? It was for your own benefit that I terminated your employment with me. I recognized in you a germ of talent. I was convinced that if you were *forced* to fend for yourself, without being overshadowed by me, you would do well. Your success proves I was right. I am proud of you.'

Jonathan knew instinctively that Mr Farquhar was lying.

It did not disturb him. It added to his feeling of power over the man who had moulded him.

'Dammit, Jonathan! Don't you have anything to say?'

'Your Excellency, why have you sent for me?'

'Let's not be formal! I want you to be among the first to share my good news. I know you can keep a secret. I have accepted a baronetcy. You may call me Sir Robert now.' He paused as though expecting Jonathan's congratulations.

'Of course, I regard this honour as a tribute to the fine help I have received over the years from you and the others in the governing of this colony. Actually King Louis of France offered me a decoration but I was not permitted to accept it.'

The false modesty did not hang well on Mr Farquhar's shoulders. Jonathan waited while he stood up and walked to the window, gazing out at the Place d'Armes.

'The truth is,' the governor said, losing his façade of geniality, 'I have a problem. Only you can advise me.'

At last Jonathan allowed his sullen expression to lift. He had savoured the pleasure of defying Mr Farquhar's charm, and won. He felt that he could not be cowered by him again. It was a heady experience to discover that even a man like the governor had feelings of insecurity too, just like himself.

'What can I do?' he said brusquely. Mr Farquhar turned.

'I knew I could rely on you.'

'Perhaps.'

'You are the only one I *can* rely on.'

'What is it?' Jonathan drummed his fingers on the arm of his chair to show his impatience. It was amazing what he could get away with.

'Madagascar. Sergeant Hastie has succeeded in renegotiating my treaty, *our* treaty. King Radama's agreed to stop shipping slaves. Devil's own job it was, but you know Hastie. He's a determined man and the King likes him.'

Jonathan nodded. He had already learned of Hastie's success from Verette. The King had been ecstatic to see the

Sergeant again. At their first meeting he was overwhelmed with laughter and barely able to keep his seat, hugging and pulling Hastie in his excitement. Cannons had been fired and there was music and dancing in the King's court.

'It took him days, Jonathan, to seal the agreement. The renewal of the slave-trade brought in money. Some of the King's kinsmen were opposed to him trusting us again. We have General Hall to thank for a new proverb among the Hovas. *False as the English* they say to describe a cheat.'

'Mr Hastie probably agreed, being Irish.'

Mr Farquhar glanced at Jonathan but seeing no glint of humour in his eyes, continued. 'The Karbary was called, the British flag unfurled, the proclamation read to shouts of joy from the people. Freedom from the bloody stain of slavery was hailed as a gift of the British nation.'

'What is the price?'

Mr Farquhar sat down, disappointed by Jonathan's reaction to his speech. 'I had not realized,' he said, 'how astute you have become. It impresses me.' Jonathan waited, unblinking.

'As I said, the King has opposition.'

'Ratsitatane?'

'Good heavens! How did you know that?'

Jonathan permitted himself a sly smile. He remembered the desperate features of the man who at first wanted to kill him, then nursed him to health. Without Ratsitatane he and Verette would never have survived when Captain Lesage abandoned him. He owed that man his life.

'Ratsitatane is being sent here in exile. He is the king's prisoner. I am not happy with the arrangement but what can I do? I *must* have that treaty! Ratsitatane represents the slave-traders and can easily be sacrificed so that I can get it.'

Jonathan rose to his feet in disgust. 'That's not true! Ratsitatane is *fighting* the slave-traders. It's because he's a challenge to Radama for the throne that he's being exiled, isn't it?'

'I had hoped for your cooperation, Jonathan. It is King Radama's wish that he be imprisoned. I do not question the reason.'

'If you keep that man in the Port Louis jail, *Sir Robert,*' Jonathan said mockingly, his eyes blazing defiance, 'you'll have to put me there too!'

He strode out of the room, shaking with fury and shock at his own angry challenge to the man he used to serve without question.

The regulars in Massey's listened to Jonathan with mixed feelings. As he spoke he tried to assess their reactions to what he was saying. He stood at the foot of the staircase with one hand on the banister rail, surrounded by groups of planters, businessmen, minor officials, merchants, visitors and army officers sitting in the marble-floored lobby. Some of them kept their eyes averted, others stared at him without bothering to disguise their astonishment at what he was saying.

Whatever they thought of his arguments, the Massey *habitués* paid Jonathan considerable attention. His change from being a sly observer sipping coffee in a corner and speaking to no one had been gradual over the years. He had progressed from exclusive conversations with the shifty George Allen to mixing with a wider circle of business acquaintances. As his prosperity increased, so did the attention paid to his views.

This morning's outburst was unique. It was the first time Jonathan had made a speech. It was spontaneous. After his interview with Governor Farquhar he had hurried to Massey's intending to calm his temper with a snifter of brandy. He wanted to consider the fate of the man who had saved his life.

His frenzy, however, was too great to contain. When he saw the regulars complacently grumbling about their business affairs, or guffawing over the latest scandal, paying no heed to the important matters happening around them, he leaped to his feet and demanded their attention.

As he spoke and they listened without interrupting him, his panic diminished and the words came easily. He wondered how much of his boldness was due to Emma's ghost. The presence that haunted him when he was on his veranda at night was driving him to distraction. He was doing irrational things, out of character with the caution he usually exercised in his daily conduct. Having the nerve to address the town's most influential citizens in the lobby of Massey's was part of it.

He spoke eloquently, with the passion of outrage, about Governor Farquhar's intention of imprisoning an innocent man – an honourable, noble man – for the sake of his policy of stopping the slave-trade with Madagascar. His listeners were fascinated. All of them had slaves. Unless more came into the island from Madagascar they were unable to replace those who died or grew too feeble to be of use.

His theme interested the Massey crowd. Jonathan sensed he was gaining their support against the action the governor was contemplating. It was a heady feeling. He continued to speak, emboldened by the power of his own words.

Had he been an experienced politician, he would have stopped when he saw his listeners were on his side. He did not. He wanted to impress everyone with what a fine man Ratsitatane was.

He told them how Ratsitatane was a leading opponent of the slave-trade, a more genuine advocate of freedom than King Radama was.

'Then he *should* be in jail,' someone heckled from the group of drinkers gathered around a table in the centre of the lobby.

Jonathan paused to see who had spoken and other voices joined in agreement. The spell was broken and he had lost the crowd. He realized it when he saw Ward challenging him. The planters would follow Ward, not him.

His mistake was in telling them too much about Ratsitatane. After Ward spoke, everyone was convinced the Hova prince should be imprisoned regardless of how honourable a man he was.

'There'll always be Hovas we can bribe to sell us slaves,'

shouted another man, notorious for shipping negroes into the island's bays at the dead of night and smuggling them onto plantations.

'Or you can buy from me,' said Ward with a broad grin. 'My stock's breedin' well.'

'Lend us a wench and I'll give you a whelp!' cried another planter to an outburst of coarse laughter.

Jonathan's nerve failed him. The crowd returned to their drinking, slapping one another on their backs and exchanging ribald remarks. The point of his plea was forgotten. Some of the merchants eyed him charily, probably thinking he was drunk. They were his rivals, the men who would profit by his downfall.

He himself wondered if he had been mad to speak out. His competitors obviously thought so. He clung to the banister rail, afraid to release it.

'Sit down, Jonathan.' Ward gripped his elbow and led him over to a table. The men seated around it rose quickly.

At first Jonathan was flattered at this sign of respect. When the men murmured excuses to leave, he realized his crazy speech had made him a social outcast.

'Take no notice,' said Ward gruffly, pushing him into a seat. He snapped his fingers and a brandy was placed before him. He stared at the glass glumly without touching it.

'That was damn impressive,' said Ward, raising his own glass and waiting for him to do the same. 'Let's drink to Ratsitatane.'

'You're only mocking me. That man saved my life.'

'And you want to save his. Very commendable.'

'It was you who turned them against me. They were listening to me until you interrupted.'

'Yes, they were. They were also wondering if you had gone mad.'

He started at Ward's words and reached for the brandy glass, taking a quick swallow. Was it coincidence that Ward pin-pointed so accurately the doubt that now troubled him?

'We're an insensitive bunch here, Jonathan. Pioneers

with no time for feelings. There's only one man in this colony who finds it as easy as you to make money. That's me. The rest are struggling, most of them have slaves mortgaged up to their ballocks, and liens on their homes and crops. Your competitors are in the same straits.'

Jonathan listened. He hated Ward yet, despite the man's objectionable personality, his words made sense. Jonathan suspected at that moment he was the only friend he had.

'What did you expect to do, Jonathan, by stirring them up? Would they march with you on Government House? It's their old ally Governor Farquhar in power again, not General Hall. Sir Robert's on their side, you know that. I saved you and your business.'

'What do I care about that when this man's done nothing to merit jail?'

Ward's frown warned Jonathan he had spoken too rashly. There was a flicker of anger in his eyes. His lips tightened.

'Are you serious, Jonathan?'

'Well ...' He fidgeted under Ward's gaze. Suddenly he wondered why he should feel ashamed to defend what he believed in. 'What's it matter to you?' he demanded. 'It's my business, I owe no one.'

Ward was silent for a moment, then he sighed wearily. His face seemed careworn, older, as he smoothed back his hair.

Jonathan was puzzled to see sorrow misting Ward's eyes. He realized with a jolt that this vile, loathesome man who terrified the colony's slaves and held the settlers in thrall was not insensitive after all.

'We all owe someone,' said Ward softly, hurriedly leaving the table.

Perhaps it was his embarrassment at having to imprison Ratsitatane to preserve King Radama's cooperation that made Governor Farquhar willing to accede to Jonathan's requests.

That was the only reason Jonathan could find for Sir

Robert's obliging attitude. He could not believe that his threat to be incarcerated with Ratsitatane was taken seriously, nor that his speech at Massey's had worried the Governor.

In this, as in most matters, Jonathan was underestimating himself. He had shown he could stand up to Sir Robert and to Ward. He was confident in his business dealings. He had grown in stature and was respected for his views. It was only because he thought of himself as a clerk that he was unable to appreciate his importance.

Sir Robert granted his requests because he believed that if he did not, he would have trouble on his hands. Jonathan demanded free access to Ratsitatane and was granted it. He approached his first meeting with Ratsitatane in a state of excitement. He was pleased at the thought of seeing him again but was nervous about the circumstances.

The Hova prince was in a cell by himself. Jonathan's immediate response was to think of him as a caged animal. He was naked apart from a strip of torn cloth around his loins. He glowered from the corner of his cage where he stood fiercely proud, his hands on his hips.

He showed no sign of recognizing Jonathan and refused to answer his greeting. Jonathan was dismayed that his overture of friendship was rejected. The sight of the once magnificent warrior trapped in a small cell angered him. He left the jail and went directly to the governor.

His further requests were granted. On his second meeting he found Ratsitatane in the army barracks with a large cell and a quadrangle where he could exercise. His clothes had been returned to him and he had two Hova warriors with him as attendants.

'Now you look like a prince,' said Jonathan, pleased by the transformation. 'I arranged this.' He gestured around the courtyard, expecting praise.

At Sir Robert's insistence two soldiers guarded the door to the quadrangle. On its battlements other soldiers patrolled. Jonathan felt no fear from his old friend.

'I'm sorry for what's happened,' he said. 'I'll do my best for you.'

Ratsitatane regarded Jonathan haughtily from the centre of the quadrangle. His scornful mien confused him and he felt offended after what he had done on the prince's behalf.

'Damn it, man,' he said crossly. 'Do you think it was easy? You know who I am, don't you? Jonathan Rendye, the man you were going to kill on the way to Tananarivo. Instead you saved my life. I'm going to help you.'

'I should have killed you then!' Ratsitatane stamped on the ground and spat at Jonathan.

Although he was deeply hurt, especially as word was bound to reach the governor and the Massey regulars, Jonathan refused to be cowered. Ratsitatane was the size of Brutus. Jonathan had learned from his experience with Brutus how even a savage could be controlled by a firm voice.

'Prince Ratsitatane,' he said sternly. 'I owe you friendship. You have no friends in Mauritius so don't abuse me. Let me know what you want and I shall request it.'

'Your head.'

Jonathan flushed. 'Oh dear,' he murmured, his confidence evaporating. 'Whatever for?'

'You're the one who bewitched Radama. You destroy my people with treaty.'

'No! That's wrong. A treaty with the British will help your people!'

'I'd rather treat with the devil.' The Prince turned his back on Jonathan and refused to say another word.

He made several visits to Ratsitatane but he was unable to soften the prince's resentment and persuade him that he was his friend. His attitude made him ashamed and despondent.

When he heard the prince was unhappy with his food, he arranged for special foodstuffs to be shipped from Madagascar for his attendants to prepare the dishes he was used to. He arranged for trusted Malagash slaves to visit his cell regularly so the prince would have other Hovas to speak with and not get lonely. He did everything possible and told Ratsitatane of what he was doing. His only reward was rebuff.

After his fifth fruitless visit to the prince, Jonathan sat on his veranda in the stillness of the night and wondered what he had done wrong. Ward would have advised him not to spoil a nigger, but this man was a prince.

Kindness is weakness was Ward's maxim. Jonathan's nature was kindness but perhaps Ward was right. Where Ratsitatane was concerned, he *was* weak. He longed for the prince's approval; it would absolve him for his failure to prevent his imprisonment.

As Jonathan sat thinking of the prince's fate, he stared out into the garden. He was reclining on the chair that was Emma's favourite. Suddenly he was overwhelmed with foreboding; it chilled his heart. He became convinced that Emma was near, watching him, coming for him ...

He leaped up from the chair and hurtled across the balcony, driven by fear. He gripped the railing until his knuckles whitened, peering with crazed eyes into the darkness.

'By all that's holy!' he shrieked. 'Go away! You're dead. Dead!' He collapsed over the rail, his head hanging down. His shoulders shook as he wept uncontrollably.

A shadow passed from the shaft of light thrown by the veranda lantern as Brutus slipped deeper into the bougainvillea bushes.

TWENTY SEVEN

Nicole opened the letter with trembling fingers. Since Fidou's departure from Mr Duncan's plantation, she had heard very little about Port Louis. It was only through Fidou's absence that Nicole realized how much she depended on her for companionship. Without her she had only Mr and Mrs Duncan, the children and God.

By day that was enough. The children were boisterous and Mr Duncan demanding in the way he wanted his house run. She paid her twice daily obeisance to God in the prayer sessions conducted by Mr Duncan and felt happy for it. At night she ached.

The letter arrived late in the afternoon. Although she tried to discipline herself to wait until she was alone in her room to read it, she was too excited. She stood in the kitchen and scanned it quickly. The writing was like a clerk's, full of flourishes used to soften the message it contained. She glanced first at the signature, amazed that her heart was thumping loudly. It quietened when she saw the signature was not Jonathan's.

The letter was signed *Arthur Didcott.* She frowned and read it through once, not fully understanding it until her eye fell again on the passage which read:

> 'Please do not be alarmed. We are aware that Jonathan has a number of problems, particularly his desire to see justice shown to his imprisoned friend from Madagascar, Prince Ratsitatane. His distraction, we believe, is due to stranger causes … Fidou and Verette have urged me to acquaint you with this. At times he shows signs of delusion, believing he is spied on by the ghost of dear Emma … Fidou insists that a visit from you would serve to alleviate his depression as well as lighten the burden under which we are all labouring because of our regard for him and our inability to assuage his distress …'

She began to pack her travelling-chest immediately. Two days later she was walking with the chest balanced on the head of a barefoot urchin along the Champ de Mars Street. She was dressed soberly, in grey, and people moved out of her path, impressed by the urgency of her stride. Her years in a religious atmosphere administering to the troubles of the Duncan family lent her the aura of authority. Her concern for Jonathan added a sense of mission.

The cooks and maids of the town houses noticed her progress towards the Champ de Mars and tried to outguess each other as to who she was and where she was bound.

When Fidou was sighted darting along the opposite side of the street in a hurry to reach the house before she did, the slaves realized something important was about to happen. Nicole hastened on unaware of the interest her arrival aroused.

She was shocked by her first glimpse of Jonathan. He was slouched on the *chaise longue*, staring into the garden. His eyes were sunk in their sockets, dark shadows spread beneath them. His hair, she noticed with regret, had been trimmed short and the boyish forelock no longer tumbled across his forehead. His jowls were dark where his beard had not been shaved. His mouth hung open and pearls of saliva glistened in its corners.

'Jonathan!' she cried in horror, hurrying up the path towards him. A spasm jerked him and his hands clawed at his throat.

'Fid ... Fidooo!' he called tremulously. He shrank back, bringing his knees up to his chest and curling up with his arms around them. The terror in his eyes made her halt. Fidou bustled onto the veranda.

'She's coming!' Jonathan screeched in a high pitched voice.

'That's right, Massa.'

'She's there! Can't you see her? Hold me, Fidou. Don't let her take me.'

'Of course she there, an' thank the Lor' for it too.'

Nicole took another step up the path. Jonathan screamed and clutched Fidou, pulling her so she stood between him and Nicole. She pulled away irritably and looked out at Nicole in despair.

'It's all right, Jonathan,' Nicole called softly. 'I'm not a ghost. I'm real. Watch.' She beckoned Fidou to come to her.

'Embrace me, Fidou,' she whispered. 'He trusts you. Let him see you welcome me, that I'm flesh and blood.'

Fidou hugged Nicole without hesitation. 'You see the poor man, miz. He worryin' so much he goin' out his mind.'

Jonathan's yelps of panic quietened as Fidou took

Nicole's hand and led her to the veranda. 'Tell him who I am,' she whispered to Fidou, 'in case he still thinks I'm a ghost.'

'Miz Nicole come from Mahebourg, massa. Ain't she prettier than ever? You see clearly now, don't you, Mas Jonathan?'

'Nicole?' He wiped his eyes furiously then tugged at his nose. He frowned. 'Nicole?' He rocked backwards and forwards on the *chaise longue*, still hugging his knees like a child.

'Yes, Jonathan, it's really me.' She smiled warmly, waiting on the veranda step. 'May I come in?'

'Lor', of course you can,' said Fidou trying to hustle her into the house.

'No,' Nicole whispered. 'It's important that *he* asks me. For his self-respect.' Fidou nodded without understanding.

'I'm feeling tired after my journey, Jonathan.'

'Journey?' He stiffened. 'Where from?'

'From Mr Duncan's plantation. Mr Duncan sends his regards.' An idea occurred to her and she reached into her reticule. 'He's given me an order for winter clothes for his slaves.' She offered the paper to him.

He eyed it suspiciously, but did not take it. 'Does he want a discount? My prices are the lowest. We don't give discounts.'

'Then he must accept your terms.'

'Come in,' Jonathan said, putting his feet on the ground and leaning forward. 'Let me see that order. We've not got many winter suits left.'

Nicole was relieved her ruse worked. It showed her that Jonathan was lucid despite his fear. She likened him to a frightened child and proposed to deal with him as she would a scared little boy, by distracting his attention until she found the cause of his distress.

She handed over the paper. He took it without looking at her, needing time to adjust to her unexpected arrival.

Nicole indicated the slave with her chest, who stood on the path watching them with interest. 'Fidou, please deal with him. Where's Verette?'

'At the barracks with Ratsitatane. I blame him for all this.' She nodded her head at Jonathan. 'He's put some Malagash magic on him.'

'Stuff and nonsense!' Nicole took off her bonnet and shook her ringlets out so they fell around her shoulders. She saw Jonathan watching her from the corner of his eye. She handed the bonnet to Fidou and stood patiently. He was pretending to read the paper and she waited, frowning Fidou into silence.

'Hah,' he said, pulling his nose. 'I wonder if Mr Duncan's credit is good?'

'I should think so,' Nicole said to humour him. 'There's a mortgage on his property but all his slaves have clear title. He's a very efficient and thrifty man.'

'You've changed, Nicole,' he said, brightening. He stood up and waved her to a seat. 'I don't know what it is. Age, perhaps.'

'That's not much of a compliment.'

'I've never been a lady's man.'

She watched him as he returned to his seat. Apart from the strain he was under, his instincts seemed sounder than ever. There was a boldness about him that was new. It contrasted with the shyness she remembered. She decided to probe to see how much he knew of his own condition.

'Do you know why I came, Jonathan?'

He eyed her sharply. 'To gloat?'

She was taken aback by his bitterness. 'Why should I do that?'

'Because you hate me.'

'That's ridiculous!'

'Why didn't you reply to my letters?'

'Because I wanted you to forget me,' she said. 'For my own silly reasons.' How wrong she had been, she thought. Was it too late?

'I *had* forgotten you,' he said. 'I thought you were another damn ghost when I saw you on the path. I was nearly asleep. You frightened me.'

'Why aren't you at the warehouse, Jonathan?' She sensed the key to his recovery lay in reviving his interest in his work, just as she would amuse a child by giving him something to do.

'Because it's here.'

'What is?' She looked around with exaggerated curiosity.

'The ghost of Em –' He stopped. 'It doesn't matter. You'll think I'm mad, just like everyone else.'

'Do *you* think you're mad?'

'Yes, Nicole.' He plunged his head in his hands. 'Sometimes I do.'

'You're certainly untidy,' she said. 'I couldn't believe it when I came up the path. You always took great care over your appearance. Aren't your slaves looking after you?'

'Yes,' he said defensively. 'I've been too preoccupied.'

'Is there someone to shave you?'

'Brutus sometimes does it.'

'Brutus?' A *frisson* of suspicion shook her. 'I'll do it for you today.'

She was pleased when he regarded her with surprise because it showed he had not given up completely. 'I used to shave Mr Duncan,' she added to reassure him.

Nicole spent the rest of the afternoon concentrating on Jonathan. She shaved him, discussed with him what he should wear for the evening and did everything possible to revive his interest in normal living.

By the time night fell, and Mr Didcott and Verette had returned from the town, she had him looking better than he had done for weeks. His mood improved and he was relaxed in her presence.

That evening, after supper, when he wanted to sit on the veranda, Nicole suggested a hand of *brelin*. Verette and Mr Didcott joined in and soon it was midnight.

'I'll take a turn on the veranda before retiring,' Jonathan announced when they finished playing.

'Won't you take me to my room, Jonathan?' Nicole said smoothly. 'Verette can lock up.' She winked at him behind Jonathan's back.

Jonathan was reluctant but his manners had returned with his improved mood and he escorted Nicole up the stairs. She wondered if he remembered the time he had burst into her room because he was jealous of Ward. Now she could think of those days without feeling ashamed.

'Aren't you going to bed?' she asked when he paused outside her room.

'I thought I'd take some fresh air.'

'Then I'll come with you.'

'It's all right.'

'Come on,' she said, taking his arm. 'Let's go.'

'Perhaps I'll go to bed after all.' He pulled away from her.

'Very well.' She walked along the passageway so he was obliged to follow her to his own chamber. She opened the door and waited for him to enter.

'It's wonderful to see you again, Jonathan. I'm truly sorry I did not write. I should have done.'

'Yes.' He stood in the doorway, watching her uncertainly. 'Are you trying to seduce me?'

'No, you silly boy,' she said, gently pushing him so he entered the room. She wanted to slap his face but that was not part of her cure. 'Go to sleep.'

She pulled the door shut on him and hurried downstairs to where Arthur Didcott and Verette were waiting. Fidou came out of the dining-room to join them.

'It's incredible,' said Verette. 'He's back to normal.'

'No, he isn't.' Nicole sighed and led the way out to the veranda. 'What is it out here that's worrying him?'

'He says he feels someone watchin' him.' Fidou rolled her eyes. 'He thinks Emma.'

Nicole stared out into the darkness. She sniffed the air, frowned and walked to the edge of the veranda. The breeze was blowing gently from the plain. There was a soft moaning in the air, almost eerie, as the wind shook the boughs of the Madagascar fir-tree that grew at the garden's edge.

She breathed in deeply to take in the scent of the night blossoms. There was an unusual smell and she frowned again, trying to identify it.

'Verette,' she said, turning around. 'Get lanterns hung in those trees. Have the garden lit up at night, everywhere.

Make sure there are no shadows where someone can hide. Let Jonathan *see* no one is spying on him.'

Even though her instructions were carried out, so convinced was Jonathan that evil lurked in the garden that it took time before he regained his normal rationale and accepted that his fear was only in his mind.

Curiously Nicole herself began to sense she was under scrutiny, especially when she walked in the garden during the day, when Jonathan was at his warehouse. Whenever she turned to see who was watching her, there was no one in sight.

Jonathan's other problem, his desire to get Ratsitatane to trust him and treat him as a friend, was beyond Nicole's ability to solve. Verette was scornful of Jonathan's consideration for the Madagascar prince.

'Ratsitatane's stirring up trouble,' he told Nicole. 'He's trying to make the Malagash slaves feel dissatisfied at being here. He tells them how much better they'd be if they were free in their homeland instead of slaving for white masters.'

'How can he spread dissatisfaction if he's in jail?' Nicole asked as she sat on the veranda with a sampler.

She enjoyed talking to Verette and he often came to sit with her. She decided she had been wrong about him. He conducted himself like a gentleman when he was with her and he was obviously fond of Fidou.

'Jail? It's like a court in exile thanks to Jonathan, not a jail at all. Every day slaves from his tribe visit him. Most of the town slaves are Malagash. The field slaves are Mozambiques, less trouble.'

'What's Brutus?' she asked, trying to sound casual.

Verette's eyes flickered and she knew he detected her interest, even if he misunderstood the reason for it.

'He's a Mozambique. Emma liked him a lot.'

She sighed. 'I know.'

Fidou interrupted them as she came up the path after a shopping – or gossiping – expedition to the market. 'Verette,' she said breathlessly. 'Mas Jonathan goan sell some silk too low in price. The Creoles will think it no good and won't buy it. It *is* good, I see it myself. You must tell him.'

'Thanks, Fidou.' He stood up and smiled warmly at Nicole. 'I must go,' he said with a grin. 'Before the Company loses some profit.' He patted Fidou's bottom and kissed her farewell.

Nicole watched him go. He and Fidou made a fine couple. They were good for each other. If they married, she thought, Verette could have a house of his own, perhaps one of the villas Jonathan had built at the other side of the plain. Fidou would care for Verette better than any Creole could. She had loved him from the beginning, before he was prosperous.

It was natural that Nicole's thoughts, as she was alone on the veranda, should turn to herself and Jonathan. Alas, he seemed to have forgotten his idea of marrying her. She could not blame him. He knew the truth about her despite her matronly clothes and guarded behaviour.

The only reward for her devotion was seeing his energy and equilibrium restored. Whether it was through her companionship or the sensible way she handled him, she could not tell. She endeavoured to preserve a distance between them.

Quite naturally she slipped into the role of housekeeper and it suited her. She brought a routine to the household that everyone, including Fidou, appreciated. The only resistance to her authority came from Brutus.

She believed she understood slaves. A kind word and interest in their welfare was usually sufficient to win their allegiance. With Brutus it had no effect. He was a chilling character, without warmth. His eyes were blank, he did what he was told without protest but she sensed the undercurrent of resentment within him.

He lurked about the house upsetting the other slaves and at night he disappeared when he should have been watching for intruders. He was grumpy, curt in his responses and showed no loyalty to Jonathan, Verette or Fidou.

Nicole always addressed him in Creole, using a brand of

baby talk to humour him into carrying out his chores. She wanted Jonathan to sell him to a plantation since he was so obviously unhappy out of the fields. Verette advised her to wait before she said anything. Jonathan liked to have Brutus around in memory of Emma. To suggest selling him could cause him to have a relapse.

She did as he advised, making it clear when she spoke to Brutus that she would tolerate no nonsense from him. He was at least a foot taller than she was and glanced down at her with an evil gleam in his eyes before he shuffled off without a word.

She watched the muscles rippling across his bare shoulders as he swung his cutlass at an imaginary clump of sugar-cane. His dark blue breech cloth was stretched tight across his buttocks, revealing the massive size of his thighs. She felt a vague shiver of fear when she watched him.

Some days later, when Jonathan seemed quite normal again but still very reserved towards her, she was alone on the veranda. She was sitting where Emma used to sit on the *chaise longue* reading a Walter Scott novel that had recently arrived from London.

Jonathan was working late that evening checking a new consignment of cargo with Mr Didcott in the warehouse. Verette and Fidou were strolling together in the Champ de Mars. Lanterns, placed in the trees by Brutus, blazed brightly in the garden.

Although she was alone in the house, Nicole was unperturbed. She was used to solitary moments and enjoyed them.

A gust of wind rattled through the veranda setting the lanterns swinging. She took no notice until an odd aroma assailed her in its wake. She sniffed without paying much attention. The odour made her frown as she tried to identify it. She placed her book aside and glanced up.

It was a smell she was familiar with, emanating from the darkness. She peered out into the garden. The lanterns revealed the hibiscus, the frangipani, the bougainvillea and the flamboyant trees. Moths fluttered around them, attracted by the light. In the darkness of the boughs above the lanterns fireflies darted. From the plain came the murmur of laughter.

It was a tranquil scene. Nicole wondered why she should be shivering with fright as though some unknown menace were hovering near her. She sniffed again and gasped. The source of that aroma was Brutus.

She stared into the shadow at the end of the veranda. The outline of his huge body lounging against the wall of the house was partly concealed by a potted palm. She shivered again in the evil of his presence.

Quickly she rose to her feet and choked back her fear. The book fell to the floor. 'Brutus!' she said sternly. 'I know you're there. Come out at once.' Too late she remembered she was alone in the house.

He stepped forward so the lantern revealed him. He was naked, his body pulsing with lust. She bit her lip to calm herself. Brutus took a step towards her. She tried to speak.

He lunged and caught her in his arms, scooping her up from the floor like she was a sack of flour. She shrieked, lashing out with her fingers and scratching his face.

He grunted and trotted off the veranda, carrying her into the darkness beside the house.

She screamed again but no one heard.

TWENTY EIGHT

'Where the devil are your slaves? I want a drink!' shouted Ward. He stamped on the veranda to announce his arrival.

Jonathan looked around apprehensively and saw Nicole's book on the floor.

'There's something wrong,' he said as his heart filled with dread. 'Nicole's too particular to leave her book like that deliberately.'

'Perhaps Rats has got here already.' Ward drew a pistol from his belt.

'No.' Jonathan shook his head as the familiar sense of

foreboding gripped him. 'It's something else. Ratsitatane doesn't know where I live.'

'That's easy for him to find out,' Ward scoffed. 'He's bright enough to be a Malagash princeling. No one's more cunning than a smart nigger.' He strode along the veranda deck, sniffing suspiciously.

Jonathan picked up the book Nicole had been reading and twisted it unhappily in his hands. She had been sitting where Emma used to sit. He shivered. Perhaps Emma had come for her because she was jealous? He moaned aloud with fright.

'Dammit, keep quiet,' hissed Ward, his head held alert and tilted to one side as he listened at the end of the veranda. Jonathan fell back into a chair with a loud crash.

'What ails you?' snapped Ward crossly. 'Are you going to swoon like a frightened virgin.'

Jonathan clutched his head and wailed. 'I don't want her to go.'

'Maybe she's inside the house?' Ward was exasperated at not being able to listen for unusual sounds in the dark.

'Emma's got her! I can feel it.'

Ward stared at him scornfully. 'Emma's dead. Pull yourself together, man.' He gripped Jonathan by his shoulders and shook him roughly. 'You're too much of a molly sometimes.'

He stopped and held his finger in front of his mouth as a warning. Jonathan gulped back his fear and cowered into silence.

They both heard a woman's cry before it was abruptly stiffled. 'Come on,' said Ward, pulling him to his feet. He dashed to the end of the veranda and plunged into the darkness.

'Bring a lantern!' he shouted as he disappeared, waving his pistol in the air.

Jonathan stood on the veranda and wondered what to do. Ward had escorted him home that evening because Ratsitatane had escaped from his quadrangle an hour before. The town's police and the militia were looking for him.

Ward had offered to stay in the house in case Ratsitatane should come there. The Prince's anger at Jonathan was public knowledge. It added to his agony at his loss of face with Massey's elite.

In a daze, convinced it was Emma not Ratsitatane who had taken Nicole, he obeyed Ward's shout. He unhooked a lantern and carried it in a shaking hand to the end of the veranda. He leaned out. There was nothing to be seen except the darkness beyond its rim of light. He had an uncanny feeling that when he stepped into the garden he would be letting go of everything he valued.

Slowly he put one foot down, then the other. He was on the lawn and held the lantern up. There was a rustle in the bushes ahead. He walked towards it in a trance, remembering the time he had walked in the garden at Tamarind with a lantern in his hand.

He had hidden from his mind the sight he saw that night: Brutus lying on top of Emma. The slave was plunging into her, his black buttocks heaving and thrusting against the limp thighs of her pale flesh.

In the shadows thrown by the lantern, he saw Ward pointing his pistol into the darkness beyond. He moved closer. Brutus emerged from behind a bush. He was naked and held Emma in his arms.

Jonathan froze, unable to move as he stared uncomprehending at the slave and Emma.

'Release Nicole!' shouted Ward, his pistol directed at the slave's chest.

Brutus shook his head. His eyes were narrow with hatred as he gazed from Ward to Jonathan and back again. Nicole in his arms lay still, her ringlets awry and hanging down.

Ward's shout roused Jonathan. He blinked and saw it was not Emma but Nicole in the slave's arms. He was confused, memory merging with the present and fading away again. His nostrils took in the powerful odour of Brutus. He shivered as he realized he was confronted by the source of all his fear.

'Release her,' said Ward again, levelling his pistol.

'Don't shoot!' Jonathan rushed forward.

Ward put up his free hand to fend him off. 'Ain't no black buck in heat goin' to best me!'

'You'll shoot Nicole.'

'I'm surprised you care,' sneered Ward, keeping his eye on Brutus as the slave held Nicole so she shielded his body. 'She's nothing to you.'

'She is!' he cried, shocked by the contempt in Ward's voice. 'I love her!' He felt a tremendous sense of relief as soon as he blurted out those words. Nicole quivered in Brutus's arms.

'Keep still,' ordered Ward. She lay without moving. 'Hold that lantern steady,' he said to Jonathan, giving vent to his anger.

'I'm sorry,' mumbled Jonathan, shaken with emotion. Brutus was eyeing him balefully, obviously thinking he was safe as long as he held Nicole between him and Ward's gun.

'Massa,' he said mockingly, 'she taste good.'

Ward fired low. The explosion made Jonathan drop the lantern. It lay on the grass, throwing out grotesque shadows as Brutus dropped Nicole's body to the ground. He fell beside her, clutching his knee where the shot had wounded him. Ward raised the second pistol to fire again.

'No!' It was Nicole who spoke. She held up her hand, scrambling to her feet. 'Don't shoot him. I'm all right. He didn't do anything.'

'By the devil's ballocks!' roared Ward. 'Why protect him? Is he your lover too?'

'No!' She shrank away from Brutus and stared at Ward with outrage. 'He's not happy here. He needs to go back to the cane fields.'

'I'll say he does!' Ward strode over to where Brutus was crouched.

The slave showed no sign of fear, nor pain. His hand rested lightly on his knee, the blood oozing between his fingers. He was watching Nicole sadly. Ward pushed her aside.

'Go to Jonathan,' he said scornfully. 'He says he *loves* you.' He made it sound like a curse. 'You ought to tell him about yourself some day.'

He turned his back on her as Jonathan stared at Nicole and wondered what Ward meant.

Brutus grinned when Ward kicked him to his feet.

'What are you going to do with him?' Nicole asked anxiously.

'He must be in league with Rats.' Ward motioned with his pistol for Brutus to move.

'He's wounded. Let me bind it.'

Ward sneered. 'Wouldn't that be kind!'

'I've bandages in the house. Jonathan, help him walk to the veranda.' She glanced at him to see if he would obey. He stared back at her in a trance.

'Hurry up!' She raised her skirt and scurried across the lawn to the house.

Jonathan did not move. Ward sneered. 'Bossy, ain't she? Do you know what I do when a slave ruts with a white woman?'

He shook his head. Brutus was standing naked only inches away. His superb body was a magnificent sight as the light from the fallen lantern played on his hips and thighs.

Jonathan sighed. Brutus was looking right inside him, seeking his soul.

'It was you!' he said, knowing at last. 'You were the one watching me every night. You were the one driving me insane!'

'By the devil!' Ward's patience snapped. 'The buck's too troublesome.' He raised his pistol and fired a single shot.

The ball tore into Brutus's lower abdomen, parting his penis from his body. It flopped to the grass between his feet in a rush of flesh and blood. Brutus sank to his knees, his eyes fixed on Jonathan questioningly as life gurgled away from him.

'Usually,' said Ward walking away and blowing at the pistol, 'I castrate troublesome bucks. I'll pay you his market value so you'll have no loss.'

Jonathan was sickened by the smell of charred flesh. The dying look in Brutus's eye would haunt him for the rest of his days. He followed Ward slowly. His mind had been unhinged by the sight of Nicole in his arms. Had Brutus done to her what he did to Emma's dead body?

Verette and Fidou rushed onto the veranda as he reached it with Ward. Before Verette could speak, Ward ordered Fidou into the house to tend Nicole.

'Tell her the buck's dead,' he said. 'Good rid –'

'Ratsitatane's escaped and started a revolt!' Verette cried. 'He's coming this way with a gang of Malagash slaves.'

'Don't interrupt.' Ward shook his head with exasperation. 'We're aware of that.'

'I heard shots,' said Verette, unabashed by Ward's temper.

'Ward shot Brutus.' Jonathan sank into a chair and cradled his head in his hands. He needed time to think. 'Brutus was carrying off Nicole ...' The picture of Brutus and Emma, Brutus and Nicole, ran through his mind again and again.

'Did he do anything to her?'

Ward chuckled. 'She didn't seem very pleased when I flushed them out of the bougainvillea. She was probably seducing the poor bugger. I knew her when she was a virgin. Did the same thing to me. A regular cane grinder, that wench.'

His words shattered Jonathan's brooding. He looked at him with loathing. Ward Trenchard had respect for neither man nor woman. He bullied his way through life, ruining those he could not buy.

'I don't believe you,' said Jonathan softly.

'For God's sake, get me a drink,' Ward ordered Verette. 'I need it if I'm to convince your partner here what a fool he is.'

'I may be a fool but I'm not a whore-monger.' Jonathan clenched his fists.

Ward's sigh of scorn reverberated around the veranda. In the distance they could hear chanting; it was an African sound, compelling and insistent. The beat of drums had a fast, hypnotic rhythm.

For a moment Jonathan felt the drums were calling him.

He shrugged the feeling aside and turned to Ward. He wanted to know the truth about Nicole.

Since her arrival at his house, he had been in awe of her. She had rescued him from his madness and taken over his life. He was in her hands, yet she remained aloof. It was as though the night they shared during the cyclone had never happened.

He dreaded Nicole's return at the same time that he longed to see her. Now that she was back, she was so different. He wondered if it had all been a dream.

'Nicole is no virgin on a pedestal, Jonathan,' Ward said gruffly, tilting his ear to listen to the chanting as it grew closer. 'You might as well know that now before Rats gets here. Any weapons in the house?'

'That's a lie.'

'Ask her. I'm the one who burst her maidenhead. In the forest at Tamarind.'

A cloud descended on Jonathan's mind. He was in the storm again. Nicole's words about a forest floor and how she was no better than a whore came back to him. He wanted to die.

The beat of the drum was growing more furious. The pounding was in time to the throbbing of his heart. He saw Ward's eyes glittering with excitement. Verette dashed out and said something to him.

Through the fog of his mind he saw Nicole and Fidou clinging to each other in the doorway. Nicole was murmuring but what she said was drowned out by the noise of the drums. He gazed at her forlornly. Her eyes were red with crying, her ringlets dishevelled. Her bosom, under the strictures of her severe corsage, heaved.

He was no longer fooled by her false respectability. He saw her now as she really was: Ward's whore.

From the expressions of the four of them on the veranda he knew they were laughing at him. The drum beat was louder. The crowd was chanting his name: '*Rendye, Rendye, Ren ... die, die ... die!*'

Yes, he knew what to do. He dashed away to the edge of the veranda, brushing aside Nicole's hands when she reached out to grasp him. For months he had heard someone calling him from the garden, from the Champ de Mars. He thought it was Emma, then Brutus. Now he knew it was Ratsitatane. The Prince was at the gate with his gang of slaves and his drummers. He was shouting his name.

He leaped off the veranda and ran down the path, his hands outstretched in front of him. He wanted to deliver himself to Ratsitatane so he could escape from the shame, the ridicule, the scorn and the dishonour that bedevilled his life.

'I'm ready!' he shouted, echoing the chanting of his name: *Rendye, Rendye*. 'I'm ready to die!'

There were about fifty slaves in the mob, males and females. They jostled around Ratsitatane, blocked from attacking the house as he stood in the gateway. He was a tall man, majestic in the regalia of a Hova chieftain. In his hand he carried a spear. The slaves were armed with clubs, cutlasses and stones. Some carried flambeaux. The drumming ceased and the chanting disintegrated into wild shouts and bloodthirsty yells.

Nicole flinched, aghast at the sight of Jonathan rushing down the path to confront this angry crowd. If they turned violent there would be no saving him. She wanted to run after him and bring him back. Ward, standing at the edge of the veranda with his pistols resting on the balustrade, pushed her away.

'He doesn't know the risk he's taking,' she said. 'I must save him.'

'You can do nothing,' said Ward. 'If he dies you'll be free of him. Nicole, you could be mine.'

She was only dimly aware of what he said. 'The slaves, why have they come here?' she demanded in despair.

Verette put his arms around her and drew her away from Ward's side. 'Ratsitatane wants revenge against the British. Jonathan's the target for his hatred instead of the governor.'

'He'll kill him.'

'Damn right,' snapped Ward. 'And you too if you don't get inside.'

Without the drum beat to inspire them, the slaves were fidgeting at the delay, unable to understand what Ratsitatane was doing.

The prince had led them to this house with a promise that their slavery would end. They were to rise up and slaughter whites, gathering other slaves with them, setting fire to the town and sacking it. They milled around impatiently, frustrated by this unexpected halt. They wanted to attack the house and kill.

'Wait!' Ratsitatane held up his spear. His Hova henchmen formed a bodyguard at his rear so he was facing Jonathan alone.

Nicole, trapped in Verette's arms, stopped struggling and held her breath. She was unnerved by Ward's words and prayed silently for Jonathan's madness to lift so he could save himself.

Jonathan flung himself to his knees in front of Ratsitatane. He pulled open his shirt, exposing his chest. The flames from the torches lit up his face. It was glistening with sweat. A strange peace had descended on him and his eyes were calm as he looked up at the Prince.

'Kill me, Ratsitatane,' he said softly. 'I'm yours.'

Ratsitatane raised his spear, ready to thrust it down. The point glittered in the flames. The crowd roared when they saw what he was going to do.

Jonathan raised his head, holding open his shirt for the spear to plunge into his heart.

Ratsitatane tensed, poised with the spearhead like a cobra ready to strike.

'*Kill, kill!*' Jonathan echoed the chanting of the rabble.

Ratsitatane faltered. The spear quivered in his hand.

'Kill me!' Jonathan's voice became a whine, lost in the shouts of the slaves surging behind Ratsitatane. To the Prince it was a cry of defiance, not a plea.

'You are willing to die?' A frown crossed Ratsitatane's brow. 'You sacrifice yourself?' Nicole saw the consternation in his eyes.

'Yes,' said Jonathan with a sigh of ecstacy.

Ratsitatane was disconcerted. He and the Hovas expected resistance and were eager for a fight. By offering himself as a sacrifice Jonathan had robbed them of their triumph.

Hova tradition put Ratsitatane in an awkward situation. There were procedures for sacrifice that had to be observed scrupulously to appease the victim's spirit. If he killed Jonathan without ceremony after he had the courage to place his fate in his hands, Ratsitatane would suffer eternal disgrace.

'Get up!' he said, leaning down to help Jonathan to his feet. 'You win honour by offering your life to save the others.'

'No!' shrieked Jonathan desperately. He fell forward and banged his head on the ground. 'Kill me, kill me!'

'I cannot.' Ratsitatane knelt beside him. 'You are Radama's blood brother. By giving yourself to me you oblige me to kill you according to Hova code, with the honour due to an honourable man. There is no time for that.' He gestured at the mob behind him. 'They are thirsty for blood.'

'Give them mine.'

Ratsitatane rose to his feet, pulling Jonathan up with him. 'I misjudged you,' he said softly. 'You are a man of consequence, not a weak fool.' He embraced him.

At that moment Ward fired. The ball struck Ratsitatane in his back. He sprang from Jonathan, a startled look in his eyes. He twisted around to face the veranda and raised his spear to hurl it. Another shot cracked behind him, spinning him towards Jonathan.

The agony of his wounds made his lips curl, exposing his gleaming teeth as though he were smiling. Jonathan caught him in his arms and fell under the weight of his body to the ground.

More shots rang out. Soldiers had taken up positions in the darkened plain behind the mob of slaves. From the veranda Nicole heard the orders shouted for the soldiers to fire. She saw slaves leap into the air as they were shot from behind.

The others scattered, leaving their drums and torches on the plain as they disappeared into the night, fleeing into their quarters before they were missed by their masters. The prince's revolt had come to an undignified end.

Nicole ran to Jonathan when the firing ceased. He was lying with his arms clasped around Ratsitatane as though trying to protect him.

'He's dead,' she said, taking his hand.

Jonathan pulled back from her and raised his head. She was dismayed to see his eyes sparked with a hatred that was directed solely at her.

'It's me, Nicole,' she said, frightened that his madness still governed his mind.

'I know.' His voice was soft. 'Get away from me! This brave prince died, yet a whore lives.'

He extricated himself from Ratsitatane's embrace with the help of Verette. Together they laid the Prince out on the ground, folding his hands across his chest.

Nicole walked back alone to the veranda, puzzling over Jonathan's words. What he said made no sense yet he spoke without a trace of the madness she feared. She trembled with misgiving. When Ward offered her his hand to help her onto the veranda she took it gratefully.

'Yes!' shouted Jonathan at her back. 'Go to him!' In a trice he was at her side. His face flushed and his clothes were soaked with Ratsitatane's blood. He leaped to the centre of the veranda and pointed an accusing finger at Ward.

'He's your lover, isn't he?'

She shuddered. The accusation made the years of penance she served on the Duncan plantation, the hundreds of prayers she had mumbled for her purity, the denials of her body's fierce yearnings seem wasted. Her struggle to become respectable, despite her mother's reputation and her own sins, had been in vain. She knew now why he despised her.

Strangely, at that moment when he was lost to her for ever, she loved him. He was strong, not weak. His foolhardy action had saved their lives. By defying

Ratsitatane and so delaying the attack, he had given the army time to rescue them.

If she could win his love, she would be the level-headedness he lacked. Together they could share his difficulties and he would no longer doubt himself.

She moved in a daze towards him, ignoring the sneer on his face and the bitterness in his eyes. 'Jonathan,' she said, 'I love you.'

The back of his fist smashed across her cheek. She stopped, stung by the pain. 'Why?' He struck her again and the tears welled in her eyes.

'You lie with him, that's why!' He pointed at Ward and she ducked, thinking he was going to strike her again. 'You can't deny it!'

'No, I can't.' She sighed, the pain in her cheek blending with her relief that he accepted the truth at last. A tranquillity embraced her, banishing the pain.

She would leave his house, his life; she would go to the Chaussée, where her mother once lived, and become what she was destined to be: a whore.

'She did it for you, old boy,' drawled Ward, watching them both with a sardonic smile. 'Ask her about that.'

Jonathan's eyes flickered. 'I don't want to know! She is no good!' His voice cracked with sorrow.

Nicole seized Ward's remark as a chance, just a small chance, to explain her behaviour. She did not expect Jonathan to forgive her, she was not worth that, but if he knew the truth, he might understand.

She stopped holding her cheek, where his blows still warmed her, and drew herself upright, summoning her courage.

'It's true,' she said. 'Listen to me, even if it doesn't matter now. You were destitute then, Jonathan, without money, with no friends. People laughed behind your back at your pathetic attempts to keep up appearances. I wanted you to show people your strength, to rise up and succeed.'

He was scowling at the memory she roused, hating to hear what he knew was true. 'Lying with this lecher was a strange way to do it!' he snapped, glaring at Ward.

'I was young, Jonathan.' She was surprised how easy it was to confess now that she had made up her mind what to do. There was no remorse.

'I thought if I let him take my virginity, he would help you with a loan. You could have used it to start up your business, as you dreamed.'

She sighed before adding with a wry smile, 'Ward spurned me! He said I was a whore like my mother. Your aunt helped you instead.'

Jonathan sat down with a groan on the *chaise longue*. He stared from her to Ward and back again.

She desperately wanted to run over and hug him. He looked baffled and so alone.

'Is it true?' he asked miserably, nodding to Ward for reassurance.

'Almost.' Ward laughed cynically. 'Except her effort *wasn't* in vain. It intrigued me that she loved you so much she would do anything for you. I won the bet but I've lost the race.' He chuckled at the thought of what he had done.

'It wasn't your aunt who lent you the money, Jonathan. I arranged it with the governor so you'd *think* it was. For Nicole's sake. Damned good investment too!'

Verette's loud gasp broke the silence. 'I thought it was Gina,' he said in astonishment. Ward glared at him and he moved away anxiously.

Nicole hovered on the edge of the veranda. Soldiers were searching the garden. They dragged away the corpses of Brutus and Ratsitatane and the other slaves who died in the senseless uprising. Her mind was in a daze.

Fidou touched her arm. 'Nicole,' she said warmly. 'Don't cry. The governor comin'.'

She raised her eyes to the path. Sir Robert Farquhar, followed by his entourage, was striding up to the house. Verette seized the opportunity to escape Ward's suspicious glance and dashed out to meet him. He danced at his side and spoke urgently in his ear. The governor listened grim faced.

Nicole made an effort to gather her shattered wits. She remembered Mrs Didcott's dictum to show good manners at all times. She swallowed her tears, disguising her disgust with herself in a formal curtsy as Sir Robert stepped onto the veranda.

He ignored her and walked straight over to Jonathan, seizing his hand and shaking it enthusiastically.

'Oh, you brave man, sir!' he cried, beaming with genuine affection. 'Saving everyone here single-handed without a thought for your own safety! Verette's told me everything. I admire you, Jonathan, the whole colony does. You're a man after my own heart!'

Nicole gaped at Jonathan's rudeness as he brushed the governor's hand aside. 'Thank Ward Trenchard,' she heard him say churlishly. 'For every damn thing.'

Through a mist of tears she saw him walk towards her. She cringed, waiting for another blow to smash into her face.

'Jonathan,' she pleaded in a low voice, praying to herself that she could avoid a scene. 'I shall go away. You'll never see me again.'

'You won't!' His voice was firm with resolve and his blue eyes clear.

She blinked and saw he was smiling. He put his arm around her waist.

'I love you,' he said. 'You're never going away from me again.' He lowered his lips to hers and held her tightly in his arms as he kissed her.

She trembled, feeling the madness fly from him and knowing that at last, in front of Ward and Sir Robert and Verette as witnesses, he was hers, her man of consequence.